The Tooth Fairy

THE

Tooth Fairy

JAKE HART

SpringStreet Books
Philadelphia

SpringStreet Books
PO Box 1042
Philadelphia, PA 19105

Printed in the United States of America
ISBN 978-0-9795204-2-6

Printed on acid-free paper.

This book is a work of fiction. Any resemblance to actual events or persons is entirely coincidental.

Contents

Prologue

1984

Six am Saturday, September 8, ten miles south of Stroudsburg, Pennsylvania

THE PILOT LOOKED AT his watch and calculated that he had at least a half hour left. In fact, he had less than ten minutes.

He had begun circling the grass bowl about forty-five minutes earlier, just about the time he was supposed to have landed. On the first pass, he had seen the runway lights flicker on briefly, then go dark as another clap of thunder rocked the tiny cabin of his Cessna 140. There was no way he could land at that moment, even had the lights stayed on. Less than a thousand feet of grass field separated the east and west stands of trees. Even under ideal conditions, with a perfectly executed power-controlled descent—final approach speed between 50 and 55 mph, rpms about 1400, two notches of flaps—the ancient tail dragger would barely touch down before reaching the west woods. In the storm that now raged around him, a short-field landing would be suicide.

The cabin was almost silent as he held the Cessna and its 85 horsepower engine—barely louder than a lawn mower—just over stall speed, circling slowly above the passing storm, waiting it out, trying to conserve fuel. On the radio, he picked up bits and pieces of weather data. Two or three more thunderstorms were scheduled to pass through the area before daybreak at 6:30 AM. These would precede a Canadian high sweeping in from the northwest, driving out the rain and humidity, but doing so with 35 mile per hour winds. If the forecast was right, he could stay aloft until then, but barely until then.

On most days, the pilot loved to fly the 140. Even though it was old, its cockpit horribly cramped for a six-foot-one, 235-pound frame, there was a simplicity in its mechanics, a joy in its handling. But this was a plane for visual flight and visual landings. It was not built for instrument weather. There were no shoulder harnesses, not even separate seats for pilot and passenger, only a single, leather-covered bench that the pilot was sharing, at this particular moment, with a 200-pound package. It was strapped in next to him, a silent copilot. It was the reason he was here.

He concentrated on the airspeed gauge, forcing his body to relax against the seat back and his hands to relax around the control wheel. Like other marques of its vintage, the Cessna had been manufactured without a stall warning light or horn. It was entirely up to the pilot to sense the exact moment when the fabric wings of the old plane would lose lift, and the aircraft would stop flying and start falling.

He knew he was close. Ten, maybe even fifteen miles per hour below the normal speed for final approach, at the very edge of the stall envelope. He had been through it before, just a subtle aerodynamic warning before the stall would occur, nose suddenly dropping toward the perpendicular. The only precursor would be a slight mushiness in the controls, and perhaps a light buffeting through the Cessna's control wheel and metal frame. He thought about increasing the airspeed, but this would only increase the landing and stopping distance, already critically long for the field below. He couldn't take the chance.

When the Cessna had taken off two hours earlier from Milton, Delaware, the pilot had decided against topping off the two fuel tanks that sat embedded in the wing roots of the old plane. He knew his own weight, the weight of his cargo, his designated time of arrival. More fuel than necessary would take him over the gross limit. So he opted to fill each tank with 8.5 gallons rather than their capacity of 12.5. It should have been more than enough.

What the pilot didn't realize, however, was that he had already used more than half his fuel by the time he passed over Allentown, about 150 miles into the journey. Everything was on schedule, except for the sudden arrival of the storms. The headwinds had cut down on his mileage. Only six usable gallons remained in the two tanks, not the seven he calculated.

On the other side of the clouds, the duck hunter was also listening to the radio.

"Good morning, all you sleepyheads, it's mayhem in the AM on WPOC, Pocono Radio, Stroudsburg. I'm Lionel, the Biiiiig Train, Hagerty and this here's Country Sunrise, playing all the very best in country and western music to start off your weekend. Well it suuuurre looks like a good one for ducks out there, now don't it? We got ourselves some big old thunder boomers passing through. But don't you worry 'cause the weatherman says it's gonna turn out to be a reeeeaaaal nice day."

The duck hunter clicked off his transistor radio and stuffed it down the front of a muddy pair of green coveralls. He was lying almost prone on the bottom of an old coffin blind set permanently into the marshy bank on the south shore of his favorite lake. He knew he was trespassing every time he came to the blind, but it didn't really matter since the place had been deserted for so many years. Besides, he had long ago justified his illegal forays by reminding himself just how pitifully he had been paid during the years he worked there.

His watch read five past six. He stared directly upward toward the dark gray sky now turning to the lighter gray of a rainy morning, his hands resting on the middle hatch cover that was pulled up to his chest like a wooden blanket. He stretched his fingers forward just enough to feel the cold barrel of the twelve-gauge Ithaca autoloader lying crosswise on top of the hatch. He loved his shotgun—the only remotely valuable possession he had.

At first, the duck hunter tried to convince himself that the birds were refusing to decoy because of the airplane droning above the clouds. He couldn't see the plane, but he could tell it was circling, over and over, the pitch of its engine rising and falling, as if the pilot were having trouble keeping his craft aloft. Of course, the hunter knew it wasn't really the plane; single engines were common in the Poconos, nothing out of the ordinary even for flighty pintails. The problem was his own decoy rig. He had known it for the past half hour, but it was just too damn windy and too damn wet to crawl out of the coffin blind to fix whatever was scaring off the ducks.

A large flock now appeared overhead, started down, then suddenly flared. The hunter finally accepted that if he was to bag anything on this rainy morning, he would have to crawl out of the coffin blind and do something about the rig.

He saw the problem as soon as his eyes focused on the horizontal. The tail-up feeder decoy, one of twelve wooden pintails he had anchored to the bottom an hour before, had keeled over on its side. There wasn't a duck in the world that would land near something that bizarre.

The hunter said "shit," then began wading out into the water.

At exactly 6:09 AM, which he knew only because he was looking directly at his watch when it happened, the pilot heard the first cough of the Cessna's little engine. By the next cough, a few seconds later, his pulse had already jumped to something over 145 and a terrible pounding began in his head.

He screamed into the radio. "Get the damn lights on, now. You hear me, now."

A thousand feet below, at a junction box just inside the western stand of trees, a heavyset man in a black double-breasted suit threw a switch, activating exactly 200 bright yellow bulbs, strung out across the grass bowl in two parallel strips sixty feet apart. The pilot strained to make them out through broken clouds now rapidly running to the east, just ahead of a wind curtain blowing thirty miles per hour directly at the Cessna.

At 400 feet, he suddenly saw the hole in the clouds he had been waiting for, about a quarter mile east of the lights. He dove for it, his angle of descent steep, but still able to clear the eastern stand of trees. He cursed loudly as he came out to the right of the runway, not enough fuel left even to consider a second approach. The only thing he could do now was pull up the aircraft's nose, put in some left bank, and pull the Cessna back around to the runway, just enough to get over the grass strip. If only the headwind would continue for another thirty seconds, he would be able to yank off power at 200 feet, then set down in a three point attitude about 75 yards from the end of the makeshift runway.

The duck hunter, by now waist deep in tepid lake water, snapped his head sharply over his right shoulder at the sound of the plane almost directly overhead. At the same time, he felt the wind suddenly stop.

He watched, open mouthed, as the tiny plane burst through a hole in the clouds, passing just over the trees, its fixed gear brushing the topmost branches. Then he saw it turn dramatically to the left, its left wing sixty degrees to the ground. The nose followed, down and to the left. The Cessna spiraled to the ground, the air now so still that the duck hunter could actually hear the pilot's muffled screams from inside the cockpit.

Impact was surprisingly quiet. No explosion. No engine roar. It looked gentle, almost slow—the Cessna, fifty degrees nose low, burrowing itself into the field, left wing tip first, then prop. And then it was at rest, suddenly halted by the earth, its nose section crushed back into the aircraft, its tail stuck up in the air, just like a feeder decoy.

The duck hunter furiously splashed his way back to shore, instinctively racing toward the dark green wreckage not more than 300 feet away. He would not realize, until he was close enough to smell the gasoline fumes, that the cockpit and its occupant were now a single piece of matter. The instrument panel had taken the pilot's head, the control wheel his chest, the engine his legs. It didn't matter. The duck hunter still called out, half-screaming, half-crying, running around the wreckage in a helpless dance.

And then it was the duck hunter's turn. The last thing he would see was a black sleeve flash from his left side across his throat. The last thing he would hear was a familiar voice, yelling, "For god's sake, no!" The last thing he would feel was heat spreading over the top of his head, as a .22 caliber bullet came to rest just inside his right temple.

Ten Years Later

ONE
Friday, August 19, 1994

THE BAR ON THE FIRST FLOOR of 4641 Hixon Avenue, Lancaster, Pennsylvania, sat directly below the headquarters of Teamsters Local 664. Its 45-year-old proprietor could still make the customers look twice if she really worked at it; and on most Fridays Jennifer Alston DeLone really did work at it. But not tonight. Just too damn hot. She did manage, however, to tug on her best pair of jeans, the ones with roses embroidered on the left butt cheek that she did herself. And she carefully tied off the bottom of her white oxford shirt so that just enough bare tummy—still tanned and taut—was visible when she leaned over to swab the bar.

Jenny's Rathskeller Bar & Grille, formerly Lifetime Oilless Bearing Company, opened for business on a chilly Friday in March of 1984. It was, from the start, all bar and no grille. Beer nuts and pre-fab pizza made up most of the menu, but the suds flowed like Niagara Falls in a thunderstorm, and the juke box—a fully retro neon Wurlitzer complete with a tiny tone arm and 250 45s—pumped out country and western music every day from noon to closing. What made the place work, however, was Jenny DeLone. Six nights a week she personally tended the plain wooden bar, making sure to remember every casual customer's name and every regular customer's brand.

But it was a struggle. Running a restaurant—even one in a building inherited free and clear from her father, even one that specialized in Doritos and Slim Jims—required the work ethic of an Amish farmer, the brass cullions of a riverboat gambler, and the charm of a New Orleans madame. Jenny had all three. Still, it was not until the great fire of 1990 that Jenny Rats, as it quickly came to be known, settled comfortably into a pool of black ink.

There was almost no one in Lancaster who thought the fire at 182 South Acorn Street, then the headquarters of Manufacturing and Transport Workers Local 664, I.B.T., had been an accident. The police arson squad certainly didn't think so, but they could never come up with enough evidence to satisfy the persnickety Lancaster County district attorney. Every piece of paper belonging to the infamous Teamster local was lost in the December blaze—every piece of paper that could have officially crowned Secretary-Treasurer Joe Greist as the heavyweight payoff champion of central Pennsylvania.

For the next thirteen months, Local 664 bunked out in the back of Engine and Ladder Company 8. Then Greist, in one of his last official acts before the International Union threw Local 664 into trusteeship, managed to make one of the only honest deals in two decades of dictatorship. He signed a ten-year lease for the second floor of DeLone's building. Jenny's first purchase with her new rent money was a full-sized, slate top Brunswick pool table. Immediately, it became the centerpiece of Jenny Rats.

On this particular Friday night in August, the centerpiece was being monopolized by Thomas Jefferson Trice. T. J., as he would have been known to his friends if he had any friends, had his pool shooting paraphernalia neatly laid out along one of the Brunswick's mahogany rails. Closest to the shooter stood the ever-present Budweiser longneck, its seven empty brothers still upright around the table. Then came Joe Cool, the Camel butt, ash teetering dangerously over the green felt playing surface. Next to Joe sat mister talcum powder, and finally the tiny square block of chalk that T. J. screwed with his custom cue after every shot.

The shooter was definitely on a roll. "Eight ball, corner." Trice slowly drew back the cue with his left hand, then fired it smartly through the thumb-forefinger gully of his right. Like a wooden frog tongue flicking at a fly, the cue shot forward, launching the white ivory ball toward its prey. The eight ball disappeared. Another game over; another victim fleeced.

"I've had enough, T. J." The vanquished opponent flipped a crumbled ten dollar bill across the table. "You're out of my league."

"Bullshit, you're just too cheap to have another go. Never know, you might get lucky."

"Yeah I'll get lucky, Trice, and you'll grow tits and become a nun."

The man shuffled off toward the bar. Trice laid down his cue, stretching his arms down and slightly out, palms up, turning to the small cluster of patrons around the table. He looked like a dashboard saint in jeans and bandanna, chumming for converts. "Well," he implored, "who's next?" Nobody moved. "What's this—amateur night at the Rat?" Still no movement. "Well, anyone changes their mind, I'm in the last booth by the jukebox."

If Thomas Jefferson Trice actually had a friend, it would have been Stuff Johnson. Steven Ufland Johnson, to be exact, though practically no one at Jenny's knew him as anything other than Stuff. At 10:30 PM he coasted his beat-up 1973 Sportster into Jenny's side lot, carefully backing the old Harley into a space directly next to the gleaming Springer Softail that belonged to T. J. Trice. Stuff knew the Springer the way a high school nerd knows the head cheerleader. He had studied every inch of her body from afar, but she was still something only to dream about. Stuff had long since given up trying to figure out where T. J. got the money he lavished on the big teal and white bike. But he suspected it had to be pushing twenty-five grand by now.

Johnson slid into the last booth across the table from an already drunk pool shark. Trice was slumped on the seat, his bandana'd head barely visible though the prism of brown glass bottles stretched out before him.

"Springer looks terrific, T. J., you been adding more chrome or what?"

"Just washed, that's all. And don't you be fucking with it, either."

"Not me, bro. I know better." Stuff ordered a Stroh's lite. "'Nother beer, T. J.? I'm buying."

"Yeah, but not that shit you drink. Tastes like piss."

"So I guess you heard about the rotating shifts down the street."

"Yeah, I heard about them." Trice was slurring his words, but the anger still came through. "Fucking ties got nothing better to do than bust our balls I swear."

"Oh, I don't know." Stuff was usually a bit more brave when T. J. was on his way to becoming wasted, like now. "I think I'm gonna like seeing the sun come up before work now and then, 'stead of after it."

With great effort, Trice slowly hauled his slender body into an upright position. Fuzzy as his brain was, his eyes still managed to bore into Stuff Johnson like little black BBs. Trice reached for the pack of Camels, tapped one out, and hammered the mouth end of the cigarette twice against his thumbnail to tighten the tobacco. Then, with one hand, he opened up the matchbook, bent a match almost in two and struck it with a snap of a filthy thumb and index finger. His words blew into Stuff Johnson's face along with the first puff of smoke.

"Yeah, well you listen here. I don't work nights for that fuck, Harry Greene, so I already wrote out the grievance. There ain't gonna be no god-damn rotating shifts."

"I thought the union contract says they can do it."

"You sound just like that limp dick Secretary-Treasurer up there." Trice gestured with his middle finger in the direction of the second floor. "When we had Greist in here, we didn't give a damn what the contract said. And I still don't, as a matter of fact. Besides, the union's got its Jew lawyer from Philly, what's his name, Rothberg, Rothman, something like that. Never seen a labor arbitration he couldn't win."

"What makes you think Pete Werner's even going to arbitration? This local's not exactly rolling in it. That's what they say, anyhow."

"Oh, is that what they say?" Trice opened a hole in the beer bottle dam with his elbows. "Well, let me tell you what I say. Werner don't take this case I'm suing his ass. Talked to a lawyer downtown does work for the Harley club. Says the union's gotta represent everyone the same, even ones they don't like."

"Then I guess you don't care about the rest of us." Stuff was way out on that limb now.

"Fact is, I don't. But even if I did I'm still going all the way on this and I'll tell you why. You don't stop this kind of crap it just gets worse. Like that fucking incentive deal Greene made us eat in the '87 contract. You weren't here, so you don't remember all the pious bullshit his butt-kissing ties were shoveling. 'You're all going to make more money. We can show you.' Yeah, they showed us all right. Fucking bosses had us ratting on each other inside a month. All it took was one boot lick faggot on a crew, goes running to the foreman. 'So and so's taking extra breaks, sir; the crew isn't going to make bonus, sir; may I stick my tongue up your ass, sir.' I'm telling you, damn near tore this union apart till we got it the hell out of there in '90."

Johnson knew it was time to stop pressing the point.

Jenny Rats on Friday nights usually hit its stride around 11:45. The last shift of the week down the street, at Greene-Pitowsky Smelting & Battery Company, had been over for almost an hour, plenty of time for the serious players to get seriously tuned. By now at least one piece of local talent had thought about doing it on the Brunswick, there had been two shoving matches, and some amateur ralpher had already missed the men's room commode.

At T. J.'s booth, there were so many empty Bud bottles it was hard to see any tabletop at all. Even Stuff had given up on the Stroh's lite by eleven, and was now equally into inebriation courtesy of Anheuser-Busch. T. J.'s woman for the evening was hanging on to Trice, trying to stay awake. Fake auburn hair, looked to be in her late thirties, J. C. Penney's cowboy shirt opened about four inches down her chest, just enough to show no bra. Even in her own foggy world, she slapped T. J.'s hand away every so often. But she didn't mean it. Her name was Gloria Partridge. Worked pack and inspect at Armstrong Floors. Into bikes. T. J. almost liked her.

Stuff Johnson was still single for the evening and by now was too far gone to keep trolling. So instead he amused himself by trying to catch a glimpse of Gloria's nipple. Trice helped by sliding open another purple glass button. "Quit it," Gloria said. "You're drunk."

"That is correct," T. J. replied. "I am most definitely drunk. Not too drunk, though, to kick your ass out of here." Gloria laughed, then buttoned up her cowboy shirt all the way to the top. She was not the least bit intimidated by the great Thomas Jefferson Trice.

But Gloria Partridge was certainly one of the few at Jenny Rats who weren't. Trice worked on intimidation. That was obvious. Even without trying, he had the image down so pat that people just naturally wanted to give him a wide berth. The ever-present bandana stretched tightly across his bald head, the scruffy beard sawed off square across the bottom like ZZ Top, the collection of almost obscene t-shirts praising death, drugs and America, and, of course, the teal and white Springer Softail, with its illegal drag pipes that echoed every night off Lancaster's finest factory buildings and run-down houses.

T. J. was not a big man, barely five-nine; and he was certainly not a heavy man, 155 with pipestem legs. But his fish belly white arms were strong, his bantam chest broad for its size, and there was hardly an ounce of fat on his 47-year-old frame. He was also smart—much more than he cared to let on; so if, by chance, one were lucky enough to be invited inside T. J.'s one-story log house in Fivepointville—a tiny town twenty miles northeast of Lancaster and so obscure that even most natives couldn't find it on the map—the visitor would see, at once, the built-ins lined with hundreds of books. The owner had read every one. The visitor would also see the racks of jazz and classical CDs, the exquisite Bösendorfer concert grand and, finally, the large format Hasselblad camera sitting on a glass-topped coffee table in the middle of his living room. But, of course, almost no one ever got an invitation to T. J.'s house.

Gloria Partridge was obviously correct about T. J.'s current state of intoxication. Had he tried, he couldn't have even blown up the balloon, though his breath might very well have melted the rubber before he could even start. So this particular Friday in August ended for Gloria at one AM, with a simple peck on T. J.'s cheek, and a knowing nod to Jenny. It was time to harvest the empty longnecks.

Trice seemed to perk up after Stuff Johnson helped him outside into the night. One o'clock in the morning and the temperature still had to be in the eighties. Humidity was even higher. The crickets roared on like so many tiny jet planes, suddenly stopping, then starting, then stopping again, as if their thousands of little bodies were wired into a common insect brain. During the crickets' silent measures, Trice could faintly hear Jenny Rats' muffled Wurlitzer, at last into its final hour. He fumbled for the keyhole in the top of the Springer's Fat Bob tank, clicked it right to glowing dash mode, pulled out the enricher, turned on the gas, and kissed the starter.

The big V-twin struggled through a few electrically assisted revolutions, then settled into its familiar potato-potato-potato cadence. After a few solo bars, Stuff joined the band, kicking the old Sportster to life; the two big Harleys now sitting riderless, side by side, warming to their appointed rounds.

The engine noise helped clear Trice's brain. He tugged the tiny turtle-shell helmet over his bandana, then flipped the throttle twice, to make sure at least some of the neighbors were awake. Johnson answered with a growl from the Sportster.

"You sure you're okay to ride?" Stuff meant it as idle chatter, but Trice naturally took it as a challenge. He eased the big bike onto Fourth Street, then swung left fifty feet to the corner. The Sportster pulled up beside.

Trice pointed to the east, down two blocks to Second and Hixon, toward the long metal battery breaking building—Greene-Pitowsky's first structure inside the Hixon Avenue gate. "You see it, Stuff," he said, gesturing upward with his chin toward the building, outlined with naked light bulbs. "It's empty. No more trucks till Monday. I say we ride through and fuck with Charlie Carpool."

"What are you, nuts!" Stuff felt suddenly sober.

"What are you, scared?"

"No, I'm not scared. It's just stupid. Anyhow, how are you going to get through the gate?"

"We're not going through the gate. We'll go down the access road next to Sharpe Street. Nothing to it. Road ends, there's twenty-five feet before the fence starts up. You coming or what?"

"Listen, Trice, you might not need this job, but I do. You wanna play Evil Kneivel down Battery Boulevard, you go ahead, but just leave me the hell out."

"All right, look." Trice stumbled off the Springer and started rooting around in one of the saddlebags. He pulled out two rubber masks. One was a generic zombie, the other a Richard Nixon. He tossed the zombie to Stuff. "Here, put this on. Your own mother'll think you're the bogeyman."

"I can't believe you carry shit like this around. You really are nuts, just like they say."

T. J. started to laugh. Then he started to cackle. "That's right, little boy, I'm nuts, just like they say." He spoke in a fake falsetto, like the Wicked

Witch of the West. "But this isn't Kansas anymore, Toto. It's the yellow Greene Road. Hey, that's not bad. The yellow Greene Road. Get it."

"I don't know what the hell you're talking about, T. J., and I'm not hanging around to find out." Stuff Johnson swung the old Sportster around and gunned the throttle.

Trice pulled on the rubber Nixon mask and continued in a muffled cackle. "That's right, little boy, you just ride on home now. Don't want to get into any trouble with Mr. Greene now, do you?"

And Trice was gone, the drag pipes screaming angrily in the humid air, down Hixon Avenue, past the battery building. Stuff Johnson watched over his shoulder just long enough to see the big Springer turn right onto Sharpe Street.

Then he faced front and raced home.

———⊷◦⊶———

Toothless Charlie Carliner couldn't even remember when the men first started calling him Charlie Carpool. And he certainly couldn't remember why. He didn't mind the nickname, though. In fact he almost liked it.

For as long as most of Greene-Pitowsky's finest could remember, Charlie Carpool sold the *Lancaster Daily Times* outside the Hixon Avenue gate. Even he couldn't remember when he started doing it, but he remembered very well the day in 1985 that Harry Greene offered him a job as weekend night watchman. "Wish you wouldn't always be so down on the man," Charlie would say to the members of Local 664. "Mr. Greene's got a good heart, I tell you. Don't know where I'd be without him, that's for sure."

The watchman job was about as close to charity as Greene ever really got. It was, after all, hard to figure out quite what a person might want to steal from a smelting and salvage yard, much less how they would go about it. Still, Greene felt it was a good idea to have someone keeping an eye on the place, and at $4.50 an hour Charlie Carpool was almost as cheap as a Doberman.

He was supposed to patrol the entire site, but he spent most of his time just sitting in a beach chair at the exit end of the long narrow battery house, listening to the radio. Years ago, the breaker men started calling the paved strip down the center of the metal house "Battery Boulevard." The name stuck, and eventually someone even had a friend in the Streets Department make up an official green and white sign. It hung on a chain across the top of the north entrance.

The old watchman was nervous anywhere near the smelting furnaces to the south, and was downright petrified of the black casing mounds, lined up along the eastern perimeter of the property, beyond Sharpe Street. At night their huge shapes dominated the skyline, some of them fully a hundred feet high. And on windy nights, particularly if there was a moon, Charlie could actually see clouds of lead dust blowing off their tops. Most of the time, the dust blew out toward the Conestoga River, but when the wind turned easterly, as it so often did before a storm, the deadly blanket would settle silently on the row of tiny clapboard houses, huddled together like wooden waifs, down the north side of Hixon Avenue all the way to the Rat.

There was no traffic on Battery Boulevard from Friday night to Sunday afternoon. The hydrocleavers all hung in neat rows from the ceiling, their merciless blades at rest. On the back wall behind one of the silent machines a neatly painted sign read: "Axel Kinnard, September 3, 1978. You're Still The Man." Below the sign, in spray paint, someone had written "Thumbs up," with a line through the *s*.

Charlie Carpool was fighting sleep and he was losing, despite non-stop country music squawking from the speaker of his ever-present portable radio. He managed to keep himself awake by concentrating on an unforgiving aluminum cross member pushing up on his tailbone.

When he first heard the motorcycle, Charlie was amused. "What kind of an idiot," he thought, "is out riding down here at one in the morning?" He looked up just in time to see the bike shoot down Hixon Avenue past the open north end. The big twin downshifted to second, then Charlie heard it again, this time starting down the east wall of the battery house. "What the hell's he doing on Sharpe Street," Charlie muttered to himself. "Damn fool must be drunk."

And then he swore the bike was right behind him, just outside the exit end. It had to be on the property now. He spun around toward the south end of the building, the open exit not twenty feet from his chair. He was close enough to see the color of the big Harley as it shot, left to right, across the stern of the battery house. Charlie Carpool jumped out of his chair, trying to follow the bike by its sound. He heard it slow and turn again, this time heading north along the west wall toward Hixon Avenue. Circling the building now, its running lights blinking—off and on and off and on—shining in like a ragged strobe as the motorcycle tore past the open windows of the battery house. The old watchman had gotten about half way down Battery Boulevard when the white headlight of the Springer suddenly swung into view at the Hixon Avenue front entrance.

He was blinded by the high beam. He could hear the throttle being gunned—once, twice, three times—the drag pipes reverberating off the tin roof and sides of the building, the sound so loud it was painful. Then it was quiet again—just the burbling of an engine. He called out.

"Building's closed. You can't come in here."

"I have come for you, Charlie Carpool." The voice was high and raspy, a muffled falsetto.

"What the hell you doing? I said the building's closed."

"I am your maker, Charlie Carpool, and I have come for you." The voice let out a high-pitched cackle; the V-twin burst back to life; the big Harley roared into the building, nothing in its way now, down the whole length of Battery Boulevard, except the watchman.

"Get out of here!" Charlie started backpedaling down the cement strip. The bike was almost on him, its rider screaming in a hideous soprano: "Charleeee, Charleeee, here I come Charleeee!"

The watchmen flattened himself against one of the cutting tables just as the motorcycle sped past, its rider all in black except for the head. Charlie Carpool would later tell police that the rider had on a rubber Richard Nixon mask. The police would laugh.

The Springer reached the south end of Battery Boulevard, slowed, then spun about for another run. Again the noise of the pipes, again the delirious cackle of the rider. Charlie Carpool was running now, toward Hixon Avenue, the bike within twenty yards. He felt himself begin to slide in a puddle of crankcase oil. He felt a sickening pull as something snapped under his kneecap. Then the pain yanked him hard to the cement floor.

Had he been sober, Thomas Jefferson Trice would have known to stay down on the rear brake when he felt the back wheel of the Springer lock. But this was Thomas Jefferson Trice pulling a point one nine. This was Thomas Jefferson Trice pouring sweat behind a rubber mask. The panic of the novice took over, and he released his right foot from the brake pedal while his right hand still squeezed the front brake lever. Six hundred pounds of Harley down in less than a second, the Springer's huge rear tire gracefully sliding out and to the left, pulling the hot drag pipes onto the inside of Trice's right calf. Rider and mount now sliding, out of control, down Battery Boulevard toward the crumpled body of a 74-year-old man.

Charlie Carpool remembered the headlight coming toward him out of the darkness. He didn't remember the impact. He didn't remember the back of his head clacking like a ball peen hammer against the metal leg of a chopping table. He didn't remember the flash of lightning going off in his brain before he lost consciousness.

T. J. Trice could only remember that he had somehow ignored the burning in his right leg after he hauled the fallen Harley to its tires and rode out of the building. He had no recollection, however, of how he managed to find the hole in the Sharpe Street fence.

TWO
Sunday, August 21

THOMAS JEFFERSON TRICE HEARD the door. But he decided to make his visitor wait until the piece was over. So Harry Greene, founder and president of Greene-Pitowsky Smelting & Battery Company, stood in the dusk and listened to muffled piano music coming from inside the log house. By his Rolex, he stood there for seventeen minutes.

Harry had gotten the phone call three hours earlier, while he was shaving, getting ready for a relaxing Sunday dinner at the club. As usual, his wife, Minna, raced to pick it up. "There's a man on the phone, honey. Says he's got to talk to you."

"I need to see you right away. It's important."

"What's wrong with tomorrow at the plant?"

"I'm not going to be at the plant tomorrow. And I'm sure you know why."

"I don't know why, and anyhow I can't talk to you here." Harry was almost whispering, but she was still all over him.

"What's the matter," Minna was chattering in his ear. "Is anything wrong? Nobody died did they? It's not Eric, is it?"

"No, sweetheart, it's not Eric ... Look, where can I reach you? I'll call you back in five minutes."

"Don't bother. Just be here at 8:30. You understand?"

Thomas Jefferson Trice hung up before Harry Greene could say he would be there on the dot.

"Sorry about that." T. J. laughed as he opened the door. "You waiting out there all that time? Got lost in the Beethoven, I guess. Moonlight Sonata. Third movement is unbelievable, don't you think? Every kid takes piano lessons gets to play the Adagio, but nobody does the Presto—hardest thing I ever tried to play. That's Alfred Brendel you're listening to. Never could figure out if he's a Kraut or a Jew. What do you think, Harry. He one of yours?"

Greene did not answer. It would start soon enough, anyhow. So he just stood in the doorway and watched as Trice turned away and walked slowly back into the living room, practically dragging his right leg. Eventually Greene followed but didn't sit down. His host turned down the massive sound system, reducing Alfred Brendel to barely audible background music, then poured two fingers of Remy Martin VSOP into a large crystal snifter.

"I'd offer you one, Harry, but I know you don't drink. Why is that, anyhow?"

"Why is what?"

"The booze, Harry. The elixir of life. Why don't you people drink?" T. J. immediately answered his own question, while Harry suddenly flashed on his dead father-in-law, Big Irv Feinstein, passed out drunk on the red leather couch in his office. "Must be the spiked grape juice they make you guzzle on holidays. I had to drink that slop, I'd abstain the rest of the year too. Sit down, Harry, you make me nervous."

The two men sat, twelve feet apart, in matching Wassily chairs that squared off across the short ends of a Kashan silk rug in front of T. J.'s fireplace. The room was huge, twenty by thirty at least, but it was lit by only two lamps and a hidden spotlight, throwing its beam across the original Hopper oil that hung above Trice's mantle. Harry could hear T. J. more clearly than he could see him.

"You realize we have a serious problem here, Mr. Greenberg. A very serious problem, particularly if the old man dies."

"He's not going to die, Trice. Doctor called me this morning."

"Is he conscious?"

"Don't know, didn't ask. Anyhow, I'm surprised you'd care."

"Come on, Harry, course I care. How am I going to find out what he remembers if he hasn't come to yet?"

"He remembered plenty already before he passed out in the ER Friday night."

"So you do know, don't you? All that baloney on the phone this afternoon about seeing me at work, and here you already know. You must think you're very clever."

"All I know is that you were riding a motorcycle inside my plant Friday night and that you damn near killed an innocent man."

"It was an accident. Dropped the bike on some grease. I was just having fun with the old guy."

"That's not the way I hear it. I hear you tried to scare him to death before you ran him over. I hear you were drunk. I hear you even wore some kind of mask so you wouldn't be recognized."

Trice got up from his chair and walked to the other side of the rug. He stood close to Harry, almost touching him, then bent down and pulled up his right pant leg.

"Nice, isn't it, Harry."

The wound was still undressed, a trail of burnt red flesh, blackened where it joined the undamaged skin, running from the inside of Trice's ankle halfway up the right calf. T.J. had pushed down on Harry's head, forcing it so close to the open wound that, even in the dim light, Greene could see droplets of clear fluid beaded on the shiny red surface. Harry spoke as his head was released.

"You know that thing's infected, don't you? You better have someone look at it."

"I just did. You looked at it."

"Can we just get to the point, Trice. Why am I here tonight? What is it that you want? It isn't September yet, so what's the deal?"

Trice dropped the pant leg and limped back to his chair. "You really don't know, do you, Harry? I got fired this afternoon. Just like that. I can't believe Breitenfeld would do it on a Sunday, but I guess he just couldn't keep it in his pants until Monday. Would you like to hear the details, Harry?"

"Does it matter if I want to hear them or not?"

"Not really." Trice paused to pour himself a fresh Remy. Then he approached the stereo. "What are you in the mood for, Mr. Greenberg. Little Bach maybe? Some Mozart? No, don't answer. It's Schumann, I can just tell. The Symphonic Études. Perfect music to get fired by." T. J. slid in the disc, then took a position in the center of the Kashan. He spoke to the ceiling as the music began.

"It's another sultry Sunday afternoon in Lancaster. Young Mr. Trice has just begun washing his trusty pickup, when all of a sudden the phone rings inside his modest log home. 'My goodness,' he thinks, 'who could be calling me at home on a Sunday?' Why, it's Mr. Breitenfeld from the plant. Seems, he needs to see Mr. Trice in the personnel office, right away. It must really be some sort of emergency, because Mr. Breitenfeld says it can't possibly wait until Monday. Like it so far, Harry? Music's not too loud, is it?"

Harry Greene said nothing.

"So, anyhow, young Trice immediately stops washing his truck and heads for Mr. Breitenfeld's office—on the double, as always. And guess who he sees the moment he walks in? Why, he sees the whole mafia. There's Lady Irene, the ice queen of personnel, and Gruppenführer Hamilton of security, and Shift Foreman Jeff Leiter, and, of course, Mr. Trice's dedicated shop steward, Lawrence T. Douglas. 'Whoa,' says young Trice to himself, 'all these people called in on a Sunday. This looks serious.'

"Mr. Breitenfeld is sounding particularly stern as he opens the proceedings. 'Thomas, do you know why we've called you to the plant on a Sunday?'

'No sir,' says young Mr. Trice in his most polite voice. 'Is anything wrong?'

'You don't have to say nothing, T. J.,' says the dedicated shop steward.

'It's okay, Lawrence,' says Mr. Trice. I can handle this.'

'Something is very wrong, Thomas,' says Mr. Breitenfeld. 'And I think you know exactly what it is.'

'Actually, I don't, sir.'

'You know, Thomas, it'll go a lot easier if you just tell the truth. We already have the police report.'

'What police report?' says Mr. Trice. 'I don't know what you're talking about.'

"All of a sudden Breitenfeld gets angry. You with me, Harry? And he starts making all these terrible accusations against Mr. Trice. He says Mr. Trice got drunk at Jenny Rats on Friday night, then put on a rubber mask and rode his motorcycle down Battery Boulevard. Right through the building, he says. Can you imagine, Harry, saying such things to a lowly forklift driver?

"And then it gets even worse. Mr. Breitenfeld says that young Trice lost control of his bike and ran smack into poor old Charlie Carpool. Knocked him out and everything. Even put him in the hospital!

"Well, Harry, you can just imagine the shock on Mr. Trice's face when he hears all these terrible things being said about him. 'No, Mr. Breitenfeld,' he says. 'That's just not true, I would never ...'"

Harry Greene had suddenly heard enough.

"Look Trice, you called me at home, half-scared my wife to death. Now I'm here, all right? So just cut out the genial host bullshit and the storytelling bullshit and all the other bullshit, and tell me what it is you want so I can go home."

"What I want? Really, Harry, a man of your intelligence? You shouldn't have to ask me that question. It should be obvious. I want my job back. That's all, Harry, just my insignificant little job driving your insignificant little forklift."

"I'm sorry, Trice, it's out of my hands. You go and pull a damn fool stunt like that, almost kill an old man, what do you expect me to do, tell Breitenfeld it was just a big mistake? You think he's that stupid?"

"Oh, Harry. Poor, poor Harry." Trice had poured himself a fresh cognac and returned to his Wassily. "No, I don't think you can tell Saint Joseph to forget it. We're talking about the greatest moment in his life here. Do you have any idea how much Breitenfeld hates me? He hates me almost as much as you hate me. So I know he's not gonna sit still for you just pulling the plug. He'll start asking questions, and we can't have that now, can we Mr. Greenberg?"

"Well then, what do you expect me to do?"

"Be creative, Harry. Go see that Philadelphia lawyer. Your mick war buddy. Just tell him he's got to take a dive in front of the arbitrator."

"You think it's that easy? How do you know there's even going to be an arbitration? You want to start listing people who hate you, try Pete Werner."

"Tell you what. Why don't you let me worry about Werner. You just worry about making sure Local 664 wins the arbitration."

"Jesus, Trice, my cat could win this case for the company. Half the neighborhood knows you were in Jenny Rats last Friday. We've got an eyewitness who says he saw your beard sticking out from under that stupid Nixon mask, practically everyone in Lancaster knows the bike, and your right leg looks like it's ready for amputation.

"But don't you see, that's what makes this whole thing so delicious. You're going to get me my job back in spite of the facts, and no one's even going to suspect that Mr. Harry Greene himself had anything to do with it. What do you think, Harry?"

"I think you're sick, Trice." Greene suddenly stood up, Trice still slouched in the Wassily. The words came out almost like an invisible hand had pulled a cork from Harry's mouth.

"And I must be even sicker, way I put up with it. What are you going to do for kicks after I die, Trice, rob collection plates? I swear I just oughta let you tell the whole damn story to the whole damn world and be done with it. Only reason I don't is my family."

"Come off it, Greene." Trice slouched a little deeper into the leather chair. "Only reason you don't is because you're a greedy bastard. So don't give me that pious crap about your family. You got it good here, Harry. Big business, big reputation, Mr. Jewboy of Lancaster County. Even got a dead partner who never existed. How'd you ever come up with a name like that anyhow, pull it outta some phone book?"

"What are you talking about?"

"Oh, please, Harry. C. Oliver Pitowsky, co-founder of Greene-Pitowsky Smelting & Battery Company. Born March 17, 1898. Died August 1, 1957. Hunting accident in Montana as I recall. What'd you think—name like Pitowsky gonna help you get all that good Christian business? You're so dumb, you couldn't even think of a good WASP name, could you? And the portrait. Where'd that come from, a garage sale?"

In point of fact, the portrait came from Samuel T. Freeman's in Philadelphia, a not-so-prized possession of the estate of its owner and likeness, Brewster Keating, an Associate Justice of the Pennsylvania Supreme Court who actually died of adult onset mumps in 1946. Harry had his cousin Artie, the jeweler, make him up a new plaque.

Trice was rolling. "Yeah, I know all about that deal now, don't I? Not that it matters, of course, seeing as how everybody works for you knows it too, only they all have to kiss your ass to keep their lousy jobs. But then, that other dirty little secret. That's a bit different, isn't it? That's just between you, me, and our dear mutual friend, Mr. Failsafe."

"And I pay you, so what more do you want?"

"I thought I just told you, Harry. But apparently you're having some trouble with your ears. So pay attention."

And then Trice screamed as loud as he could, his face not more than an inch away from Greene's. "*I want my job back!*"

Harry wanted to scream too. But, he was just so tired of it all that he made himself speak softly.

"Just tell me, Trice. Why do you stay here? Why can't you just take the money and leave me alone? Why do you want to keep a crummy job driving a forklift?"

"Three questions, Mr. Greene? I'd love to answer those three questions. Even put on some fresh music for the occasion." Trice pulled out Bach this time.

"Glenn Gould, Harry. Plays *The Well-Tempered Clavier* on piano, you know. Much more soothing to the ear than the harpsichord. Real nut, Glenn Gould. Never appeared in public. Just recorded in the studio, moaning while he played. Always wore a big overcoat and sat on a real low stool so his face was right in the keys. Upped and killed himself one day. Shame. Best Bach player ever lived." Again piano music filled the big living room.

"Question number one. 'Why do I stay here?' That's an easy one, my friend. I stay here because I was born here. Not a carpetbagger like you. You know I lived most of my childhood not two miles from that plant of yours. I remember Hixon Avenue when it was just houses, nice neat little houses full of good working folk. We had a big old park on your land back then. Had a creek running through it and everything. Used to catch salamanders in that creek, Harry. Know what I did with them?"

"I really don't care, Trice."

"Oh, but you should, Harry, you really should. I used to kill the slimy little critters. Taped them to arrows and shot the arrows into trees. Guts came squirting right out their mouths when the arrow hit. I'm sure it was quick and painless, not like the slow way you do it to people. Come on, Harry, sure I can't interest you in some of this fine cognac?"

"All right, get it."

Trice pulled a fresh crystal snifter from the liquor cabinet, covered its bottom with the warm golden liquid and handed it to his guest. Harry Greene swigged it down like medicine. No smelling, no sipping.

"Christ, Harry, that's expensive stuff. You're supposed to savor it, not chug it. Please, can we drink the next one just a tad slower?" Trice filled Greene's snifter again, then went back to his narrative.

"Now what was that next question. Oh, yes. 'Why can't I just take your money and leave you alone?' But I do, Harry. I do leave you alone, except now I need just this one extra little favor." Trice pursed his lips and slowly stroked the long square beard. "In fact, tell you what. You get me my job back and this year's a push. No money. Whaddya think?"

"I don't know what I think, you want to know the truth. You don't need the damn job. You don't even like it."

"Ah, the third question. Why do I want to keep—what did you call it—a 'crummy' job? I want to keep it, Harry, because I can do damn near whatever I want and not get fired. Who wouldn't love a gig like that? It's the power, Harry. The power to strut around, to make Breitenfeld and all his Hitler youth look like a bunch of Barney Fifes. And I can cheat, Harry. Just like you. I fake my time card. You cheat your salesmen. Always telling them you're shipping orders short so you can pocket some of their commissions. And the best part is, they all know you're screwing them, but they can't do a damn thing about it or else they'll get fired, right Harry?"

"No it's not right. I don't know who told you that. I don't cheat my men."

"Well I think you do. I think you cheat your men. I think you cheat your customers. I think you would cheat your own mother if you had to—and the fact is, you do have to. Because you still can't stop spending money, can you, Harry? Thirty-eight years in the junk metal business, and you still think you're some kind of Rockefeller."

Harry Greene, now deep into his second cognac, knew Trice was right. He did live over his head, and he did cheat. How many times, when he couldn't sleep at night, when he wandered though his dark house deep into the early morning hours, did he ask himself the very same question that seemed now to so amuse his tormenter. He could have lived well without the craziness. But he had to buy the kids' camp. He had to have the boat, and the lake house, and the condo in Margate, and the country club. And that was precisely how it all started, or more accurately, how it all ended.

Harry peered into the shadows of the huge living room. In a distant corner he could make out the silhouette of Trice's Hasselblad camera. He saw it and wondered if Trice really meant the words. Would he really be spared next month? Would there really be no annual bill? And what about the photograph? Was it possible that Trice would spare him that as well? He didn't know, one way or the other. But what Harry Greene did know was that, somehow, he had to fix it so the union would win Trice's arbitration.

For that, he knew it was time to visit Jack McKeon.

THREE
Monday, August 22

HARRY WAS TRYING TO take his blood pressure while driving. He had paid $168 for the portable model from Hammacher Schlemmer which was now giving him a systolic of 250, then shutting off. After the third try, with the circulation all but cut off from his right index finger, Greene shook the little gizmo off his hand in disgust and tossed it to the floor of his black Buick Park Avenue.

He was taking the southern route to Philadelphia today. Some days he just aimed the big sedan east, down Route 30, past the Dutch Wonderland, past Mr. 3-L's bookshop in Paradise, its bright red and yellow sign inviting passersby to "come in, browse and enjoy." He had never been there. He would mark the journey. First third to the Downingtown bypass, through the Amish country. Next leg the highway. Finally the Philadelphia Main Line, starting at humble Frazer, building through Paoli, Malvern, Devon, Bryn Mawr, tapering off to Ardmore and Narberth, then slumming across City Avenue to West Philadelphia itself, to his alma mater, Overbrook High School, which he never looked at anymore, now that it was sprayed solid with graffiti.

But today he was in a hurry, so it had to be the southern route. He slowed the Buick only briefly outside Strasburg to admire the old steam locomotives parked forever behind the Pennsylvania Railroad Museum on Route 741. He took a commuter train to work after the war, pulled by a steam engine just like the rusted 2-4-0 parked closest to the highway. Took it every day from 30th Street Station to Bridgeport. Then he would walk nine blocks to Bridgeport Metal Traders, on his way to learn the smelting business from his father's brother, Nate.

At sixty-nine, poised to enter his eighth decade on November 2, Harry Greene was suddenly having a lot more trouble not thinking about dying. He tried to stay in good shape. Worked out every other day at the club. Stair climber, Nordic Track, Nautilus. His forearms were still massive, a last vestige of torture from his Uncle Nate. But the upper arms were starting to crease and flatten, like old balloons with half the air gone; and the legs, he swore, just kept getting thinner and thinner each year, no matter what he did. He particularly hated the hairy white skin, streaked with sky blue rivers of varicose veins. Most days at the club he kept his sweatpants on during the whole workout, no matter how uncomfortable it got. And he always showered alone.

At the same time Harry and his pressure cuff were making their way to Philadelphia, Jack McKeon, senior partner of McKeon, Tingham & Marsh, was busy stapling a large cockroach to a brown transmittal slip. McKeon had tried just about everything else to get the office manager's attention concerning the Lincoln Building's infamous bug problem, but nothing seemed to work. Today he decided to try a more direct approach. He checked the box on the slip marked "Handle," walked out to his secretary's desk and dropped the animal into the out box. Marjorie Hewson looked like she was about to throw up.

"What time is Harry Greene due?" he asked.

"In ten minutes, Mr. McKeon, and does that–that horrible thing have to stay here?

"No, Margie, you can take it to Ms. Rice's office right now if you want."

The secretary was not amused. McKeon told her to hold his calls pending Harry Greene's arrival.

Greene had sounded unusually flustered on the phone when he called to make the appointment. It was well after ten PM when McKeon's oldest client called the lawyer at home, practically begging to be seen first thing the next morning.

Often, after calls like that, Jack McKeon would ask himself why he had ever decided to practice labor law, particularly on the management side. His partners regularly teased him about spending endless hours in assorted Motel 6's with packs of thugs and reprobates, while they dined at the Four Seasons with the Wazzir of Swat and talked of mega-deals. Most of the time, the senior partner would just shrug it off and laugh. The one thing they couldn't tease him about, however, was his book of business. The best known and most widely respected labor lawyer in the city of Philadelphia was on his way to another two and a half million in billings for 1994, and 1995 was looking to be even better.

A meeting with Harry Greene, however, always took Jack McKeon back to earlier times, sometimes as far back as the summer of '43, when the Irish Catholic from Lansdowne and the Jew from West Philadelphia huddled together in wet, shallow foxholes overlooking tiny Sicilian towns reduced to rubble, pledging eternal friendship if only God would let them live one more day. They were linked only by the constant fear of death, and their hatred of George Patton, who mugged for news photographers with his ivory-handled revolvers, while the Seventh Army, filled with legions of McKeons and Greenbergs sleeping in dirt and brushing maggots off their dinners, lost lives from Palermo to Messina, just for the glory of allowing their leader to upstage Field Marshal Montgomery.

Despite their promises, the two young veterans, both with Purple Hearts and chests of ribbons, at first drifted apart after the war. Harry was busy shortening his name to Greene and flailing about, looking for something to do with his life. Jack knew precisely. By 1951 McKeon was sitting for the Pennsylvania Bar exam, already assured of a judicial clerkship in Common Pleas Six, the most prestigious trial court in Philadelphia City Hall. Harry was pouring lead pigs for Bridgeport Metal Traders, cursing his overbearing Uncle Nate, never realizing that he would someday become a multi-millionaire just by using the knowledge his uncle was force-feeding him, day after filthy, hot day.

Harry and Jack reunited in the summer of 1951. Like most things in Harry's life, it was an accident. On a rainy night in July, the world's worst dancer ducked into Wagner's Ballroom at Broad and Olney just to stay dry. Within an hour, Harry not only bumped into Jack McKeon, but also met the slender brunette with white skin and blue eyes who would, in two years, become Mrs. Greene. Minna Feinstein and Harry were inseparable for the rest of the summer. He cried openly when she returned to Lancaster after Labor Day.

By the end of October, Harry was selling cars for a living—in Lancaster, of course, at Big Irv Feinstein's Buick/Oldsmobile, of course. Harry Greene was a terrible car salesman, but it didn't matter a bit to Big Irv, so long as his daughter was happy. And she certainly was.

⸺⟐⸺

All the way from Lancaster, Harry had been trying to stay calm. He kept telling himself that McKeon would have a solution, that his old friend would lean back in that big leather chair and squint those big Irish blues and smile that confident way he always did, and tell Harry to just settle down and relax. But every few minutes, he imagined another scene. In this one, McKeon would look troubled. Then he would get angry at Harry, and would start berating him about not ending it years ago.

Greene was still playing the two tapes in his head when the elevator opened to the twenty-fourth floor. The lobby was quiet this morning, with just the pendulum of the firm's antique grandfather clock and the distant burbles of telephones to break the silence. Even the receptionist was missing, her massive art deco desk empty, except for the ever-present vase of fresh flowers adorning the left front corner. McKeon loved to tell Harry how much he hated the lobby's decor. "Too many purple wizzits shaped like conch shells," he would mutter. "Never should have let Jocelyn hire that fag decorator. Used to look like a law firm in here—now it's a beauty parlor."

The receptionist, painfully thin except for her huge breasts, pushed open a smoked glass door at the end of the lobby, saw her visitor, and immediately began reciting her lines. "Oh, Mr. Greene, I'm so sorry. Have you been here long? I'll tell Mr. McKeon you're here. Can I get you some coffee?"

Before Harry Greene could say "black," the senior partner magically appeared in the lobby. McKeon's manicured right hand practically disappeared into the fleshy palm of his old friend as they greeted, then embraced.

The lawyer and the smelter: John Joseph McKeon, sixty-eight years old, small, tan and fit, with a full head of silver hair, no strand out of place, with his narrow, straight nose and his cleft chin, and his slim lips, and his custom-tailored blue suit, set off, as always, by a monogrammed white shirt and perfectly knotted rep tie; Harry Greene, one year older, burly and bald, his shirt already opened at the collar with the tie knot pulled down, two thick hands never quite able to come clean, no matter how often they were washed—one ring finger displaying a massive gold wedding band, the other a silver circle topped with the Star of David made of diamonds.

McKeon never sat behind his desk when he met with a client. "You are there to help that person," he would remind his associates, "not lecture them. This isn't teacher-student. It's a meeting of equals. If your office isn't big enough to carry on a conversation without you hiding behind a desk, then use a conference room." Of course, McKeon's office was more than big enough. The twin couches and easy chairs alone could seat eight people.

McKeon settled neatly into one of the easy chairs, while Greene sunk into the flanking couch, his coffee cup resting on a large glass-topped table covered with miniature trucks—trophies of the successful labor lawyer.

"It's Trice again, isn't it, Harry? What's he done this time, run over Breitenfeld with a forklift?"

"That's not funny, Jack. I've got a real problem here."

McKeon leaned forward in the chair, his knees almost touching Harry. "Whatever it is, we'll deal with it, you understand that?"

Greene reached for the coffee, drank deeply from the steaming cup, then started.

"Last Friday night, Trice got drunk down at the Rat. He ended up putting on a rubber mask and riding his motorcycle into the battery building, lost control in the grease and smashed into that night watchman, Charlie, the one they all call Carpool. Anyhow, the old man's still in the hospital, with a fractured skull and a really bad concussion. Doctors say he'll be all right, but he's going in and out of consciousness and they've got him in intensive care."

"Has he talked yet?"

"That's one of the problems, Jack. He was still conscious when they took him to the emergency room. Told the whole story to the cops. Said he recognized Trice even with the mask on because of that stupid beard he's got with the square bottom. And everyone in the neighborhood knows the motorcycle."

"I take it you've talked to our friend?"

"Right before I called you last night. I got the full treatment, the cognac, the classical music. He even showed me his burned-up right leg, where the exhaust pipe went over on him when he fell. Then this morning, he calls my secretary and has her give me a message that one of his biker buddies, Stuff Johnson, also knows about it."

"Stuff Johnson? Never heard of him."

"Works in the warehouse. Night shift. Just another punk, but he's Trice's only friend at the plant. Must have been at the Rat with T. J. when it happened, that's all I can figure."

McKeon leaned back in the easy chair. "All right, Harry, I get the picture. Now what's the punch line?"

"The punch line is that Sunday afternoon Breitenfeld fired Trice. He had the police report with Charlie Carpool's statement, and he just went ahead and did it. Never even called me."

"I still don't see the problem. Breitenfeld's been waiting for years to get rid of that guy. Now it's out of your hands. You just keep paying him his lousy blood money, but now he's not there in your face every day."

"It's not that simple, Jack. Trice wants his job back."

"You've got to be kidding. Christ, you're giving him a hundred thousand a year now, what the hell does he want with ..."

Harry didn't wait to hear the rest of the sentence. "Look, you're the one keeps telling me the guy's a lunatic. So you're right, that's all. He's a lunatic. All I know is, Trice says that's the whole bill for this year. Says he doesn't even want the money, just the job."

"Come on, Harry. Get some sense into that bald head of yours. You think this guy's going to derail a one hundred K gravy train just so he can keep busting your supervisors every day in a warehouse?"

"Would you bet against it? Look at the guy, Jack. Look at what he did in 1984. Look at the pictures he sends me every year. Look at the way he lives. I'm telling you, I think he's serious. I don't know what to do. I tell

Breitenfeld to lay off, the whole plant's gonna smell something. The sonofabitch practically killed a man right in my battery building. And there's an eyewitness."

"Christ, Harry. Even if you could figure out a way to lose the arbitration, that assumes there's going to be an arbitration. My guess is, Pete Werner's going to take one look at this dog and bail."

"That's what I thought, but Trice says no. And I think he's right. Werner's up for re-election next March and that's going to be a real fight. Plus he's got the Rapid Freight contract coming up in October, and mine after that. No, he'll take the case. Can't afford not to. Members'll start calling him a wimp if he doesn't. Trice will threaten to sue the union. Werner's got two bad choices here, and walking away from T. J. is the worse of them. Besides, if the union loses, he can always blame Rothstein or claim I bought off the arbitrator."

"You think getting him his job back is going to be the end of it?"

"No, Jack. I don't think anything's the end of it. For all I know he'll change his mind and want to be paid double next month. But right now I know he's serious, and you've got to do something."

McKeon stood up and walked slowly to his large picture window overlooking the statue of William Penn atop City Hall. He kept his back to Harry as he spoke. "You know how many lawyers there are in Philadelphia, Harry? Over twelve thousand. Twelve thousand esquires chumming for a bag of business can't keep half of 'em employed. Look down there. Lawyers selling insurance, lawyers tending bars, lawyers driving cabs. Every time one of my clients gets sued, half the firms in Philly send them brochures; union files a representation petition at the NLRB, ten slimy labor consultants mail out demo tapes bragging that they can win the election cheaper than a lawyer. And you expect me to lay down on a can't lose case against the toughest union in Lancaster County?"

"I don't know what I expect you to do, Jack. But you're in this too, you know."

McKeon spun around on his heels. Suddenly, there was no twinkle in the eyes. "What the hell are you talking about? I'm not the one getting blackmailed? I'm not the one wets himself every time the phone rings after nine o'clock at night."

"No, but you're still in it. This thing goes down, I'm telling everything. You understand me, everything. And that includes who introduced me to those bastards in the first place. See how that sits with your buddies at the Union League."

"I can't believe I'm hearing this Harry. You came to me, remember? You were the one ready to commit suicide you were so deep in debt. You just about begged me. 'I need money bad, Jack. I'll do anything, Jack. The bank's going to pull my line, Jack.' All I did was put you in touch with some people."

"Some people? You put me in touch with the goddamn mob. Except you didn't tell me it was the goddamn mob."

"I've told you a thousand times. *I* didn't know it was the mob, either. But it wouldn't have mattered if I did, because *I* just said I had some people might be interested in that abandoned kids' camp of yours. It wasn't me who turned Camp Pocono Sunrise into the northeast terminal of Cocaine Airways. You managed to do that one all by your little self."

Harry Greene suddenly felt the blood rush to his ears, as his 69-year-old heart kicked into overdrive. He could not deal with McKeon making remarks about the cocaine, even though he knew the lawyer was dead on, as usual. It was true. McKeon was only the matchmaker. But Harry could never completely accept his friend's professed innocence. Jack McKeon was a labor lawyer. He knew those people. Hell, he knew every shady character in Philadelphia.

Harry pulled his heavy body up from the depths of the lawyer's sofa. He reached for one of the miniature forklifts on the coffee table and began playing absentmindedly with the tiny lift chain mechanism. "I'm sorry, Jack. That crack wasn't fair. It's just that I don't know what to do. Trice is out of control, and I'm scared, that's all."

The twinkle was back in McKeon's eyes and he rested his hand on Greene's shoulder as he spoke. "You know, Harry. When I first got into this crazy business in 1953, I worked for a big fat slob, with a face like a old bloodhound, named Percival Morgan. Guy would come back every day from lunch with stains on his tie and gin on his breath; but he was one smart son of a bitch. He always calmed me down when he thought I was too pumped up about an arbitration. 'Funny kind of trial, a labor arbitration,' old Percival used to say. 'Not like a courtroom, you know. None of those nice Marquis of Queensbury rules for lawyers, with all the bowing and curtseying. More like a gunfight in Dodge City. Damndest things can happen in a labor arbitration. Never saw one yet couldn't be won. Never saw one couldn't be lost, either.' I learned a lot from Percival Morgan, Harry. We'll think of something."

FOUR
Tuesday, August 23

AXEL KINNARD HAD TO finish the job before Pete Werner returned from shop-level grievance hearings at the plant. He chopped furiously at an ice glacier clinging to the vents of an ancient Admiral air-conditioner rammed into the only window of Werner's steaming office. The old unit leaked out a whisper of tepid air that only seemed to make the cluttered office even more uncomfortable. Werner was going to be in a terrible mood. He always was after shop-level grievance hearings, particularly in August.

"It's the goddamn heat down there," he would say. "Place already stinks from acid fumes, then you throw in the goddamn heat and it's a wonder no one drops dead. I keep telling the ties, there's gonna be a riot in this factory one of these days if you don't get some decent fans. But it doesn't matter, 'cause the ties got no power, and everybody knows it."

Kinnard looked up from the dying Admiral and peered out the window of Werner's office. Just a few hundred feet down Hixon Avenue he could see the main gate of Greene-Pitowsky Smelting & Battery Company. It was almost three. Shift change. A wave of sweat-soaked bodies about to pour through that gate, escaping at last to the sanctuary of a Tuesday afternoon. Many would just file in downstairs, clamoring for a Bud at the bar of Jenny Rats. Kinnard liked having the union hall in the same building as the Rat. That way he could work them both. It also kept the Rat pretty much off limits to the ties. "Us against them," he would say. "Just the way God made it."

The ice glacier was starting to peel away now—surrendering to the stainless steel tentacle that disappeared up the right cuff of Axel Kinnard's shirt sleeve. Finally, the Admiral's condenser settled in to its familiar vibrating groan, the air stream regaining a cool edge, helped along by the only two digits remaining on Kinnard's other hand—a powerful vice of thumb and forefinger ripping away at the stubborn foundation of ice crust.

He pulled off his shirt, exposing the shiny mechanism of springs and cables that mated the flesh of his powerful forearm to the steel of his hand. A slurry of sweat and dust glinted off the hair of his chest, tufted and black above the rim of his white sleeveless undershirt.

Even in disfigurement, Kinnard was a decent-looking, if not a handsome man. At forty-six, gray was just beginning to show at the temples and in the hairs of his walrus mustache. But the head of hair was still thick and shiny, combed back with just a bit too much grease to look natural. The upper body was broad but not fat. And the left bicep still showed the faded remnants of the Rolling Stone tongue that Kinnard let a drunken friend tattoo on him in memory of Altamont.

Axel knew immediately that the Secretary-Treasurer of Manufacturing and Transport Workers Local 664 was in the building.

"Chopper, you lazy piece of gristle, that damn air-conditioner better be blowing ice cubes by the time I get in there."

Pete Werner stomped up the old wooden stairs and threw open the door of his office. In almost the same motion he swiped at the Windsor knot choked around his size seventeen shirt collar, let his gray Samsonite attaché fall to the floor and propelled himself to the shiny clean faceplate of the groaning Admiral. He shoved his face so close to the brown plastic grillwork that he could feel his thinning locks of hair, the color of wheat, flick at his scalp like tiny wet bullwhips. He didn't move for more than a minute.

It had been over two years since the union election in which Pete Werner had defeated Rapid Freight's Chief Steward, Dickie Romanowski, for the top spot in Local 664: the dilapidated corner office overlooking Hixon Avenue, plus all the aggravation a man could eat. And even though it was 94 degrees in the shade on this particular August day in Lancaster, Werner had still worn his tie and jacket to the grievance meeting.

"Never take the damn things off in front of them," he would preach to his business agents. "I don't care how hot it gets or how long you're in there. You're a businessman, just like them. You're their equal. Hell, you're more than their equal. Never let them forget it."

Axel Kinnard broke the silence.

"Tough one today, Pete?"

Werner slowly pulled his face from the air-conditioner. "They're all tough, Chopper. Last six months before a contract and all of a sudden everyone's a goddamn lawyer. Least little thing goes up their butt, I gotta get the contract changed.

"Now it's the night shift. Can you believe that, the freaking night shift. Company decides to start rotating shifts in the warehouse and half of 'em want to take it to arbitration! Say they all got important matters to take care of at night, so they can only work steady first and second. Some important matters. Most of those dumb bastards sit in their garages all night with their willies up the tailpipe of some motorcycle."

Kinnard started toward the door of Werner's office. "You want a beer? I'm going downstairs."

"Sure. Get one for yourself too, Chopper. Put it on my tab."

Axel yelled back over his shoulder from the hall. "I wouldn't get too comfortable, boss. I think we're gonna have a visitor. Tell ya in a minute."

Despite the warning, Werner kicked off his shoes and put two size thirteen feet up on his seedy glass-covered desk, awash with miniature forklifts, loose paper, and assorted office junk. He was finally alone for the first time all day. If he just leaned his head back on the threadbare captain's chair the old Admiral could drone him to sleep in five minutes. But he couldn't relax. Beat as he was, he just couldn't relax.

So instead he yelled out the door. "Visitor. What the hell kind of visitor?" Axel couldn't hear him. So he returned to his worrying.

Why did he ever let Harry Greene have a two-year labor contract in 1993? Joe Greist might have been crooked as a dog's hind leg, but he had set it up just perfect at GPS&B way back in 1969. A contract never expired in an election year. But Werner, newly elected Secretary-Treasurer, negotiating his first contract with Harry Greene, let himself get sucked into a two-year deal. And in just six months he would be square up against it.

The contract between Local 664 and Greene-Pitowsky Smelting & Battery Company expired on February 15, 1995. Elections for local union officers were March 15. One month. Not enough time for the men to appreciate a good deal, but plenty of time to get revenge for a bad one. Especially with Romanowski looking to get even for '92.

Axel trundled upstairs and kicked open the door, a pair of longnecks squeezed firmly in his two-finger vice. He had been thinking of just how to tell his boss about Thomas Jefferson Trice.

Werner beat him to it.

"I guess you heard Breitenfeld fired our bearded friend day before yesterday. On a Sunday, no less, can you believe that."

"Everybody heard it, boss. Heard about Charlie too. Poor sonofabitch. He ain't gonna make it, ya know."

"Bullshit. Man's too pickled to die. He'll make it, trust me." Werner took a long pull on his beer, then let the springs of the old desk chair propel him to vertical. "So who's this visitor you're so hot and bothered about."

"Who do you think, Pete. Picked up a blank grievance form first thing out of the chute this morning. Said he wants to deliver it to you in person."

"You're fucking with me, Chopper. Say you're fucking with me."

The voice in the office doorway beat Kinnard to the answer. "Wrong, Werner. The man is definitely *not* fucking with you." Trice was folding the grievance form into the shape of a paper plane as he spoke, now launching it with a flick of the wrist, now watching it gently sail across the room and touch down square in the middle of Werner's desk blotter. "Read it, bro. Read it and do that fancy job we're all paying you for."

Pete Werner didn't move a muscle. He didn't reach for the airborne grievance form. He didn't raise his voice. He didn't even bother to look up at his visiting member. He just spoke to the blotter.

"I'm going to give you a choice, Trice. Column A or column B. Column A, you walk over here like a good boy, take this piece of garbage off my desk and go file for unemployment. Column B, Axel shoves a certain grievance form about halfway up your sorry ass, then sails you and it down those steps out there. You got that—bro?"

T. J. Trice walked slowly toward his elected leader. He was limping badly, his right leg dragging more like a nuisance than a functioning limb. Werner raised his large blond head, trading his view of the blotter for one of Trice's foul-smelling beard. He knew, at once, that he had made a mistake.

Trice reached for the paper plane. Then he carefully unfolded it, placed it flat on the blotter, and signed it slowly and clearly with the big Mont Blanc he extracted from Werner's desk set. "Column C, Mr. Secretary-Treasurer. Would you like me to quote the labor contract verbatim, or will an executive summary suffice?"

"I know what the goddamn contract says." Werner hated himself for going on the defensive, but he couldn't help it. "And I also know what vehicular homicide is. So you better hope he doesn't die. Let me ask you, Brother Trice, did it give you a thrill running down a helpless old man? Was it better than getting drunk downstairs? Was it better than diddling your slutty girlfriend from Armstrong? Tell me, Bro, how was it? How did it really make you feel?"

Trice was already limping toward the office door while Werner was talking, but he wasn't quite ready yet to make an official exit. Instead, he stood in the doorway, facing back into the office, his white arms stretched upward, hands gripping the top of the door jamb. He looked like a withered ape hanging from his perch.

"You got till next March, cuz. You know it. I know it. Every damn member of this local knows it. Then it's back down the street—you and your bionic friend there—sucking Harry Greene's dick so you don't get laid off again. What was it, Werner, third shift kettle room? Dirtiest job in the plant? And you'll gobble it up like chocolate pudding, because it's still better than selling cheese on Route 30 like your old man."

Werner lost it.

"You get the hell out of here. You mention my father again, I'll rip that fucking beard off your fucking face."

Trice relaxed his grip on the door jamb. "Just process the grievance, Mr. Secretary-Treasurer. Do what you're still getting paid for. I want my job back, you got that?"

"I'll tell you what I got. I got a grievance form that's just about to go into my toilet. You want a job with Harry Greene? Go ask Romanowski to help you fill out an application next spring."

T. J. Trice didn't hear Werner's parting shot, because he was already down the stairs. Axel clipped the neck of Werner's spent beer in his metal hand. "You want another?"

"Yeah, I do, but maybe I ought to just start saving my money. You heard the man."

"It'll never happen, boss. The members love you."

"You think so? Let me tell you something. They don't love dick. Something goes up their ass sideways with the Rapid Freight contract, or Greene's after that, we're all out on our keisters. It's the way this business works. Hooray for me and fuck you. Sometimes I actually think I'd be better off back down the street with Harry's stinking kettles."

"What, and get walking pneumonia, again. You know how many times I've heard that story."

Pete Werner knew Axel was right. Right about Greene, and right about the story. He had told it often.

In the middle of February of 1986, Werner had almost died of pneumonia. He was convinced Harry Greene did it on purpose. How much could it have cost to put in some kind of covered walkway between the end of the breaker building and the kettle room? It was only about a hundred feet. But, of course, Greene was too cheap. So when the breaking crew left the post and connector carts at the south end of the long open breaker building, Werner had to leave the overheated kettle room, drive his tractor into the frigid night air to the waiting cart, hook on and drive back. Hot to cold, cold to hot, night after freezing night.

The doctor figured Werner had been carrying the pneumonia for about three weeks. Werner knew it was longer than that, just from the coughing and chills. But he was afraid to take off. He needed the OT, especially with the wife pregnant, plus he only had three more points to burn under the plant attendance program before Breitenfeld would be able to give him a three-day suspension.

It was the third week in February before Werner finally gave in to the coughing and fever. Sure enough, first day back Breitenfeld slapped him with a three. On day one, he sulked at home. On day two he yelled at his wife for no good reason. On day three he was sitting in Local 664's office, filling out a job application.

He never returned to work for Harry Greene.

"On second thought, Axel, maybe I could use another beer."

Werner felt himself returning to sanity. But there was no way he was going to process Trice's ridiculous grievance. It was one thing to get jobs back for stupid members who did stupid things and got themselves fired by stupid supervisors. Ike Rothstein would be doing just that tomorrow for a poor slob named Henry Koza. Trice, however, was something else.

FIVE
Wednesday, August 24

PETE WERNER WAS WATCHING his lawyer perform a ritual disembow-eling in Lititz, Pennsylvania. The victim was Jack McKeon's handpicked protégé, David Castelli, Esq.—young, eager, and, on this particular day, completely overmatched.

As soon as the case of *In re Rapid Freight, Inc. and Teamsters Local 664 (Discharge of Henry Koza)* had convened in the Mardi Gras suite of the Sleep-Tite Motor Inn, the neutral arbitrator, Professor G. Arnold van Auten, had to make a command decision. Jack McKeon's favorite asso-ciate, representing Rapid Freight, had opted for air-conditioning. Isaac Rothstein, attorney for Local 664, insisted on quiet.

"I'm not surprised Mr. Castelli wants that air-conditioner on," Rothstein had said, even before he sat down. "If the union had his witnesses we would want their testimony drowned out too." When the arbitrator laughed, then decided to proceed without air-conditioning, Werner knew it was going to be a very long day for Mr. Castelli.

What Werner didn't know, of course, was that Jack McKeon had told his senior associate that the Rapid Freight case was cake, a perfect oppor-tunity to notch a nice win four months before Castelli came up for partner-ship. "Henry Koza got caught red handed, off route, selling merchandise out of the back of his truck," McKeon had said.

But that was two weeks ago, when McKeon had given the Koza file to the handsome blond Italian who, Jack had promised, would be the next partner in the labor department of McKeon, Tingham & Marsh. Today David Castelli wished he had joined the firm's corporate department when he got out of law school in 1987. The Mardi Gras suite, no circulating air anywhere to be found, was now at a temperature of about 85 degrees and it was climbing.

Werner knew that his young opponent was powerless to stop the execution now in progress. Whenever he was in the presence of Isaac Rothstein, the Secretary-Treasurer found it difficult not to stare at the old lawyer's lips; they were so full and puffy, and they were always wet, glistening with saliva as though their owner were constantly licking them, even though he wasn't.

The words that came from the lips had some sort of a distant accent. Werner was never completely sure if it was real or fake. The accent was fungible European, a little German, a little Hungarian, maybe even a little Yiddish; and even when it was trying to be friendly and helpful, the voice of Isaac Rothstein always sounded as if it were on the verge of an argument.

Rothstein was also the best seat-of-the-pants cross-examiner Pete Werner had ever seen; and at this moment Local 664's lawyer had his hook firmly planted in the mouth of Rapid's chief witness, Gregory Newell. He played with his victim like a cat with a wounded field mouse—knowing he can kill at any moment, but just having too much fun to stop.

"In other words, Mr. Newell, you threatened Mr. Galenkos, didn't you?"

Sweat was all over the face and bald head of the supervisor. "No, sir, I wouldn't call it a threat."

"Oh you wouldn't? Well what would you call it, then?"

"It was more like a suggestion."

"A suggestion, Mr. Newell? Mr. Galenkos just said ten minutes ago that you threatened to have him arrested for receiving stolen goods if he didn't agree to testify against Henry Koza, and you call that a suggestion? Surely you can make up a better story than that."

Castelli interrupted. "Mr. Arbitrator, union counsel is badgering the witness."

Rothstein didn't even wait for van Auten to rule. "This is cross-examination, Mr. Arbitrator. I have a right to expose this witness for what he is—a lying ..."

"Whoa!" Castelli was on his feet. "I resent that remark. Professor, I demand that you instruct union counsel to behave himself."

"All right, gentlemen. Please." Professor van Auten turned to the scion of the Philadelphia union bar. "I understand that this is cross-examination, Isaac, but if you wouldn't mind keeping it just a bit less emotional."

"I'm sorry," Rothstein lied. "Sometimes I just get carried away when I see an innocent man about to lose his job."

Castelli felt like screaming at the top of his lungs. He wanted to stand up, like Howard Beale in *Network*, and just say it: "I'm as mad as hell and I'm not going to take this anymore. Henry Koza is a no-good thief and everyone in this room knows it. He stole merchandise, sold it to the Crystal Acropolis Restaurant, and got caught red handed." But, of course, David didn't stand up. He didn't scream at the top of his lungs. He just sat there, mindlessly unbending paper clips, as he always did when he was losing.

Rothstein jumped back on the soapbox.

"You knew, didn't you, Mr. Newell, that Plato Galenkos is a Greek immigrant who speaks very little English?"

"He has an accent, but I understood him."

"That's funny, Mr. Newell, I just heard Mr. Galenkos testify in this very room and I could barely understand a word he said." Rothstein turned toward the arbitrator. "You heard him too, didn't you, Professor? Could you understand him?"

The arbitrator looked sheepishly at Plato Galenkos, sitting at the end of the table, still wearing his greasy white apron with its maroon Parthenon logo. "How long have you been in the United States, Mr. Galenkos?" the arbitrator asked.

"Due year. I bin due year."

Castelli rolled his eyes toward the ceiling, then flipped his Sleep-Tite Motor Inn ball-point pen in the air. It came down in a plastic cup, spilling ice water all over his notes. Across the room, Henry Koza couldn't stop snickering. He whispered something in Dickie Romanowski's ear and the big shop steward started to shake with laughter.

"You think this is some kind of joke, Mr. Romanowski?" David said across the table.

"I think you're some kind of joke," said Romanowski.

"It's all right, Dickie," said Rothstein. "Mr. Castelli is always rude when his case is going down the toilet."

"Gentlemen, please," said Professor van Auten.

For the next hour and a half, Isaac Rothstein, defender of the downtrodden working man, pin-striped crusader against fascist supervisors everywhere, put Rapid Freight Incorporated on trial for the high crime of denying industrial due process. Not a word was said about the three dozen chianti bottle lamps with electric candles that Henry Koza sold to Plato Galenkos for twenty-five dollars in cash and four cold gyros.

When it was his turn, of course, Koza denied everything. He never met Galenkos, was never anywhere near the Crystal Acropolis, and had no idea how Rapid Freight merchandise boxes got into the restaurant's dumpster. All he knew is that his supervisor, Greg Newell, always hated him.

Throughout Koza's testimony, practically everyone in the room had their eyes fixed on the grievant's right forearm. The tattoo of Pluto the Pup had a huge erection. Every time Koza flexed, the penis rose and fell.

Castelli had no questions on cross-examination.

The arbitrator dutifully set the briefing schedule at two weeks, turning down Rothstein's usual suggestion that the case was so obvious it deserved a bench ruling on the spot. "That's a good one," Werner thought to himself. "What arbitrator in his right mind is going to give up two and a half days of billable time for reading the briefs and writing an opinion?"

Even though he had no direct involvement in Henry Koza's actual discharge or the grievance that followed it, Werner had been present for the entire arbitration. It was another inflexible rule he preached to his business agents, like the rule against removing your necktie.

"Nothing this union does is more important than handling discharge arbitrations," he would say. "Men can't remember a contract dispute one month after it's decided, but they never forget when a brother gets fired. They might hate the bastard and know he's guilty as sin. But come that arbitration, they want the company to lose. And it's our job to make sure they do. So you be there."

Counsel for Rapid Freight, sweeping up debris from the carnage as the room emptied, was startled when he heard Werner's chair creak behind him. He assumed everyone had already left the room.

"I want to apologize for Romanowski," Werner said. "That's not the way we train our stewards to behave."

"Forget it, Pete," said Castelli. "I don't pay any attention to Romanowski."

"Well you better," replied Werner. "You know he's running for Secretary-Treasurer next spring."

"Come on, Pete. Your members aren't gonna vote for that loudmouth and you know it."

Pete Werner looked tired. "I wish it were that easy," he said. Then he turned and left the hearing room.

It was just past three in the afternoon when Pete Werner looked at the dashboard clock of his Lincoln Town Car—late, but not quite late enough to blow off the rest of yet another soaking hot August day. He wanted to go straight home, maybe take Dorothy and the kids out for ice cream at the mall, and he would have done exactly that if only Ike Rothstein had blustered just a bit longer or Castelli had called one more witness. Then the clock would have read four o'clock, not three, and his guilt over the pile of paperwork waiting at Hixon Avenue would have succumbed to the rationalization that he had already put in a full workday. But five past three didn't quite cut it, so he just headed east on Marietta Pike.

At first, he couldn't see what was causing the traffic jam. It was too early for rush hour and too hot for the permanent crew that seemed to be fixing every road in Lancaster County every day of the year. It wasn't until the Town Car crested the hill before him that he could make out an Amish buggy, its left wheel missing, flopped over on its axle just far enough so that the roof blocked part of the driving lane.

On the shoulder of the road, where the square carriages usually traveled, Amish buggies were part of the scenery, curious conveyances filled with unsmiling people dressed in black. But this buggy, crippled and wedged into the highway like an unwelcome visitor, was obviously a nuisance on a busy afternoon. Pete had once read in a Lancaster County guidebook that the Amish traveled in horse-drawn vehicles because they believed that automobiles pulled families apart. He always liked that notion, even though he couldn't quite comprehend its logic. And many times when he would pass a buggy, on his way to the next confrontation on Local 664's daily schedule, he would peek inside to see if, indeed, a whole family was there together. If it wasn't, he would always feel momentarily sad.

The buggy without a left wheel was just ahead now. Pete watched as the father struggled with a long wooden lever placed across a rock, trying to lift the naked axle far enough off the blacktop so that his teenaged son could slide the wheel back on, both men in shirtsleeves, suspenders hiking up the waistlines of their black pants. Off to the side stood the mother and daughter, another set of twins in black long dresses and white gauze bonnets. Nobody in the family was speaking, and nobody driving by was stopping to help.

It bothered Werner to see an Amish family in trouble. Mishaps were just not supposed to happen in a culture so devoted to simplicity. It was almost as if God were welshing on a deal. "You folks over here—you get the cars and the computers and the booze, plus you get cancer and plane crashes. You others get nothing but earth and, in exchange, I'll leave you alone."

He knew, of course, that there were no deals. He saw the proof every time his friend Axel Kinnard pinched the neck of another Bud between the two steel hooks at the end of his right arm.

Kinnard had been working as a breaker man on the hydrocleaver the day it happened. He was doing a double, now fourteen hours into the shift, his mind numbed by the repetition of guillotining the tops off a thousand junked batteries. Turn to the flat bed, grab the battery, lay it on the chopping table, line it up, right hand on the safety, left hand on the trip lever. Push. Hard. Air release. The hydrocleaver blade thundered down like a steel curtain. It clanged on the chopping table, returned at once to the ceiling. Spring release. A severed battery top yawed forward, acid spilling across the table, puddling on the floor about his rubber boots. Throw the posts and connectors in the trough. Upright the case, send it along. Turn to the flatbed, grab the battery, begin again.

He knew the machine—its rhythm, its pulse, its every squeak and groan. At hour ten he had jammed the safety. Ties not looking. Everyone did it. At hour twelve he began to rest his right hand on the chopping table. At hour fourteen, he picked another battery off the flatbed. It was an old six volt, a big, black briefcase of hard rubber, took special positioning on the cutting table, must shove it further back so the blade didn't slit the case down the middle. Lean forward. Push. Hard. Air release.

It felt only like a punch when it happened. Not a sting, just a punch. Blade up. And then the spurts, arcing like crimson tracer bullets fired from the barrel of his severed radial artery, slamming rhythmically against the cement wall behind the hydrocleaver. He was cold, dizzy. But still no pain. Suddenly, he saw it on the cutting table. Himself! A piece of himself, still throbbing. Must rescue it. He reached in with his left hand, leaning forward. Safety still jammed. Air release. Spring. Second punch. Three fingers this time. And then, at last, at merciful last, the searing and burning of pain. He felt someone twisting rags around his arms. He heard himself scream, "Oh my god." Then he fell to the battery house floor curled like a fetus.

In his dreams over the next two months Kinnard's mother made it better. She sat on the blood-soaked bed sheet beside her only son, pushing the severed right hand tight against the stump, gently stroking his forearm at the point of union. Softly she sang the "I lu lu" lullaby of his childhood, sometimes pausing to hold his head for warm milk in a glass. And all the while, Axel Kinnard cried softly. The hand stayed magically attached when she bent down to kiss him goodnight. He felt so loved, so little, so safe. Then she would leave the hospital room, and as the wide door slowly closed, the pain returned, burning and stinging, and the hand again fell softly to the floor.

Most of the time Kinnard knew it was just the morphine, but it did not stop him. Awake, he screamed constantly for the floor nurses, demanding again and again to be reassured that they still had the hand in a jar, waiting to be reattached. The nurses humored him. The staff psychiatrist would decide when to tell Kinnard that there was no jar, that the right hand was never even recovered from the cutting table.

———◦◦◦◦———

Werner was fairly certain that the pickup parked in the side lot of Jenny Rat's belonged to T. J. Trice. A bumper sticker that read "I'd rather be riding my Harley" was slapped across the rear window of the cab, exactly where it would best interfere with the driver's attempt to use his rear view mirror. Another bumper sticker, this one actually affixed to the bumper, said "I Graduated from Fuck U."

Pete was hoping, though not really believing, that T. J. was just in for an early brew. Axel Kinnard wasted no time delivering the truth. Werner was still coming up the stairs when Axel appeared at the top of the landing.

"Boss, we got a problem," he said. He followed Pete into the corner office without even waiting for a response.

"Well at least the air's on in here, Chopper. So how bad can it be?"

"Trice is back. He's waiting for you in the conference room, Pete. This time he says he not leaving till you talk to him about his discharge."

"Oh is that right? Well you just go on in there and tell Mr. Trice that we already talked about it yesterday. I got nothing more to say to him." Werner sat down at the large glass-covered desk and started thumbing through his mail. "Dumb bastard is lucky he's not in jail."

"But he's got a lawyer with him today, Pete."

Werner's head snapped up. "What are you talking about?"

"Trice is here with a lawyer. I think it's the same jerk sued us last year on account of Mike Twardzik getting videotaped over at Rapid without pants on."

Pete Werner stood up. In the same motion, he threw down the letter he was holding and snapped off his reading glasses. "O'Conner? Trice has that fucking Brian O'Conner in my union hall?"

"I think he's the one, boss."

Pete was around the desk and out the door. In two giant steps the Secretary-Treasurer reached the closed door of the conference room and threw it open.

T. J. Trice had his right leg up on the table. Next to him stiffly sat Brian O'Conner, Esq., Executive Director of the Lancaster County Public Interest Law Center. A large ACLU button was pinned to his left lapel.

Pete Werner got directly to the point. "All right, Trice, what is this all about?"

"Now just what do you think it's all about, Mr. Secretary-Treasurer? It's about my getting fired last Sunday."

Werner sat down and worked hard at not raising his voice. "I already told you, T. J., there's nothing this local can do for you. You got caught, plain and simple."

"Oh," said Trice. "Just like that, ey? Some half-drunk, senile watchman says he recognized me under a mask and now there's nothing this local can do?"

Brian O'Conner decided it was his turn to speak. "Mr. Werner," he said. "I find it difficult to believe that we have to go through all of this again."

Trice broke into a grin. "I'm surprised too, Pete. Mr. O'Conner told me all about the Twardzik case. Invasion of privacy, failure to represent a union member."

"What happened with Mike Twardzik has nothing to do with you, Trice. Someone at Rapid was vandalizing lockers. They put in a secret camera to catch whoever was doing it, then Mr. O'Conner here made up some bag of bullshit about his client's privacy and us not taking it to arbitration. He got lucky."

Brian O'Conner counterattacked. "What I got, Mr. Werner, was a jury verdict against Rapid Freight and Local 664 for thirty thousand dollars. And I assure you it was not luck. Now Mr. Trice swears to me he was not the person who ran down Charlie Carliner last Friday. I believe him, but you apparently don't."

"Goddamn right I don't believe him, and no arbitrator will, either."

"I don't think, Mr. Werner, that you can be the judge of that. My client pays dues to this union; he says he is innocent; he's filed a timely griev-ance; and we demand that Local 664 take this case to binding arbitration."

"I'm really glad you demand it, Mr. O'Conner. Then maybe you can pay for it too? Do you know what it costs this local to take a case that far?"

Brian O'Conner reached into his briefcase. He looked almost bored as he pulled out the blue-backed wad of paper. "I'm not really interested in debating the proper uses of your union treasury, Mr. Werner. All I know is that you're on a big hook here, and I think you know it too. We're talking back pay, front pay, punitive damages and attorney's fees. So don't force me to file this." O'Conner slid the draft complaint across the table. "Because I assure you it will make the Twardzik case look like chump change."

The lawyer and his client slowly stood up from the table. As Brian O'Conner shut his briefcase, Thomas Jefferson Trice opened his mouth. "Just so we're clear, Werner. I filed my grievance yesterday, August 23.

Contract says you've got seven days to request a shop-level hearing down the street or the case is dead—no arbitration, no nothing. I make that August 30. You dig?"

Werner didn't even raise his voice when he answered, "You get the hell out of my union hall, Trice. And take your slimy friend with you."

Trice and O'Conner walked through the door of the tiny conference room. On the way out Trice said, "That's good, Pete, real good. Let's just see if it's still your union hall next spring."

Werner thought, but he couldn't be sure, that Trice slammed the door shut as he left. It was good, however, that it might have been just the wind; otherwise, Pete would have gone after both of them. Instead, he leaned his elbows on the now empty conference table and cradled the sides of his head against his palms.

Axel reported for duty without having to be summoned. "You didn't need that, boss, I'm really sorry."

"It'll pass, Chopper. Everything passes sooner or later."

"But he's such a prick. Everything this union's done for him and he comes in here with O'Conner."

"Yeah, I know. But let me tell you something. In this line of work, you have to learn how to eat it."

Werner was back in his seat now, handing O'Conner's complaint to Axel. "Fax this pile of garbage to Rothstein. And tell him to call me as soon as he gets it."

"Didn't he just have an arbitration out here this morning?"

"So?"

"So maybe he didn't go back to his office."

"Oh, he went back all right. There may be a fee check waiting for him."

"Well I hope he doesn't make you sit here all day waiting for his call, boss. If you need me, I'll be down at the bar helping Jenny."

Alone now in his office, Pete leaned back in the desk chair, kicked up his feet, and closed his eyes. Sometimes he just liked to sit quietly and do absolutely nothing. If he got lucky, he might even be able to take a nap. Someday he must get around to buying a couch for the office. But maybe he would wait until March to see if he still had an office.

He knew he shouldn't have let Trice get him so aggravated yesterday with the comment about Pete's father selling cheese. It made him look vulnerable. Even worse, it made him face the truth—that what happened to his father, and before that his grandfather, was floating in his mind almost every day.

Whenever he passed the railroad museum in Strasburg, Pete would look at the old steam locomotives sitting outside. His father built those monsters. His grandfather too. Two generations of Werner's busted their stones for the mighty Pennsylvania Railroad, and all it got them was nothing.

First they took out his grandfather. Gustave Werner went up to Altoona, Pennsylvania, from Missouri after the first war and signed on at the Juniata shops—built the boiler for the last K-4 Pacific in 1928—best steam loco Pennsy ever ran; but then he got sick. Doctors said it had something to do with all the dust he breathed, soldering inside the boilers. The railroad made him quit. No pension, no health insurance. Just quit. Thank you very much for the use of your lungs, Mr. Werner. Now, don't let the door hit you in the ass when you leave.

Pete's father, Wilhelm, thought he'd do better. He wasn't about to let the railroad do the same thing to him it did to his father; so he helped get the boilermakers union in. Became the shop steward. Wilhelm "Bill" Werner was going to set everything straight at the Juniata shops. Except the poor sonofabitch didn't know he was building the last steam locomotive ever in 1946.

In 1948, the railroad brought in a fourteen carat cocksucker named Clair Clugh to manage the works. Turned out he was in charge of switching the whole locomotive fleet over to diesels. Five years later, that was the end of the boiler shop.

Bill, of course, thought he had a pension coming, even if he got laid off. But Pete's dad didn't read the fine print in the labor contract. He didn't read the part where it said if you got fired for misconduct, the railroad could take your pension credits away. So he was in a meeting with management in 1953, trying to save the boiler shop from being shut down, trying to help his members, and he got a little carried away. He lost his temper and called Clair Clugh a cheap bastard. Under the rules of conduct, if you called Clair Clugh a cheap bastard just because he was about to put you and all your friends out on the street, that was insubordination. End of job. End of pension.

———≈◦≈◦≈———

It was after six when the phone finally rang in Pete's office.

"All right, Isaac, so give it to me. We take the case to arbitration, we don't. What are the odds?" It was almost early evening by now, but Werner wouldn't go home until Isaac Rothstein had gotten back to Philadelphia and returned Werner's call. The old lawyer refused to own a car phone.

"The odds of what," Rothstein said. "You're not making any sense."

"The odds that O'Conner can actually win this bullshit lawsuit he's talking about."

"Look here," Rothstein said. Werner felt the lawyer winding up for a lecture. "I'm not a racing tout. I don't give odds. But that's not the point anyhow—at least as far as the union is concerned."

"Well then, what is?"

"It's the aggravation, Peter. And the legal expense, and the publicity. You don't need that sort of thing, especially now. What do you think Mr. Romanowski's going to do when he finds out the union was sued for failure to represent a member?"

"But Isaac, the sonofabitch is drop dead guilty. Half the damn plant knows what he did last week to that old man."

Werner could almost touch the silent pause at the other end of the phone. Finally the lawyer spoke.

"How many times, Peter? How many times do we have to go over the same ground? You've got O'Conner's papers right there in front of you. It's called a failure to represent suit. It'll go before a federal court jury. Trice will take the witness stand and swear that you have a personal vendetta against him because of all the grievances he files. Then he'll claim to be supporting Romanowski and try to make the whole incident look political. And for the finale, he'll swear on his grandmother's grave that he was nowhere near Harry Greene's battery house on August 19, 1994, despite what some half-dead night watchman said just before he went unconscious. Now do you get the picture?"

Werner picked up the wad of paper lying on the center of his desk blotter. He flipped mindlessly though the pages of O'Conner's complaint, each paragraph reciting yet another baseless allegation, slathered with a coating of legal drivel. He picked one out and read it slowly to himself:

> 12. Despite the fact that Defendant Werner knew, or should have known, that Plaintiff had been improperly discharged from employment without just cause, Defendant Werner intentionally, and in bad faith, failed and refused to process Plaintiff's grievance, as required by Article XIX of the Collective Bargaining Agreement between Defendant Local 664 and Greene-Pitowsky Smelting & Battery Co.

Werner put the wad of paper back down on the desk. "Yes, Isaac," he said finally and quietly into the receiver. "I get the picture."

SIX

Friday, August 26

THE DUNGEON, ROOM 37C in the basement of Building 102, had no windows. Its dead fireplace had been bricked up for as long as anyone could remember, and the badly installed dropped ceiling was adorned with rust-colored water spots. Most of the room was furnished in American Government, dominated by the six new deal tables arranged in a squared-off U, with a seventh table for the hearing officer bisecting the open end. The chairs around the table had wooden seats with no cushions. Behind the closed end of the U were the spectator chairs. Unlike the official furniture, the gallery seats were made of original issue salmon-colored plastic with tubular legs. There were no smoking signs on the walls and tiny aluminum ashtrays strewn about the floor.

The actual grievance language of the Greene-Pitowsky collective bargaining agreement was dignified and orderly. The shop-level hearings themselves, however, more closely resembled the final session of parliament in a fatally wounded banana republic. That was why Harry Greene insisted that all such hearings be held in the Dungeon. The room's thick plaster walls kept most of the screaming and cursing bottled up inside. Greene also insisted that arbitration hearings be held there as well. Even though the union could have demanded a neutral site for arbitrations, they willingly used the Dungeon because it saved them sharing the cost of a hotel room.

Greene-Pitowsky's Director of Human Resources, Irene Henderson, called the hearing to order at precisely 10:00 am. At precisely 10:01, Shop Committee Delegate Lester G. Schenk accused the company of a conspiracy to bust the union by falsely and deliberately injuring the reputation of Thomas Jefferson Trice. Pete Werner told Lester to shut up.

The grievant had worn his favorite t-shirt for the occasion. Underneath a cartoon of several brown cylindrical objects with wings, the shirt said "If shit could fly, this place would be an airport." T. J. cleaned his fingernails with a pen knife as Irene read the grievance and the company's answer.

"Grievance 94 dash 238, filed August 23, 1994. Grievant Thomas J. Trice, clock number 74211, Shipping & Receiving. Statement of grievance. 'Protest unjust discharge. Company says I rode a motorcycle inside the plant and injured the night watchman. This is untrue and defamatory. Request apology, reinstatement and full back pay.' Statement of company answer. 'Grievance denied.' Mr. Breitenfeld will present the case for the company."

"Thank you, Ms. Henderson." Warehouse Superintendent Joseph Raymond Breitenfeld stood stiffly behind the table as he spoke. He was a small man, barely five-six, with thin hairy arms and hands that appeared to tremble slightly as they held his written statement. His high tenor voice, while fitting his body, seemed curiously at odds with the mouth from which it came, mustache covered and protruding just a bit too far from jowls that were already sprouting a five o'clock shadow even though it was barely mid-morning.

"On Saturday morning, August 20, 1994, I was at home when I received a call from the Lancaster police. They told me that our night watchman, Charlie Carliner, had been injured the night before when he was struck down by a motorcycle inside the battery house."

Lester Schenk stood up screaming. "That's hearsay. How do you know what happened, Breitenfeld? Were you there?"

"Mr. Schenk, sit down." Irene Henderson outweighed the shop committee delegate by at least thirty pounds and, had she wanted to, could have out-bellowed him by thirty decibels. But it wasn't necessary. "We do not have rules of evidence here, Mr. Schenk. But we do have order. Do you understand that?"

Pete Werner knew he had to come to his member's defense, even though Lester, as usual, was acting like an ass. "I'll worry about my men, Irene.

Not you. This isn't the Supreme Court here, it's a grievance meeting."

"Then I suggest you tell Mr. Schenk to control himself. The union will have its chance to respond as soon as Mr. Breitenfeld is finished. Please continue, Joe."

"Yes. Thank you. I went directly to the police station where Sergeant Bilosky gave me this incident report. Would you like me to read it?"

"Just the part that has Mr. Carliner's statement."

"It's a bit hard to read, because it's in the officer's handwriting, but I have copies."

Werner suddenly became interested in the proceedings even though he didn't even intend to hold this hearing until Rothstein convinced him he really had no choice. His interest, of course, had nothing to do with Trice's guilt or innocence. Everybody at the union hall already knew that T. J. had run down Charlie Carpool. Werner was coming to life only because he couldn't believe what he was hearing from the company. They didn't even have a statement from Charlie. All they had was handwritten notes from some cop who supposedly talked to Charlie.

He couldn't control his urge to interrupt. Hating Trice wasn't enough now that the old shop steward in Pete suddenly had firm control of his brain. "Do you people mean to tell this union that the company doesn't even have a statement directly from Mr. Carliner? Is that what I'm hearing?"

"What did you expect us to do?" said Breitenfeld, now off the script. "Drag the poor old man in here from intensive care so Trice could attack him again?"

"You'd better be able to back that up, Breitenfeld," Werner replied, "or you're gonna be the one ends up in intensive care."

Irene Henderson took control again. "Gentlemen, if there is one more outburst, I will clear this hearing room."

No one said a word, as the Dungeon quickly filled itself with the uncomfortable tension produced by total silence in a hostile meeting. The Director of Human Resources played the moment just long enough, then mercifully popped the bubble. "Mr. Breitenfeld, would you like to continue?"

"Yes ma'am. I would like to read the officer's statement for the record: 'Notes taken by Sergeant F. Campbell of interview with C. Carliner, 0240 hours, 20 August 1994, Garden Spot General Hospital Emergency Room.

Victim is employed as night watchman for Greene Petcock Company, Lancaster. At approximately 0130 hours, 20 August 1994, victim saw a motorcycle enter open end of building by Hixon Street. Rider was yelling victim's name in a high-pitched voice. Victim recognized rider as Thomas Trice, a worker at Greene Petcock Company. Victim said that he also recognized Trice's motorcycle, a blue Harley Davidson with lots of chrome. Victim said rider was trying to run him over on Battery Street. Victim pulled something in his knee and slipped on some oil. Motorcycle also fell in oil and slid toward victim with rider trapped. Victim heard rider scream. Victim lost consciousness when struck by motorcycle.'

"That's the end of the officer's notes."

Irene Henderson thanked Breitenfeld for his statement, then turned to Pete Werner. "Does the union want to ask Joe any questions?"

"We certainly do," said Werner. "Joe, have you actually talked to Charlie Carliner since last Friday?"

"He's still in intensive care, Pete."

"I take it that means no."

"No what?"

"No, as in, no, you haven't talked to Carliner."

"We have his statement. What's there to talk about?"

"And you didn't talk to Mr. Trice either, before you fired him, did you?"

"We had him in first thing Sunday afternoon."

"But you had already made up your mind to fire him by then, isn't that right?"

Breitenfeld didn't answer. "Well," said Werner, "isn't that right?"

The warehouse superintendent turned to Irene Henderson. "Do I have to keep answering these questions? I mean, what's the point?"

Werner spoke to the room. "The point is that you people got nothing here. Absolutely nothing. Where's Mr. Carliner? Where's Sergeant Campbell? You think this union is going to roll over just because Joe Breitenfeld's got a piece of paper? We're talking about a man's job here."

Irene Henderson was not impressed. "Mr. Trice, would you like to tell us your side of this?"

"There ain't no side," said Trice, still cleaning his fingernails. "I don't even know what the fuck this is all about."

"Well," said Irene, "you did file a grievance, didn't you?"

"Yeah. I filed a grievance. I filed a grievance like I said, 'cause I don't know what the fuck this is all about."

"Are you denying that you drove your motorcycle through the battery house?"

"Goddamn right I'm denying it. You think I'm crazy?"

"We're not here to judge your mental state, Mr. Trice," said the hearing officer. "We just want to find out what happened last Saturday at one in the morning."

"How the fuck should I know?"

"Because there's a man lying in the intensive care ward at Garden Spot General Hospital who says he recognized you and your motorcycle. And I would very much appreciate it, Mr. Trice, if you would try and control your language."

The grievant put his hand to his mouth and coughed. "Fuck you very much," he muttered under his breath. The Greene-Pitowsky Smelting & Battery Shop Committee, all seven men, snickered in unison. Pete Werner decided it was time to close the proceedings.

"Look," he said, rising up from the old wooden table and beginning to gather his notes. "The man said he didn't do it and you don't have a witness."

Breitenfeld was on his feet, waiving the police report. "You don't call Charlie Carpool here a witness? What do you think, the police made all this stuff up?"

"I think Charlie Carpool is a fucking liar," said Trice. "That's what I think."

"Forget it, T. J.," said Lester Schenk. "We'll just take it to arbitration and let them all make fools of themselves."

With the invocation of the A word, the Shop Committee triumphantly stood as one and silently filed out of the Dungeon. T. J. and Werner followed them out as Irene Henderson called to the grievant. "That's a nasty limp you've got there, Thomas. Must really hurt having a Harley fall on your leg."

SEVEN

Monday, August 29

EVEN THOUGH IT WAS only five miles from Jenny Rat's to Garden Spot General Hospital, T. J. Trice was in serious pain. Simply pushing down on the gas pedal of the pickup made him wince. Braking was agony. The burn was only a nuisance by now, and while it stung and throbbed under the gauze pads he had taped to his right calf, he still didn't believe it was really infected. But the knee scared him. At first T. J. had thought it was just a sprain. But now, ten days after the accident, it was swollen to the size of a small grapefruit. It was tender and red. And he could feel something clicking back and forth deep inside whenever he kneaded it with his fingers, which was constantly, every chance he got, hoping each time that he wouldn't feel the clicking.

Trice hated doctors and believed them powerless. He was twelve when his mother had died of lung cancer. At the end, a nurse just propped her up in an easy chair, in the little dark living room, in front of the TV, where she could watch "Queen for a Day" and Art Linkletter. Jane Trice, forty-two years old, seventy-three pounds at the end, still smoking Raleighs and saving the coupons.

He sat on an examining table in the tiny cubicle, dressed in a green paper gown, sitting on a white paper sheet, waiting for the emergency room resident to reach his stall. The hem of the gown lay across his skinny thighs, the two knees poking out over the edge of the table, one normal, the other grotesque. He tested the joint of his right knee, trying to straighten it, but the pressure of the grapefruit was unrelenting.

"What have we got here?" The resident was in his mid-twenties, red hair; he looked like a serious Howdy Doody.

"Motorcycle accident. Slipped on some grease." Trice had thought about a better story, but didn't feel like taking the trouble to make one up. "Besides," he had said to himself on his way to the hospital, "it's Greene's problem anyhow."

"When did this happen, Mr. Trice?" Dr. Doody did not look up as he methodically swabbed the right leg with alcohol to ease removal of T. J.'s homemade dressing.

"I don't know, last week, week before, what's the difference?"

"This wound is badly infected. Definitely should have been taken care of before now."

"I was busy."

"You shouldn't be fooling around with this kind of thing, Mr. Trice. If an infection like this becomes systemic, you can have a serious problem." The doctor turned and opened a small door in the medicine chest behind him. He pulled out a vial and syringe. "This is mezlocillin, Mr. Trice. It's an antibiotic."

"I don't take needles, doc. You can put that away."

"What do you mean, you don't take needles?"

Trice reached for the vial in the doctor's hand. He snatched it away, the syringe falling to the floor. "Just clean the leg and check out my knee."

Dr. Doody picked up the syringe, threw it in the trash, then placed both his hands around the grapefruit. "You're a grown man, Mr. Trice. I can't make you do anything, but I'm telling you that leg's in bad shape. I really think ..."

"Look, I told you. I don't take needles and that's the end of it." The young doctor shrugged, then began manipulating Trice's swollen right knee. Immediately, T. J. winced and sucked in his breath. "Jesus, what the hell are you doing? That hurts."

"This knee's going to have to be x-rayed. Then I want you to see an orthopedic surgeon. I don't think anything's broken, but there could well be some ligament or cartilage damage in here."

"What's that mean?" Trice felt the tingle of fear race through his body.

"We won't know until you've seen the orthopedist. In the meantime, I want you off this leg completely. The nurse will give you some painkillers and some penicillin to take for the infection."

He did see an orthopedist two days later and let him x-ray the knee. But when it came out negative, as Dr. Doody had predicted, Trice decided his medical treatment was over. The orthopedist, a kind enough looking old man who resembled Wilford Brimly, then delivered his own obligatory lecture about the evils of declining medical treatment and sent T. J. Trice home.

On the morning of what he thought was the second day after he saw Wilford Brimly, Trice awoke and bent his right knee. The grapefruit had shrunk to an orange and the field of needles under the bandage had dulled themselves to a field of paper clips—still pointed, but no longer searing.

He remembered the first night fairly well. He had chosen *Carmina Burana* for the occasion. It was a terrible piece of music and Trice knew it. But when he cranked up the gigantic Bose system as loud as his ears could stand, there was something about Nazi composer Carl Orff's lumbering tribute to medieval dropouts that T. J. actually found hypnotic. The gutter Latin mixed well with the fifth snifter of Remy, he had thought.

The second night was more difficult to remember. Now, as he moved through the rooms of the log house, finally able to walk almost without a limp, Trice reconstructed the past two days, sifting through debris the way an archeologist pieces together an ancient civilization.

He knew it had been maudlin. That he could tell just by the CD jewel boxes strewn about the living room. The entry of Fasolt and Fafner from *Das Rheingold* he remembered; the Strauss *Death and Transfiguration* he thought he remembered; Siegfried's Funeral Music and the Prelude from *Tristan und Isolde* and Steve Reich's *Different Trains* he could not remember at all.

Sheet music was piled in disarray at the feet of the Bösendorfer grand. Snifters, some empty, others still cradling tiny puddles of the amber liquid, sparkled in the morning sunlight. The opened cans, each with a spoon antenna poking out, chronicled Trice's diet for the past two days: Spaghetti-Os, cheddar cheese soup, hot 'n spicy salsa, yellow cling peaches in heavy syrup.

It was only when Trice finally noticed the Hasselblad camera, opened and lying precariously close to the edge of the coffee table, that he remembered something vividly. He had definitely started the project, but how far had he gotten? Suddenly, he was running, ignoring the pain still pulsing from the knee, out of the living room, through the kitchen, stumbling out the back door across the rocky yard to the shed. He stopped short, relieved. The padlock was still on the door.

For most of the year, Trice was able to will the multiple-day blackouts out of his life. In fact, for the last half decade, he had kept them so much under control that they were now down to a mere annual event, just a nuisance, no longer the *leit motif* of every weekend. There was still the pattern, however. The blackouts and the picture taking, one each, practically every September.

It had come a bit early this year, the blackout, and this one had been particularly virulent: a day and half, plus two full nights. Perhaps, he thought, it was the accident, or maybe the loss of his job. It didn't really matter, though. What did matter to Thomas Jefferson Trice on this particular morning in early September, and it was the only thing that mattered, was the project.

The old Norge freezer chest in the shed held mostly ice. Defrosting the ancient appliance was never a very high priority for Trice, so each year the ice walls thickened and the old freezer's capacity shrunk. Every so often, if he thought the temperature was going up, he would take a few whacks at the ice wall with a hammer, breaking off the bigger pieces. But since he didn't keep any food in the freezer, its cubic feet of storage space was mostly irrelevant. Just so long as there was enough room to hold the box.

In the beginning, the project had been much more difficult. He could still remember the first year, 1984. Willis Tucker's head had been detached from the rest of his body for less than twenty-four hours when Trice had taken the first photograph. It wasn't just a jawbone, then; it was the actual head of an actual person. It had skin and hair and blood still oozing from the hole in the right temple. It had a stench so horrible that Trice had to bury his nose in a gasoline-soaked rag every thirty seconds, just to deaden his sense of smell. But worst of all, it still had a face with an expression, with open dead eyes and the tip of a blackened tongue poking through its teeth, as if in some act of final defiance.

He had to use an electric saw that year to sever the maxilla and mandible from the rest of the head. He threw up twice before finishing the job, and almost passed out at least a half-dozen times. But as soon as Willis Tucker had been reduced to just a jawbone, and the rest of the head pulp and bones had been buried in the yard, Trice knew he could finish the project.

By year eleven, Trice knew the freezer wasn't necessary. In fact, the last strings of skin had dried to dust years ago, and there was no smell left at all. Still, Trice kept the jawbone in the cloth bag, and the cloth bag in the wooden box, and the wooden box in the Norge—just as he had since 1984, almost as if he feared that, once exposed to air and room temperature, Willis Tucker would somehow re-emerge, growing like a film run backwards from jawbone to skull to face to person—though Trice had never actually seen the live person, even from the beginning.

He carried the cold wooden box carefully back into the house, gently placing it on the free-standing butcher block, covered with black construction paper, that formed a two-foot-square island in the center of an otherwise useless kitchen. Then his hands began to shake, just as they did every September when it was time to open the box. How many years, he thought, would he have to go through the same ritual of reminding himself that he did not kill this man, that he didn't do anything, except just happen to be there when Willis Tucker was laid to rest? That, of course, and cut off his head. Now, for the eleventh time, he ran the events of the night of September 8, 1984, through his mind, playing them over and over until he once again knew it wasn't Trice who committed murder, and he was able to open the box and extract its contents.

The smaller pouch came out first. It was purple velvet and once held a fifth of Pinch scotch. Now it held the eight teeth from Willis Tucker's upper right jaw, and the first two from his upper left. Trice laid a fresh dental exam chart on the blacked out surface of the butcher block, then carefully placed each tooth atop its corresponding outline on the chart. Upper jaw, right to left, starting with tooth number one, the wisdom tooth, all the way around to number ten, extracted September 6, 1993, the left upper lateral.

Again he reached into the box, this time drawing out the white cloth bag that held all that was left of Willis Tucker. The two pieces of Tucker's jaw had come apart years ago, which actually made photographing the jawbone much easier. Trice carefully placed the lower jaw, its sixteen teeth still intact, on the butcher block next to the chart, then took the upper jaw into a tiny workshop, just off the kitchen. There, under a bright tensor lamp focused on his tiny work table, Trice began working a dental extractor back and forth against the surface of tooth number eleven, the left upper canine. It took longer than he thought, for even with no more skin or muscle left to hold it in place, the dog tooth's single fat root only reluctantly surrendered its long grip on Tucker's maxilla.

Trice went back to the butcher block and completed his 1994 still life. Tooth number eleven now in place on the chart, the maxilla lying next to it, butted up against the mandible—real jaw and chart jaw, side by side, different from last year's picture only by the addition of one more extracted tooth. Finally, the paper label, generated by his computer: "Seasons Greetings from the Tooth Fairy, September, 1994."

The large format Hasselblad was fitted with a close-up lens that allowed Trice to bore in so near to his subject that he had to be careful not to sneeze or cough, lest his breath dislodge one of the carefully placed teeth on the dental chart. He had loaded high resolution T-max film into the Hasselblad for the occasion. Twenty-four exposures. He used them all, varying the distance from lens to subject, his tripod holding the camera perfectly still as he pointed its nose directly down on the grisly still life.

When the last of the exposures had been spent, Trice went directly into his darkroom, tucked behind the workshop. The tiny windowless cell, more like a closet actually than a room, had just enough floor space to unfold the cheap aluminum and nylon beach lounger that Trice kept outside the darkroom's door. Although he owned an impressive array of high-end developing equipment, T. J.'s favorite time in the room was not spent producing photographs. What he mostly did in the tiny space was lie on the chaise smoking bongs, listening to music piped in through two small, but incredibly powerful ProAc Studio One speakers mounted high on the wall, under the ceiling—and always, of course, with the red developing light on, to give the room its proper ambiance.

But on this day in September, as he did on one such day every September, Trice handled the developing equipment with the same confidence and dexterity that marked his piano playing: always in control, never a wrong note. The very first picture came out textbook right, exactly the way he wanted it.

Trice smiled. The 1994 jaws of Willis Tucker would be as real as if Harry Greene were holding them in his hands; the teeth would glimmer with porcelain highlights and perfect little shadows on the dental chart. They would look almost three dimensional.

Carefully he slid the picture from developer, to stop bath, to fixer, each treatment locking the final, perfect image into place. The first picture completed, Trice repeated the process twice more—one for the archives, the other for the failsafe. All that remained now were the letter and the annual delivery.

EIGHT
Monday, september 5

THE TAN BREASTS OF Vanessa Reynolds fit snugly into David Castelli's hands as she rocked above him, neck arched back in the anguished moment just before orgasm. They were perfect breasts, sloping gently out from the smooth skin beneath her collarbone, turning up to small dark nipples, then sharply dropping off to half globes, down then up, back into her chest. He concentrated on her firm, thin body, as it jerked and twisted on him.

David squeezed his eyes shut, straining to keep the picture of Jocelyn Marsh's beautiful black secretary locked in his mind, knowing that the imaginary scene on Marsh's office couch, late at night with Vanessa, was the only way he could stay aroused until Leslie Castelli was finished.

His wife's climax was probably fake, David thought, a polite way of excusing herself from the love table without making obvious what both of them knew but never discussed. It had been that way ever since Ashley was born three years ago. David stretched his arms above his head, gripping the brass bars of the headboard, his eyes appearing to be closed, but actually watching through slits as Leslie quickly hid her nakedness in terry cloth and escaped the bedroom. Then he quietly slipped his hands beneath the covers and returned to Vanessa.

Castelli always hated Labor Day. It meant it was time for school to start again, time to get serious and put away summer for another year. David hadn't seen the inside of a classroom since he left Temple University over seven years ago, but his mental calendar still always flipped on Labor Day, never on January first.

The fall semester was going to be particularly unpleasant. In December, his class at McKeon, Tingham and Marsh would be considered for partnership and Castelli knew the final exam was going to be a ball buster. He had gone over the numbers so many times during the past few weeks that they were becoming more like a mantra than a calculation. Twenty-nine partners, thirty-three associates, three up this year.

The valedictorian of the class was Melissa Cohen, litigation, age thirty-one, *Harvard Law Review*, personal pet of Jocelyn Marsh herself. Cohen was a lock, even though she had never actually seen the inside of a courtroom except when carrying Marsh's trial bags.

Next, the salutatorian, Carl Merriweather, tax department, brain in a bottle, personality of a lima bean. Didn't matter. Merriweather was supposedly the only human being on Earth capable of even explaining, much less defending, the Fluxite Chemicals merger. No, Carl Merriweather was untouchable—at least until the statute of limitations ran on the client's IRS audit.

Castelli knew the leverage game better than most of the partners. At slightly better than one to one, the associate/partner ratio was just about perfect for Philadelphia. But three new partners in one year would slide that magic number below break even. There would be more members of the firm than fungible associates. Jack McKeon controlled a lot of things at McKeon, Tingham and Marsh, but the partnership election process was one sacred ritual still dominated by secret ballot and the four partner blackball. It was going to be a very tough semester indeed.

And it was going to start immediately. Castelli dragged himself out of bed. It may have been Labor Day for normal human beings; but for a senior associate standing on the precipice of partnership it was just another day in the office. The Koza brief was due in forty-eight hours.

Castelli's office was next door to McKeon's, a long thin rectangle that his fellow associates often referred to as "Castelli's Lanes" for its bowling alley dimensions. According to the plans drawn up for the twenty-fourth floor renovations last year, the associate's office had actually been two feet wider; but when Jack McKeon realized that this made his own corner of-

fice two feet smaller, the senior partner simply ordered the interior de-
signers to move the wall. McKeon never denied making the last minute
switch. In fact, he was rather proud of it.

From the minute the Koza case had ended, David could smell reinstatement with full back pay, despite the fact that every person at Rapid Freight,
from the president to the janitor, knew that Henry Koza had been selling
off the back of his truck for years. When David had reported the events of
the hearing, Jack McKeon just laughed and reminded Castelli that Rapid
Freight had the dumbest collection of supervisors on the planet.

"Don't worry about it, David," he had said. "Those idiots could screw up a
one car funeral. Just do the best you can with the brief and let it ride."

"But what about the other twenty-eight partners?" David had thought
then, and was still thinking now. None of them had ever gone through the
hailstorm of a labor arbitration. They would know only that David Castelli
had lost an important case for an important client on the very eve of his
nomination for partnership. They would, of course, all listen politely as
McKeon defended his protégé. But, when it came down to the precious
ratio and their secret ballot, would he get twenty-five votes? "Not without a big win between now and December," he thought. "Not a fucking
chance."

———◆———

Sixty-five miles to the west of the Lincoln Building, Harry Greene was also
waking to an unwelcome Labor Day. As usual, Minna had planned the tra-
ditional end-of-summer barbecue without consulting Harry—not that it
would have mattered—only this year she decided that a lawn tent and live
music would finally guarantee at least some mention by Trish Campbell in
the *Lancaster Daily Times* "Chatterbox" column.

Once he realized the inevitable, Harry had suggested a quiet jazz
combo, but Minna wouldn't hear of it. And that was why the first sound
Harry heard, as he came to consciousness, was the amplified bleating of a
Fender Stratocaster tuning up in the hands of a definite amateur.

"For goodness sake, Harry, do you realize it's after eleven. There's going
to be company here in less than two hours." Minna Greene was standing

at the foot of the gigantic bed, tugging the blankets off her husband as if she were trying to rouse a stubborn teenager.

"In a minute, I'm getting up in a minute."

"That's what you said an hour ago, then you fell back to sleep."

"Well you don't have to worry now, because I sure as hell can't sleep any more with that juvenile delinquent outside."

Minna Greene at sixty-five looked about as perfect as a woman halfway through her seventh decade could. Her body was still firm, though she had taken of late to wearing nothing but pants suits, ever since she decided one morning, in front of the mirror, than her calves had officially shrunk to old woman thin. Forty-three summers of sun had also taken their toll on the once milk-white skin of Harry's bride, but two expensive lifts managed at least to smooth out the wrinkles, and every miracle face cream known to woman softened the texture.

Despite her uncontrolled extravagances, Harry Greene truly loved his wife. He knew, of course, that he had contributed to her lifestyle by not reining it in from the start, but he always justified that lack of discipline by reminding himself that it was not really his fault. She had, after all, been to the manor born. And he had, after all, become a bit addicted too.

It was the 1952 Buick Roadmaster convertible that started it. That, and the accompanying three-week honeymoon at Grossinger's. Harry could still remember the beautiful fall morning in 1951 when Minna honked the dual horns of their new, custom-ordered car, waking him up not like today, but with a sound as rich and stately as the car from which it came.

Big Irv was riding with Minna on the morning Harry first saw the Roadmaster. He had never remembered his future father-in-law looking so proud and happy. His beautiful daughter and his beautiful car—both about to be given away to the poor boy from West Philadelphia. Harry had never quite been able to explain, much less justify, such amazing good fortune.

It was impossible not to like Big Irv Feinstein. The New Car King of Lancaster was one of those people who simply took over a room as soon as he entered it. The size helped. Six foot four, over three hundred pounds. But it was more than just physical presence. He almost seemed to twinkle, like a gigantic Christmas tree ornament with legs.

So when Big Irv toppled over on his office floor, at precisely 11:00 AM on May 31, 1952, it seemed as if the entire Jewish community of Lancaster went into collective mourning. The man who never met a meal he didn't eat was stuffing a lebanon bologna and ketchup sandwich on white bread into his mouth when the grim reaper called. He had just taken the delicacy from the full-size refrigerator he kept in his office. Suddenly, his eyes bulged, bread and meat flew out from between his lips, he made a loud sucking noise, and life was over at fifty-three.

They said that Irv Feinstein's funeral procession was the longest ever to wend its way from Abroms-Levin Funeral Home to Beth Sholom Memorial Park. Harry had never seen a Buick hearse before, and he wondered if it too had been custom ordered for the occasion.

Greene was thinking about Big Irv's Buick hearse when he first saw the large white envelope lying on the front seat of his own Buick. He had just put on his favorite Nike jogging suit and was about to head out to the gym for a quick workout before the mob arrived under the tent. He figured out immediately what was inside the package.

But this year he was wrong.

He expected the horrible photograph of Willis Tucker's jaw. It always made him sick to look at what was left of the old caretaker, even though—and today was no exception—he was compelled to count the extracted teeth just to make sure it really was a fresh picture. He also expected instructions about the upcoming discharge arbitration. And that, too, didn't take long.

September 5, 1994

Mr. Harry Greenberg
17 Great Stag Drive
Lancaster, PA

Greetings, Harry!

As you can see, my dear Mr. Greenberg, your old friend Willis
is still vacationing in T. J. Trice's freezer, only it seems he's lost
yet another tooth, poor fellow. I think that's number eleven.
Only twenty-one more to go!

My strong advice, today, is that you forget about Minna's little
bagel brunch and start thinking about my beloved job—the one
that you will ensure is returned to me, in good working order,
with all back pay and benefits.

And just to show what a good guy I am, here's a little help. I've
been told that Mr. Carpool's statement isn't pretty. Maybe
someone should have a talk with him. So have a nice Labor Day,
Mr. Greenberg. I'll be in touch.

The Tooth Fairy

P. S. The Union meets on the first Tuesday of each month. That's
tomorrow if I'm correct. They'll be voting to take a most important case to arbitration, so you don't have much time. By
the way, you did get my message about Stuff Johnson, didn't
you? I don't want to see him show up at my arbitration, so you
better take care of that little problem too.

The final piece of paper in the envelope was the one Harry Greene didn't expect.

September 5, 1994

INVOICE

For confidential storage of W. Tucker during the period September 1993 to and including September 1994.

AMOUNT DUE $100,000.00

Because he was inside the car with the door shut, and the car was inside the garage with the door shut, Harry was able to yell as loud as he could. He did. "You lying, no good son of a bitch!" Harry shouted into the air. Then he picked up the car phone and dialed McKeon's office, forgetting that it was Labor Day.

————❦————

Castelli was startled by the ringing in the office next door. For two hours it had been tomb quiet on the twenty-fourth floor of the Lincoln Building, except for the droning sound of his own voice as he dictated the Koza brief. His first thought was to run into McKeon's office and answer the call. It could be an emergency for a client. But by the time he came around his desk and jogged into the big corner office, the ringing had stopped.

"Damn," he thought to himself. He stood and stared at the little red light now blinking on McKeon's phone. "Phone mail's on." It was too late to answer, now. So, instead, he just lifted the receiver quietly. At least that way he could hear the message and break in if it really was a client emergency.

"... bastard still wants the hundred grand!" The voice sounded vaguely familiar, but it was so loud and angry that Castelli couldn't be sure. "Did you get that, Jack. The job *and* the money. And he says I'm supposed to take care of Johnson too. I think he wants me to murder the guy. You gotta help me here. Call me if you get this and in the meantime I'll try you at home."

David stood there, holding the phone, even though there was only a dial tone now. Whatever that was, Castelli was certain of one thing. He wasn't supposed to have heard it. He quietly placed the receiver back in its cradle, treating it almost as if there were still a live caller on the other end. Then he walked across the senior partner's huge office and sunk into one of the twin leather couches, closing his eyes and trying to decide what to do.

By the time he got up a few minutes later and returned to his own narrow cell, David Castelli had neatly sorted out the possibilities and concluded the obvious. There was no way he would tell Jack McKeon that he had heard even part of the phone message. But he did decide to scribble down some notes, just to make sure he didn't forget all the details. It was true that Jack McKeon practiced a tough brand of law. Still, the word "murder" was not part of most phone mail messages received at McKeon, Tingham & Marsh, even those left on the phone of the big corner office on the twenty-fourth floor.

Castelli wrote only a few words on a yellow post-it note before pasting it in the center drawer of his desk, for reasons he could not, at that moment, even begin to fathom. "Hundred grand *and* job. Think he wants me to murder Johnson. You have to help me here." Then he picked up the dictaphone and did his best to finish the Koza brief.

Jack McKeon was sitting on the toilet in his two million dollar townhouse overlooking the Benjamin Franklin Bridge when the phone rang. It was just for moments like this, when the lawyer was comfortably perched on the throne and nobody else was home, that he had insisted on the bathroom telephone. He always enjoyed having serious conversations with serious clients about serious legal matters when nobody knew his pants were down.

"If you would just shut up for one minute," he was saying to Harry Greene, "we'll go through it, step by step."

"All right, I'll listen," Harry said. Then he added, "Are you okay, Jack? You sound out of breath."

"I'm fine," he answered and laughed to himself. "Just finishing up some business when you called. Now here's how it works. Tomorrow night is the union's general membership meeting. If Werner's lucky, not too many of the lunatics will show up. Trice's case'll be somewhere on the agenda. Knowing T. J. he's already put the wrath of god in Werner, so one way or the other Pete's going to have to get the vote he needs to take this thing to arbitration.

"Once that's done," McKeon went on, "Rothstein will notify the American Arbitration Association and they'll send both of us a list of arbitrators. We'll take turns striking names and the one that's left hears the case."

"But what if the one that's left is pro-management? Isn't that the whole idea?"

"Not this time, Harry. You got to trust me. I'll make sure we end up with one of Rothstein's best bitches. There's always at least one or two of them on these lists."

"Won't he get suspicious?"

"He might, but so what? The guy's a zealot, a true believer. If he thinks about it at all, he'll probably just assume it was a gift from God."

"Then what."

"Then the Triple A will schedule the hearing on a date we're all available. It'll be easy. Rothstein's gonna want to get it done right away, but I'm going to start begging off dates because of the Rapid Freight negotiations. That will give you time to make sure everything comes out right, you understand?"

"I understand that part, Jack, but what about your precious reputation? All that stuff in your office the other day about looking bad?"

"Who said anything about me, Harry? You think I'm going to try this case myself? Not a chance. I've got an associate in the office, David Castelli. I'm sure you've seen him around."

"You mean that blonde dago kid? The one always looks so serious?"

"That's the one. Anyhow, Castelli's up for partner this year, which means he'll just about kiss me when I give him a chance to handle a case for Greene-Pitowsky Smelting & Battery. Particularly when I tell him it was going to be my gig, but I got stuck in the Rapid Freight negotiations, so he has to do it."

Harry had now calmed down enough to start thinking like a businessman again. He never really expected the great Jack McKeon to take a dive, but he worried about Castelli. Now that he could focus, he did remember seeing the young lawyer around the office. What's more, he also remembered McKeon going on and on about this guy. That was why he came right out and said it.

"Jack, isn't Castelli the one you're always talking about, the one you're grooming to take over the practice when you retire?"

"So?" came the lawyer's voice from the telephone.

"So that means you must think he's really good. And he's going to want this one bad since you tell me he's up for partner. What if he wins?"

"Harry, my friend, I'm sure that by the time you're done with Charlie Carpool, F. Lee Bailey couldn't win this case for Greene-Pitowsky. Besides, Rothstein just kicked Castelli's butt last week, and that was a *fair* fight."

NINE
Tuesday, September 6

HAD IT BEEN NECESSARY, over seven hundred people could have found a seat in the auditorium of Milk Drivers and Dairymen, Local 199. But because the local only had 450 dues-paying members by 1994, the large room had become more shrine than meeting place.

Pete Werner felt sad whenever he visited Local 199, which he did on the first Tuesday of each month when Local 664 borrowed the shrine for its general membership meetings. Despite his modest quarters atop Jenny Rats, it was Werner's local, with over three thousand members, that now dominated the Central Pennsylvania Conference of Teamsters. Local 199 was nothing more than a bad joke, a ghost local hanging on to the past, just like the hundreds of black-and-white photos of horse-drawn milk carriages neatly hung on the auditorium walls.

Pete Werner parked the town car in front of 123 Penn Street at precisely 7:15 PM. The meeting wasn't scheduled to start until eight, but Werner always made sure he and his fellow union officers were early for general membership meetings. "You never want to let them start yapping among themselves without you being in the room," he told them. "Particularly a night meeting when they can all get tuned up first. They come in the hall and see us sitting there on the stage already, shuts them right up. Works every time."

"You got that banner?" Werner was yelling over the roof of the Town Car to Axel Kinnard.

"It's in the trunk. I was hoping you'd forget it."

"You know we can't do that, Chopper. Order come straight from O'Dwyer." Werner flipped his keys to Axel. Kinnard's silver right hand glinted in the lights of the parking lot as it flicked upward to snatch the key ring from the air.

"Well I don't care if he is the goddamn International president. He don't know this city and he don't know this local. We don't need suedetops in here."

Pete winced at his friend. It was one of the only sore spots in the relationship between the two.

"How many times I have to tell you to cut that shit? I don't like it and I won't have it in this local."

"But look at this stupid banner, 'Where Have All the Minorities Gone?' What are we running here, a labor union or a church?"

Werner said nothing at first, just started walking from the parking lot, Axel following close behind with the rolled-up banner clenched between the thumb and forefinger of his left hand. They had almost reached the back door of the building when Werner turned to his friend.

"Look, I know this banner is for show. Except I don't do it for show, Chopper. I do it for what's right. So I've got six men from Ironclad Trailers over in Columbia coming tonight. And we're going to treat them with respect. You get it?"

"Yeah, boss, I get it just fine."

If Pennsylvania ever needed an enema, they could stick the nozzle in Columbia, a full square mile of urban decay on the east bank of the Susquehanna, less than ten miles west of Lancaster. But despite its proximity to Local 664, and despite its thriving population of union companies, there wasn't a single Teamster barn in the whole town.

Tonight, thought Werner, that too was going to change. The International had poured five thousand dollars of its own money into Local 664's campaign to organize the mostly black workforce at Ironclad.

Werner himself had logged over a hundred hours in the two broken-down taverns that flanked the trailer manufacturer's hulking plant on River Street. Almost got his teeth knocked out one night in the Blackbird Lounge; but he had hung in, handed out his membership cards, and was now ready to demand that the company recognize the Teamsters as the collective bargaining representative for all 180 of Ironclad's production and maintenance employees. Bringing the Ironclad workers to the monthly meeting, letting them see firsthand how a strong union fights for its members, was going to be the final step in pushing Local 664 over the top.

Standing at attention for the "Star-Spangled Banner" was required before all meetings of Manufacturing and Transport Workers Local 664. At precisely 8:00 PM Axel Kinnard turned on the gigantic floor fan and dropped the tone arm of Local 199's ancient Magnavox. The wind from the fan made Old Glory stick out straight as a board, while four hundred white males, and a half dozen nervous-looking black visitors, doffed caps and covered their hearts for the scratchy sounds of Francis Scott Key.

Up on the old wooden stage, strung out in a line behind the old wooden table, stood the Secretary-Treasurer and his five officers. Immediately to Werner's right, Union President Roger Daulton had already booted up his laptop to take notes. Pete had never quite gotten used to having a college graduate—Cornell Industrial Relations, no less—as his second in command; but the membership seemed to like Daulton, and he was certainly no threat ever to lead a *coup d'état*.

As soon as the post-anthem coughing, mumbling and moving of chairs had died down, Pete called the meeting to order. He had just invited Recording Secretary Ed Bruckenbauer to read last month's minutes when Dickie Romanowski entered the auditorium—not from the regular back door, of course, but from a side door just off the stage so that he could make a grand entrance across the front of the wooden table, then down the stairs, stage left. He turned to Pete as he crossed before the row of officers. "Keep it warm for me, Werner," he said, mostly for the benefit of the front row minions from Rapid Freight, all of whom snickered as if on command.

And then, as soon as Romanowski had finished insulting the incumbents, another figure emerged from the side door, crossed the stage, then sat down on the front row, right next to the big Rapid Freight steward. Werner could tell immediately that Thomas Jefferson Trice was already drunk.

Romanowski threw out the first monkey wrench just as Local Treasurer and Business Agent, Ken Quinlan, was about to finish reporting on the

1995 dues increase ordered by the International.

"Point of order, Mr. Secretary-Treasurer. I've got a point of order here."

"The only order you got is 'out of order,' Dickie. You got something to say, you can wait until we take questions on Ken's report." Werner nodded to the Treasurer, signaling him to resume.

"General President O'Dwyer has written to each local, apologizing for the increase. His letter states, 'While we regret having to place this added burden on our members and their families, all of us must realize ...'"

Romanowski was on his feet. "This is bullshit. Why do we have to listen to bullshit? What I want to know is what this local is doing with them fucking dues—other than buying Town Cars." Another on-cue snicker came from the front of the hall.

"Sit down, Romanowski, or I'll have you removed from this meeting." Werner could feel his ears beginning to redden. "I said you could comment *after* the Treasurer's report."

Axel Kinnard moved slowly from the shadows beneath the apron of the stage. He took just a single, small step closer to the front row of seats; but it was clearly enough, at least for the moment. Romanowski sat down, letting out a huge belch as his bulk squeezed back into the seat.

When it came time to introduce his visitors, Werner walked out from behind the long table and stood at the very edge of the stage holding the microphone.

"We got some special guests in the hall tonight. These men work over at Ironclad Trailers in Columbia. Guys, could you stand up for a second."

Six men, looking somewhat embarrassed, rose from the back row—a cluster of black in Local 664's sea of white. The bravest of the group took a battered porkpie hat from his head and gently waved to the audience.

Werner went on. "You all know this local's been organizing at Ironclad since the summer. Taken the usual crap from management, couple guys got roughed up in a place called the Blackbird Lounge, few tires slashed—but nothing real serious. Anyhow, I'm happy to report we now got ninety percent cards and we're filing with the Labor Board down in Philly this week."

Pete waited for the raucous cheering that always followed an announcement that Local 664 had successfully organized a new barn. It took him only a few seconds to realize that, this time, polite applause was all he was going to hear. The six men still standing at the back of the room also got the message and slid carefully into their seats. Werner did his best to continue as though nothing unusual had happened.

Werner continued. "On open and pending grievances, there was an arbitration hearing August 24th on the Henry Koza discharge by Rapid Freight. I was there. Case went real good, I thought. We expect Brother Koza to be reinstated with full back pay. As usual, Rothstein did a terrific job."

Then someone yelled from the back. "Way to go, Ike the Kike." Pete chose to ignore the statement, as well as the ensuing laughter, which he immediately began talking over.

"Tonight we're voting on a Greene-Pitowsky discharge—Brother Thomas J. Trice, forklift driver."

Another voice from the audience. "Take it all the way. Fuck Harry Greene."

Next came a dissent. "No way we're taking that piece-of-shit case. Trice ran over an old man."

T. J. was helped up by Dickie Romanowski so he could turn and bellow. "Who the fuck said that?" When there was no answer, Trice upped the ante. "Come on, asshole, right now. Stand up and we'll take care of this outside."

The audience began to hoot. Then someone started a chant. "T. J., T. J., T. J." Werner quickly went behind the table and banged his gavel for order. He managed to get the room quiet, but it was the kind of quiet everyone knew was just looking for a chance to erupt.

"Brother Trice was terminated for allegedly riding his motorcycle through the plant and injuring a night watchman, Charlie Carliner. Brother Trice has denied the charges and is asking the union to go to arbitration. We will take comments and discussion from the floor—one at a time. Brother Thomasson."

Sig Thomasson, tall, quiet and respected, addressed the group. "I hear Mr. Trice has a lawyer from the ACLU who's going to sue us if we don't take his case. Is that true?"

"Mr. Trice does have a lawyer, but that has nothing to do with the question on the floor."

Dickie Romanowski stood up and said, "The fuck it don't." Then he turned to the audience. "The lawyer is Brian O'Conner, and he's a prick. You men remember Mike Twardzik, faggot used to work at Rapid?"

Someone called out, "Took it up the ass for lunch in the locker room." The rising laughter was just on the verge of not being funny when Werner banged his gavel.

Romanowski tried to sound serious. "Go ahead, laugh. But let me tell you what happened. Twardzik filed a grievance. Said someone took a picture of him naked. Mr. Werner thought it was a joke. Wouldn't take the case. Why don't you tell them what happened, Petey."

"What does this have to do with Trice?" Werner said.

"It has to do with thirty thousand dollars of this union's money, that's what it has to do with. And T. J.'s got the same lawyer." Again to the audience. "That's right, the same lawyer who made Local 664 pay Twardzik thirty thousand dollars, just because Mr. Werner up there thought it was a joke." Now over his shoulder to the Secretary-Treasurer, "You think this case is a joke too?"

Thomas Jefferson Trice had decided to use this brief interlude to stagger up the stairs to the stage. He leaned over the table, directly in front of Werner, his rear end wiggling to the audience making them laugh all over again. He took the microphone from its stand and faced the crowd.

"How many you men work for Harry Greene?"

About seventy-five hands went up, along with a few catcalls and assorted grumbling noises.

"Well I ain't talking to you, because I don't have to. You already know what a sonofabitch he is, right?"

The remark was greeted with a combination of laughter and cheering, punctuated by Pete Werner's gavel.

"So let me talk to the rest of you, who don't know what it's like at Greene-Pitowsky Smelting & Battery Company." Trice had to lean against the table to keep his balance, but his words were surprisingly clear and powerful.

"I started working in that hole in 1968, right after I got outta Nam. Helped bring this union in. Lot of you don't know that I bet. Twenty-six years, and in all that time not one of them bastards ever learned how to treat a working man. We call them 'ties,' the bosses, because Greene makes them all wear neckties. Ask me, it cuts the blood off to their fucking brains.

"Two weeks ago yesterday, the worst tie of them all, a little Hitler named Breitenfeld, calls me in his office and says I run over Charlie Carpool on my motorcycle. Then he fires me, just like that. No trial, no nothing."

A voice from the audience interrupted T. J.'s narrative. "Come off it, Trice. Everybody knows you got wasted at the Rat and went after Carpool."

"Oh, is that right, everybody knows it? Well let me tell you something. I was nowhere near that battery house when the old man went down. You ask me, he was drunk, slipped on the grease, then made up the whole story just to keep his own damn job. And I'll tell you something else. Not one of them fucking ties even bothered to talk to Carpool before they went and fired me! They just took the word of some dick at the police station who says he talked to the old man when he was half unconscious."

It was at this point that Henry Pelletier stood for the first time, rising from the middle of the room, a gigantic gnarled tree, suddenly sprung full grown from the earth.

"It isn't working, Trice, so why don't you just shut up." Pelletier's voice sounded more like it came from a subwoofer than from human vocal chords. It was a voice felt rather than heard, and it immediately brought the huge auditorium to absolute silence.

Had it not been for his size, Henry Pelletier would have looked almost comical in his bib overalls and no shirt. Thick clumps of black hair squirted from every area of skin not covered by greasy denim. On his head, the beard and hair were indistinguishable, combining to frame a round face whose dominant feature was a bulbous nose latticed with red veins. In the mouth, more teeth were missing than present.

As if on cue, every person on the row stood as Pelletier moved past them toward the aisle. He took more time than even a man of his size actually needed to traverse the distance. Then he slowly approached the stage, stopping only when he had reached a spot directly below the apron. He beckoned for the microphone. Trice obliged without a word. Axel Kinnard again emerged from the shadows.

"Most of you men know me. If you don't, my name is Pelletier, Henry Pelletier. I work in the furnace room at Greene-Pitowsky. I've been a member of this local since 1976 and I ain't never filed but one grievance all them years. Won it second step. Now, Mr. Trice here wants us to take his case to arbitration. But, see, Mr. Trice isn't telling the truth, are you, T. J.?"

Trice was on the defensive for the first time all night. "I don't know what you're talking about, Henry."

"Yes you do. You know what I'm talking about. I'm talking about the other guy seen you ride that Harley into the plant. He saw the whole thing, even saw you put on the Nixon mask."

Werner stood up behind the table and said, "Henry, if you know anything about this case that we don't, we'd like to hear it."

"Can't do that, Mr. Werner. Can't rat out a brother. But I'm telling you, there's another man saw this thing and if Breitenfeld finds out and makes him talk, this union's going to look awful dumb."

Dickie Romanowski knew he had a problem, but he had to be careful not to get his face rearranged trying to solve it. He decided to change the subject.

"What we're doing here's all wrong," Dickie said. "Henry says there's another witness, I believe him, but that's what we got Rothstein for. Far as I'm concerned, Brother Trice says he didn't do it, that's the end of it. Besides, we don't take this thing all the way, Brian O'Conner's going to shove it up our ass all over again."

Pete Werner took the bait in spite of himself. "Goddammit, Romanowski, I already told you once, Brian O'Conner doesn't run Local 664."

"And you ain't gonna be running it either after March. Now you already lost one case on account of that sonofabitch, shit all over the newspapers, remember? We get sued again, that'll be oh for two." Romanowski, on a roll, stood up and started to jab his index finger at the stage. "That's a zero, Werner. That's an F down at Saints Cyril and Methodias where I come from, and you ask me, we got enough fucking Fs in this union already."

Axel Kinnard said, "Well it's not March yet, Dickie, so if I were you I'd just sit down and show some goddamn respect."

Romanowski shot back, "Nobody's talking to you, Robocop, so butt out."

The metal claw at the end of Kinnard's right arm was just supposed to push Romanowski back into his seat, not also rip open his t-shirt and draw blood. So when Dickie felt the stinging pain in his chest, then saw a red stain forming above his left nipple, he naturally went berserk.

"You motherfucker," he screamed. "You no-good motherfucker." Axel was flat on his back with the big Rapid Freight steward astride him before anyone in the room could even move. Romanowski reached back to plunge his fist into Kinnard's face, but immediately, the two-finger vice of Axel's left hand shot upward from the ground. It seized Romanowski's right arm, twisting his wrist back over his forearm, making the bigger man scream in agony and leap up from his fallen victim as if he had been shot through by an electric charge.

Werner, screaming "order, order in this hall," reached the auditorium floor just in time to see the first chair go airborne. He bounced from one brawling couple to another, trying to separate combatants, but having little success inside the suddenly formed mass of bodies that were pushing, shoving and cursing at each other, often for no apparent reason other than the thrill of the moment.

For the next few minutes more objects were thrown than punches, and if there was any order at all to the proceedings, it had only to do with union politics, certainly not with the merits of Thomas J. Trice's discharge. T. J., in the meantime, was sitting cross-legged on the stage laughing to himself. Henry Pelletier stood between Axel and Romanowski, keeping them apart as if he were holding two little kids by the scruffs of their necks.

Shortly after nine, three carloads of Lancaster police were unloaded in the parking lot of Local 199. The fifteen officers, dressed in full riot gear for the first time since 1989 when they broke up a gay rights rally in front of the Dutch Wonderland Theme Park, marched into the great hall just as six disgusted black men were marching out. One of the men from Ironclad Trailers looked up at the blue and gold banner stretched over the doorway: "Where Have All the Minorities Gone?"

"I'll tell you where this minority's going," he said. "This minority's going home. No way I'm joining up with those crackers." The other five men agreed.

Pete Werner decided to proceed with the Trice arbitration without a vote.

TEN
Wednesday, September 7

ONE OF THE WIVES at the two breakfast tables, fifteen miles apart, was listening intently as her husband read from the September 7 edition of the *Lancaster Daily Times*. The other, still fuming over the paper's failure to print even a single word about her Labor Day party, was only pretending to listen. She was doing her nails at the moment, pausing now and then to say "very interesting," but placing the vast majority of her concentration on not painting polish onto her cuticles.

The husband of the wife who was listening spotted the error first.

"Jesus Christ, the election's not for six months and the papers already think he's in. Listen to this crap. 'Richard Romanowski, a union officer.' Did you hear that, they call him a union officer."

The wife said, "Pete, I'm sorry. I really am. But can't you watch the language in front of the kids?"

Werner tousled the blond head of his ten-year-old son, Mack, The gesture signaled both apology to his wife and affection for the boy. Dorothy Werner smiled, but the boy heard nothing his father said. He was much too intent on hiding behind a cereal box so that he didn't have to watch his sister eat oatmeal.

The quote from Romanowski was in the third paragraph of the front page article.

Three Men Hospitalized As Riot Mars Union Meeting

Police in riot gear were called out last evening to break up a vicious fight at the monthly meeting of Teamsters Local 664, the county's largest, and most notorious, labor union. Although no one was seriously hurt, the meeting hall of Teamsters Local 199, where Local 664 holds its membership meetings, sustained heavy damage.

The fight erupted over a dispute involving a member who is accused of seriously injuring a night watchman at Greene-Pitowsky Smelting & Battery Company during a wild motorcycle ride through the factory. The member, Thomas Trice of Fivepointville, has denied the charges and has demanded that the union start proceedings to exonerate him. Union members hostile to Trice were apparently upset over the recommendation of Union Chief Pete Werner that the Local defend the accused member.

Richard Romanowski, a union officer, blamed the fracas on Werner. "I think Mr. Werner let the whole thing get out of hand," Romanowski said. "It's just one more reason this union needs new blood." Romanowski expects to challenge Werner for the powerful Teamster Local's top spot next Spring. Secretary-Treasurer Werner called the incident "regrettable" but denied that union politics played any part in the melee. The injured watchmen remains in serious condition at Garden Spot General Hospital.

"Is that all you said, honey, that the incident was regrettable?" Dorothy asked.

"What do you think? Of course it's not all I said. It's just all those bastards decided to print. Fight in a union hall's not enough to sell papers, I guess. Have to find the 'story,' you know, the 'angle.' And good old Dickie couldn't wait to oblige. You think he's gonna tell the newspaper what really started the fight?"

"Which was?"

"There was a witness to the whole motorcycle thing. We got a member name of Henry Pelletier. Biggest pile of hair and beef you ever saw. But dumb as a brick. Anyhow, Henry gets up last night and says there was a witness. Problem is, Henry thinks he'd be selling out the holy brotherhood if he said who it was. That's what got the fur flying. Trice's enemies wanted to know who saw the thing. And Henry's friends—well, what the hell's the use."

"So what are you going to do, now?"

"I'm going to have a talk with Pelletier, what else can I do, even though I know I'd be better off if I just forgot it, let it ride."

"Why do you say that, Pete?"

"Because I'll be pissed off if he won't talk, and maybe even more pissed if he does."

"Peter, for goodness sake."

Mack Werner started giggling uncontrollably behind the cereal box.

Dorothy Werner said nothing for the rest of breakfast; but after the kids left for the school bus, and Pete was going through some notes at the kitchen table for his meeting with the shop committee from Rapid Freight, she walked quietly behind her husband, put her arms around his large chest, and gently kissed the top of his head.

"So why do you keep doing this?" she said.

"Because if I don't, who will?"

"A lot of people will. There'd be a line around the block."

"A line of what, Dickie Romanowskis?"

"So what if it's Dickie Romanowski. Maybe that's all the lot of them deserve."

"Well it's not what I deserve, goddammit. And it doesn't matter anyhow, because there's no way I go back down that street and work for Harry Greene."

"And that's it? There's only two jobs in Lancaster County? Run the union or work for Harry Greene? Peter, there's lots of things out there. Besides, the kids are old enough to let themselves in after school. I could get something too."

"Dorothy, listen to me. We've been over this too many times. Our labor agreement requires Greene to hire me back if I leave the union office. He's got no choice. But everyone else *does* have a choice. And to them, I'm AIDS, cancer, TB. Don't you understand that? Hire the guy who ran Local 664? Jesus, honey, I'd have a better chance if I were the former president of Lancaster County Hitler Youth. Look at my father, for god's sake. And he was just a shop steward."

"He got a job."

"Yeah, he got a job all right. A job selling cheese at Lengacher's for minimum wage. Is that what you want?"

"Oh, Peter, that was over forty years ago. I wasn't even born yet. You were five years old. How do you know what happened?"

"Because I watched him get drunk every night. I watched him pass out. I watched him hit my mother. And I watched him die when he was forty-eight." Pete stood up from the table. "I don't mean to start yelling, sweetheart. But we've been over this so many times now. I'm a union leader. That's what I do."

"And I'm just supposed to sit quietly and let you do it."

"It's one hell of a lot better than selling cheese."

"Or working for Harry Greene?"

"Especially working for Harry Greene."

———⊷◈⊶———

Fifteen miles away, at a breakfast table in the Old School Lane Hills section of Lancaster, Harry Greene was focusing on what was missing from the story. He had already read it through once, start to finish.

"What about the arbitration vote, dammit." Harry Greene was talking out loud to himself by now, even though Minna was physically present across the glass breakfast table by the kitchen picture window. Greene, clad in silk pajamas and a monogrammed bathrobe, stood and peered through the window, looking out beyond his swimming pool and tennis court to where the aluminum frame of Monday's Labor Day tent still remained, awaiting today's scheduled dismantlement. He continued the monologue.

"There's not one word in the whole article about what happened with the arbitration vote. Doesn't say whether the union's going to take the case or not. Reporters. I swear to God. Make my company look like some kind of goddamn zoo, that's fine. But don't bother with anything important."

Greene walked back to the table, picked up the portable phone, and dialed the plant. "This is Mr. Greene, let me speak to Joseph Breitenfeld." The warehouse supervisor picked up on the first ring.

"Breitenfeld here."

"Joseph, it's Harry Greene. You got a minute?"

"Sure, what's up?" Breitenfeld would have had a minute even if he had been in the middle of fighting a five alarm blaze when Greene called.

"I take it you've read the paper by now."

"Are you kidding, it's all over the plant. We can't get a thing done in here this morning."

"Yeah, but what about the arbitration. They taking it, or what?"

"Of course, they're taking it." Breitenfeld couldn't hide his disgust. "Why should it matter the bastard almost killed an innocent old man? Union says we're just supposed to kiss and make up and put him back to work. That is the American way, isn't it?"

Harry had to work hard to make his voice sound sympathetic. "What'd you expect them to do, just roll over and die? You know Werner's got opposition next year."

"I know, but you'd figure just once."

"Never happen, Joseph. Brother gets fired, they go. It's a religion, don't you understand that?"

"I understand it, but this is Trice we're talking about. Their own members hate him more than we do. I'm telling you, we get that bastard back in here now, there's no way we run this warehouse."

"Well, I wouldn't worry too much about that. McKeon's the best labor lawyer in Philadelphia. That's why we use him, just for punks like Trice."

Twenty-five minutes later Harry Greene was nosing the big Buick slowly down Hixon Avenue toward the main gate of Greene-Pitowsky Smelting & Battery Company. He passed Jenny Rats, looking up as he always did toward the faded blue and gold sign swinging out from the corner of the old brick building, just below the second floor windows. "Manufacturing and Transport Workers, Local 664, I.B.T.C.W.H.A." Greene was always a bit bemused by what the initials stood for, "International Brotherhood of Teamsters, Chauffeurs, Warehousemen and Helpers of America." He had never actually met a union chauffeur, though he was sure such a person must have existed somewhere in Teamster history. One of the men told him recently that the union dropped the "Chauffeurs, Warehousemen and Helpers" part when O'Dwyer took over in '93, but Harry was sure the sign above Jenny Rats would never change. Things in Lancaster seldom did.

Harry wondered what kind of night Pete Werner must have had over at Local 199. The Secretary-Treasurer had been such a pain in the ass to Greene when he had worked for the company during the seventies, but now, Harry had to admit, he had actually grown to like the leader of Local 664. It was just too bad Werner had to represent so many worthless drones and champion so many bogus causes. And it was especially too bad that he had to rely on Isaac Rothstein to help him do it.

Harry Greene had only spoken one time in his life to Rothstein. He never got over it. It happened on the same day in 1990 that Harry testified at his only labor arbitration. He never got over that, either.

McKeon had tried hard to dissuade the owner from taking the witness stand.

"I don't care if the incentive system is the greatest idea you ever had, you have any clue what Rothstein's gonna do to you?"

"What can he do, Jack. He's a lawyer. He don't know a damn thing about the battery business. I'm telling you, every one of those men is going to make more money, not less. Union's out of its mind."

"They don't like change, Harry. How many times do we have to go over this? You rammed the first incentive system down their throats in '87. They just got it out of the contract, and now you're trying to put in a different version. Doesn't matter if they all make enough money to buy Cadillacs, union's gotta fight you. It's not about money. It's about power."

But Harry wouldn't listen. And by the second hour of Rothstein's cross-examination, McKeon had no choice but to call a time out.

"So what it all boils down to, Mr. Greene—after your time studies and your industrial engineers and your wage projections—what the bottom line really is, Mr. Greene, is that the faster you make these men work, the more money goes into your pocket. That's the real deal, now, isn't it, sir?"

"The men make more too."

"Just answer the question, Mr. Greene. The faster the men work, the richer you get. Yes or no?"

"Well, yes, but that's ..."

"That's what? That's not the whole story? Is that what you want to tell this arbitrator?"

"My men make a good wage, Mr. Rothstein, and you know it."

"Good like what, Mr. Greene? Like the million dollars a year you make?"

McKeon was off his chair. "Mr. Arbitrator, union counsel isn't questioning here. He's baiting this man. I demand that you stop it."

"Or what Mr. McKeon?" Rothstein said. "You gonna take me outside to the woodshed?"

It was at this point that the arbitrator called a recess. Harry Greene sat motionless in the witness chair while the union delegation filed out of the hearing room. Then his side left, then the arbitrator, and all of a sudden, the owner was alone—except for the frail figure of Isaac Rothstein, carefully repacking his briefcase. The union lawyer was startled when he looked up and saw Harry, still sitting in the chair.

"Shut the door, Mr. Rothstein, I have to talk to you."

"I'm afraid I can't do that, Mr. Greene, you're still under oath."

Harry was shocked at the sudden politeness in Rothstein's voice. "It's not about the case. Please. Just shut the door."

Rothstein shrugged but complied. Then he sat down in one of the spectator's chairs, so Harry had to twist around in his own seat to make eye contact.

"Why do you have to do this?"

"What are you talking about, Mr. Greene?"

"Come on, cut the Mr. Greene stuff, will you. There's nobody here but us. Just tell me what you're doing."

"My job. What does it look like I'm doing?"

"You really want to know? I'll tell you what it looks like you're doing. It looks like you're selling out your own people."

"I represent these people."

"I'm not talking about those *goyim*. I'm talking about me, dammit. I'm your people. Me. Harry Greenberg from West Philly. How old are you, anyhow?"

"What's that got ..."

"Just answer me, please. How old are you?"

"Sixty-four."

"A year younger than me. D'you know that? You a Philly boy?"

"Suburbs."

"What do you mean suburbs? Drexel Hill? Lansdowne?"

"I was born in Cheltenham."

"Oh, one of them rich boys. Don't tell me. Latham Park."

"Look, Mr. Greene, where are we going with this?"

"Going? I'm just trying to figure out why a Jew fucks another Jew for a bunch of *shkotzim*. Where do you think these people would be without my company? You ever think about that?"

"They have rights, Mr. Greene. And no one is going to trample on those rights, I don't care what religion they are."

"You really don't get it, do you. Rights? It's a nothing but a joke to these people. You're nothing but a joke to these people."

"I resent that."

"Well you can resent it all you want, but that don't change a damn thing. You want to embarrass me in this hearing, strut around like a rich Cheltenham boy with the big words and the law degree, suck up to your precious clients, go ahead. Have a party. Long as you remember you're just another Heeb to them." Then he added, "Ike the Kike."

"How dare you."

"How dare I, Mr. Rothstein? No, I don't think so. That's not my nickname for you. That's their nickname for you—those wonderful people you're so busy protecting in here. They're the ones call you Ike the Kike behind your back. What do you think of that?"

"That is not only a lie, it's a disgusting lie. And you, sir, are a disgusting man."

And then the arbitrator came back into the room. Isaac Rothstein made it a point to keep Harry Greene on the witness stand for another full hour.

"I have to talk to Jack McKeon right away." Harry barked the order to Shelia even before he said good morning. That didn't happen often, but when it did she knew Greene was a man best left alone.

"It's crazy, Jack. They busted up the whole damn place just on account of Trice. We're gonna get it. I can feel it." Harry Greene was talking fast, jumping from one subject to another, making no sense.

The sincere-sounding baritone of John Joseph McKeon was, as always, quick to soothe and even quicker to reassure. "Harry, Harry, Harry, my oldest friend. It couldn't be better, don't you see?"

"Tell me why it couldn't be better."

"Because Werner's got to win, now, that's why. Romanowski challenged the guy, right there in front of the membership."

"But they hate Trice, and Werner hates him more than anybody."

"Doesn't matter. Werner can't afford to lose this one anymore. Trice could walk in that hall today and piss on Pete's shoes, still wouldn't matter."

"I don't care, Jack. There's something wrong. I can feel it. I can't take it anymore. First the guy says no money, then he sends the same damn picture with the same damn blackmail note. I tell you, Jack, I'm getting to the point where I'm actually thinking about taking the guy out, I really am."

"Why don't you then? I keep telling you that failsafe is bullshit."

"That's not even funny, Jack. Jesus, I don't know what the hell to do."

"Okay. Then let's go over it again. Thomas Jefferson Trice is a nutcase. We both know that. For ten years, he's been telling you that someone else gets a copy of the new picture each year. For ten years, he's been telling you what's going to happen the first time this guy doesn't get his copy. For ten years, you don't have a clue who this guy is. And for ten years, you've been paying. Now, nothing has changed this year, except Trice also wants his job back. It's no big deal, so just calm down."

"You're right, Jack. You're always right."

"Good, then listen to me. I've been thinking about how this has to go down."

"You already told me how it's going down. We're gonna fix the case, remember?"

"I'm talking about the 'when,' not the 'how.' I figure Rothstein gets the call from Werner this week. Ike calls Triple A, I get the list next week, say Monday or Tuesday. Time we go through the usual dance, striking off names and all, agreeing to a date, it's going to be another week. That's when I give the file to Castelli. Now I don't want you talking to Carpool until the last possible minute, you understand?"

"I don't get it."

"I'll draw you a map. Castelli will want to win this case really bad. He starts over-preparing and finds out it's a dog, he's going to go nuts. God knows what he'll turn up. So it's gotta look like a boat race. Carpool's gotta stay clean right till the very end. Last thing we need is for the kid to make one last check with the old man and smell something. No, this boy has to waltz into that arbitration thinking he's got the winner of his life, you get it?"

"There's not going to be time, Jack. I've got to talk to Charlie now."

"Are you listening, dammit? There'll be plenty of time. Trust me."

<hr>

When T. J. spun Stuff Johnson around by the shoulder, the force was so great that Stuff's torque wrench flew across the garage and knocked over a large open can of motor oil. Black ooze started running along the floor, heading straight for the custom chrome rear wheel of Mr. Boneyard's Fat Boy.

The President of the Devil's Disciples M.C. was not pleased. "The fuck's going on here?" he screamed, throwing fistfuls of sawdust in the path of the petroleum river.

T. J. mumbled something that sounded like "sorry." Stuff Johnson leaped to his feet and began pushing the Fat Boy out of harm's way.

Boneyard threw them both out. "You assholes got a problem, you take it the fuck outside." Mr. Boneyard was holding a forty-pound clutch assembly in his hands while he was saying this, so there was no argument from either man.

Stuff Johnson tried to change the subject even before Trice got on the subject. "You gotta be outta your mind, going in there like that. Guy coulda killed you, fucking with his bike." It didn't work.

"Every person you told, Johnson. Right now."

"What are you talking about?"

"Don't play dumb with me. You know exactly what I'm talking about."

"I swear T. J. I didn't talk to nobody."

"Then you tell me how that big slob, Pelletier, could stand up last night and give 'em all a fucking play by play."

Stuff Johnson looked at the ground. T. J. kept talking. "That's right, motherfucker. Pelletier told it all to the membership just before the fight started. He told it all, you hear me, right down to the Nixon mask."

"I swear T. J., I never said a word to Pelletier. I never told no one. Why would I?"

"Because you're a dumb bastard with a big mouth, that's why."

Stuff was trying very hard to think now. "Could have been anyone talked to Pelletier," he said. "You think no one knows the story? Think again. Carpool told the cops ten minutes after you went in there."

T. J. was out of patience. He twisted a handful of Johnson's t-shirt in his fist, turning it until the larger man almost lifted off the ground. He spoke in a low voice, his stale Camel breath mixing with Stuff's own shallow breathing.

"The man wasn't talking about Carpool. The man was talking about you. He told the whole union there was another witness, you get it? He said this other witness saw me put on the Nixon mask, you get it? So you tell me who else beside Pelletier knows, and you tell me right the fuck now."

"All right, all right." T. J. untwisted the t-shirt so that Stuff could come clean unencumbered by not being able to breathe.

"I don't know what got into me, T. J., I really don't. But I swear to God it was only Henry. I told him last week on midnight shift. It was just him and me. I was taking a load of iron in for Bessemer Three. Well, you know how he is, with that voice and all."

"I want all of it, you little shit"

"That is all of it. Henry starts asking about that night. Says people saw us together at the Rat. Says it's all gonna come out sooner or later. Then he's talking about how much he's worried about the old man, and I just got scared. I'm figuring he thinks I went in there with you."

"So you ratted me out to save your own ass, is that what I'm hearing?"

"For god's sake, T. J., what was I supposed to do? The guy's a fucking loop job. Anyhow, you know Pelletier's never gonna tell the ties."

"It ain't the ties I'm worried about."

"So what's the problem then?"

"Werner's the problem. Pelletier thinks the guy's some kind of god. Oughta hear him. Mr. Werner this, Mr. Werner that. Suck your dick, Mr. Werner? Kraut bastard must have pictures of Henry doing the family dog or something."

"I still don't get it. Why would Pelletier drop the dime on me? What the hell's that gonna get him?"

"A fucking hard-on for all I know. I'm just telling you, Pelletier loves our honorable Secretary-Treasurer. Last night he wouldn't give your name. But that was in front of the whole damn hall. Werner gets him alone, that big bear'll tell him anything he wants to know."

"Okay, so Pelletier tells Werner I was a witness. What's he do with that, go help Breitenfeld prepare the company's case?"

"You don't know much about our wonderful Secretary-Treasurer, do you."

"Not really."

"Well then maybe you oughta learn. Might help you keep your big trap shut one of these days. Werner thinks he's too good for the rest of us. Gets that corner office and all of a sudden he thinks he's some kind of avenging angel. Gonna clean up the Teamsters, he says. I'll tell you what the cocksucker's gonna do, you mark my word. He's gonna get his ass whipped by Romanowski next spring, then run straight down the street to that big nose Jew looking for work. And I'm not talking kettle room work, either. Not Pete Werner. He's gonna be one of the fucking ties. No, I take that back. He's gonna be the worst one of the fucking ties. He'll make Breitenfeld look like a shop steward."

"I don't believe it."

"You don't? Tell you what. You come back here in a few weeks, after fat Hamilton from security starts leaning on you to testify for the company. Ask me then how the company found out you were a witness."

<hr>

When Jenny Rats was open for business, it was quite impossible to hear the rhythmic ticking of the Regulator clock over the bar. But at noon on a Wednesday, the voice of the old timepiece left over from the Lifetime Oilless Bearing Company was the dominant sound in the empty saloon. And it was also the tempo setter for Jenny DeLone and Axel Kinnard, as they methodically prepared for the evening ahead.

Axel put down his push broom and peered out one of the tiny, eye-high windows onto Hixon Avenue. He was looking for the truck from Lancaster Beverage.

"You did call them first thing this morning, didn't you?"

Jenny looked up from the bar sink. "Yes, mother," she mocked. "First thing."

She loved his devotion, even as she felt terribly sad for it. Axel Kinnard, the Quasimodo of 4641 Hixon Avenue, keeping paper forever in the copiers upstairs, Budweiser forever in the coolers downstairs. Often, she wondered if he had a life at all outside the old brick building, for despite their years together, Jenny DeLone had never seen his house, didn't even really know where it was.

The two worked on in silence, moving to the rhythm of the Regulator, until Jenny finally asked the question.

"You talk to Pete?"

"This morning, saw him for a second on his way up." Axel pointed with his head and neck toward the second floor. "He's really down, not that I blame him."

"I take it he's seen the paper."

"He saw it, but I don't think that's the problem."

"Not even that garbage from Romanowski?"

"What's he supposed to do, ask for a retraction? Anyhow, nobody gives a damn about reporters. It's Henry Pelletier's got him upset."

Jenny put down her dishrag and came around the bar. She motioned to Axel and they slid into the end booth. "I heard Henry said something last night about a witness in the Trice case, that true?"

"Damn right it's true. And Pelletier knows exactly who it is."

Jenny lowered her voice, even though there was no one to hear it, other than Axel and the Regulator. "So do I, Axel. At least I'm pretty sure. It's gotta be that biker creep Trice hangs out with all the time—Stuff Johnson."

"Yeah. Works down the street, night shift."

"Well the two of them were here, right in this booth, just before Charlie Carpool got run down."

"You saw them leave together?"

"No, but I heard them leave together. Damn Harleys practically peel my paint off the walls."

"But you don't know if Johnson went in the battery house with Trice, do you?"

"Of course I don't know that. How could I possibly know that? But you figure it. Johnson and Pelletier both work down the street, so they probably know each other. Johnson was with Trice the night it happened. Left this bar together. Now Pelletier says there was a witness and he knows who it was. Jesus, Axel, even you should be able to figure that one out."

"You gonna tell Pete?"

"I don't know, I really don't. I'm running a bar down here; he's running a union up there. I start messing with his business, first thing you know it's gonna be bad for my business. Besides, what's he supposed to do with it, even if he does know?"

"Well I'm telling you, he does want to know. Tried to get Pelletier to dime the guy out right there at the meeting. Didn't work, but he did try."

"You ask me, he's better off not knowing. Follow me here, Axel. Pete hates Trice. But the guy's still a member. He files a grievance and the next thing you know that creep, Romanowski, starts acting like Trice's godfather. You were there. You know what dear old Dickie's gonna do if Pete doesn't back T. J. So right now, it's Trice's word against the old man. Doesn't matter if Pete thinks T. J. did it. He washes his hands, then lets some arbitrator decide. But I go and tell Pete that Stuff Johnson knows the whole story, now what? The poor guy is suffering enough with this thing. You want me to make it worse?"

Axel Kinnard listened carefully to what Jenny was saying. He didn't like keeping anything from Pete Werner, and he wasn't exactly sure how knowing about Stuff was going to be bad for Pete. Then again, he knew Jenny would never hurt the Secretary-Treasurer and he also knew Jenny was very smart. So he changed the subject.

"Charlie Carpool's getting out tomorrow, you heard?"

And Jenny DeLone knew she had made her point, so she let him change the subject.

"Already? It's not even three weeks, and half of that was intensive care."

"Well I don't know nothing about intensive care. All I know is Charlie said he couldn't take it in there no more and he wanted to go home."

"But who's going to take care of him, Axel? He can't stay sober even when his head's not half cracked open."

"You're not going to believe this, I know, 'cause I didn't when I first heard it. But it's all over the plant that Harry Greene hired a nurse for Charlie."

"You're right, I don't believe it."

"Well, someone down at employee health says she saw a paper with Greene's signature on it ordering some kind of nurse for C. Carliner. And Charlie is getting out of the hospital awful early."

"If Harry Greene's handing out money on account of someone other than Harry Greene, there's gotta be a profit in it somewhere"

"A profit from Charlie Carpool? Not a chance. I don't think the old man owns a blessed thing except that old beach chair and his boom box."

"Then I'll go back to what I said," Jenny stood up and returned to the bar, saying over her shoulder, "I just don't believe it."

———◦◦◦◦———

Isaac Rothstein started screaming for his secretary the second he glanced down at the first piece of his new letterhead.

"Florence, get in here. Did you look at this stuff?"

Florence Daley put her head into the great one's cluttered office.

"Is there a problem, Mr. Rothstein?"

Isaac spun around in his wooden chair so that he was no longer hunched over the old rolltop desk. In the same motion he stood up and began waving a piece of Rothstein & Glabberman's new stationery wildly back and forth in the air.

"Look at this, Florence. Look at what that idiot printed right in the middle of the page."

Florence Daley reached out for the paper. Then she started to laugh.

"You think it's funny?"

"I'm sorry, Mr. Rothstein, but I can't help it. It has the words 'Union Bug' right here under your name."

"I can read it, Mrs. Daley."

Florence was finding it difficult to talk between giggles. "Well, I guess the new printer didn't understand me, sir. I told him just what you said. You know, about you having labor unions for clients so a union bug has to be on the letterhead. I suppose if he had been a union printer, this wouldn't have happened."

"Well you just call him back and tell him that if this job doesn't get re-done correctly in twenty-four hours I'll make sure he is a union printer. You got that?"

"Yes, sir."

"And send him a piece of the old stuff so he can see that a 'union bug' is a printer's mark." Then he added, "Damn fool."

The offices of Rothstein & Glabberman, P.C., not quite half a floor in the class B Jefferson Tower Building, were appropriately spartan. Ringing the small lobby were pictures of Walter Reuther, Eugene V. Debs and a half-dozen other icons of organized labor. Behind the receptionist's desk, a large oil depicted the inside of some mythical factory, where handsome men in undershirts with bulging muscles hoisted objects of great weight upon their shoulders.

Rothstein was still fuming over his new letterhead when Pete Werner called from Lancaster. Isaac had never been comfortable with the Secretary-Treasurer, though he did his best to conceal the blend of frustration and contempt he felt for Werner, as he would attempt to hide such feelings from any client as lucrative as Local 664.

"We had a little problem up here last night, Isaac."

"I'm waiting."

"Romanowski and Axel got into it during the membership meeting."

"What do you mean, 'into it.' You're not talking about a fight or anything, are you?"

"Well as a matter of fact, I am talking about a fight."

"All right, how bad?"

"Bad, Isaac. Three guys ended up in the hospital. Nothing serious, but the cops came and it's in the paper this morning."

"Let me see if I can guess. Mr. Trice had something to do with it, didn't he."

"Yes, Isaac." Werner's voice had the flat edge of a sullen teenager admitting that he just dented the family car. "Mr. Trice was right in the middle. Matter of fact, the whole thing started on account of his grievance."

Werner paused instinctively to receive Rothstein's next barrage of criticism. When it didn't come, Pete quickly seized the chance to tell his side of the story, which he did in great detail as Rothstein returned to the morning mail, looking for an overdue retainer check from the Clothing and Textile Workers Health & Welfare Fund.

But the ears of the old lawyer were still tuned, so when Pete got to the part about Pelletier and the secret witness, Rothstein immediately put down the stack of mail and took over the conversation.

"Absolutely not," the lawyer snapped. "I do not want you talking to Henry Pelletier, you understand that?"

"But, Isaac, the man knows ..."

"The man knows nothing you need to know. You start grilling him, first thing happens he tells you the name of some witness. Then you can't stand it, so you go talk to whoever it is Pelletier says was there, and then that guy starts thinking it's all over town and the next thing he's spilling his guts to one of those, whatdya call 'em?

"Ties, Isaac. Men call the supervisors 'ties' because Greene makes 'em all wear neckties."

"Whatever. Anyhow, I know how these things work, Peter. So just stay out of it. Let it die. We go into that arbitration with Trice's word against the old man, we win."

"Maybe that's the problem, Isaac."

"It sounds to me like you're the problem. You want to stay in that corner office or would you rather go back down the street and take orders from Harry Greene?"

"You know something, Isaac. You're really beginning to tick me off. You act like Romanowski's already got one cheek of his Polish ass in this chair and it's only September. And I'll tell you something else, sometimes I think you're more worried about your win-and-loss record than you are about my job."

"I resent that. Do you know how many years I've represented this union?"

"A hundred and ten, how's that?"

"Fine, Peter. You want the files, just tell me and I'll resign today. Handle your own arbitrations."

Werner felt the power working. He hated it, but it didn't matter. There was nothing he could do. "I'm sorry, Isaac. You know I didn't mean that. It's just the sonofabitch is so damn guilty."

"Maybe yes, maybe no. But that's not your job. You are paid to represent the members of Local 664, and I am paid to help you do it. Thomas Trice is a member. So when he gets in trouble, we defend him. You can't do that, Peter, there's lots of men out there will, and I'm not just talking about Mr. Romanowski."

The Secretary-Treasurer felt like asking the great one who had the job of defending Charlie Carpool, but he knew better, so instead he just told Rothstein to call Triple A and get a list.

Five minutes later, he was walking down Hixon Avenue, on his way to speak to Henry Pelletier.

"Dammit, Patterson, all I want to know is when the guy goes on break. I just have to talk to him for a minute." Werner could feel sweat dripping down the back of his buttoned-up shirt collar. Over the shoulder of Hubert Patterson, furnace room day shift supervisor, he could see the glow from the top of Bessemer Three, bathing the room in red orange.

The two men stood chest to chest on the ingot car tracks, Werner trying hard to keep his dress shoes away from the grease pools that lay between the rails, reflecting off into the distance toward the gigantic furnaces.

"Look, Werner. I just work here, you understand. You got rules, we got rules." Patterson pulled the tiny book from his back pocket. He knew the collective bargaining agreement by heart, but still he made a point of carefully turning the pages until he reached Article XXI, Union Visitation. "You got no grievances going down in here, you didn't go to HR or else Ms. Henderson would have called me, so I don't think we have anything to talk about."

"Do I understand that you are refusing me access to this facility?"

"That is precisely what I'm doing. You want to bullshit with Henry Pelletier, you do it on your time, not mine."

Pete Werner reached out and grabbed the book from Hubert Patterson's hand. He did it so fast, and so unexpectedly, that the supervisor just stood there with his mouth open. Now Werner flipped pages. He shoved the open book back against Patterson's chest.

"You want to play by the rules, Patterson. Fine, we'll play by the rules.

This is a safety inspection. Article XIX." Pete reached into his pocket, pulled out his cell phone and hit the speed dial. Five seconds later he was telling Axel Kinnard to round up any business agents he could find in the hall and send them down the street to the furnace room. Then he said, "never mind" as Patterson turned to walk away.

By the time Werner found Henry Pelletier, the Secretary-Treasurer had almost violated his own sacred coat and tie rule. Even in the break room, where he was now sitting with the gigantic furnace tender, the temperature had to be close to ninety. Pelletier leaned against the cool metal of the soda machine, a glistening mound of hair, sweat and denim, inhaling his Diet Coke.

"I only got a few minutes, Mr. Werner. They don't like us taking too long on break."

"That took a lot of guts, what you did last night, Henry."

"Thanks, but I only talked on account of Charlie. He still ain't right, you know."

"I don't understand."

"They say his brain's swelled up or something like that. Can't feel his feet neither."

Werner started boring in. "Old man's pretty popular down here, isn't he?"

Pelletier laughed. "Yeah, Charlie's all right. Guys bust on him and all, but he don't mind, ya know what I mean."

"Well, at least he's out of the hospital."

"That's true, Mr. Werner, but like I said, he's still in bad shape."

Werner decided it was time to get to the point. "You know, we got ourselves a real problem down the hall with this one."

"I don't understand, Mr. Werner."

"Sure you do, Henry. You were there last night. You heard the two of them, T. J. and that slob Romanowski."

"You mean about them suing the local if we don't try to get Trice his job back? Shit, that dog ain't gonna hunt."

"It will if you don't help us." The Secretary-Treasurer did not pause for Henry's reply. "Way it stands now, we gotta take his case. Trice's word against the old man. And I'll tell you something else, union's gonna win it too. T. J.'ll be coming back in here like shit through a goose. You think he was trouble before they fired him, just wait till some arbitrator puts him back to work with full back pay."

"Well, then, maybe someone in here's gonna have to fix it themself. Lot of bad things can happen in a place like this."

"You really *are* nuts, aren't you, Henry. Next thing you know we'll be talking about your case. Look, it's so damn simple. There's another witness out there and you know who it is. Christ, you told the whole damn union last night."

"And I shouldn't a done it, neither. Just got so sick of that lying sack of shit I couldn't sit still no more. But like I said, I ain't going no further. You wanna find the man saw Trice doing the deed, that's your business. Fact is, I hope you do find him. Hope he sings his brains out. Only don't be asking me to help you 'cause I can't do it."

"You mean you *won't* do it."

"Look, Mr. Werner. You worked in here, same as me. Folks say you kicked them ties all over this factory. That's how you got to running the union in the first place."

"So?"

"So don't start forgetting now what's right and what's wrong."

Werner slowly stood up. Again he was conscious of the stifling heat, and the noises, and the smells—all three intruding into the tiny break room, as if they had even more right to be there than the men trying to escape. He looked over Henry Pelletier's shoulder, though the dirty glass window, separating room from factory, out toward the figure of Hubert Patterson as it lumbered slowly toward the break room door, clipboard in hand, pencil on ear, scowl on face.

Patterson was able to push the door open with his foot because the lock and knob assembly had been missing for years. "All right, Werner. You boys had your little club meeting, okay. Now I got a factory to run, so why don't you just run along home to your tree house and let Mr. Pelletier get back to work?"

"This room stinks, you know that, Patterson?"

"You sure it's the room?"

"I'll tell you what I'm sure of. These men are supposed to have a break room here, not a goddamn toilet. When's the last time anyone cleaned this place out?"

"Well, now, Mr. Werner. I can't rightly say when the last time this place was clean. But I know when the next time'll be."

"Yeah, when's that?"

"When you get the hell out of it."

ELEVEN
Wednesday, September 28

ON THE MORNING PROFESSOR G. Arnold van Auten's decision in the
Koza arbitration arrived, David Castelli had already been through a fifty-
minute back-up on the Walt Whitman Bridge, caused by an overturned
tractor trailer hauling 85,000 pounds of french fries to every Willie
Whopper drive-through in the Delaware Valley.

It didn't get any better at the office. Castelli knew immediately that the
envelope from the American Arbitration Association contained bad news.
van Auten's decision wasn't even due for another week, so when it arrived
early the postmark might as well have been the mark of death. The professor believed that an employer who was about to have a "reinstatement
with full back pay" shoved up its corporate behind would somehow be less
upset if the grievant came back sooner so that the back pay would be less.
The professor just didn't get it.

As he was tearing open the envelope, Castelli's secretary was saying.
"Youse got a call from Mr. McKeon 'bout half hour ago. I told him I didn't
know where you were. Anyhow, he said he wants to see you soon as you
come in."

Maribeth Kryselski, already drinking Diet Coke at 9:45 in the morning,
was wearing her turquoise jumpsuit today. David said, "I thought Eleanor
Rice had a rule about pantsuits in the office, not that I care, of course."

"It's not a pantsuit, Mr. C., it's a jumpsuit. Youse want some coffee?"

Castelli glanced toward the ceiling and shook his head back and forth, which had nothing to do with coffee, but it didn't matter because Maribeth thought it did. "I don't want any calls for the next twenty minutes, you got that?"

"Don't youse want me to stamp that in?" Maribeth said, pointing to the half-open envelope in David's hand.

"Just hold the damn calls."

Like Don Corleone in *The Godfather*, David was a man who liked to receive bad news fast—which is why he read the last page of van Auten's opinion first.

AWARD

The grievance is sustained. Rapid Freight, Inc. did not have just cause to terminate Henry Koza. The Company is ordered to offer Mr. Koza reinstatement to his former position as truck driver, with all seniority rights intact. The Company is further ordered to make Mr. Koza whole by giving him full back pay, less interim earnings, from the date of his discharge to the date on which he is offered reinstatement. In addition, the Company is directed to make all back payments on Mr. Koza's behalf to the Teamster Local 664 Pension, Health & Welfare, Legal, Scholarship and Vacation Funds in accordance with the terms of the parties' collective bargaining agreement.

G. Arnold van Auten
Arbitrator

David knew it was coming. He knew it when van Auten turned off the air-conditioning a month ago. Still, he could not control the familiar tingly chill that ran up his back as he read the award. Furiously, he tore through the opinion, looking for the hook that van Auten used to put a lying thief back to work, complete with $35,000 in back pay for bragging rights. He found it on page six.

Unfortunately for the Company, the issue here is not solely the guilt or innocence of the grievant. Industrial due process is no less a part of the fabric of modern labor relations than is the right of an employer to terminate employees for cause. And in this area, even scoundrels have rights.

This arbitrator is particularly troubled about the cavalier manner in which the Company handled its investigation of the case.
It is perfectly clear that supervisor Gregory Newell made up his
mind to terminate Henry Koza based solely on the presence
of Rapid Freight boxes in the dumpster behind the Crystal
Acropolis, and the unsworn statements of Plato Galenkos. There
was no meaningful attempt made even to hear, much less credit,
the grievant's side of the story before management imposed
industrial capital punishment on Mr. Koza.

Castelli was very close to crumbling page six into a ball and stuffing it
into the wastebasket. The only reason he didn't was that he had to send
a copy of the opinion to his client, and van Auten had been too cheap to
send him an extra one. The arbitrator did send his bill, of course: Five days
at $750.00 per day. One hearing day, two study and prep days, two days to
write the opinion.

The bill was van Auten's final insult. Castelli figured it actually took the
sonofabitch about twenty minutes to kiss off the company's brief, then
maybe two hours to write the decision.

Just once, he thought, he would like to see an honest reinstatement
with back pay award, one that explained what was really going through the
arbitrator's mind. He actually thought about changing the last page of van
Auten's opinion before sending it to the client. And he would have, too, if
Gregory Newell had half a sense of humor.

AWARD

The grievant was caught red-handed selling off the back of
his truck. Moreover, he lied under oath, showed no remorse
whatsoever, and had an obscene tattoo.

On the other hand, Isaac Rothstein sends me twenty cases a
year and is vindictive as hell. David Castelli, by contrast, is still
an associate whom Jack McKeon would never have thrown in
here if he thought management really needed a victory. Besides,
McKeon is getting ready to retire.

My wife says the kids need braces and I want a new car.
Accordingly, the grievant is reinstated with full back pay.

Typing the revised award on his computer made David feel a lot better. He was even starting to laugh when Jack McKeon called, wanting to know where he was.

The senior associate said, "No, I didn't get any message." David was not comfortable lying to his mentor, but this year he was feeling the strain. Besides, Maribeth missed half his calls anyhow.

McKeon was uncharacteristically sitting on one of his white leather couches when David entered the corner office. But the old man's Irish blues were still twinkling brightly, so Castelli didn't get too suspicious over the senior partner's change of normal venue.

McKeon spoke first. "Saw Arnie van Auten last night at the Industrial Relations Roundtable. Says you did a terrific job in the Koza hearing."

"Well, actually ..."

"So I immediately said to the little shit, 'That's great Arnie. Now, tell me, how far *did* you shove it up the kid's rear end?'"

"You really want to know, Jack? The opinion came in this morning."

"Let me guess. Good old Professor Arnie gave Ike Rothstein the whole enchilada, right? Reinstatement, back pay, money to the funds—all of it."

"I'm sorry."

"What sorry. I told you last month Gregory Newell was a half-wit. Anyhow, I got something much more important to talk to you about."

The senior partner stood up from his couch and returned to the mahogany aircraft carrier that doubled as his desk. He slid on the half glasses that hung around his neck on a golden chain then began paging mindlessly through a file in front of him. Castelli followed to the crew's quarters of the desk, pulling out the wooden tongue to take notes.

"Just listen. Don't write."

"Sure."

"I know these last few months have been tough on you, David. But we're gonna get you through it, you understand?"

"I understand how you feel, Jack. But that's not all of it, not in this place."

"You mean the secret ballot? Crock o' shit. Besides, what are you worried about, Melissa Cohen and Carl Merriweather? Rub 'em both together they couldn't make sparks in a desert. Geek and a freak."

"Except that's not the way it's going down, Jack. I hear the whole litigation department has been ordered to vote for Cohen. They don't get another woman partner in there, Jocelyn Marsh's gonna cut off some major balls. And you know that little nerd in tax is keeping half of Tingham's clients out of jail, so what the hell you think that department's gonna do?"

"Well neither one of them is half the lawyer you are, David, and every partner in this firm knows it. So just relax and listen to me."

"I'm listening."

"You know Harry Greene, don't you?"

Of course I know Harry Greene. Biggest labor client in the firm."

"Well, he's got this forklift driver, Thomas J. Trice. Real piece of garbage. Been soldiering down there for years. Anyhow, the guy got drunk about a month ago and decided it would be fun to ride his Harley through the factory. Only it turns out he must have been a little too drunk, because he dumped the bike and damn near killed the night watchman. Old man's still not right, they say."

"I take it they fired him."

"You take it absolutely right. Now Trice, of course, says he didn't do it, but the whole factory thinks that's bullshit. Apparently he's got this fancy motorcycle everyone in Lancaster knows, and the watchman can identify him *and* the bike."

"Don't tell me Werner's taking the case to arbitration."

"Got no choice. You ever hear of a lawyer named Brian O'Conner, little pinko out of Lancaster?"

"No, give me a hint."

"How about the Lancaster County Workers' Rights Project?"

David pursed his lips together in a tight little smile, then nodded his head in recognition. "Michael Twardzik," he said. "What'd he get? Twenty thousand?"

"I think it was thirty."

"And Trice's got the same lawyer?"

"Bingo! The Lancaster County Workers' Rights Project is on Werner's case again. Anyhow, Harry Greene says it's all over the plant that Trice's bragging he'll be back with full pay, and then O'Conner's gonna sue everyone in sight for libel. You know the union almost had a riot over this case?"

Jack McKeon tossed the folded-up newspaper across the carrier deck. He kept on talking as David scanned the front page article.

"So, as you can now plainly see, Mr. Werner doesn't have much of a choice in this one. But I know his heart's not in it."

Castelli had already figured out that the Trice case was about to be his. He just didn't know why. Jack's favorite client. High local publicity. Eyewitness. Perfect slam dunk.

McKeon continued. "Harry wants this case on a fast track. Says it's distracting the hell out of half his plant and ruining production. So Rothstein and I struck arbitrators last week, and the case is on for October 5. Only problem is, I got Rapid Freight negotiations."

"Jack, that's next Wednesday."

"You can't do it, I'll get someone else."

"I didn't say I couldn't do it. It's just not a lot of time, that's all."

"Baloney, Whatd'ya have to do? One trip to Lancaster. Check out the scene, talk to the witness, interview the boss who pulled the trigger. Done."

"And who, may I ask, is the boss who pulled the trigger?"

"The warehouse supervisor himself, Joseph F. Breitenfeld. Guy's a bit of a Nazi, but his heart's in the right place."

"And the arbitrator?"

McKeon took something that almost looked to David like a deep breath. Then he cleared his throat about three times and pulled a piece of letterhead from the file. David could see the red American Arbitration Association logo though the paper. "Damndest Triple A list I ever saw. They must have been trying to drive the both of us crazy." McKeon skimmed the letter to Castelli, who caught it, looked down at the name with the big circle around it, and dropped the paper to the floor.

"You've got to be kidding."

"I wish I were. But look at the other six names they gave us to chose from. Besides, the guy owes you big time."

David retrieved the list of arbitrators, trying to make sense out of McKeon's selection. Seven names on the list. Each side can strike three, taking turns. It took him just a few seconds to figure out why G. Arnold van Auten ended up the winner.

"That's right," McKeon said. "The three best management arbitrators in town, Rothstein's three biggest whores, and Professor van Auten. So you tell me."

"You're right. I can't believe it, but you're right." Castelli put the letter in his lap and his forehead in his hand. "Felix Gomberger. I thought the guy was dead. He must be ninety."

"David, he was the best of the ones I struck. How about Victoria Pershing? Never upheld a discharge in her life. And Scott Mund? That guy would give Rothstein a hand job in the middle of City Hall courtyard if he asked."

Castelli couldn't resist. "And Oliver Winthrop would give you one, Jack, so those two are a standoff. All right. I get the old professor again and one week to prepare. Any other good news?"

"Yeah. I'm giving you a drop dead winner for McKeon, Tingham & Marsh's biggest labor client just in time for the partnership vote. That good enough news for you?"

⸻⸻◈⸻⸻

The eastern border of the city of Lancaster is shaped like the mandibles of a gigantic insect, reaching out from the town's north and south boundaries, east across the Conestoga River, as if they are trying to grab and eat a large section of Manheim Township. On the west bank of the Conestoga, just inside the city's northern mandible, lies Hixon Avenue, its four-block length dominated by the dark gray buildings of the Greene-Pitowsky Smelting & Battery Company.

Driving south on Conestoga River Drive, off the Walnut Street exit from Route 30, river on the left, a traveler's first glimpse of the gigantic battery plant comes just over a crest in the road, looking down a long sloping grade toward the water. The traveler notices the mountains first, strung out along the river bank like so many gigantic Indian tepees. At first the traveler suspects them to be merely mounds of blue-gray sand, perhaps piled there by the Street Department to await the winter storms. It is only later, when the traveler is close enough to catch the twinkling glints of late afternoon sun blinking on and off against the west sides of the mountains, that he realizes these are not innocent mounds of sand. They are burial grounds for the decaying exoskeletons of millions of dead car batteries.

David's pewter gray Honda Accord nosed the crest of Conestoga River Drive just after four Thursday afternoon. The casing mountains looked even larger than the lawyer remembered, though, in fairness, it had been almost two years since Jack McKeon last let his prize pupil handle a matter for Greene-Pitowsky. It was a small unemployment compensation dispute, hardly worth a senior partner's time; still, it was unusual for anyone other than McKeon himself to represent Greene-Pitowsky, no matter how small the case, and David had felt extremely flattered. Also extremely worried.

And that, of course, was why the young lawyer had felt oddly ill at ease, when he headed off from Center City Philadelphia, two hours earlier this day, on his way to the first significant encounter he would ever have with the venerable Harry Greene.

That morning, David told his wife he had to go out to Lancaster the night before the scheduled interviews with Breitenfeld and Charlie Carliner, so that he could see the buildings in the dark, the way they looked when Trice ran down the watchman. There could actually have been some truth to his explanation, although the real reason was just so David could get away for a night.

Surprisingly, there was a decent hotel in the area, less than a mile from the factory. It was called the Lamplighter House, and it was listed in the Almanac of Historic Buildings of Pennsylvania. The 150-year-old wood frame hotel had been faithfully restored to the exact way it looked in the summer of 1863 when, according to unconfirmed legend, the great Confederate cavalry general J.E.B. Stuart holed up there in a drunken stupor for two days when he was supposed to have been out scouting the Union Army before the battle of Gettysburg. Jack McKeon had told David about the hotel just after he assigned Castelli to the Trice case. Even called ahead to make sure David got the J.E.B. Stuart suite itself.

Castelli could smell the sulfuric acid leitmotiv of Greene-Pitowsky Smelting & Battery Company even before he made the left turn from Conestoga River Road onto Hixon Avenue. Once he made the turn, the acrid odor attacked his nostrils like the smell of a high school chemistry lab. He felt immediately depressed, as if the sun had suddenly gone out, which it almost had from the perpetual haze that rose over the factory, still four blocks away.

Kids trundled mindlessly back and forth on the sidewalks, riding assorted plastic tricycles. Occasionally one would dart out from the dim porch of his tiny row house, exploding down the patch of brown grass that served as his front lawn. The kids seemed oblivious to the haze and the stench, their lifelong companions. McKeon had told David to stop in and introduce himself to Harry Greene before he began nosing around the factory grounds. Said the man would be expecting him and not to be late. He wasn't.

By the time David reached the dilapidated perimeter fence that half-heartedly separated Greene-Pitowsky from the rest of Hixon Avenue, the acid fumes were practically overwhelming. He was also immediately aware of the rhythmic thunk that called out every two seconds from inside the long metal-sided building just beyond the guard shack, then answered with its own echo, bouncing off from somewhere in the distance toward the river—over and over and over, like the mating sounds of two gigantic animals. None of the employees at Greene-Pitowsky smelled the acid or heard the hydrocleavers—they had long since grown numb. One of them, a hugely overweight slug of a man, squeezed out from the guard shack and stared into the driver's window of Castelli's car.

"You got business in here?" It was definitely not a pleasant greeting.

David realized immediately what was going on. His first instinct was to come back with some snotty remark about *not* being from the government so the guy should just chill out. His second instinct was to say, "Yes, sir. I'm a lawyer for the company and I have an appointment with Mr. Greene." When he chose the second answer, the fat man suddenly relaxed and reached for a filthy phone hanging on the wall, just inside the guard-house door.

David sat stiffly in a wooden chair facing Harry Greene's desk. Moments earlier, a secretary who introduced herself as Shelia told the lawyer to just go on in and sit down.

Greene was shouting into the receiver. "I don't give a damn what the American Metal Market Daily says, you want me to take that shit off your hands, it's three cents a pound. You think you can get more from Weinstein, do it, only I know you can't 'cause he's an even cheaper Jew than me."

David watched as Harry Greene tapped his fat fingers against the receiver, listening to his customer's rebuttal. Then, slowly, his angry expression slid into a smile. Not a jovial smile. More like the smile of an old alligator, sated with the afternoon sun, fresh prey still steaming in its belly.

"Now you're getting some sense in that thick head. For a minute there, I thought you was coming down with Alzheimer's." Again Greene paused, listening to the surrender. Then he looked across his cluttered desk.

"Who the hell are you?"

Stammering was not exactly the way Castelli had expected to meet the firm's most important client. "Y–your secretary told me to just come in, I'm really sorry if I ..."

Greene stood up and stuck out his paw. "Just kidding, David, I know exactly who you are. Forgive the mess." Harry swung his hand in a broad arc around the office. "One of these days, I gotta get Shelia to straighten out this place." He yelled toward the office door. "Right, beautiful?"

The owner sat back down in his chair, bit off the end of a huge black cigar, then spit the tiny piece of tobacco leaf toward the corner of his office. The lighter was one of those old silver relics shaped like a .45 automatic that shot out flame from the end of the barrel when Harry pulled the trigger. He spoke from behind the first cloud of smoke.

"So you're the man Jack McKeon sent me to slay the dragon. Ever gone up against Ike Rothstein, before?"

"Yes, sir."

"Ever beat him?"

"Absolutely."

"That's not what I hear. I hear he just cleaned your clock."

David stiffened in the wooden chair. He couldn't believe Jack McKeon actually told Harry Greene about the Koza case. Again he went on the defensive, this time trying to shrug off the defeat with humor.

"Yes, I'm afraid he did, sir. Now he's only got to beat me five more times to get even."

Harry laughed again. "I like you already, David. So just for that, I'm gonna make that number six." Then he turned off the smile. "We have to win this one, you know. I'm sure Jack told you."

"You mean about Trice being problem in the plant?"

"A problem! Is that what the old Irish bastard told you Mr. Trice was, a problem? How about a cancer? How about a no-good, lying sonofabitch who gets up every morning just to screw this company? I don't even want to tell you how long I've waited to fire him. Anyhow, this time he finally went and did something really dumb. And this time, somebody saw him do it."

"He was wearing a mask, though, wasn't he?"

"Look, David. I'm not going to tell you how to do your job. You're the lawyer. But I wouldn't worry about the mask. Wait till you see this guy. Right out of one of those biker magazines. Has this wacky-looking beard, cut off straight across the bottom. Man he hit swears he saw the damn thing sticking right out from under the mask. Swears he recognized his voice too. And I'll tell you something else, there's nobody in Lancaster County has a motorcycle like Trice's. No, I wouldn't worry about this case. Matter of fact, *you* oughta be paying *me* for this one. Jack says it's gonna make you a partner."

By the time Harry was finished with his pep talk, the cigar smoke had so enveloped him that he looked almost like the *Alice in Wonderland* caterpillar. Greene looked at the nervous young lawyer, head down, furiously scribbling on his yellow pad. Harry almost wished he hadn't laid it on quite so thick, Castelli being so earnest and all, but McKeon had been emphatic on the phone earlier in the afternoon.

"The kid's a digger, I'm telling you. He starts thinking there's a chance this case is a loser, he's gonna dive into stuff we don't want him worrying about, you got that."

"I understand, Jack. I really do. But I can't control everything he does."

"I know you can't. And that's exactly why he's gotta think there isn't anything *to* do except check out the scene and interview the old man. I take it you have that covered."

"Castelli's seeing him first thing tomorrow morning. Before Charlie can get a load on. Nurse says she's even gonna make sure he takes a bath."

David finished writing and looked up from his notes. "I understand you've set up a meeting for me tomorrow morning with Charlie Carliner."

"It's at his house. Joe Breitenfeld will give you directions. Just remember, the old man's still a bit weak from the accident."

"So I'm told."

"But his memory's sharp as a tack, David. Especially when it comes to Thomas J. Trice."

"I hope so, Mr. Greene. You know Charlie's our whole case."

Then David rose, shook Harry's hand, and left the office. Harry couldn't help thinking that the young man, so handsome, so ramrod straight, was just about the same age as his own son, Eric, five years younger at most. Probably had a perfect family and a beautiful home. Eric had three D.U.I. arrests in the last eighteen months. But Harry never blamed Eric for the shambles of his young life. With extra helpings of Jewish guilt, Harry blamed only himself. Himself, and the high wire act his own life had become when Eric was still almost a child.

———————

It had begun in the fall of 1980. Greene was on the verge of losing his empire. Twenty-four years of whacking the GPS&B treasury for everything from limos to condos, and there it was, all about to crash down on his head. Minna was out of control; Eric couldn't hold on to a job even if it was made of iron and the kid had a fifty-pound magnet strapped to his ample waist, and Princess Loni-Jo, twenty-three years old and spoiled to the core, was planning the most elaborate wedding since Grace Kelly laid siege to Monaco.

So Harry turned to Jack McKeon, the man who knew everyone and could do anything. McKeon could not have been more understanding. Within a week he had called Harry with the idea.

"You still own that kids' summer camp up near Stroudsburg?"

"What do you think," Harry answered. "Of course I still own it. Worst investment I ever made. Been closed for years."

"Well, what would you say if I told you I have someone who's interested in looking at it?"

"I'd say he's an idiot. Place has been rotting for nine years. Only thing I've done is put a fence around it to keep off the trespassers and even that doesn't work. Damn duck hunters sneak on anyhow."

"I don't know these guys, Harry, but I don't think they're idiots. And if they are, they're sure as hell rich idiots."

"What are you talking about?"

"I'm talking about investors. And they need a piece of property in the Poconos. I haven't the slightest idea what for, but the other night I'm in my favorite South Philly restaurant having dinner, place called the Saloon, you'd love it, and this palooka I know from the Pipefitters, fella named Corky something or other, comes over to my table to shoot the breeze. We start talking, and all of a sudden he says, 'Yo Jack, you're a rich lawyer. You know anybody has land in the Poconos?' Right away I think of you."

"I'm listening but I don't like it already."

"For chrissake, Harry, I'm trying to help you."

"You're right. Keep going."

"So anyhow, I tell Corky I may know someone and he says, 'Great, I'm having dinner over in the corner with some friends, can you talk to them?' I say 'sure.' Corky disappears for a few seconds, comes back for me, and the next thing you know I'm sitting with two characters who look like they're right out of central casting. Thousand dollar suits, Gucci watches—the real ones, mind you—white on white on white monogrammed shirts. One of them is even wearing sunglasses.

"Corky doesn't even bother with their names and right away the one without the sunglasses, real skinny guy with a suntan, starts asking me about the property. What town is it in? How many acres? Is it flat? I say, 'Whoa, slow down a minute. It's not my property. It belongs to a friend.' So then Mr. Sunglasses hands me this business card. Nothing on it but a phone number and the words 'Mountaintop Investment Properties.' Not even an address or a name. He says, 'Tell your friend if he's serious, call this number.' That was the end of the conversation."

There was silence at the other end of the phone. Then Harry spoke. "That's it? I'm supposed to call some number, talk to god knows who, and sell them Camp Pocono Sunrise just like that?"

"All I know, Harry, it's a lead. You tell me you're desperate. You tell me the camp's rotting away up there. What do you have to lose?"

He called the number Jack gave him within five minutes of getting off the phone.

Harry knew only that the man was named Fontini. He had arranged to meet him at Kitty's Tavern, just south of Stroudsburg on Route 191. Greene rarely visited the site of Camp Pocono Sunrise anymore. He knew he should be checking the property more often, but the whole experience was just too painful.

The old camp was like the rotting corpse of a once beautiful woman. Less than a year after he had closed her up in 1971, a powerful late summer storm called Agnes had torn through northern Monroe County, taking dead aim at the old girl, tearing the roof off her dining hall, splintering her boat dock, littering her ball fields with tree limbs, blowing the shutters off her bunk houses, then skimming them like gigantic flat stones across the grounds.

In its early years, Camp Pocono Sunrise would open each summer, crammed full of spoiled Jewish kids from Philadelphia and New York. Harry loved to parade about the grounds, bare from the waist up, flexing his tanned biceps. Each Friday evening from late June to mid August he would end the drive from Lancaster to Stroudsburg, slowly gliding his big Buick Roadmaster down the dirt road, past the dining hall, right onto one of the ball fields—lord of the manor surveying his spotless plantation.

Then, in the late sixties, Camp Pocono Sunrise contracted a case of terminal liability insurance. Lawyers had taken over the world; a rustic, unsafe camp, overflowing with the coddled offspring of wealthy parents, was the perfect breeding ground for litigation. All it would take was one contagious illness, one drowning, even one good fall off a horse, and Camp Pocono Sunrise would be history. The precarious balance between black ink and red started to tip. Tuition had to go up. Enrollments began to decline. By 1971, the camp was only half filled. Harry Greene, a businessman if nothing else, knew it was time to strike the set.

It was close to 3:30 in the afternoon when Harry pulled into the parking lot of Kitty's Tavern. Fontini wasn't due until four, but Harry was almost always early for appointments—especially ones that could rescue him from financial ruin.

Camp Pocono Sunrise may have become a ghost town in the last nine years, but Kitty's hadn't changed at all. When the camp was in its prime, Harry figured that the one-story white wood tavern, its dilapidated neon sign blinking a pussycat logo on and off to passing motorists, probably doubled its profits from June to August selling beer to underaged camp counselors with fake IDs.

It was too early on this Saturday in October for the regulars; just a pair of black Harleys and a few pickups in the lot, their owners quietly guzzling shots and beer at the already dark bar. Each man was staring intently at the TV high on the corner wall. Game four of the World Series was quickly slipping away from the home state Phillies.

"Oh and two the count to Brett. Dickie Noles kicks, delivers ... and Brett goes down in the dirt! That one sure looked like a message." One of the Harley guys peered up from his shot glass. "Atta boy, Dickie, stick it in his ear."

Harry settled into a corner booth facing the front door and waited for his guests to arrive.

At five minutes past four, the front door of Kitty's Tavern opened. Blinded by the late afternoon sun streaming into the dark room, Harry could barely make out two tall broad-shouldered silhouettes filling up the entrance. It was only after the door had closed and his eyes had readjusted that Harry realized three men were walking toward his booth. The short man in the lead had at first been invisible against the hulking backdrop of his companions; but it would have been obvious to anyone paying attention to the trio that it was the short man who was in charge.

He was dressed in the most expensive suit Harry had ever seen. His body, thin almost to the point of looking sick, slid into the booth across from Greene. One of the bookends filled up almost all of the other side of the booth, except for the tiny space between his right leg and the wall that suddenly imprisoned Harry. The third man sat alone in the next booth, on the far side, his round, fat face undistinguished except for two small dark eyes that peered at Harry over the short man's left shoulder. They were dead eyes, revealing no emotion, pasted into their whites like raisins on a Christmas cookie.

The short man extended his hand across the table—bony and tan, a large diamond pinky ring dwarfing the delicate finger it encircled. "My name is Mario Fontini, Mr. Greene."

Harry took the hand cautiously and nodded.

Fontini said, "And this is my associate, Tony Angelo." The bookend muttered something that sounded like "Howyadoon," then Fontini took over.

"So Mr. Greene."

"Harry, please."

"Okay, Harry. I understand you own some property up here."

"Two thousand acres, Mr. Fontini. Used to be a kids' camp, but I closed it in 1971."

"And since then?"

"Nothing, hardly even come up here anymore. The county made me put a fence around the place a few years ago to keep the duck hunters out. Actually they didn't make me put it up, just suggested. It was my lawyer convinced me. Told me the place was an attractive nuisance. Said I might get sued if one of those damn hunters shot himself in the foot. Something like that, anyhow."

Fontini smiled. "Never use lawyers, myself. Don't believe in them."

"Well, the one I use is an old war buddy, Jack McKeon. You know him?"

"Yeah, I know him. Big-time labor lawyer, though. Wouldn't think he'd be giving out real estate advice."

"He didn't. Got the advice from his partner, British fellow named Tingham. Talks like he swallowed a sweat sock." Harry wasn't really interested in continuing the small talk, but at least it helped him take his mind off the gorilla sitting in the next booth.

Fortunately, Fontini was also ready to move on. "This land you own, far from here?"

"Just up the road. About two miles."

"That's good. We'll go in my car."

Harry sat in the middle of the limousine's rear seat. He could see the fall colors, dimmed but still visible though the blacked-out windows. The man with the dead eyes drove slowly south on 191 while Fontini tried in vain to tune in the World Series on the tiny TV mounted behind the driver's seat. Tony Angelo stared straight ahead.

"These things never work. Fancy antenna poking out the back of the car and still all you get is fuzz. Next week we take it back, Tony, you got that?"

"No problem, Mr. Fontini."

"Gadgets, Harry. I love gadgets, except most of them don't ever do what they're supposed to. Kinda like employees. Fontini laughed out loud. "Isn't that right, Tony, gadgets like employees? Never do what they're supposed to."

"Right, Mr. Fontini."

"You got employees, Harry?"

Harry knew, almost as if by instinct, that he should say as little as possible to Mario Fontini. "A few," he answered.

"A few! That's not what I hear. A few hundred is more like it. Teamsters too. Biggest lead smelter in Pennsylvania, you know that, Tony? Mr. Greene's got quite a business down there in Lancaster. Matter of fact, Mr. Greene's a famous man—number one polluter on DER's most wanted list, isn't that right, Harry."

Harry felt his stomach muscles grow tight. The sudden chill that transforms anxiety into fear raced up his body, smashing into the top of his head from inside as if it wanted to burst through. He knew his voice was shaking, but he could do nothing to stop it. He tried to make a joke of the remark.

"Yeah, that's me all right. A regular Jesse James."

"Self-righteous sons of bitches too, aren't they, Harry? Bunch of granola bar chomping do-gooders, picking on hard-working businessmen. Damn shame if you ask me."

The white Cadillac rounded a bend in the road and the wire fence appeared. "Up there on the right," Harry said. "I have to get out and unlock the gate."

Even though the four men walked mostly in silence through the dilapidated, unkempt site, it was obvious that Mario Fontini was pleased with the layout of Camp Pocono Sunrise. Several times Harry saw him nod his head up and down, lips tightly pursed, as if he were mentally giving an exam to some feature of the grounds, then grading it an A. Fontini spent a particularly long time walking the open field that was once the centerpiece of Harry's beloved camp, a vast green expanse, totally surrounded by tall oak trees. The field was large enough for several softball games to be played at the same time. Four rotted wood backstops still stood, back to back in the center of the field, the quartet laced with fragments of rusted chicken wire; but the infields they anchored had long ago gone to eternal rest beneath a tangle of undergrowth.

Harry followed a respectful few yards behind Fontini and his body-guards as the group made their way slowly back from the ball fields, along the shore of the lake, to the waiting limousine parked next to Camp Pocono Sunrise's decapitated dining hall.

Dead eyes held open the left rear passenger door. Fontini said, "Why don't you get in, Harry. We'll talk."

Fontini and Greene sat alone in the back seat of the limo, now suddenly silent as the door thunked shut. The bookends flanked the car, their large gray-suited backs pressed against the two rear windows, blotting out most of the fading late afternoon sunlight. Fontini turned toward Harry.

"I like the place, Mr. Greene. I like it a lot, especially the ball field. It's going to be perfect."

"Perfect for what?" Harry's stomach was quickly filling with a bouilla-baisse of equal parts fear, curiosity and impatience. The recipe was causing him serious indigestion.

"That, my friend, is not for you to worry about. All you have to do is be here once a month to let us in and collect your share."

"What are you talking about, 'let us in?' You mean you don't want to buy this place?"

Fontini threw back his head and laughed out loud. "Buy? Who ever said anything about buy. I'm just a poor renter, Harry, a mere tenant. Two hours a month, that's all we need."

"Look, Mr. Fontini, I don't know what this is all about, and I don't care, either." Harry heard the words coming out, but he seemed to have little control over them. "I was given a phone number, Mountaintop Investment Properties. I called it. I arranged this meeting. Then you show up with those two creeps out there and tell me you just want to rent this place for a lousy two hours a month. Why don't you just take me back to my car?"

"Of course, Harry. We'll take you back. But at least listen before you make a hasty decision."

"I'm listening."

Fontini started speaking very softly. He rested his hand on Harry's knee as he talked. "We know everything, Mr. Greene. We know all about Greene-Pitowsky Smelting & Battery—both sets of books. You're in trou-ble, Harry. Deep, deep trouble. Wouldn't even surprise me if the banks were beginning to get suspicious. Would it surprise you?"

Harry tried to speak, but he could not utter a sound. He could feel the acid rush into his mouth. He swallowed and tried to control breathing that was suddenly labored. Fontini continued.

"You need money, Harry. We need Camp Pocono Sunrise. It's really simple. You come up here once a month. We'll let you know when. You open up the place and we all just sit quietly and wait for a little Cessna to land in that beautiful old ball field. We pick up a package from the pilot, and you get five thousand dollars in cash."

Harry forced himself to speak. He was on the verge of hysteria. "You can use the place yourself. I don't care. I'll give you the keys right now. Just leave me out of it."

"Now you're really being silly, aren't you." Fontini squeezed his hand on Harry's knee and leaned even closer. "You know we can't turn you loose now, just like that. We need you as a partner. And besides, no one walks away from five thousand in cash every month, do they, Harry?"

"Well I do. I don't care what happens to the company. It's not worth getting mixed up in any crime, you understand that."

The slender hand with the gigantic ring relaxed on Harry's knee. "Who said anything about crime? Did I say anything about crime?"

"Just take me back to my car and I'll forget we ever met each other."

"You don't get it, Harry, do you?" Fontini's voice no longer had its fatherly calmness. "This isn't a quiz show here. You don't get to choose an answer, see if it's right, then decide if you're coming back in a week to go for the next plateau. Besides, you've got a family down there in Lancaster who are depending on you. Even have a wedding coming up I understand. Loni-Jo. Beautiful name, Loni-Jo. I'll bet she's a beautiful girl too."

It was then that Harry Greene suddenly began to cry. His 56-year-old body shook like a child. Mario Fontini took out a silk handkerchief and told him not to worry. He said that Harry was going make a lot of money and that Loni-Jo was going to be a lovely bride.

TWELVE
Thursday, September 29

JOSEPH BREITENFELD WAS YELLING in David's ear, just to be heard above the pounding of the hydrocleavers. Before the walk around, they had made David put on big rubber boots that came up to his knees, like a trout fisherman. Breitenfeld said it was for the acid. Pools of it were polka-dotting the floor of Battery Boulevard as Castelli and the warehouse supervisor made their way past the rows of water-powered guillotines, each one tended by an operator wearing similar boots and a respirator. Up close, the hydrocleavers at speed were deafening. They thunked and wheezed like old asthmatic giants, methodically decapitating their already dead victims.

"Had to start wearing the masks last summer," Breitenfeld shouted. "Damn OSHA."

David had declined the respirator when it was offered to him about ten minutes earlier. Now he wished he hadn't. The smell of sulfuric acid tore through his nostrils. And even though he was wearing rubber boots, he could sense heat each time he stepped in one of the puddles.

As the two men walked the length of Battery Boulevard, toward the spot where Charlie Carliner had been sitting when he first heard Trice's Harley, Breitenfeld was working hard at trying to be friendly.

"Don't even ask about the workers' comp. claims in this place. Blue collar lottery, you ask me. Had a secretary on it last year. Bet you'll never guess what for."

David played along, also yelling to be heard. "I won't even try."

"Acid burns up her joy trail," Breitenfeld laughed. "I swear to God. Turns out one of the battery men was diddling her every afternoon down the locker room."

"Don't tell me she got comp. for that."

"You tell me, you're the lawyer. Referee said it was an on-the-job injury."

At the south end of Battery Boulevard, the two men stopped, David turning and looking north, down the long line of flatbeds toward Hixon Avenue. "Trice actually rode in here on a motorcycle?"

"That's what the old man said. Course there weren't any trucks in here at the time, it being Friday night and all. Just a long open aisle from here up to Hixon."

"The old man must have been scared out of his mind."

"Wouldn't you be? Some screaming maniac wearing a Richard Nixon mask, coming at you on that damn Harley. Course it's no wonder Trice dropped the bike. You oughta see the oil slick in here when them trucks pull out."

It was at this point David knew he had to come back after dark. There really wasn't any choice. He had wanted just to check in at the Lamplighter, have himself a couple of extra dry Beefeater martinis and a big steak, then watch "Thursday Night Football" on TV in his room. Instead, he ended up back on Battery Boulevard at 8:30 PM, trying not to slip on the oil slick.

Breitenfeld said, "Oh, I don't know about *that*. We got a schedule here."

It was obvious to David that the warehouse manager didn't even want to be in the plant after his regular shift, much less do anything. Castelli decided to try the humble approach.

"I understand it's a pain, Mr. Breitenfeld. But it would really help me if I could just see the place empty for a minute or two."

"Look, young man. It's not like I'm trying to be uncooperative or nothing, but these men are on bonus. I pull these trucks outta here five seconds I'm gonna have grievances up the wazoo."

The lawyer looked at his watch: 8:35. "Well, how about during break? Aren't they supposed to get one in the sixth hour of the shift?

Breitenfeld's look was just barely shy of disgust, mixed also with a touch of resignation. "Let me see what I can do," he said. Then he walked away toward the foreman's office cubicle.

As soon as the first truck engine started up, just after the rest whistle, one of the breaker men said, "What the fuck!"

Another, obviously noticing David, yelled out, "Hey, faggot, someone put you in charge here all of a sudden?"

Breitenfeld had to calm them down. He didn't try to hide his displeasure. "I told you they weren't gonna like it. If I were you, I'd make it fast."

Had he been a partner, Castelli would have picked this moment to say something like, "You know, pal, if I were the same Joseph Breitenfeld who's gonna look like the town dope when Trice comes back with full pay, I'd be trying to make my lawyer's job easier, not harder." Instead, he picked this moment to say, "It'll just take a few seconds. I'm really sorry."

As soon as the last flatbed had backed out onto Hixon Avenue, David, now sitting in Charlie Carpool's folding chair at the south end of Battery Boulevard, peered up the deserted indoor road and saw exactly what he hoped: a clear, unobstructed view running the entire length of the long metal building, out the door to the entrance area, then out to Hixon, then even to the houses across the street.

David tried to imagine Charlie Carpool's fear. The old watchman was alone that night in the quiet building. Suddenly he heard the unmistakable rumble of a Harley, echoing off the metal walls as Trice circled the property. He called out to the figure astride the bike as Trice roared through the Hixon Avenue entrance, cackling like an old witch, wearing the bizarre Nixon mask, his squared-off beard sticking out from beneath the former president's rubber chin. David could picture the old man trying to run on hobbled legs through puddles of crankcase oil, then falling in front of the bike.

The warehouse supervisor broke the lawyer's concentration. "You seen enough now," he asked, obviously not intending to be influenced by Castelli's answer, since he immediately yelled up to the shift foreman, "All right, start bringing 'em back."

David did not bother saying good night to Joseph Breitenfeld.

Nine-fifteen was too late to find a decent restaurant in Lancaster, but it was too early to go to bed. Besides, David was still torqued up about Breitenfeld's lousy attitude. As he drove slowly down Hixon Avenue, he looked up at the sign sticking out from the corner of a red brick building:

"Manufacturing & Transport Workers' Local 664, I.B.T.C.W.H.A." Then he saw the bar. A bar right underneath the union hall.

Under normal circumstances, the thought of even walking into such a place, much less drinking there, would never have crossed David's mind. It was one thing to litigate against the Teamsters, quite another to fraternize with them. But something seemed to propel David toward the parking lot of Jenny Rats. Maybe he was just too tired and too disgusted to worry. Maybe he was simply curious about an upcoming opponent. Whatever the reason, he parked the Accord next to a pickup, then smiled when he saw the bumper sticker: "I Graduated from Fuck U."

Thomas J. Trice did not notice the man in the suit who came in quietly, sat at the bar, and ordered a double Jack Daniels on the rocks. David had wanted a martini, but he knew that in a place like Jenny Rats, at best "dry" would mean soaked with vermouth rather than drowning in it. So he settled for his winter drink, figuring that it was, after all, almost October.

The reason Trice didn't look up from his corner booth when the front door opened—the way he usually did, so as not to miss an opportunity to start trouble—was because he was deep into a conversation with Dickie Romanowski. From the number of empty Bud longnecks scattered about the table, a knowledgeable observer would have realized that T. J. had been holding court for some time.

By now, Romanowski was making what had to be his fourth pass at the pair's favorite subject for the evening, each time laughing harder and slurring his words more. "Did you see Werner up on that stage Tuesday banging his weenie gavel, screaming 'Order, order.' I thought he was gonna shit himself."

Trice flicked his Zippo at the fresh Camel dangling from his lower lip. "No, I didn't see Werner, Dickie-Do. I was having too much fun watching Pelletier keep you off Axel. You know, you're lucky Henry was in there."

"The fuck you talking about?"

"You know exactly what I'm talking about. Kinnard's a maniac. He'd a killed you right there wasn't for Pelletier."

"Well it don't matter anyhow," Dickie said. "Come March there ain't gonna be no more Axel. No more Werner either—long as you don't keep pissing in the soup."

"What's that supposed to mean?" Trice's smile vanished in a cloud of cigarette smoke.

"It means that goddamn arbitration of yours. Werner wimps out Tuesday, I make him look like a pussy. 'Cept you have to go and make a big fucking deal over a shit job with Harry the Jew. I told you I'd get you something down at Rapid."

"Oh, is that right? You gonna get me twenty-five years seniority down at Rapid? You gonna get me the biggest tit job on the floor down at Rapid?" Romanowski sat mute as Trice berated him. Then there was silence. Then Trice started in again. "Anyhow, you were on his case same as me. All that shit about Brian O'Conner and that pillow biter you got down there, what's his name, 'Twat-dick'?"

"Twardzik. His name is Twardzik. But you know damn well Werner's not taking your case just on account of a lawyer scoring 30k for some faggot who got his picture took naked. That was just for show. Give me something else to bust his balls about. There's only one reason Werner's taking your case—'cause *you* embarrassed him into it. Only it don't matter anyhow, since there's no way in hell you win it."

Trice dragged deep on his Camel, tilted his head back and drained about half a longneck down his gullet, beer dripping into the thick gray beard whenever his glottis could not keep pace with gravity. Then he pounded the empty brown bottle onto the table, a judge calling for quiet in his court.

T. J. was just about to begin his lecture. He was just about to explain to Dickie—whom he would repeatedly call a fat dumb polack—why the grievant would soon be back on his forklift at Greene-Pitowsky, with full seniority and a fat check for back pay, when the big Rapid Freight steward suddenly looked over toward the bar. Romanowski's flabby forearms lifted their owner half off the booth seat, just so he could be sure. He was.

"I can't believe it."

"You talking about?"

"Castelli. Peckerhead lawyer's sitting right over there at the bar."

Trice turned to look over his left shoulder. He saw the man in the suit for the first time. "Well I'll be goddamned," he said. "Don't think I ever saw a necktie in *this* place, and I been coming here ten years. You sure that's him?"

Romanowski was already squeezing his stomach out from between the table and bench. "I never forget a lawyer, Trice, specially when he's a clown spills water all over his notes." Dickie popped free from the booth, then hiked his jeans over the southern hemisphere of his gut. "David Castelli in Jenny Rats, I can't fucking believe it."

Had Castelli known what was about to go down, he might never have walked into 4641 Hixon Avenue; but, at this particular moment, he was glad he did. The dark-haired woman in the baseball cap behind the bar was no more than a foot away from him. He could see her clearly even while he appeared just to be looking into an amber reflecting pool of Jack Daniels and ice. The lack of eye contact made it easy

He had noticed her forearms and hands first, as they rose to, then disappeared from, the top of the bar, rhythmically washing glasses, one after another. They were tan, slightly muscled forearms, covered with just the finest down of blond hair. The hands were large for a woman, but they were slender, with long curved fingers. There was no wedding ring.

Just above the elbow, the sleeves of her white silk shirt strained tightly around her upper arms, also tan, also muscled, yet also feminine. The sleeves were neatly folded, like in the World War II posters of Rosy the Riveter. Finished with the washing, the woman now began reaching up to hang the glasses, one by one upside down from their racks.

She was no longer young, mid-forties, which is why, perhaps, David could almost read her sensuousness. The eyes deep green even in bar light, their corners laced ever so slightly with creases. They sat wide apart over high cheekbones, looking down on a nose too thin only for perfection. Her voice, contralto in timber, just barely husky, came from a wide mouth of bright teeth.

David was startled when she suddenly spoke to him. "I think you've got some friends."

Dickie Romanowski lowered his ample butt over the bar stool immediately to David's left. "Now lookie here. One of Philadelphia's finest lawyers, come to pay us a visit. You writing a paper 'bout working folks or something?"

Castelli thought it would go away if he just played it straight.

"I'm here on business," he answered.

"Business, Mr. Castelli? Just exactly what kind of *business* brings a powerful man like you to a simple country bar like this?"

"Labor arbitration down the street."

Then Romanowski spoke to Jenny DeLone. "This fine-looking young fellow here is a very important Philadelphia lawyer. Only thing is, he spills a lot, so maybe you ought to get him a bib."

Jenny said, "Why don't you just leave him alone and go sit down. He's not bothering you, is he?"

"As a matter of fact, sweetie, since you asked, I don't think he's bothering *me*, but I do think he's bothering my friend, here." Romanowski spun clumsily on his stool as T. J. came out of the shadows. "Isn't that right, friend, isn't this boy bothering you?"

Castelli looked at the thick gray beard squared off at the bottom, at the bandanna tied tight around the head, at the black t-shirt emblazoned with a skeleton riding a flaming motorcycle. Even had he not seen Trice's ID badge clipped inside the personnel file a few hours earlier, he would have known immediately.

"Well, Mr. Trice," David said. "Is Mr. Romanowski right? Am I bothering you?"

"That's a hard question to answer, counselor. See 'bothering' really isn't the proper word here. Proper word is 'nauseating.' Fact is, I suspect you're nauseating every decent workingman in this establishment by being here. So why don't you just get out and save us all some trouble."

"I got a drink to finish, you mind?"

Romanowski laughed. "Don't worry T. J., I think he's just about done."

Castelli sat motionless, as if in a trance, watching as Romanowski's big right hand picked up the glass of Jack Daniels and poured its contents into David's lap.

Before he could even react, David's two visitors disappeared back into the shadows of the dark room. Jenny DeLone, towel in hand, raced around the bar to where David was just sitting, watching the cold liquid roll off the end of the bar, feeling it seep through his slacks, then through his briefs.

"I'm so sorry," she said. "We'll pay to have the suit cleaned. Really." Without even thinking, Jenny started dabbing David's crotch, rubbing to get his pants dry. All of a sudden, the lawyer began to laugh. He couldn't help himself.

"I think I'm falling in love," he said to the strange woman between his legs.

Jenny looked up, red in the face. "Oh my goodness, what am I doing." Then she, too, started to laugh, a deep throaty laugh trailing off into a "brother, what a mess."

Castelli watched as Jenny walked back around to the business side of the bar. It was the first time he could see her from the rear, hips and legs showing athlete even through her black parachute pants. He couldn't resist when she got back to her work station. "Double Jack Daniels on the rocks, hold the glass."

"I really am sorry," she laughed. "I don't know what's the matter with those two." She poured David a fresh drink, mostly bourbon, little ice.

"Don't worry about it, whoever you are. See, me and Mr. Romanowski go way back together. He's the head cretin over at Rapid Freight."

"And you?"

"Well, you heard the man." Castelli reached across the bar. "David Castelli, Esquire, oppressor of little people. Pleased to meet you."

She took David's hand firmly. Hers was warm, holding his just an instant longer than necessary. "Jenny DeLone. I own this place."

"The bar?"

"Whole building, union hall and everything."

"Interesting line of work."

Since he emphasized the first syllable of 'interesting,' and since she noticed it, she replied, "Would it make you feel better if I were a nurse at Garden Spot General like my sister?"

"No, please. I didn't mean anything by it, really. It's just that meeting a union landlady isn't something I do every day. And the bar too. Ready-made customers, I suspect."

"You see it. Fact is, I don't remember the last time a coat and tie walked in this place."

"I think you just saw the last time. I was down the street, checking some stuff out."

"You were checking out the battery house, weren't you?"

"How did ..."

"This is a very small town, David Castelli. I'll lay odds every person in this bar knows who you are and why you're here."

"And I'm sure that includes Mr. Trice."

"It especially includes Mr. Trice," she said.

David looked down at his own wedding ring, wishing all of a sudden that he wasn't wearing it. He was drawn to the sound of Jenny's voice; he wanted to hear more of it. But politeness took over. "Listen, I know you've got a bar here to run, so don't think you have to hang out with me. Besides," he said, looking down into his lap, "it'll be dry by morning."

"I can do both, you know—bar tend and talk. Part of the job description. Plus I got Axel over there."

"Okay, Ms. DeLone, since you already know who I am and why I'm here, you might as well also tell me if I'm going to win."

"Well, I assume you know he did it. I mean everyone knows that."

"Everyone may know it," David said. "But the trouble is only one person saw him do it, and they tell me Charlie Carpool wasn't wrapped too tight even before the accident."

Jenny DeLone tensed imperceptibly, thinking about Stuff Johnson. "Oh, I don't know," she said. "Everybody really likes old Charlie. He should be all right. Trice is the one you got to worry about."

"You mean because he'll lie under oath? My line of work that's business as usual."

"You obviously don't know Thomas Jefferson Trice."

"What's there to know? Another slimeball trying to get the union to save his job?"

"Slimeball? I don't think that for a minute. No, this guy is much too scary to be a slimeball. Lives by himself over in Fivepointville, about twenty miles from here. I've never been in his house, of course, but the rumor is—now get this 'cause you just saw him—that he plays the piano like a pro and has an IQ of about a million."

"Right, and I play shortstop for the Phillies."

"No, I'm not kidding. And I'll tell you something else. He gets away with murder down that plant. Everybody's scared to death of him."

"Does that include you?" David asked.

"Yes," she said. "As a matter of fact it does. And the funny thing is, I don't even really know why. I mean look at him. Comes in here just about every night. Sits in the same booth, gets drunk and obnoxious ..."

"Hassles the paying customers," Castelli added, and then, without thinking, covered both of her hands on the bar with his own.

And she made no attempt to free herself, saying only, "I said I was sorry."

"It was supposed to be a joke," he answered. "Anyhow, I'm actually glad the two of them came over here. Gave me a chance to hit on the bartender."

Jennifer DeLone looked directly into David's eyes. Then she turned her still imprisoned hands palm up, wrapping them around David's with a sudden squeeze. "You're very sweet, Mr. Castelli." She toyed with his wedding band for just an instant, before letting go and moving on down the bar. "Next time you come in," she laughed back over her shoulder, "I'll have the bib ready."

<hr />

On the map, 315 Magnolia Street could have been anything: a freshly painted, yellow-trimmed wood frame on a tree-covered lot; a split-level ornament from the sixties; maybe even a garden apartment. But, even when his destination was still several blocks away, Castelli knew it would be none of these.

The southwest corner of Lancaster—King Street to Hershey, West End to Prince—between those boundaries a latticework of sorry streets and sorry houses. Despite its name, Magnolia had no trees at all. What it did have was mostly abandoned.

On the corner of Magnolia and Water Streets stood the corpse of what looked like it had once been a drug store. Castelli assumed the store was called SWANK'S from what was left of the gold leaf lettering on the one remaining picture window. He parked the car.

Between SWA K' on the corner, and 315 in the middle of the block, Castelli counted six single homes, each on a lot so small that a man walking between them could not even have lifted his arms to horizontal. Two of the houses were boarded shut. The other four should have been.

On the porch of 307 Magnolia sat an old refrigerator with no door, and next to it, in a chair looking quite unable to hold her weight, a gigantic woman in a house dress, 300 pounds at least. She stared into the street without expression, smoking a cigarette, red faced. Castelli looked up at her, thinking about saying good morning. But the woman offered not the slightest sign of recognition, even though the lawyer passed within a few feet of her. He flicked his eyes toward the ground.

The house at 315 had no porch. It was set back from the street just far enough to allow for a set of wooden stairs. At the top of these stairs was a brown door that looked more like it was meant to separate a bedroom from its closet rather than an entire house from the world. Someone had done a bad job of stenciling 315 on the door with white paint.

David pushed gingerly on the black doorbell button in its cheap round frame. He heard a faint buzzer, then a cough, followed by a muffled voice.

"Who's out there?"

Castelli pressed his lips almost to the wood. "David Castelli. I want to talk to Mr. Carliner."

"Just a minute."

The lawyer stood by the door far longer than it should have taken even a slow-footed person to traverse every inch of 315 Magnolia. Then, finally, came the litany of locks and chains, clicking and thunking their way down the inside of the door. Charlie Carpool pulled open the flimsy barrier to his house, squinting into the sun as if he hadn't seen daylight in weeks.

"Mr. Carliner?"

"Maybe."

Charlie Carpool could not have been more than five foot three, most of it torso. A cane was helping out a pair of barefooted legs, bowed almost to the point of dwarfism. They poked out from baggy bermuda shorts. Above the shorts stretched a plain white t-shirt, actually more gray than white from years of sharing a washing machine with dark clothing. Then came the chest and neck, pale skin sprouting tufts of gray hair. And finally, a large square head, jowls covered with stubble, top covered with a green baseball cap, "Greene-Pitowsky Smelting & Battery" scrolled across its crown in gold script.

David looked down at the tiny figure almost a foot below his own seventy-four inches. "Harry Greene sent me," he said, sounding nothing like a lawyer. "We're supposed to talk about the arbitration."

"Don't know nuthin bout no arbitration."

"Well, Mr. Greene told me yesterday I was supposed to come talk to you. Didn't he tell you anything about that?"

Charlie Carpool looked like he was trying very hard to put his thoughts into some kind of order. He cleared his throat, a deep wet rumble from inside his chest. Then he reached into his pants pocket and pulled out a filthy old handkerchief, putting it up to his mouth as he hocked into it. David was already conscious of the musty smell wafting out from the darkness behind the old man's shoulders.

"Oh yeah, you're the lawyer."

"That's right, I'm the lawyer. David Castelli. Mr. Greene said he told you I'd be coming by this morning to talk about the accident. Remember?"

Charlie stepped away from the door and motioned for David to follow him. They walked into the darkened house, down a narrow corridor that smelled to Castelli like some kind of unpleasant medicine. Charlie led his guest into the living room, where a metal-sided hospital bed had been pushed up to the front window. An old wooden chair, doubling as a night table, stood next to the bed, its seat awash with half-empty glasses, used kleenex wads and dirty spoons.

"Sorry about the mess. Mr. Greene got me a nurse, but she ain't been in to clean since Monday. Just came in yesterday to give me a bath."

"Don't worry about it, really."

"Can't go up the steps, ya know. Busted my knee up pretty bad." Charlie sat down on the edge of the hospital bed, then propped his left leg up on what little space remained on the wooden chair. The knee was wrapped in a blue rubber sleeve. "Still getting the headaches too."

"I'm sorry, I really am."

"Not your fault," Charlie said.

David sat down on the fuzzy brown sofa next to the bed. He sunk deep into ancient cushions and springs, his long thighs suddenly angled upwards from his hips.

Jack McKeon once said that the best way for a lawyer to start a conversation with a working man was with small talk. "Baseball and pussy," he would say. "Start 'em off with baseball and pussy. Let 'em see you're just like them." David never took it literally, but he did get the plan.

"Got any idea when they're going to let you go back to work?"

"When my head stops hurtin', I guess."

"Still bad?"

"Long as I sit quiet here, no problem. Gotta watch though when I stand up, like when you rang the bell back there. Damn near fell on my rear end. Room starts spinnin', I feel like I'm gonna puke and all, you know."

"I do know, as a matter of fact. Got your hospital records." Castelli pointed toward his briefcase.

"Ain't they supposed to be private?"

"Mr. Greene got them for me. Thought it might help our case. Course I told him that's fine, but we don't have any case without the real Charlie Carliner, which is why I'm here."

"I don't understand. You mean that sonofabitch is gonna get his job back?"

"Depends on you, Charlie. You were the only eyewitness. Arbitrator believes it was Trice ran you down, we win. He doesn't, your friend is right back on his forklift with a three month paid vacation."

"So what do you want me to say?"

"The truth, Charlie, that's all. Same thing you said that night at the police station to Sergeant Campbell."

Charlie Carpool leaned forward again. He scrunched his brow into deep creases, then reached for one of the jelly glasses on the chair: red and blue polka dots, dirty, half full of water.

"I didn't talk to no cop."

Castelli felt his pulse start to race. He pulled the statement out of his briefcase and thrust it into the old man's hand. "Sure you did, Charlie. This came right out of the police file."

Carliner took the paper in his hand and stared at it. Castelli could see the old man's lips slowly moving, silently trying to form words as he nodded back and forth over the text. Then he started shaking his big head side to side. "What *is* this?" he said.

"What do you mean, 'what is this?' It's your statement to Sergeant Campbell. Says so right on the top."

Again Carliner dropped his head toward the paper. He spoke without looking at David. "Okay, I see it. 'Cept like I say, I didn't talk to no cop."

"Well I'm sure they didn't make all that up, Charlie. You probably just can't remember giving the statement because you passed out right after. Doesn't really matter, though, so long as you can remember now what happened. Look at it again. Maybe it'll refresh your memory."

As David watched the old man, now for the second time struggling with the statement, he realized that his star witness couldn't read a word of it. Castelli reached out for the paper, which Charlie surrendered, almost like he was a vampire and it was a cross.

David covered. "I know the light's bad in here, so maybe if I read it to you."

"Yeah, that would help."

When Castelli was finished reading Sergeant Campbell's statement, he looked at the old man, searching in Carliner's eyes for a spark, a sign, however slight, that this only witness to Trice's escapade would somehow be able to withstand the cross-examination of Isaac Rothstein. He was rewarded.

"Yeh, yeh, that's right, yeh. I guess I *did* talk to that cop. Must have, 'cause he sure got the story down exact. Specially that voice, like some kind of witch."

David was on the scent now, nose down, through the details. "And the mask, you could definitely see Trice's beard under the mask?"

"Never forget it. Ain't no one in this whole town got a beard like that bastard. No one got a bike like his, neither. Big blue Harley, all painted up custom. Got a naked woman right on the gas tank.

"You remember that too?"

"Remember it! Last thing I seen 'fore I got hit. Big old bush coming right at me on the ground. Thought I was dead."

David laughed out loud at the image. Impulsively, he reached over toward the bed and chucked the old man on his knee. "You're going to make a fine witness, so long as you tell the arbitrator the exact same things you're telling me now."

"Just gonna tell it like it happened, Mr. Castelli. Ain't no big deal, you know."

THIRTEEN
Sunday, October 2

CASTELLI ALWAYS LOOKED FORWARD to Sunday dinner with his parents. Leslie hated it. The house was too small; the whole downstairs smelled like pasta gravy; nobody talked about anything except sports and church. But at least Leslie knew enough to keep quiet most of the time. It was an Italian thing, she kept telling herself—a man had to bring his family to his mother's house every Sunday, and that was the end of it.

Except on this particular Sunday, as the Castelli family drove across the Walt Whitman Bridge from New Jersey to Philadelphia, David was hardly in the mood for melon and prosciutto. He was too busy thinking about dead wood.

"Dead wood." David was saying the two words over and over to himself. Jack had taught him the expression several years before, about the same time he had taught him "big headaches, big fees" and "you never know till you ask" and all the other McKeon maxims that made the young associate feel like a real labor lawyer.

Leslie turned toward her husband. "You're being awfully quiet, David. What's the matter?"

"Nothing's the matter. I'm just worried about the Trice case."

"You mean that creep with the motorcycle? What's there to worry about?"

"I got no dead wood. That's what there is to worry about."

"Huh?"

"Dead wood. You know, a piece of hard evidence that can't be torn apart on cross-examination."

"You mean like a picture?"

"Right, a picture. A picture is exactly what I need. Maybe a nice eight-by-ten glossy of Thomas Trice riding his Harley into the factory. You wouldn't happen to have one in your purse, would you?"

"I was only trying to help. David, you don't have to get snotty."

"I'm sorry. It's just that this case is so damn important, and all I've got is one crazy old man."

"I thought he saw the whole thing?"

"He did see the whole thing. Except he didn't see it with Isaac Rothstein yapping in his ear. And he didn't see it with a court reporter taking down everything he says. Charlie Carliner is just not enough. I know it. I've got to have at least one piece of dead wood—something else to tie that biker to Harry Greene's battery house."

And then, suddenly, it hit him. The accident. Charlie said the motorcycle went over on Trice just before T. J. and the bike rammed into the old watchman. Six hundred pounds of Harley-Davidson falling on its rider, skidding along a cement floor. A blistering hot engine, trailing even hotter exhaust pipes. Trice had to have been hurt. Knee sprain, broken ankle, exhaust burns. Maybe all three. And just maybe, if Castelli was lucky, T. J. went to the hospital. And just maybe, if David was really, really lucky, there would be a record in the files of Garden Spot General.

———◦◦◦◦———

Minna Greene was saying, "For chrissake, Harry, I wish you'd shut that window. It's October already."

"I like fresh air. What's the big deal?"

Minna drew on the sash of her purple terry cloth bathrobe, then yanked the lapels together. They were sitting at the glass table in the breakfast room. It was early afternoon but Minna still wasn't dressed. Harry reached into a large wicker bowl and drew out the last bagel which he then smartly sliced in half.

"Who are you kidding with that?" Minna said. "You know you're going to eat the whole thing. Just go easy on the cream cheese."

"I got to go down to the plant."

"On a Sunday? You're going to the plant on a Sunday?"

"We're getting bad pigs out of number three furnace, shift foreman wants me to see it."

"You can see it tomorrow."

"I can't see it tomorrow, Minna. Only happens when we start up the furnaces and that's on Sunday."

"Well how long are you going to be? You know the Pearlsteins are coming for early dinner."

"I don't know how long I'm going to be and, no, I don't know the Pearlsteins are coming for early dinner."

"It's on the calendar. You could look at it once in a while."

"Look at what?"

"The calendar, Harry. Everything we do is on the calendar."

Greene reached for the other half of the bagel. "I'll try to be home by four."

Charlie Carliner had been asleep when Harry had called him three hours earlier. Greene hoped that was why he had to give his name three times before there was even the slightest hint of recognition from the old man. If Charlie was already drunk at that hour on a Sunday morning, Greene knew the meeting was going to be even more difficult.

Now he looked over at his map, spread out on the passenger seat of the big Park Avenue. He was trying, at the same time, to keep his eye on the road and pick out the yellow highlighter line he had drawn on the paper just after he had spoken to McKeon, which was just after he had spoken to Carliner.

"So what are you going to tell him?" Jack had asked.

"How the hell should I know. I'll think of something."

"Well it'd better be a good something. Castelli tells me he prepped the old man for over an hour last Friday. Says he's good. Remembered facts that weren't even in the police report."

"You know I don't like this, Jack. I don't like it at all."

"You like going to jail better?"

"That's not funny."

"It's not supposed to be funny. You think Trice won't pull the pin on you if he doesn't get that job back? You've got a lot more confidence in the bastard than I do."

"But I'm asking a man to lie under oath. Isn't that some kind of crime?"

"Yeah, it's called subornation of perjury. You get caught, maybe you get probation." There was silence on Harry's end of the phone. So McKeon added. "What do you think you get for murder?"

"Goddammit, I didn't commit any murder, Jack. You know that."

"I do? I'll tell you what I know. I know you let some two bit goomba mash your fingerprints all over a gun, then put a dead body in the trunk of your car. Then you drove that car a hundred miles, got out and buried the poor bastard under ten tons of busted up battery casings. If you're lucky, the D.A. will believe you about the gun and be satisfied with accessory after the fact. Of course if he doesn't, you're looking at conspiracy. Murder one."

"What the hell was I supposed to do? Tell them to get rid of their own corpse?"

"Look, Harry. You're losing focus. It was ten years ago. Anyhow, there's nothing you can do about it now. You just gotta make sure Charlie Carpool tells the right story next Wednesday. Then you gotta hope van Auten is as big a whore as I think he is, and that Trice gets his rocks off enough to leave you alone."

Harry Greene stood before the battered wooden door with its stenciled 315. Suddenly, he was back in Stroudsburg, Pennsylvania, back on a street just like Magnolia, at a door just like Charlie's, about to pay a condolence call on the widow of Willis Tucker.

The authorities had declared him legally dead on September 8, 1985, one year after the disappearance. Harry had driven in silence that day from Lancaster to the Poconos. He had forced himself to stay for an hour, sneaking glances at his watch the entire time. They drank apple juice and talked about Camp Pocono Sunrise, about how much Willis had loved his job as camp caretaker, especially in the summer when he could joke with the kids. And they talked about duck hunting, Mrs. Tucker breaking down when she told Harry that nobody ever found the shotgun or the beloved decoys her husband had carved by hand. She confessed that day that Willis trespassed on the old camp grounds almost every weekend. She hoped Harry wouldn't be too upset; it was just that the lake was such a perfect place to shoot. Harry said it was fine.

He never returned to Stroudsburg after that visit, not even to check on the carcass of Camp Pocono Sunrise. But, inside his mind he was still there every day, there on a windy, gray morning in 1984, watching a tiny plane fall from the sky, watching the gaunt, familiar figure of Willis Tucker stumbling up from the lake bank, trailing water from the tops of his waders as he rushed innocently to the aid of a pilot already dead.

Tony Angelo had yanked off the runway lights the moment the old Cessna plowed into the ball field. Behind him, Harry and Mario Fontini stood in shock, neither man yet fully comprehending that death was occurring just a hundred yards away. Angelo had spoken first.

"What a stupid fuck!" Then he started to run toward the wreck, not waiting—or even thinking to wait—for Mario's permission. Harry followed, twice almost tripping in the tangle of weeds that ringed the woods where the three men had been awaiting the plane's arrival.

Harry tried to focus on the cockpit as he ran and panted. But then his eyes were distracted by movement from beyond the plane—another man running toward the wreck, coming from the lake.

Tony Angelo also saw the movement. He stopped short and knelt to the ground, using the wreckage of the plane to shield his body from the running man. Harry dropped to all fours, trying catch his breath.

The two men watched as the running man circled the Cessna, calling to the wreck. "Hey. Hey, you all right in there? Oh, Jesus. Somebody! Jesus!"

"It's Willis Tucker!" Harry was whispering between shallow breaths.

"Who the fuck is Willis Tucker?"

"Used to work at the camp. Caretaker. What the hell's he doing here?"

"Getting in the fucking way, that's what." Tony Angelo reached into the left armpit of his suit and pulled out a silver Walther .22 TPH. It was the closest Harry Greene had been to a gun in forty years. Angelo spoke without turning his head. "Don't move and don't talk, you hear me." The bodyguard did not wait for an answer.

Harry watched as the large figure in black began to stalk Willis Tucker, the old caretaker still dancing about the wreckage, crying out to no one in particular. When Tony Angelo looked to be almost on top of his prey, he suddenly stood up and grabbed Willis around the neck with his left hand, freezing the stunned man's right temple against the nose of the Walther.

"For God's sake, no!" The plea sprang from Harry's throat without a conscious thought. It coincided exactly with the crack of the .22, echoing off the trees around the ball field. Tony Angelo held Willis Tucker in his arms for a brief moment, then gently laid him to the ground.

"You sonofabitch. He didn't do anything." Harry was banging the sides of his fists against the chest of Tony Angelo. The bodyguard stood perfectly still, letting Harry spend himself, watching as Greene slowly deflated from rage to fear.

"Done now, asshole?" Tony took Harry by the wrists, stopping the older man's pitiful attempt at beating, lowering Greene's arms to his side as if he were straightening the limbs of a mannequin. Then he spoke.

"He was the caretaker, boss. Used to work here."

"That's unfortunate," said Mario Fontini. He had just finished his slow walk from the woods to the wreckage as the last echo of the .22 spent itself in the trees. He spoke to Harry.

"So what do you think, Mr. Greene? Do we have a problem, here?"

"Yes we have a problem here. What the fuck do you think we have?"

"You don't have to curse, Harry. You just have to think. Now tell me who this man is."

Harry looked down at Willis Tucker, curled at the feet of Tony Angelo. The eyes were open, the legs tucked into a fetal position. He could have been just a man lying in a field, were it not for the spreading red circle, slowly increasing its diameter in the grass beneath his head.

"Willis Tucker. Used to work for me when I had the camp. Must have been duck hunting down there when the plane crashed." Harry pointed to the lake.

"Check it, Tony." Mario Fontini took out a cigarette and lit it. Then he watched as the big bodyguard disappeared down the bank toward the lake. "How long we been doing business, Harry, three years?"

"Four years next month, why?"

"Because you don't like it, that's why. And I just don't understand. We give you five thousand dollars every month for doing absolutely nothing, but you don't like it. Why is that, Harry? Why are you so ungrateful?"

"I'm not ungrateful, just scared."

"Of what? Me? The police? Tony? You scared of Tony?"

"Look Fontini, how often do we have to keep going over the same ground. Every time I come up here, I have to lie to someone. My wife, my employees, my friends. I told you a thousand times. Just use the damn place and forget the money."

"He was right, boss. Dumb bastard was duck hunting, all right." Tony Angelo lumbered toward the two men. He was holding the shotgun in one hand, dragging a line of decoys on a wet rope with the other. He laid the string of wooden birds at the feet of Mario Fontini, a good dog gone to fetch.

"Anything else down there?"

"Nothing but this stuff, Mr. Fontini. What you want me to do with it?"

"Keep the gun. I like it. Put the ducks in the trunk of Mr. Greene's car. Give him the keys, Harry."

"What?"

"I said, give the man your keys. Something difficult about that?"

Harry fished around in his pocket, then pulled out an army of keys tethered to a bright green and yellow fob with "G.P.S.& B." printed on both sides.

Fontini looked down at the key ring dangling from Greene's fat fingers. "You love that company, don't you?"

"So?"

"So I'm going to let you keep it? How do you like that?"

"What are you talking about?"

"Please, Harry, don't insult your own intelligence. Here's the deal. We take care of the plane. Not registered anyhow. Pilot's ours too. Trouble is Willis here." Fontini nudged at the dead man with a shiny black shoe. The corpse shifted, then exhaled for the final time. "He got family?"

"Had a wife last I knew. Lives in Stroudsburg."

Fontini dragged on his cigarette. "See, that's the problem now, isn't it? Old lady is going to report him missing. Then she's going to tell the police he went duck hunting, and they'll be all over this place. Lucky for us, of course, they won't find a trace of him. Nobody ever will."

"What are you talking about?"

"Bessemers, Harry. That's what I'm talking about."

The light suddenly went on. Harry said, "You can't be serious."

"Tony, show the man we're serious."

Before Harry could react, Tony Angelo cupped the murder weapon in his gloved hand, grabbed Harry's naked hand, then pressed the gun so tightly against Harry's palm that his fingers instinctively curled around its handle. Angelo then reached around with his other hand, forming a large fist over Harry, imprinting Greene's prints on the gun handle. Then he relaxed, carefully now extracting a plastic baggie from his pocket, and even more carefully sliding the doctored piece into the bag.

"We'll just hold onto that for safe keeping, Harry. Now, as I was saying, what do they get to, Bessemer furnaces, three thousand degrees? Lost one man already, least that's what I hear. Anyhow, it'll be easy. You go in there tonight, when the furnaces are down and the place is empty. Willis and his ducks ride up the conveyor belt, plop into the soup, then wait nice and quiet till the Sunday crew comes in to charge 'em up."

"That simple, eh?"

"You don't like it, I'm sure we can find some other way to handle the job. But I'm a generous man, so I'll throw in one more incentive."

"What's that?"

"You do this, you never see us again. Just like you wanted all along. So what do you say, Harry? Deal?"

Harry said nothing and looked at the ground. Mario Fontini nodded at Tony Angelo. The bodyguard took the keys from Greene's hand, then picked up Willis Tucker. He flung the old caretaker over his shoulder like a sack of flour. Willis' head hung down Tony Angelo's back, mouth and eyes open, a small river of blood still oozing from the right temple.

Mario said, "Harry, why don't you bring the ducks."

Charlie Carpool must have been looking out the window; he opened the door of 315 Magnolia even before Harry could push the doorbell button.

"Good morning, Mr. Greene, they told me you were coming."

"*I* told you, Charlie. *I* told you on the phone not three hours ago."

Carpool pressed his lips together and squinted. "Yeah, that's right. You're the one called me. It's the head, Mr. Greene." He tapped the point of his right index finger against a tuft of white hair just above his ear. "Head still ain't right since the uh, you know, the night." Then he added. "But I remember everything 'bout the accident, so don't you worry."

Harry entered the house without being asked. "How's the nurse, Charlie, she been working out okay?"

"Well, sir, she ain't been in but one time last week to give me a bath, so it's a bit dirty. But she been doing real good when she's here. Real good. And I do 'preciate it. You want something to drink?"

They were in the living room now. Harry looked down at the round chair by Charlie's bed, with the dirty juice glasses and sticky medicine spoons. "No thanks."

"Why did you come here, Mr. Greene?"

Harry was not expecting such a serious question, not this fast, not from Charlie Carpool. The old watchman's eyes looked straight at Harry's; they were clear and bright, much more so than Greene expected. The visitor knew at once that his host was prepared. The visitor was not. He stumbled.

"Well, I–I just wanted to see how you were doing. You know, the accident and all."

Charlie Carpool ignored Harry's dissembling. He went on as if Greene hadn't said a word. "It's the case, isn't it? You came to talk about the case. Well I already talked about the case to that lawyer you sent round here. Like I told him, you got nothing to worry about."

Harry forced himself to laugh. "That's–that's great, Charlie. Because you know I was a little worried, actually. They say you really hit that table leg hard. Sometimes a blow like that can knock a man's memory right out. Would certainly be something the company could understand."

Charlie did not reply. He just looked at Harry, waiting. The silence started to become noticeable. Greene jumped in to fill the space. "You ever testify at a labor arbitration?"

"Never testified nowhere."

"So Mr. Castelli told you all about it, then?"

"Sure did. Yes, no, I don't remember. That's what the man said all right."

"Yes, no, I don't remember?"

"Yep, that's what Mr. Castelli said. Mr. Rothstein starts asking me a lot of questions, I'm just supposed to say yes, no, I don't remember. Not all three at once, you know, 'cause that'd sound pretty silly. I mean I can't say yes, no, I don't remember, when the man asks me how old I am or something like that."

Again Harry made himself laugh. "Well, it sounds like Mr. Castelli gave you some good advice there. Real good advice. Of course you know it's harder than you think."

"What?"

"Trying to just say yes, no, I don't remember. Gonna be a whole room full of people there, you know. Lots of guys from the union, court reporter, Trice, the arbitrator. He's a college professor, they tell me."

Charlie Carpool stood up from the side of his bed where he had been sitting. "Mr. Greene, why are you telling me this?"

"Well, it's just you've really been through a lot here. So I want to make sure you're prepared. That's all."

"I thought that's why you sent the lawyer? He didn't tell you anything bad, did he?"

In an instant, Harry saw the crack and made for it. "I'm gonna be straight with you, Charlie. There is something he said."

"Fuck."

"No, it's not your fault, but we might as well get it out. It's about your statement to the police."

"What about it?"

"That's the problem, Charlie. You wouldn't know 'what about it,' would you?

"What are you talking about, Mr. Greene?"

"I'm talking about you can't read. It's no big deal, Charlie. Lots of people can't read, but don't you see what's gonna happen when Rothstein figures that out on Wednesday?"

"So he figures it out? I don't get the problem. Me not being able to read don't mean I can't remember what I seen."

"Well, I know that and you know that, Charlie, but this is a trial, and the truth doesn't always matter at a trial. Rothstein will ask if you read that statement you gave to the police. How will you answer that? You say, yes, I read it, he'll ask you to read it right then and there. You say no, he'll argue that the company had nothing but an unread, unsigned statement when they fired Mr. Trice. How do you think that's going to look?"

"What're you telling me, Mr. Greene? You want me to lie or something?"

"It's not a lie, Charlie, if it could have happened, if it could be the truth."

Charlie was agitated. He reached into his pants pocket and pulled out a cigarette, his hands suddenly shaking on the match. Harry took the matchbook and held it. "Please, Mr. Greene. Stop playing games with me. Why did you come here?"

"Okay. You really want to know, Charlie? I've been doing a lot of thinking about this Trice case. You know I hate the bastard. Everybody does. So the last thing I want is for him to make our company look foolish."

"But we're not going to look foolish, Mr. Greene. I saw the guy run me down on his cycle, I swear I did."

"I know that, Charlie. But Breitenfeld jumped the gun, don't you see? You know how criminal courts work, don't you? One bastard after another gets out on a technicality."

"So?"

"So labor arbitrations are the same way. Soon as the union shows you didn't read your statement before Breitenfeld used it to fire Trice, they'll claim Trice didn't get due process of law and Breitenfeld will look like an idiot, and so will we. But you can help us fix that."

"By doing what?"

"By just getting up there next Wednesday and telling the arbitrator you can't remember a thing about the accident."

"You mean lie and let Trice win?"

"He's gonna win anyhow. I told you that. But at least this way, the police statement won't come out. No one will have to know the company screwed up. It'll just look like you're a poor guy who got his head cracked open by somebody, and can't remember two months later what happened. Everyone will apologize and the company will agree to put Trice back to work without a formal decision."

"But I'll look like an idiot."

"Charlie, you won't look like an idiot. You'll just look like a guy who's

152   THE TOOTH FAIRY

gone through a terrible accident. People will feel sorry for you; they won't be mad. And besides, you'll be able to take a nice vacation when it's all over."

"With what?"

"With this. It's the least the company can do after what you've been through."

The cigarette dropped directly out of Charlie Carpool's mouth and onto the floor when he opened up the manila envelope and took out ten thousand dollars in cash.

FOURTEEN
Monday, October 3

THE PHONE MESSAGE FROM Maribeth said that while David was out, "Mr. Eeyore" had called. Since David hadn't remembered having any active matters at that particular time with Christopher Robbin's donkey, he decided to ask his secretary some follow-up questions.

"Did he say who he was or anything?"

"Nope, just Eeyore."

"And, of course, you didn't ask him where he was calling from."

"I did actually. He said he was calling from some hospital, but then I figured you knew what it was about, so I ..."

David didn't wait for Maribeth Kryselski to finish her sentence before going into his office and closing the door. He laughed out loud. "'Mr. Eeyore.' What an imbecile."

He scribbled the words "Garden Spot General Hospital ER" under the caller's name on the phone slip, then dialed the number.

On his fifth try the line wasn't busy. He tried to calculate exactly how much blood he could have lost in the meantime."

"Emergency Room."

"Yes, I'm calling to check on a patient."

"Name?"

"Thomas Jefferson Trice."

"Just a minute."

When the woman got back on the line, she said, predictably, "I'm sorry, we have no record of a Thomas Jefferson Trice in the ER at this time."

"That's because he's not in the ER at this time; he was in a few weeks ago."

The voice on the other end of the phone then slid instantly into "you idiot" mode. It explained to David that all records of discharged ER patients are kept in Medical Records, and asked if he would like to be transferred.

In answer to his "yes, please" the phone clicked about ten times, then disconnected and went back to a dial tone.

Medical Records answered on the eleventh ring. David took some solace in figuring that death from loss of files was less common than death from loss of blood. Once the conversation began, however, all remaining solace went immediately out the window.

"I understand you represent Mr. Greene's company, sir, but we simply do not give out that kind of information over the telephone. If you wish to subpoena the file for a medical records deposition, you may do so. Other than that, I can't help you."

"Look, would it make any difference if I told you this is for a labor arbitration the day after tomorrow. I don't have time for a medical records deposition, and anyhow, there aren't any depositions in arbitration."

"You mean this isn't even for court, Mr. Castelli?"

"Look, sir, it's the same thing as court. The arbitrator has subpoena power under Pennsylvania law, and I assure you that I will personally deliver a properly executed subpoena *duces tecum* to you in time for the hearing on Wednesday."

"Then I don't understand your problem."

"My problem is I'm trying to save both of us a lot of time and trouble."

"Let me see if I get this straight. You want to know if this Mr. uh ..."

"Trice, Thomas Jefferson Trice."

"Whatever ... Trice was treated in the Garden Spot General Hospital Emergency Room between August 19 and September 1."

"Right, and if he was, the only other thing I want you to tell me is whether it had anything to do with a motorcycle. In fact, you don't even have to tell me. I'll just ask you if the word motorcycle is in the record, and you can just say yes or no. How's that?"

"And if I say no that's the end of it?"

David used his most cheerful voice. "That's the end of it."

"Okay, no."

"You're telling me you've got the file right there?"

"Not correct, I'm telling you no, we can't release information without a subpoena. Now, Mr. Castelli, if you have nothing further, I've got to get off."

David thought once more about asking for the clerk's name; he didn't. Instead he just said, "Well thank you for your time," and hung up.

He stuck the phone slip under a paperweight, then began to run through the possibilities. He could easily get a subpoena. Could even serve it himself, though it would require him to drive out to Lancaster a bit earlier tomorrow than he had planned. The problem was what to do on Wednesday when the records custodian showed up with Trice's file, assuming there even was a file.

Rothstein would never let him get away with sneaking a look; and van Auten would be too intimidated by the union lawyer to be of any help at all. So he'd be rolling some very big dice. He'd have to call the witness, ask for the document right there on the record, then pray the damn thing didn't blow up in his face.

The other possibility, of course, was to forget the whole idea and just go naked with Charlie Carpool. He would still have the standard argument to make to the arbitrator: Trice's job is on the line; he has an incentive to lie. Charlie doesn't. He is an innocent victim with a vivid memory of the most frightening moment in his whole life. Why would he not tell the truth? David willed himself to believe it would be enough to win. And who knew, maybe Castelli would get lucky on cross-examination.

But then he pictured the man at the bar last Thursday night, the biker with the 150 IQ who played the piano when he wasn't driving a forklift. He remembered how he had looked into the eyes of Thomas J. Trice and had seen an animal looking back, an animal without feeling, without conscience. David Castelli knew that this man would be completely at ease when he lied.

The idea did not hit him until late in the afternoon. He dismissed it at first. Too embarrassing, too intrusive. She was Local 664's landlady. But then he remembered the way she had spoken about Trice, and he remembered her hands.

He had been sitting at his desk with the door closed, trying to think of some way to see Trice's hospital records before cutting the umbilical cord with an actual subpoena. He had never been comfortable in the long thin cell, knowing as he did that it should have been two feet wider.

His favorite part of the office was usually kept in the center desk drawer. It was a small plastic penis on little plastic feet. When he wound it up, it would hop around the desk. David got it from the business manager of United Paperworkers Local 4, who launched it across the bargaining table, late one night, to break the tension. David refused to give it back.

At the moment he thought of calling Jenny Delone, Castelli had been mindlessly winding up the little dick, setting it on the desk, and watching it hop.

He caught his first break of the day when Jenny answered the phone herself.

"Jenny Rats."

Then he stumbled on his opening statement. "Uh, Jenny, Jenny DeLone?"

"Speaking."

"This is David Castelli. I don't know if you remember me, but I was in your bar last Thursday night ..."

"Bourbon on the rocks, hold the glass." She laughed heartily into the phone. "Why the honor?"

"Well actually, it's kinda hard to explain, but I need a favor if you've got a few minutes."

"I don't have the slightest idea what kind of a favor I can do for you, but sure, start talking."

"When I was in the bar last week, you said something about your sister being a nurse at Garden Spot General. You remember that?"

"So?"

"Well, what I need is for someone to take a peek at an ER chart and let me know what the patient said about his accident. I was wondering if maybe your sister could get that done."

"And if I said she could?"

"It would certainly make my life a whole lot easier."

"I assume, of course, that this little favor has something to do with Mr. Trice."

"What do you think? Of course it does. Look, I'm not going to start blowing smoke here. I've got a problem."

"I'm listening, but already I don't think I like it."

"You know I've got his discharge arbitration the day after tomorrow. Right now, I've got one witness, Charlie Carliner. The union's got one witness. So I need a tie breaker, that's all, and I'm figuring just maybe that tie breaker is somewhere in the files of Garden Spot General Hospital."

"And I assume you've already talked to someone there, and they blew you off."

"I wouldn't exactly call it a blow off; it was more like a 'red tape' off. See, they'll bring the records to the hearing if I subpoena them, but then I'll be seeing them cold right there in front of the arbitrator ..."

"And the union lawyer will make you look like a fool if the records don't help your case. Am I warm?"

"Scalding. So now that you know the problem, what's the answer?"

"The answer is I think you're out of your mind. You hardly know me. In fact, the only thing you do know is that I rent half my building to the same union you're trying to screw over. What makes you think I'm not going to go upstairs and tell Pete Werner exactly what you're up to as soon as this call is over, which might, as a matter of fact, be sooner than you think."

"You could do exactly that if you wanted. But something tells me you won't."

"Yeah, what?"

"Thomas J. Trice. You know you hate him."

"That's right, I do hate him. But how do you know I don't hate Harry Greene more?"

"Well, try this for starters. You don't have Greene-Pitowsky Smelting & Battery Company down that street of yours, you're out of business. And I'll tell you something else. I've got this crazy hunch you're one of those people who can't help but do the right thing."

"And the right thing is to cheat so you can win a case?"

"No, Ms. DeLone, the right thing is to make sure somebody finally stands up to Thomas Jefferson Trice. The right thing is to make sure that bastard pays for what he did to an innocent old man."

There was then the first long pause in the conversation. It was followed by Jenny saying, "That's not bad. That's not bad at all. Ever think of becoming a lawyer?"

"Not really, I prefer honest work."

Jenny DeLone laughed, the same deep, healthy laugh that David had not been able to get out of his mind since he first heard it as she swabbed down his wet pants.

"You've got a great laugh, you know that?"

"And you've got a big set of you know whats."

"So does that mean you'll talk to your sister?"

"I don't believe you, David Castelli. For one thing, you don't even know if my sister could get those records."

"Sure I do. If she couldn't, all you would have had to do was tell me that a minute ago and it would have been game, set and match. Right?"

"Okay. Right. So, just for being so clever, I'll tell you something else, since you obviously won't go away. My sister is a head nurse on the biggest Med. Surg. floor over there. She can see any chart in the place."

"And her name?"

"Bettina. Bettina DeLone Weatherspoon. Married outside the faith, but we still love her."

"Is she there now?"

"You do go on, don't you?"

"I'm sorry, it's just I don't have much time."

"Well, I hate to disappoint such a high-profile lawyer, but I don't have the foggiest idea what her schedule is. She could be on vacation for all I know."

"In October? With her seniority?"

"You really are impossible, you know that."

"No, just a little desperate, that's all. Look, will you at least think about it and let me call you back?"

"All right. Give me an hour. But I'm not promising a thing, you understand?"

"Perfectly."

At the western end of the phone connection, Jennifer DeLone cradled the receiver, then leaned her elbows on the bar and rested her head in the palms of her hands.

For a few seconds, she actually did think about going upstairs to look for Pete Werner. Not because Thomas J. Trice was anything but scum. That was a given. It was because Pete needed the case and needed it badly, if only to keep another dangerous weapon out of the hands of Dickie Romanowski.

The problem was Trice. And it wasn't just the way he pawed over women, and got filthy drunk, and made lots of noise. When you owned a bar up the street from a factory you took the clientele as you found them. And he wasn't the only one.

But he was a different one. The others just grew up that way, tethered from puberty to a world of cheap sex and Budweiser. They worked crummy jobs to support families that were too large on wages that were too small. Thomas Trice, on the other hand, did it all for fun, even though it wasn't funny. By now, the rumors in town about his brilliant mind were more than rumors; they were accepted fact. He could have been anything, and that, in the end, is what made him so loathsome.

Jenny put off for last the entry in her equation that read "plus David Castelli." But she knew that somewhere before the "equal" sign, the company's lawyer would have to enter the formula.

When she was completely honest with herself, Jennifer Alston DeLone believed that she was probably the most attractive 45-year-old woman in Lancaster. She was used to having younger men hit on her. Happened regularly. Most of the time, she just thought it was cute, particularly when they were married men, like David Castelli. But this time, there was nothing cute about it.

She had always been proud of her sexuality—proud to be one of those women who accepted, without shame, that physical attraction to a man could sometimes be deliciously overwhelming. And she definitely felt something along those lines when she thought of the tall blond lawyer with the boyish face and broad shoulders, who stumbled into her bar and her life last Thursday.

When the phone rang precisely one hour and ten minutes after she had hung up with Castelli, Jenny knew who it was.

"Jenny Rats."

"Well, I gave you an extra ten minutes."

"Pretty damn sure of yourself, aren't you?"

"No, I'm not sure of myself. I just can't stand suspense, that's all."

And then Jenny DeLone said something that was totally unplanned, something that just came out of her mouth without giving her even a millisecond to stuff it back. "You know it's gonna cost you."

David felt his pulse accelerate. It was right there in her voice. This had nothing to do with money or anything as trivial as that. He forced himself to be coy.

"I don't make much as an associate, you know, so be gentle with me. What's it going to cost?"

"One dinner at the Lamplighter House. That cheap enough?"

In the instant she said the words, David forgot completely about the ER records. All he wanted to do was make sure he actually heard what he thought he heard. He tried to make a joke. "Am I allowed to eat too?"

"You drive a hard bargain, mister lawyer from Philadelphia. Okay, then. Two dinners. One for me, one for you." Then she added, "And one check —for you."

When David finally got enough control over himself to ask about the ER records, it was then he learned that Jenny hadn't even called her sister yet. Not that it mattered.

"Don't worry about it. It's no problem. I told you she's a head nurse over there. When do you need the answer?"

David did some quick time calculations. He could get the subpoena today and serve it personally tomorrow afternoon. He could drive to Lancaster from Center City Philadelphia in under three hours. He'd give himself three and a half to make sure. That meant if Jenny could get him an answer by 10:00 AM, assuming it was the right answer, he could have the subpoena in the hospital's hands by 1:30, then have the rest of the day to himself.

"Ten o'clock tomorrow. That doable?"

"Ten for the info, eight for the dinner. I'll meet you in the hotel bar at 7:30. Do we have a deal?"

"What do you think?"

Castelli sat perfectly still at his desk for at least five minutes. He did absolutely nothing during those five minutes except stare at the notation on his time sheet that he had made, almost without thinking, while the phone call had been in progress: "GPS&B-Trice, .2, tel. Delone re ER records."

Then he called the Lamplighter House and made a reservation for dinner, two at eight. He also booked the J.E.B. Stuart suite.

And then he thought about his wife.

Jenny DeLone spent her first five minutes swabbing glasses. Then, the one person she least wanted to see at this particular moment came down the old wooden back stairs that ended just inches from one end of the bar.

Pete Werner said, "Good, you're here. I need one bad." He helped himself to a clean pilsner, expertly tilting it against the spigot of the bright red Budweiser tap.

"You ever need a night job, P. W., you know I've got one for you."

"Already have a night job. It's the same as my day job."

"That bad, eh?"

"Yeah, that bad. Where would you like me to start?" It wasn't a question designed to provoke an answer. It was a question designed to be an overture. The Secretary-Treasurer launched right into act one.

"Damn Rapid Freight negotiations are going nowhere. Company's got more money than Joe Greist ever stole, but you oughta hear Jack McKeon. I swear they must pay that lawyer by the word.

"And I'll tell you something else, since you asked. Our side of the table is worse. Every damn caucus, Romanowski starts in. 'Put 'em down now. Fuck the contract. Only got three weeks left anyhow.' Then that starts the rest of 'em, bunch of freaking bobblehead dolls."

When Jenny saw him pause for a breath, she jumped in. "Okay, already, I get the picture." She needn't have bothered.

"No you don't get the picture. Nobody gets the picture. Do you have any idea how many times that skinny little shit, O'Conner, has called this union in the last week about T. J. Trice. Every damn day, that's how many times. 'Who's the arbitrator?' 'Is Rothstein ready?' 'I'm going to be there, you know.' I'll tell you what I know. He tries to say one word during that hearing, he's gonna find a big German fist in his ugly face. Christ, I hate lawyers."

"Even your own?"

"Especially my own. You know he's actually convinced himself that biker bastard is going to sue the union if he doesn't get his job back. Then he starts in about the Twardzik case, and Romanowski's campaign, and how bad it's gonna look if this local gets whacked again. And you know the worst part?"

"What?"

"It doesn't have a damn thing to do with Pete Werner. Rothstein doesn't give a shit if I have to go back down the street and clean out Harry Greene's toilets for the rest of my life. He's only worried about who Dickie is going to use for a lawyer if a new slate gets in."

She watched him drain the pilsner, then refill it, without, it seemed, even stopping to catch his breath. Then she asked the question. The involuntary question. The question that made her feel as if she were picking at a scab, knowing it was about to bleed but unable to stop.

"You don't really think Trice is going to sue anybody here, do you?"

"Christ, Jenny, I don't know what to think anymore."

"But he's guilty, Pete. He knows it, you know it, I know it, the whole union knows it."

Werner put down his glass and stood directly opposite his landlady. He reached both arms across the old wooden bar, then placed his hands squarely on both of her shoulders. He had been calmed by the two beers, and by the chance to vent at one of the only people he knew who would take it with a smile.

"You see Axel over there?" He gestured to the omnipresent Mr. Kinnard, sitting quietly at an empty table, in an empty saloon, playing solitaire with two fingers.

"What about him?"

"You think he cares if T. J. Trice is guilty? Local 664 saved that man's life. I don't mean physically saved it. Hospital did that. But we saved it by giving him a job in the office and some goddamn dignity. And that's the way it should be, because that's what we do. We give people dignity. We take a bunch of uneducated men like Axel, who have to go to work down there in that sulfuric acid stink hole, and we give them self-respect. So it doesn't matter if Trice ran over Charlie. What matters is whether Harry Greene wins, or whether this union wins. The only real shame of it all is that Trice happens to be no fucking good."

It was the longest uninterrupted string of words Jenny DeLone had ever heard Pete Werner utter. When it was over, she almost slipped and let him see the first tear squeeze out from the corner of her eye and roll down her cheek. But she avoided disclosure by quickly removing his palms from her shoulders, then reaching down for his glass, empty now for the second time.

"You need another beer, Pete," she said. "So do I."

FIFTEEN
Tuesday, October 4

THE FAX THAT ARRIVED on David Castelli's desk was the most beautiful piece of paper he had ever seen. It was more than beautiful enough to make him forget about the lie he had told Leslie three hours earlier, David telling her some baloney about why he had to spend the night in Lancaster, instead of driving there the morning of the arbitration.

"I just want to see the battery house one more time at night," he had said.

"What difference does it make? The old man is either going to tell the story right or he's not. Isn't that what you've been saying all week? His word against what's his name's?"

"And I also said 'what's his name' is going to be a very good liar. So I'm looking for any extra edge I can get. That's what lawyers do, for god's sake."

"Lawyers also spend time with their families, David."

"Not lawyers trying to make partner at McKeon, Tingham & Marsh. And why do we keep having to go over the same ground?"

"Because I love you, that's why. Or didn't you ever think of that? Sometimes I just miss having you around the house at night." And then Leslie had put her arms around her husband's waist, kissed him deeply, and told him to be careful driving at night. It was exactly what he did not want to hear.

But now the fax was in front of him, staring up from his desk, an absolutely perfect piece of dead wood:

GARDEN SPOT GENERAL HOSPITAL
Emergency Room Report

Date: August 29, 1994

Name of Patient: Thomas Jefferson Trice

Address: R.D. 1
             Box 26
             Fivepointville, PA 18703

Telephone: Patient refused - unlisted
Admitted: 08/29/94 15:13
Discharged: 08/29/94 16:36
Treating Physician: Marcus X. Gerhard, MD

Physician's Notes:
Patient, a white male, age 47, presented with burns and a laceration on the inside of his right calf, together with swelling and pain in right knee. Patient reports injury was the result of a motorcycle accident that occurred when vehicle slipped on grease, causing bike to fall over on patient's leg.

Laceration badly infected. Patient unable to recall exact date of accident, but from appearance of wound, and from patient's own recollection, injury probably occurred 7–10 days earlier, August 19–22.

Palpation of knee resulted in considerable pain, but no evidence of fracture. Patient referred to Dr. Ellston for follow-up arthrogram.

Patient refused injection of mezlocillin. Replaced dressing on wound. Prescribed penicillin, *per os*. Told patient to stay completely off leg for at least one week.

MXG

It was even better than he had hoped. The date was right; the description of the accident was right. It would have been enough had she merely called and told him what was in the file. But she actually got the document and had it faxed it to him, which made the reception he got when he tried to reach her by phone, to thank her, just a bit odd.

"Jenny Rats." It was a male voice.

"Could I speak to Jenny, please."

"She ain't here."

"Well, do you expect her back soon?"

"Look, pal, this is a bar. It ain't no answering service. What do you want anyway?"

"I just want to speak to her, that's all."

"I already told ya, she ain't here."

"Okay, then, could you tell her David Castelli called?"

"No, I can't tell her that, 'cause I'm about to leave. And don't be calling here any more, either."

"Why is that?"

"'Cause you're a jerk off."

Castelli tried to put the phone call to Jenny Rats out of his mind as he drove toward Lancaster. He couldn't do it. Twice he reached for the cell phone in his briefcase on the front seat. The second time he even turned it on. But he stopped short of calling the bar again.

He looked at his watch. Eleven-fifty. He was on Route 41 North now, maybe five miles from the Gap clock. Plenty of time to reach Garden Spot General by one at the latest, then a whole afternoon to himself. The Lamplighter House closed its pool for the season around mid-September; but the jacuzzi ran all year round. He had already confirmed an early arrival.

Dinner was not until eight. He could almost feel the warm spa jets that would precede a delicious late afternoon nap in J. E. B. Stuart's bed; then it would be time to shower and dress, head down to the coziest bar in Lancaster County, gently suck on his first double Jack of the young evening, and wait for the arrival of Jenny DeLone.

The nurse at the reception desk in Medical Records looked down at the

American Arbitration Association subpoena like it was some kind of a dead animal.

"What is this? I've never seen this before."

"It's a Triple A subpoena."

"A what?"

"It's just a subpoena. I spoke to someone on the phone here about it yesterday morning."

"Spoke to who?"

"I didn't ask for his name. Look, is there a problem?"

She didn't answer the question. She was a scarecrow-thin woman, he guessed in her early sixties. The name tag said "E. Klugerman, RN, Medical Records." She said, "just a minute," then turned and disappeared with the paper.

Castelli waited in the now empty reception area, waited for an annoyingly long time. When a man wearing a white lab coat finally appeared before him holding the subpoena, lips pursed, bald head glistening with sweat even though the room was quite cool, David could feel himself bracing for trouble.

"Counselor, you want to explain this?"

"Are you the person I spoke to yesterday morning?"

"I haven't the slightest idea. I speak to lots of people."

"Well, I spoke to somebody yesterday about this. If it was you, I'm sure you'd remember."

"Then I guess it wasn't me now, was it?"

David was almost sure he recognized the voice. He controlled the urge to start an argument, though it wasn't easy. "The paper in your hand is a subpoena issued by the American Arbitration Association. It requires someone from this office to bring a file to a labor arbitration scheduled for 10:00 AM tomorrow."

"I can see that, counselor." The bald-headed man wiped his brow with a dirty handkerchief drawn from the front pocket of his lab coat. "But this isn't enforceable."

"And would you mind telling me why not?"

"Well, for one thing, this isn't from a court, or am I missing something? And for another, there's no witness check."

"You know, you people are really starting to piss me off." Castelli knew it was time to stop being polite. He reached into his briefcase and pulled out a green volume of *Pennsylvania Statutes, Annotated*. "I don't understand what the big damn deal is. You all act like you've never seen an arbitration subpoena before."

"It isn't necessary to use profanity, counselor."

David didn't respond. He just opened the book. "Look, Mr. ..."

"Licata, Alexander Licata."

"Okay, Mr. Alexander Licata. This is volume 42, *Pennsylvania Statutes*. And this page is chapter 20, section 11. Do you want me to read it, or will you take my word for what it says."

Alexander Licata reached across the counter and took the book. He studied it briefly, then handed it back.

"I'm going to have to discuss this with our counsel."

"There isn't time for you to discuss it with your counsel. What do you think we're having tomorrow, some kind of a prayer meeting? It's a trial, for god's sake. You want money, here, I'll give you twenty dollars."

Alexander Licata took the twenty dollar bill and put it in the pocket of his lab coat, the same one with the sweaty handkerchief. Then it was his turn to disappear. When he returned, he pointed to a telephone on the counter. "Pick it up when it rings. It's our general counsel."

Five minutes later, David handed the receiver back to Alexander Licata. For the first time in weeks, he loved lawyers.

Licata made mostly uh-huh noises into the phone, and occasionally shook his head up and down. Then he hung up and handed David back his twenty dollars.

"I'll be there tomorrow with the file," he said. "Assuming there *is* a file." The "is" part was the closest Alexander Licata came to telling David to go fuck himself.

—————◦◦◦◦———

The music was Chopin, one of the nocturnes. There was a time when he could probably have picked out the exact one. Unfortunately, seven years at McKeon, Tingham & Marsh had dulled certain parts of his brain even while it was honing others; so today he had to be content, at least, to recognize the composer.

He had picked out a good seat, near the back wall of the wood-paneled bar, with a clear view of the doorway. The stakeout had begun at 6:50, after he had come in from the spa, napped, showered and dressed, started watching "Sports Center" on ESPN, then couldn't stand it any more. By 7:15 he had begun playing a little game with himself, seeing how long he could go without looking down at his watch. At 7:25 he gave up hoping she'd be early, instead switching gears to hoping she wouldn't be too late. He desperately wanted not to start worrying about being stood up.

When it got to be 7:40, all David could think about was the phone call he had made earlier to the Rat. "'Cause you're a jerk off." That is what the voice had said; he definitely heard it. Now he was thinking maybe he was a jerk off, sitting in this dark bar like some kind of horny adolescent.

And maybe that thought, going through his head at that very second, is what caused him not to recognize Jennifer Alston DeLone the moment she first appeared in the doorway of the bar, craning her neck looking about, at precisely 7:42 PM.

By the time he realized what was going on, she had already spotted him, flashed a smile, and begun weaving her way through the tangle of low cocktail tables and chairs. David sat still as a stone, hands wrapped around Jack Daniels number two, as she approached.

His first clear view, head to toe, did not come until she was no more than ten feet away: black, billowy slacks, cinched in tightly at the waist; a bomber length jacket of multi-colored swaths that appeared to be pieces of Japanese kimonos; it was open to reveal a white silk blouse, also open at least six inches down her neck, enough to show off a necklace of garnets laying on tan skin. Her hair, black as a raven, fell softly to her shoulders, done just enough to shape the face, but not quite done enough to keep a few strands from crossing her cheeks, so she could brush them from her green eyes as she came to the table and sat down across from him.

"I'm so sorry," she said. "What time is it, anyhow?"

"Sorry for what?" he said.

"You know, for being late. I hate being late."

"I didn't even notice, really. But I'm glad you're here."

"So am I."

"Drink?"

"Excellent idea." She reached across the table and ever so quickly placed both her hands around his, as if she were trying to divine the contents of his glass. "Looks like the usual Mr. Daniels, I see. I'll take the same, only make it neat."

Castelli sat back in his chair and relaxed for the first time since about 7:05. He said, "You know that was quite a nice surprise you sent me this morning."

"I thought you'd like it."

"Any problems with your sister?"

"That's not for you to know, Mr. Castelli. Let's just say I owe her one."

"In that case, I must owe you about ten."

"I'll just take this," she said, waving her arm in a sweep around the room.

"You know I tried to call you at the bar this morning. Got a very un-friendly response."

"Oh that. That was just Axel. He's very protective, you know."

"Protective? How about nasty?"

"What'd he do, call you a jerk off?"

"How did you know?"

"Because he calls everyone he doesn't like a jerk off. Look, you gotta un-derstand, to him you're the enemy. He knows you work for Harry Greene; he knows you're in town to beat up on his union. That's his religion for god's sake."

The cocktail waitress wore black slacks, a red cummerbund and a tuxedo shirt. She gave Jenny Delone a respectful smile as she placed a topped-off tumbler, amber with bourbon, on the table.

"I like the music," Jenny said.

"Chopin nocturnes. One of the reasons I love this bar."

Then they sat without saying a word, sipping at their drinks, listening to the chamber music, looking at each other now and then like two little kids afraid to get caught playing dirty doctor.

She spoke first.

"This is crazy, you know."

"So?"

"I got my hair done, today, David. Do you know when the last time was I got my hair done?"

"I don't know, and I'll tell you something else. I don't care. You look terrific."

"But that's the whole point, don't you see? What the hell am I doing getting all dressed up to have dinner with a married man? And what the hell am I doing helping him win a case against a labor union run by my best friend?"

"Those are very good questions. Would you like to hear my very good questions too? Or would you prefer that I just answer your very good questions?"

"Okay. You're right. I'm here because I want to be here. And this is not a very good way to start off a dinner conversation, is it?"

"No, it's not, but I'll forgive you if you'll just agree to let me refill that glass there, the one you appear to have already drained."

"Deal," she said, looking down at her first dead soldier of the evening.

The table they shared for dinner had been personally picked out by David, shortly after he came out of the jacuzzi. It was next to one of the multi-paned windows that ran down the west wall of the room, looking out over a vast expanse of lawn, still visible at five past eight because the moon was full.

David watched her head, tilted slightly up toward the waiter as he recited the obligatory list of special entrées, an endless list, carefully committed to memory, right down to the sauces and shitake mushrooms. When he finally finished, they both ordered off the menu: she, the sea bass stuffed with crab meat; he, beef Wellington. David was glad when she eagerly accepted his invitation to share a Caesar for two, prepared tableside, *with* anchovies.

"Lots of people hate those things you know, anchovies."

"Not me," she said. "Not a Caesar without anchovies."

When it came time to order wine, Jenny deferred. "Don't sell too much of that stuff down the Rat. Unless you count Gallo Chablis in half-gallon bottles with twist-off tops."

David chose well; and he chose expensive. Sonoma Cutrair, La Pierre.

"So then, Ms. Jennifer DeLone," he said, after feeling the cork to make sure it was wet, and tasting just the tiniest bit of chardonnay to make sure it wasn't poison, "what shall we toast to?"

"Alcohol," she laughed. "I say we toast to alcohol, seeing as how much of it we've already consumed."

They spoke surprisingly little during the meal. Small talk, mostly. Finding out where they each came from, and how they each got from there to here, David saying things like how much fun he would have running a bar, Jennifer answering with lists of how many beer glasses got washed in a day, and how the distributors were always trying to squeeze her margin.

Neither spoke about what they were really thinking, each one waiting for the other to start, wanting to get it on, but not knowing quite how to do it.

The Battle of Gettysburg saved them.

"You know it's funny," she said.

"What?"

"This place, the Lamplighter House. Spent my whole life in Lancaster County, all forty-five years of it, never been here."

"Every time you say that, I can't believe it."

"What are you talking about, this is the first time I said it."

"No, I don't mean the Lamplighter House. I mean forty-five. I know I've done three double Jacks and god knows how much of this stuff." He gestured toward the second empty bottle of Sonoma Cutrair La Pierre, its neck buried like an ostrich in the melting ice of a wine bucket. "So maybe I'm buzzed. But there's still no way you're forty-five."

She was fishing through her purse while he spoke, looking for her wallet, flipping it open to her driver's license, first stumbling with the catch. "Oh yeah," she said, "well just read it and weep."

David was having trouble focusing. "You've had to do this before, haven't you?"

"Get carded every week. Can't deny it. It's a fact."

He forced himself to focus on the small laminated card: Jennifer Alston DeLone. D.O.B. June 4, 1949. "You know you're almost eleven years older than I am?"

"Hey, what are you gonna do? Maybe I like my studs young."

They both laughed, she putting her wallet back, he fiddling with the dessert menu. "Tell you what," he said. "Share a Double Chocolate Death with me and I'll give you the history of this place. How's that?"

"Done."

They were taking turns being silly with the spoons, slathered with chocolate cake and chocolate icing and chocolate sauce. She reached across the table, her spoon overflowing, putting the utensil into his mouth, then slowly drawing it out while he rolled his tongue over his upper lip, biting down, making her tug to jerk it free.

"There was great movie scene like this, remember?"

"*Tom Jones*," she said, "1969. Only I think they did it with turkey parts. So are you going to tell me about the Lamplighter, or what?"

"Oh, that. Well it's actually more about the Battle of Gettysburg. See, the South should've won. Would've, too, if it weren't for this place." He paused. "That, and Robert E. Lee being a stubborn egomaniac."

"A history buff *and* a chocoholic. I'm impressed."

"Everybody who studies the battle can't understand how Lee ever thought he could take the high ground. But here's the thing. Weren't for J. E. B. Stuart, Meade's army would never have gotten up there in the first place. Stuart was this hot-shot cavalry officer. Lee's favorite. Should've been Longstreet, Lee's favorite. But the old man just loved Stuart. Maybe they were queer for each other. Who knows?

"Anyhow, week before the battle, Lee sends Stuart out to scout the Army of the Potomac. Wants the kid to tell him exactly where the enemy is. Only Stuart never does it. He just disappears. So, in the meantime, old Meade slides on into Gettysburg, easy as pie and takes the hills before Lee knows what's happening. And all the time, he's yelling at his generals, wanting to know where J. E. B. Stuart is."

Jennifer scooped up the last piece of Double Chocolate Death, and went back to feeding straight lines. "So now you're going to tell me where the handsome young cavalry officer was, right?"

"Not quite. See, actually, no one has ever figured out exactly where he was, at least not for the whole week. Best guess, he was just marching around here someplace, showing off and mugging for the women. But one thing most people do believe's true, and now we're getting to the Lamplighter House, is that on the very day of Pickett's charge, July 3, 1863, J. E. B. Stuart was passed out drunk in the actual bed I'm going to be sleeping in tonight. Right upstairs in this hotel."

"Did he look like you, J. E. B. Stuart?"

"Huh?"

"Well I figure you're going be passed out drunk in that bed too, so I was just wondering if we're going to have some kind of psychic experience here."

"Only if J. E. B. spent July 4, 1863, in the basement of Greene-Pitowsky Smelting & Battery." David looked at his watch. "Jesus, do you realize it's after ten already?"

"You throwing me out?"

"No, no, not at all. Really. It's just that you mentioned 'passed out' and then I remembered why I'm here in the first place."

"So I'm not going to see the famous J. E. B. Stuart suite, after all. What a shame."

David was signing his name and room number to the check when she said it. He almost dropped his pen.

"You're joking."

"I never joke about my work, double-o-seven." She made her voice sound deep, mimicking the movie line. "*Goldfinger*, 1964." she said. Then she looked up at him, again brushing strands of black hair from across her cheekbones. "Besides, it *is* a historic landmark, now. Isn't it?"

Neither one wanted any more games. There were no words exchanged. When he reached for the small lamp left on by the maid, Jennifer said only three words. "Leave it lit."

The first kiss was brutal. Their lips instantly opened to each other, now her tongue burning inside his mouth, thick, almost choking him, making him breathe through his nose. When they broke, her sigh was nearly guttural, her breath sucking quickly in and out, her hips locked in against his.

Then she stepped back, barely far enough so he could see. "Don't move, just look." The words softly tumbled from her mouth, as she tried to regain normal breathing. He watched, there in the dim light of the J. E. B. Stuart suite, as Jennifer DeLone began removing the top half of her ensemble.

The kimono jacket slipped to the floor; then she fumbled for the buttons of her blouse, half-opening them, half-tearing at them. The bra barely covered her breasts. It unclasped from the front, now hanging loosely by its straps from her shoulders. She shrugged; she was half naked before him, except for the necklace of garnets.

He reached for her breasts, wanting more than anything in the world just to touch them, to feel their heat. "Not yet, just stand there." The belt of her pants flashed in the semi-darkness, then slid to the floor, followed by the black slacks. Her legs were muscular, but perfectly formed as he knew they would be, angled out slightly from the leg bands of her black panties, flesh now visibly tightening as she slowly caressed the inside skin of each thigh with her finger tips.

When she beckoned for him, it was with an almost imperceptible nod, her eyes bright even in the dim lamplight, her tongue barely showing through an open mouth. By the time they reached the four-poster bed, his clothes were gone, littering the floor. Then she pushed him back, his hands instinctively reaching up and over his head to grasp two of the turned mahogany uprights on the headboard. He watched, holding himself stiff as a board, his erection straining up from his groin, as Jennifer Alston DeLone turned her back to him, then leaned forward between his knees, bracing herself against the mattress with one outstretched arm, while, with the other, she guided him ever so slowly inside her.

David had never felt anything like it before. He could only watch, through eyes half squeezed shut with his own passion, willing himself not to surrender to what was going on above him. He could see the muscles in her back, rolling like tiny waves from the top of her buttocks up to her shoulders. And he could hear her. Loud and strong, the deep moans of something almost inhuman, then a rapid series of halting tiny breaths, then another moan.

And through it all, this wonderful woman, who moved atop him like a beautiful tan goddess, remained completely in control, as if she knew the precise moment he would come to the almost uncontrollable point of release. For then she stopped, motionless, reaching behind to grasp him, hard, willing him not to finish, as she turned now to face him, looking at him for the first time, her lips drawn back tightly with her own excitement.

Seconds later, they were both out of control. Jennifer slamming up and down on him, again and again, almost separating, but not quite, each return thrust from his hips sending him deep inside her, David feeling her again as if for the first time. Finally his own scream, lost in the hollow of her shoulder as he pulled her to him, violently. Then hers, half cry, half shudder. And then, two bodies, exhaling, turning themselves hard to soft, melting into each other until they were separated only by the glint of their own sweat.

He wanted to reach for the bed table light, but she wouldn't let him. "Don't," she said. "Just lay still."

She was off him now, lying flat on her back next to his drained body, right arm crooked over her eyes. He watched her breathing rhythmically slow as the final surges of passion ebbed from inside her. She had drawn up her legs, showing the tan outside of one beautiful thigh, the pale, soft inside of the other.

"Feeling guilty?" She said it, turning to him, reaching for one of his hands and sucking gently on his fingers.

He wiggled them inside her mouth, making her giggle. "I don't know. Don't think so."

"Well you shouldn't be if you are. It's a useless emotion, guilt. Never gets anything resolved."

"You gonna feel that way tomorrow, when I shove Trice's ER record up Rothstein's ass?"

"Maybe yes, maybe no. Anyhow, I won't be there, so what difference does it make what I feel?"

"But you just said guilt is a useless emotion."

"It is, just involuntary sometimes."

Then, without any warning whatsoever, Jennifer Delone sat up, got out of bed, and started picking up her clothes off the floor. "I think I'd better be getting out of here. You've got a big day tomorrow and it's late."

"You mean, just like that?"

"Well, we could sneak outside to that lit-up lawn, then separate from each other in slow motion like in the movies, but I don't think you're dressed for it."

"Look, I just want to know if I'm going to see you again."

"I guess that depends on how guilty you are, doesn't it?"

"Yes," he said, "and it also depends on how guilty you are."

She was pulling on her clothes as they spoke, Jennifer now dressed, with her hand on the doorknob. "You're right," she said, leaving. "It does depend on that."

SIXTEEN
Wednesday, October 5

ISAAC ROTHSTEIN STOOD UP from the end of the table in the conference room of Local 664 at 10:09 AM.

Finally permitted to do so, Pete Werner and Greene-Pitowsky's warehouse steward, Larry Douglas, also rose. Thomas Jefferson Trice, who had been standing the whole time cleaning his fingernails with a pen knife, folded the blade and walked toward the door.

"I don't want any surprises in there, Mr. Trice. You understand that?"

"Then don't ask me any questions."

The union lawyer ignored the remark. He walked slowly out into the hall, then down the stairs, then out onto Hixon Avenue, turning left toward the river, his entourage trailing behind. The sky was perfectly clear, a sharp breeze, curiously free of acid, blowing toward them off the Conestoga. Isaac Rothstein paid no attention to the weather.

The walk from 4641 Hixon Avenue to Building 102, Room 37C, of the Greene-Pitowsky Smelting & Battery Company took four minutes. Rothstein had taken that walk more than a hundred times, maybe a hundred and fifty. He knew exactly, almost to the second, how to arrive for a ten o'clock hearing at 10:15.

As the union's lawyer was strolling down Hixon Avenue this fall morning, the company's lawyer was already bending paper clips. By 10:05, the small talk was over, G. Arnold van Auten asking David where Mr. McKeon was, the professor happy to see Castelli instead of the senior partner. Then he took his seat at the arbitrator's table, loading his cassette recorder, even though a court reporter had been hired by the company for the occasion, the professor a creature of habit after twenty-five years in the business.

David sat perfectly still at one of the counsel tables, his notes carefully laid out before him and his exhibits each in its own folder. To his left, Joseph Breitenfeld, chewing gum and looking terrible.

Behind the witness stand, filling up the first pew of orange plastic chairs, there sat in a silent row, left to right, Alexander Licata, Charles Carliner, Irene Henderson from personnel, and Brian O'Conner—an ACLU pin stuck in one lapel, in the other, a tiny microphone connected to the cassette recorder hidden in the breast pocket of his rumpled corduroy sports jacket.

And by himself, stuffed into a seat on the last row, Dickie Romanowski taking a personal day.

David forced himself not to turn his head at the sound of the double doors to Room 37C opening behind him, Rothstein leading the charge, starting immediately.

"I see there's still no heat in this lousy room. What's the matter Mr. Breitenfeld, company too cheap to pay the electric bill?"

David purposely spoke without looking up. "It was nice and warm in here at ten o'clock, Isaac—when this hearing was supposed to have started."

Rothstein was unfazed. "Mr. Breitenfeld," he said. "The steward is supposed to be released at 8:30 AM to prep at the union hall. If you'd bother to read your contract once in a while, we could start these things on time."

"I released him at 8:20, Mr. Rothstein."

"What time did they let you leave, Larry?" The union lawyer had crossed the room without acknowledging Castelli's presence in any way.

"8:45. Looked right at the time clock."

Breitenfeld grabbed David's arm. "He's lying I'll get his goddamn time card."

"Forget it. Just forget it."

Rothstein reached down and shook Professor van Auten's hand, then settled into his seat at counsel table. "I want the witnesses sequestered, Professor van Auten."

David's head snapped up from his yellow pad. Even the arbitrator was a bit surprised. "Is that really necessary, Isaac? I mean we don't usually do that here."

"Believe me, Professor. It's necessary. You haven't heard the company's ridiculous story yet, but I have."

"Not wasting any time today, are you, Mr. Rothstein?"

"I'm not talking to you, Mr. Castelli, I'm talking to the arbitrator. Are we going to have sequestration here or not?"

"That's your right, Isaac. You know that. It's either party's right." Then he spoke to the room. "Mr. Rothstein has asked that the witnesses be sequestered for this hearing. What that means is that if any of you are going to be testifying, I must ask you to leave the room until it's your turn.

Breitenfeld started to get up, along with Charlie Carpool and Alexander Licata. David stopped the warehouse foreman.

"We *are* permitted to have a representative of the company remain at counsel table, are we not?" David said to the arbitrator.

Isaac said, "Is Mr. Breitenfeld going to testify?"

"Of course he's going to testify. He fired the grievant."

"Then," said the union lawyer, again ignoring Castelli and speaking directly to van Auten, "I am going to request that Ms. Henderson remain as the company's representative, unless she is going to testify too."

"Mr. Arbitrator, you know that's not the way it works. He can't tell me who I pick to represent this company."

"He's right, you know, Isaac."

"Oh, so now you're on the company's side too."

David swore he wasn't going to get into it with Rothstein, but when Breitenfeld leaned over and said, "You can't let him get away with that," David was on his feet.

"That is a completely improper remark, Professor van Auten. Mr. Rothstein knows the rules on sequestration just like the rest of us."

It worked. The professor suddenly started sprouting a backbone. "Look, both of you. We're not going to have another circus here today, do you understand? Mr. Castelli has every right to decide who sits with him at counsel table. You do also, Isaac. Now, who will stay for the union?"

"Mr. Werner—and the grievant, of course."

As all of this was going on, Alexander Licata and Charlie Carpool were just standing at their chairs, looking confused. Finally, Licata spoke. "Excuse me, Professor, my name is Licata. I've been subpoenaed by Mr. Castelli and I'm on a very tight schedule. Is this going to take long?"

David said, "Mr. Licata is going to be my first witness, so there's no reason for him to leave." Then he looked over at the medical records custodian. "I'll have you out of here as soon as I can."

So, as it turned out, the only person who actually had to leave the room was Charlie Carliner, who said he didn't mind at all because he had to go to the bathroom.

David liked to style his opening statements to his opponents. If a civilized lawyer was representing the union, Castelli would ignore the courtroom etiquette about facts in the opening, argument in the closing, blending everything together in an attempt to prejudice the arbitrator in his client's favor before a single witness took the stand.

However, when Isaac Rothstein was on the other side of the room, ready to erupt at any second into one of his injured victim tirades, David rigidly stuck to the facts of his case, his opening usually dulled into mediocrity by the third sentence.

"This is a discharge case, Mr. Arbitrator. The issue is whether the grievant, Thomas Jefferson Trice, was terminated for just cause on August 21, 1994.

"The facts are simple. On Saturday, August 20, 1994, at approximately 1:15 AM, the grievant decided to ride his motorcycle through a building on the property of Greene-Pitowsky Smelting & Battery Company, known as the battery house. This building is empty from the end of second shift, Friday afternoon, until Sunday afternoon.

"The company employs a watchman, Charles Carliner, to patrol the property during this period. Mr. Carliner, who is not a member of the bargaining unit, will testify that shortly after 1:00 AM on Saturday morning, August 20, he was sitting at the south end of the battery house when he heard the sounds of a very loud motorcycle. The bike circled the entire building, then appeared at the open north end.

"Mr. Carliner heard the rider, laughing—no, actually cackling—in a very loud voice. The rider was threatening to come after Mr. Carliner, which he then did. The motorcycle drove straight down the length of the battery house, pinning Mr. Carliner against a bench.

"Now this was no ordinary motorcycle. It was a customized teal blue, Harley-Davidson Springer Softail, known throughout the company as belonging to the grievant, Thomas Jefferson Trice."

"Okay, that's enough." Rothstein was on his feet. "Do we have to listen to any more of Mr. Castelli testifying? Because, if we do, I'm going to ask that he be put under oath so I can cross-examine him too."

"It's my opening statement, Professor. I am permitted to summarize the company's case; it's just that Mr. Rothstein over there doesn't like what he's hearing."

The arbitrator rubbed his chin. "You may continue, Mr. Castelli. But just try and confine yourself to the facts."

"These *are* the facts, Professor van Auten. And every one of them will be supported by the testimony of a witness under oath, including the fact that the grievant owns a customized teal blue Harley-Davidson Springer Softail, with a naked woman painted on the tank, which Mr. Carliner was able to recognize—and which every other half-conscious human being who works for the company is also able to recognize."

"I want that stricken from the record, Mr. Arbitrator. It's impertinent and irrelevant."

"Gentlemen, please. I told you this was going to be a hearing, not a circus. Do you have much more, Mr. Castelli?"

Rothstein had done the usual damage.

Castelli finished quickly. He knew exactly what his opponent was going to do when van Auten asked if the union wished to make an opening statement. Rothstein was so predictable.

"I was planning to save my opening until the beginning of the union's case, Mr. Arbitrator. However, after hearing Mr. Castelli's so-called version of what happened here—a version which contains not a single accurate statement—I cannot allow this charade to continue without comment."

Then David had a brief moment. "Why don't you just stick a sock in it, Isaac? Either make an opening statement or don't."

The company's side of the room had its first laugh of the morning. It was a good laugh. It was needed.

Dickie Romanowski laughed too, snotting out a big goober onto his upper lip, which he rubbed off with his sleeve.

And even though Pete Werner wanted to give David Castelli a round of applause, what he said across the room was, "Just keep it up, buster. Then we'll see who's got a sock in their mouth."

That was when Professor G. Arnold van Auten turned off his tape recorder, stood up, and slammed his palm hard on the table. No one in the room had ever seen such a display before from the Chairman of St. Joseph's University's Department of Industrial Relations.

"I am *not*," he was almost shouting, "going to tell either one of you again. There will be no more outbursts of any sort during this hearing. None. Is that clear, Mr. Castelli?"

"Yes, sir."

"Is that clear, Isaac?"

"As long as he ..."

"I *said*, is that clear, Isaac."

"Yes, Arnold. I'm not stupid, just frustrated."

"Now, does the union wish to make an opening statement?"

"We'll wait till our case in chief."

"Good. Mr. Castelli, call your first witness."

He was wearing the same white lab coat, Alexander Licata slowly rising, with beads of perspiration on his bald head, walking over to the witness table, carrying a thin manila envelope as David hoped he would be.

"Mr. Licata." David was going to savor every moment. "You are here today pursuant to a subpoena *duces tecum*, signed by Professor van Auten?"

"Correct."

"Do you have it with you, sir?"

Licata reached into his favorite lab coat pocket. After he pulled out the handkerchief, he extracted the subpoena, folded into squares.

"Please hand it to the court reporter. I'd like to have it marked as an exhibit."

Rothstein mumbled into his notes. "May I see it first, counselor?"

David stood up, walked around behind his table to the witness chair, then took the folded subpoena over to Isaac Rothstein and dropped it in front of the union lawyer, still folded. He watched as his opponent unfolded the document, smoothed it down, then handed it to Trice. The grievant looked briefly at the subpoena and shrugged.

"No objection," Rothstein said.

David returned to his seat. "By whom are you employed, Mr. Licata?"

"Garden Spot General Hospital."

"And in what capacity?"

"I am the supervisor of medical records."

"Now, as supervisor of medical records, are you the custodian of the documents kept by Garden Spot General Hospital concerning the treatment of patients?"

"I don't know what you mean by custodian."

"It's a term of art, Mr. Licata. Are the hospital's medical records kept under your supervision?"

"I just said I'm the supervisor of medical records, didn't I?"

"Please, Mr. Licata, just answer the question."

"I'm trying."

"Now the subpoena you were served with yesterday instructed you to bring to this hearing any Garden Spot General Hospital Emergency Room records showing treatment given to Thomas Jefferson Trice between August 19 and September 1, 1994. Have you brought any such records?"

"Yes."

"And how many such records have you brought?"

"One. He was only in the ER once during the period."

"All right, Mr. Licata, take a look at the record you have there with you, and tell us, please, when was Mr. Trice treated."

"August 29, 1994."

"And does that record state what happened to Mr. Trice?"

"Sure. It says he got run over by a forklift at work."

"What did you say?"

"I said, he got run over by a forklift at work."

Trice and Rothstein reacted even faster than David, Trice just slightly jerking his head up and toward the witness, Rothstein leaning forward over the table, scribbling on a yellow pad.

Breitenfeld leaned over and said in David's ear, "What kind of bullshit's that?" Then David lifted up all the sheets on the yellow pad before him, to where the fax was stuck between the last piece of paper and the cardboard back of the pad, his heart suddenly trying to burst through his shirt. It was still there, still the way he remembered it: "Patient reports injury was the result of a motorcycle accident …"

"It says 'motorcycle accident,' Mr. Licata. Doesn't it? He was in a motorcycle accident."

"Objection," said Rothstein. "He's cross-examining his own witness."

Licata responded before the arbitrator could even open his mouth. "No it doesn't say 'motorcycle accident,' Mr. Castelli. I don't know what you're talking about. Here, look at it."

Then van Auten said, "You can't cross-examine your own witness. Isaac is right this time."

David was on his feet, feeling his whole body starting to shake, almost dizzy, grabbing the paper from Licata's outstretched hand, staring at it, trying to focus his eyes:

Patient, a white male, age 47, presented with burns and a laceration on the inside of his right calf, together with swelling and pain in right knee. Patient reports injury occurred when his forklift slipped into gear after he had alighted from it at work, pinning him against a stack of pallets.

Laceration badly infected. Patient said accident occurred while at work for Greene-Pitowsky Batteries on Friday, August 19, 1994, at approximately 2:00 PM. Patient did not seek treatment at that time because he thought the injury was not serious.

David went back to his seat. He showed the paper to Breitenfeld, his hands visibly shaking. "I saw the damn thing myself," he whispered. "It said motorcycle accident, I swear to God. Look." Then he placed the fax copy on the table in front of them.

Rothstein could smell blood in the water. "I'd like to see that medical record, Mr. Castelli. The other piece of paper you're looking at there, too, please."

"You're not seeing anything until I introduce it."

"Excuse me?"

"Well you're certainly not seeing my notes."

Even van Auten knew something was up. "Are you going to sponsor an exhibit through this witness, Mr. Castelli?"

"I don't know yet." He looked up at Alexander Licata. The medical records supervisor was cracking just the slightest wisp of a smile. "Mr. Licata, are you absolutely sure there are no other ER records for Mr. Trice during the period covered by the subpoena?"

The witness drew out his answer as slowly as possible. "Absolutely sure, counselor. Absolutely."

Then David did the only thing left.

"I have no further questions of this witness."

Breitenfeld said under his breath, "Brilliant. Fucking brilliant."

van Auten said, "Does the union wish to cross-examine?"

Rothstein said, "Yes, Mr. Arbitrator. It certainly does."

"Mr. Licata, who served you with this subpoena?"

"Mr. Castelli."

"And when was that, sir?"

"Yesterday afternoon."

"Had you ever met Mr. Castelli before yesterday?"

"Not in person."

"Go on."

"Mr. Castelli called me on the telephone. Day before yesterday."

David, sick to his stomach now, still made himself whisper "motherfucker" into his lap.

"And what was the reason for Mr. Castelli's call?"

David had to stop it. "Objection. This is beyond the scope of direct examination and irrelevant."

"Oh is that so, Mr. Castelli." Rothstein looked like he was about to pop a nut in his pants. "Professor van Auten," he said. "You just saw what happened here. We all did. I think we may have a serious breach of professional ethics in this case. Plus we have an innocent man who lost his job based on some imaginary charge that's falling apart right in front of your eyes. I demand the right to cross-examine this witness."

Rothstein didn't even wait for van Auten to rule on Castelli's objection. "Would you like me to repeat the question, Mr. Licata?"

"Not necessary, sir. Mr. Castelli called trying to find out what was in Mr.

Trice's medical file."

"And what did you tell Mr. Castelli when he called trying to find out what was in Mr. Trice's medical file?"

"What do you think I told him? I told him it's against the law. Said he'd have to get a subpoena like everyone else."

"Did he accept that?"

"Eventually."

"How about before 'eventually'?"

"Actually, he was rather childish."

"How is that?"

"Well, at one point he wanted me to play twenty questions with him. You know, he'd ask were certain things were in Mr. Trice's file, and I could just respond yes or no."

Isaac Rothstein slowly stood up as a quiet ripple of laughter rolled over the room. David watched the thin union lawyer make his way across the open space between counsel tables, his old body lost inside a loose-fitting blue suit, his large head, covered with blotchy skin and topped by wispy, yellow-gray hair, moving forward and back on his neck like a chicken.

Rothstein smiled down at Castelli, reached out a bony hand, and snatched the ER file off the table.

"The union would like this document marked as U-1."

van Auten said, "Any objection, Mr. Castelli?"

He could have objected. He could have launched into an interrogation of Alexander Licata about the hospital's computer system, trying to find out how the records could have been changed in barely twenty-four hours. He could have, but instead he found himself thinking of yet another verse from the gospel according to Jack McKeon. "Don't play with a turd, son. The more you do, the more of it gets on your hands."

"No objection."

Then he had to go to the john.

He sat on the last toilet by the wall in the basement men's room, feeling sweat run down the back of his collar, forcing himself to think despite the cramps now rippling deep inside his intestines.

He stood in front of the sink, suddenly thinking about Jackie Gleason in *The Hustler*, Fast Eddie Felson whipping him at pool, Minnesota Fats taking a break, washing his face, washing his hands, then strolling out of the men's room and back to the center table at Ames, now running that table, then running it again, then again, while Paul Newman is passing out on the floor with his bottle of J.T.S. Brown.

At the door to Room 37C David motioned for Breitenfeld to come out into the hall.

"Your forklifts ever slip into gear?" he asked.

"Not since the OSHA case. You oughta know about that, your firm handled it."

"McKeon does most of the GPS&B work. You tell me about it."

"Two years ago. Union sicked OSHA on us on account of the forklifts didn't have dead man switches. I tell the little government dweeb on the walk around that the lifts weren't made with no switches, but it's like talking to the wall. He says we can retrofit them with some piece of crap under the seat so when the driver gets off, the seat tilts up and breaks a circuit. Cost more to do that than we paid for the goddamn forklifts, but what does that little do-gooder care?

"So Mr. Greene says, 'No way. Fight it.' Then your man McKeon comes in and wins the case. Wins it clean. And then you know what?"

"What?"

"Greene goes and gets new forklifts anyhow. Some kind of sweetheart deal or something with tax write-offs. I don't understand that shit. Alls I know is one day about six months ago, we get these brand new Hysters, dead man switches and all."

"You can testify to all of this, I take it?"

"If I have to."

"You have to. We'll put you on after Charlie."

Trying a case against Isaac Rothstein was like sharing a bed with a porcupine. Every time David tried to get comfortable, he'd get a side full of quills. So he wasn't really surprised when the next fusillade was launched.

"Mr. Arbitrator, the union objects to any testimony from Charles Carliner."

In a real courtroom, in front of a real judge, a lawyer took a big risk making a completely spurious argument. Not that it *never* happened; it's just that there could be consequences. There were no consequences in front of an arbitrator, only more opportunities to rattle the opponent and cloud the issues. There wasn't a better rattler or clouder in the whole Philadelphia union labor bar than Isaac Rothstein.

But this one even puzzled van Auten. "I don't understand, Isaac. What's your problem here?"

"I shouldn't have to explain it, Mr. Arbitrator, it's so obvious, but I guess I'll have to anyway. The company never even talked to this witness before they fired Mr. Trice. They just relied on his so-called statement. A statement that Mr. Carliner never even signed. Never even looked at for all we know. But now they come in here and want to fix up their own inadequate case by having Mr. Carliner—after the fact—tell you god only knows what. It's post-discharge evidence and I demand that you keep it out."

As many times as Isaac Rothstein reached into his bag of dirty arbitration tricks, David still could not help getting angry. He never had a problem rebutting legitimate arguments. It was the crazy ones that set him off, arguments so silly that any response at all seemed only to dignify them. And Rothstein had just laid out a gem.

"Mr. Arbitrator. I should never be surprised at anything my opponent will say to win a case. Thomas Jefferson Trice was fired for assaulting a fellow employee on company property. The victim is right here in this room, prepared to give you direct, first-hand testimony, under oath, as to what the grievant did to him. This testimony would be admissible in any court in the country."

David waited for van Auten to overrule Rothstein's absurd objection and get on with the case. As usual, it wasn't that easy.

"Mr. Castelli," van Auten said, trying to look earnest. "I understand that Mr. Carliner was the victim here. But isn't Mr. Rothstein correct? Didn't the company fire Mr. Trice without ever talking to this witness?"

"He was in intensive care, for god's sake. This isn't post-discharge evidence. I can't believe you're even listening to this kind of bull ..."

"Mr. Castelli, may I remind you ..."

"I'm sorry." David stood up and took a deep breath. "I am familiar with the concept of post-discharge evidence. But this isn't it. Now, if the company had fired Mr. Trice for excessive absenteeism or poor work performance, then I admit we could not come before you with evidence that we later learned he also committed an assault. *That* would be post-discharge evidence. But here, the assault on Mr. Carliner by the grievant is the *only* basis for Mr. Trice's termination. With all due respect to opposing counsel's fertile imagination, he's just plain wrong."

Rothstein was on his feet. "May I be heard, Professor van Auten?"

"I don't think so, Isaac. I understand the arguments, but I don't have to rule on the issue at this time. I'm letting this evidence in for what it's worth."

David couldn't believe it. The objection was utter nonsense. "For what it's worth! Mr. Arbitrator," he said, "I'm entitled to more than that. This is ridiculous."

"You really want me to rule on Mr. Rothstein's objection?"

Castelli looked at the frail figure seated at the arbitrator's table, at the patches on the elbows of his tweed sports jacket, at the chewed-off pipe-stem sticking out from the handkerchief pocket. He wondered what van Auten would do if Isaac Rothstein just got up one day and spat on the professor's notes. He wasn't sure.

"The company calls Charles Carliner."

He looked like a condemned man heading for the gallows, Irene Henderson leading him into the room, Charlie shuffling slowly behind.

"Right here, Mr. Carliner." Then Irene whispered into his ear. "Now don't be nervous, Charlie, it's going to be fine."

The outfit he chose for the occasion looked like a softball uniform: polyester slacks, old, pressed, mustard color. The green t-shirt had gold script lettering, "Greene-Pitowsky," and a gold streak, shooting out across the shirt from the end of the Y in "Pitowsky," right to left across his gut. A green baseball cap completed the ensemble. It also bore the legend, this time in stitched block letters: "Greene-Pitowsky Smelting & Battery Co." On the side of the hat, a blue lightning bolt exploding into some sort of yellow sunburst.

A 74-year-old nervous leprechaun.

"Good morning, Charlie. Thank you for coming."

"I assume you want this witness sworn, Mr. Castelli."

"Please."

Charlie Carliner then stood and took off his hat, as if he were waiting for the National Anthem. van Auten did his duty.

Charlie did not replace his hat after the oath. He held it in his lap, already twisting the visor, his white hair plastered down with some sort of primitive hair tonic. David went slowly, as if he were stalking a deer, trying to get as close as possible before the animal spooked.

"Mr. Carliner, I'm going to ask you some questions about what happened on Saturday, August 20. It's important to keep your voice up so that the court reporter can take down what you say. If you don't understand a question, just say so and we'll try it again. You okay with that?"

"Yes sir."

"Good. Now, please tell us your name for the record."

"You mean my real name or my company name?"

When the giggling stopped, Romanowski called out to David, "Need some water there, sport?"

Castelli ignored the remark. "You can tell us both names."

"Charles Carliner, 'cept everybody calls me Carpool."

"Do you know why that is?"

"Nope, folks just started calling me that one day and I guess it stuck."

"Well suppose I call you Charlie. Make it easier. Where do you work, Charlie?"

"Nowhere actual. Just sell papers. Usual spot's outside the main gate upstairs."

"Well beside that, Charlie, do you work for anyone in a job?"

"Sure. Work for Mr. Greene on weekends."

"What do you do for Mr. Greene?"

"Watchman, pick up stuff lying around, sweep."

"I want to take you back a few weeks to Friday night, August 19. Were you working for Mr. Greene that night?"

"Guess so, work every Friday night."

"I'm afraid you can't guess here, Charlie. So I'll have to ask you to think on this. Today is October 5. August 19 was six weeks ago last Friday, does that help?"

Everyone in the room watched as Charlie Carliner shut his eyes and started moving his lips, as if he was counting. David felt the first little wave of uneasiness wash over him; but it was over as soon as Charlie answered.

"Yeah. Okay. I worked that night. See I was counting back how many weeks I been out since I got hit. I was there. Definite."

"Good. Now when you work for Mr. Greene on Friday nights, what are your usual hours?"

"Go on at seven, stay till five, six, whenever the sun comes up."

"So you were on duty at 1:00 AM on the morning of Saturday, August 20?"

"Right."

"Now do you remember exactly where you were at 1:00 AM?"

"Battery house. Sitting in my chair. See I got this beach chair Mr. Greene lets me bring. Radio too. Not much to do, you know."

"Were you awake?"

"Course I was awake. Can't be watching no building when you're asleep."

"Well I only asked because the next thing is very important. Did a motorcycle come into the battery house while you were sitting in your beach chair that night?"

"Objection. He's leading the witness."

"It's background, Professor. I'm allowed to lead." David returned to Charlie Carpool. "You may answer."

"Motorcycle? Yeah, there was a motorcycle."

"All right, Charlie. What I want you to do now is tell the arbitrator, in your own words, everything that happened beginning with when you first heard or saw a motorcycle."

In every trial, whether it is held in the fanciest courtroom or the dingiest basement, there comes a time when the undercard is over and the main event begins—when one witness, under oath, is asked a question that can determine the entire outcome of the proceedings. David sat back in his chair. He had finished with Isaac Rothstein's barrage of distractions, finished with Alexander Licata's smirking wisecracks, finished with the tedium of direct examination. He had turned his witness loose. Finally, Professor van Auten would hear what happened at 1:00 AM on August 20, 1994, between Charles Carliner and Thomas Jefferson Trice, right down to the naked woman on the cycle tank.

Except something was terribly wrong.

Charlie Carpool started moving his head around as if he were looking for help. He twisted the green baseball cap in his hands. He shuffled his feet back and forth on the floor. He cleared his throat. He did everything but talk.

And when the silence was finally over, this is what came out.

"Don't remember nothing, actually. Motorcycle come in the front door, up by Hixon, then start on down the street in there. I hear some guy screaming like a witch or somethin. Anyhow, I slipped on the grease. Next thing I know I'm in the hospital."

When David's tenth grade history class was studying the French Revolution, Ralph Robbins, sitting next to him, said that after people got their heads chopped off by the guillotine, their bodies got up and walked around. When David heard this, he got sick and had to go to the boy's room. Now, eighteen years later, this was the image in his brain, David Castelli, without a head, his body still asking questions through its neck, not yet realizing it was dead.

"Charlie, don't you remember meeting with me at your house last Friday?"

"Sure. Why?"

"Because I want you to tell the arbitrator exactly what you told me then about the accident."

"Just did."

"No, dammit, that isn't even close to what you told me Friday. What the hell's going on here?"

Professor van Auten looked over at Isaac Rothstein, waiting for the explosion. But there wasn't a sound from counsel table, just the best union lawyer in Philadelphia quietly watching one of the greatest moments in his professional life.

"Honest, Mr. Castelli. Nothing's going on. I'm telling you everything I remember. See my head ain't been right since the accident. I got good days, I got bad days. I can't help it none, really. I can't."

David stood up and grabbed his yellow pad, the one with the fax copy of Trice's ER record under the last sheet. It felt like there was a sewing needle pricking at his left temple. "Now," he said. "Right now. I want to see the arbitrator and union counsel in the hall."

He was out the double doors even before Rothstein could object. Castelli stood there, stiff as a board, his chest heaving up and down.

van Auten began. "What is this all about, Mr. Castelli?"

"I'll tell you what it's all about. Somebody is fucking with me in there and it's going to stop."

Rothstein said, "You'd better watch yourself, young man."

David was raging now, out of control. "Listen, you pompous sack of shit, I've had just about enough of you and your goddamned self-righteous indignation. And don't you ever call me young man, again, you understand."

"Please, David, get yourself under control." van Auten reached out and cupped his hand around Castelli's shoulder. "Now what seems to be the problem?"

"The problem. I'll tell you the problem. The problem is that someone's been tampering with my exhibits and playing games with my witness. And I don't care who knows it, either. Look, I got a copy of Trice's ER record yesterday. Don't ask me how, because I'm not going to tell you, and I don't give a shit how many bogus charges Mr. Rothstein here threatens me with, because none of them is equal to suborning perjury and tampering with documents."

"Are you accusing me of something, here, Mr. Castelli? Because if you are, you'll either back it up or I'll have you disbarred."

"Oh is that so? Somebody die and make you pope all of a sudden? Now listen to me, Professor. I don't know who did it, and right now I don't even care. But somebody got to that witness in there, I'm telling you. He's lying and he knows it. Good days and bad days, my ass. Less than one week ago that old man gave me details about August 20th that weren't even in the police report. This whole thing is a farce. And I'll tell you something else, the real ER report is the one I've got right here, the one with 'motorcycle accident' written all over it."

van Auten said, "How could you possibly know that, David? Look, you're just upset. Now, why don't you take a few minutes to calm down, then you can apologize to Mr. Rothstein and we'll all go back in as if nothing happened. Will that be all right, Isaac?"

"Absolutely not, Professor. I will not stand here and be libeled by an impudent pup like Mr. Castelli. He's just got another bad case. If he can't take it like a man, maybe he should go find himself another line of work."

"Like what, Isaac, representing whores?"

"You know, Castelli, if I were twenty years younger, we'd go outside right now. But I'm going back in that room, Professor van Auten. I am going to tell my clients that counsel is accusing Local 664 of criminal conduct in this case. And, quite frankly, it would not bother me one bit if someone in there took this little snot nose out back and rearranged his face."

van Auten was still trying. "No, Isaac, that is not what you are going to do. Not as long as I am conducting this hearing. Listen to me, David. You are totally out of line here. Totally. Mr. Rothstein and I are going to take a short walk outside. Give you a chance to calm down. Then we are going back in there to finish this arbitration, do you understand?"

David was trying to force himself to breathe normally. He measured out his words slowly, willing himself to stop cursing and start thinking again like a lawyer.

"All right, both of you. I'm sorry. I know I lost my temper and I apologize. But something is wrong in there. That ER record, the one Mr. Licata produced. That's just not the real thing. Think about it, Isaac. Please. You know there was a big OSHA case here not two years ago about those forklifts not having dead man switches. Then Harry got brand new ones. And they've got dead man switches. They don't just jump into gear and Trice knows it."

"So what are you telling us?" van Auten said.

"I don't really know what I'm telling you, Professor. Honest to god I don't. I just feel like I need some time."

David paused. He started mindlessly flipping the pages of his yellow pad, as if the answer to his nightmare lay buried somewhere in his notes.

Finally he said, "Look, give me a week, that's all. One lousy week. If I can't get to the bottom of this, the company will reinstate Mr. Trice with full back pay, full seniority and full benefits. And I will personally apologize to Mr. Rothstein."

"How about it, Isaac? Will you give him a week?"

Rothstein started shaking his head from side to side. "I'll agree to a continuance until Monday, not that it's going to matter. But I want counsel fees for the union."

"You know I can't order that, Isaac."

"Forget it, Professor," David said. "He wants the fucking counsel fees, he can have them. Company won't pay it, I'll write the check myself. You happy now, Mr. Rothstein?"

"No, I'm not happy, Mr. Castelli. I think you are a disgrace to the practice of law. You make me sick."

"In that case, Isaac, we both need mops."

SEVENTEEN
Wednesday, October 5

ROTHSTEIN STARTED IN EVEN before Werner was up the stairs, Isaac yammering behind Pete's right ear as the two men walked up the back steps to Pete's office.

"I want to know exactly what was going on in there, and I want to know now."

Werner ignored the lawyer until the two reached the corner office over Hixon Avenue and Werner settled in behind the huge glass-topped desk. Rothstein did not sit down, preferring instead a pestering, back-and-forth pace in front of the confused Secretary-Treasurer.

"Isaac, I don't have the faintest idea what you're talking about."

"Please, Peter, don't make a joke out of this. I've been trying labor arbitrations for over forty years. I've tried a hundred at least against that young man's very law firm, against him and his boss. They are careful people. They prepare their cases. They don't make fools out of themselves like that."

"So maybe the kid had a bad day, all right. You had a good one. What are you driving at, anyhow?"

Rothstein stopped pacing and sat down in the faded vinyl wing chair across from Werner's desk. Pete could see the saliva sheen start to form on the lawyer's lips.

"Peter, I did what I had to do in there. Because my job is to win cases, and if I can embarrass my opponent in public, put him off guard, then I do it.

But you know as well as I do that something very disturbing just went on in that basement. That young man put a witness on the stand who completely changed his story. That's obvious. And the medical report Licata produced—that was as phony as a three dollar bill."

"So."

"So I want to know what this union has to say about it. I've got a license to practice law, Peter. I support my family with that license. Castelli finds out Local 664 was fooling around with witnesses and changing documents, I won't be the one filing a charge with the disciplinary board. McKeon will gladly save me the trouble. Am I making myself clear?"

"Do I understand, Isaac, that you are accusing *me* of something here. Is that what's going on? Because if it is …"

"I'm not accusing anyone of anything. I just want to get to the bottom of it, that's all. Look, I know this case is important for the local, with the election coming up, so I just thought …"

"So you just thought I got to Carpool and made him change his story. Right?"

"I don't think anything of the sort. Peter. But Local 664's got a whole slate of officers on the payroll, and that whole slate's out of work in five months if Romanowski defeats you. I just want you to focus with me for a moment, think of the possibilities."

Werner had heard enough. He stood up from the desk and came around to the old wing chair. For the first time in his life, he was going to give Isaac Rothstein a lecture.

"You know something, Isaac. I've got half a mind to fire you right now. Do you have any idea how popular Charlie Carpool is with my members down the street? No, you don't. Because you only care about showing off how smart you are. Now, you had a great show down there this morning. Why don't you just leave it at that? Because I'll tell you something else. There's not one man on this board wants to see that bastard Trice put back to work—not one, and that especially includes me. He's drop dead guilty and you know it."

"Then who is doing this, Peter?"

"I don't have the foggiest idea, Isaac, unless maybe it's you. Could that be it? What do you think?"

"I am not even going to respond to such a statement."

"Oh, you're not, ey? Why is that, Isaac, because you're an attorney-at-law and I'm just an uneducated Teamster goon? Now you listen to me. This union had nothing to do with whatever's going on in this arbitration. And if you ever come in here again and accuse me—or anyone else on this board—of pulling a damn fool stunt like that, you will not only never represent this local again, you will never see a fee check from another Teamster union as long as you live. Now, get out of my office."

Isaac Rothstein stood up, his face ashen. He had made a terrible error in judgment, and for one of the few times in his life he had nothing whatsoever to say. He quietly turned and left the office, leaving Werner, who had now walked over to the window overlooking Hixon Avenue, as hurt and angry as the Secretary-Treasurer had ever been.

So this was definitely not the time that Pete wanted to look down at the parking lot of Jenny Rats and see David Castelli getting out of his car.

Castelli's first assault on the green metal door was direct. He almost bolted from the Honda, almost jogged across the lot, almost flew through the entrance like some ancient gunslinger entering a saloon. Then he stopped.

He stopped when he realized he had no idea what he was going to say. He was suddenly back in his row home on Tasker Street, seventeen years old, dialing the phone number of Laura Lynne Altomari, then hanging up before she could answer.

So now he was walking around his car, afraid that if he succumbed to the urge to get inside, he would simply drive away. And he could not allow himself to do that.

He forced himself to stop pacing, forced himself to lean against the side of the car, stiff arming the top of the driver's door just below the roof, his head hanging down between his shoulders. He stared at the ground so hard he could almost count the individual pieces of gravel. He made himself think.

The second assault on the bar door was deliberate and outwardly calm. David's head was up now, which was why Axel Kinnard, who had been throwing trash bags in Jenny's dumpster when Castelli's Accord roared into the parking lot, finally recognized the man he had been watching so intently.

"I thought I told you to stay the hell away from here."

David said nothing.

Axel put his body directly in David's path. "You don't listen too good, do ya?"

"I just want to see Jenny. I'm not looking for trouble."

"Oh, is that so? Well then why don't you just get your fancy lawyer butt back in the car. That way there won't *be* any trouble."

"I don't think so."

"You know, pal, you're a real brave boy for a jerk off." Axel held out his steel right arm. David stepped back.

"It's all right, Axel. Let him in." Jenny stood in the entrance, holding open the green metal door with its tiny window and its brass plaque, "Lifetime Oilless Bearing Company."

David said, "I need to talk to you. It's important."

They sat in the end booth, T. J. Trice's booth, Axel sulking behind the bar, wrestling a fresh half into place beneath the Bud tap.

"What are you doing here, David?" She kept her voice low, "You're supposed to be down the street."

"That's good, Jenny. Very good. So why don't you tell me what I'm supposed to be doing down the street, now that you flushed my whole case down the toilet?"

"What are you talking about?"

"Fine, Jenny. I'll play the game, if that's what you want. Just tell me one thing. When did your sister rewrite Trice's report, before or after you fucked my brains out?"

"She didn't rewrite anything. I swear it. Now what's going on?"

He wanted to believe Jennifer Alston DeLone. She looked genuinely shocked. She slid her hands across the table top, grabbing his tightly, bending forward to shield her movements from the eyes of Axel Kinnard.

David spoke first. "Did you look at that fax before you sent it?"

"Of course I looked at it. Why?"

"Because the report you sent wasn't the report that showed up with the witness."

"That can't be."

"Oh is that right?" David reached into his jacket pocket and pulled out the fax. "You see all this terrific stuff about a motorcycle accident? Well, guess what. The record I subpoenaed didn't say one goddamned word about a motorcycle. Not a word. It said Trice hurt his leg at work. A forklift ran him over!"

"For god's sake. Keep your voice down. He'll hear you."

"That's it? That's what you say to me, 'keep your voice down'? You realize what I'm telling you here? Somebody got into the computer system of Garden Spot General Hospital and rewrote a whole emergency room chart. And I'll tell you something else. Somebody got to Charlie Carpool too."

"David, you're paranoid. What's next? This whole thing is some big conspiracy to ruin your career? Hey, maybe it's me and Leslie. You know, scorned wife enlists aid of husband's lover."

"I don't find that very funny. And let me tell you something else, I'm still not so sure you didn't do it, so if I were you I'd stop making a big joke out of this."

Jennifer slid out from the booth, reached down and grabbed Castelli by the shirtsleeve. "I'm not going to sit here and let you accuse me of something I didn't do and don't know a thing about. So we're going outside, David. Right now. We're going to sit in your car and get this resolved like two civilized human beings."

"I'm sorry. I really am. It's just I don't know what the hell's going on here, that's all."

"Fine, then the two of us will go outside, where we can talk without hiding in the corner, and maybe we can figure it out."

They were in the car now, their arms down between the bucket seats, fingers intertwining, squeezing and stroking, while he told her what just happened in Building 102, Room 37C.

At the end, all she could say was. "I'm so sorry, David. It must have been awful. Can't you talk to Charlie, though? Find out why he did it?"

"The man was compromised, don't you see? He was fixed, altered, castrated. Call it whatever. Nobody just forgets an entire incident. Especially one he couldn't wait to tell me about less than a week ago."

"So what *do* you do?"

"I don't know. I'm trying to think."

"Well, how about the ER report? Suppose I got Bettina to set something up with the doc who examined Trice? At least that way you'd know which one was the real version."

"I'm pretty sure I *do* know. It was the cycle accident. But yeah, that would help. Nail it down, at least. You think she'd do it?"

"You tell me. She already made an unauthorized copy of a hospital record. I'll call her today."

Then David looked into her green cat's eyes, wrinkled at the corners by the passage of two score years and five, and saw something that made him uneasy. He could not have articulated what it was, had he been asked to do so, but he felt it just as strongly as if she had been wearing a sign around her neck. This is what the sign said: "There's something I'm not telling you."

"You know what separates a good lawyer from a not-so-good lawyer?"

"I thought we were talking about Dr. Gerhard."

"A good lawyer knows when to stop asking questions. But I'm not very good, see, so I'm going to ask you one more. What else do you know, Jennifer?"

There was an urgency in David's voice she had not heard before. At the same time, he was demanding with his mouth and begging with his eyes. She looked down at the car floor, avoiding his gaze. It was something Jennifer Alston DeLone almost never did.

"How well do you know Pete Werner?" She couldn't think of anywhere else to start.

"I don't know him, not really. We've had some arbitrations against each other—small talk after the hearings—that sort of thing. Busted my balls this morning but the script called for it. Tell the truth, he seems like a pretty decent guy."

"He's too decent a guy. And he's got his hands full with Dickie Romanowski."

"That fat piece of shit?"

"Yeah, well that fat piece of shit damn near started a riot at the last union membership meeting."

"McKeon showed me the newspaper article."

"And would you care to guess what that riot was all about?"

"I know what it was about. Trice."

"Right. Thomas Jefferson Trice. And now, he's got that ACLU creep, Brian O'Conner. Says he's suing the union if T. J. isn't reinstated."

"That's ridiculous," David said. "Do you have any idea what a bogus lawsuit that would be?"

"Doesn't matter. This isn't reality. This is union politics. After Twardzik, all Romanowski has to do is mention O'Conner's name and the drums start beating."

"Okay. So Werner's up against it. But, we're talking perjury here. We're talking tampering with evidence here. No way T.J. Trice is worth that much. And I want to know what you're holding back."

Jennifer could almost feel the words "Stuff Johnson" form in her brain, then transmit to her lips. It was that close. But when she opened her mouth, the two words were suddenly gone.

"I'm not holding anything back. You come over here like some kind of crazy man, accuse me of altering records. And now with the cross-examination. What do you expect from me, David?"

He did not answer.

"I'm talking to you, dammit," she said.

"I said I was sorry about blaming it on you. You wanna hear it again. I'm sorry. All right? But somebody was playing with my head down there. And don't tell me I'm crazy. So if it wasn't you, I've only got two choices left. One is Trice, and the other is your friend, Pete Werner. You got a preference?"

"You leave Pete out of this. There's no way."

"No way, what? No way a guy fighting for his own job wouldn't take a few chances? Meet with good old Charlie? Wave the Teamster flag? Maybe get one of the maintenance men at that hospital to fiddle with the computer? Local 664 represents those guys. You know he could do it."

"He *could* do it. But he *wouldn't* do it. Didn't I just ask you how well you knew Pete Werner? You said 'not very.' Well I *do* know him—very. I know him better than any human being on this earth, maybe even better than his own wife. The man turned that whole local around in less than two years." She gestured toward the building.

"And that makes him a saint?"

"No, it doesn't make him a saint. It just makes him a person who wouldn't forge a document or force a witnesses to lie under oath—job or no job."

David turned away from Jenny now and rested both of his hands on the steering wheel. He peered through the windshield, looking straight ahead, focusing on absolutely nothing. There was still something more she knew.

He remained in that position as he spoke.

"All right. Since you know him so well, answer me this. What would Werner do if he knew that someone *was* tampering with documents and witnesses. Another business agent, a member, Ike Rothstein for all I care. What would he do?"

"It's a hypothetical question."

"Not if I look him in the eye and tell him what I just told you."

"Why would you do a thing like that?"

"How about because I want to share my pain with a fellow human being? You tell me the guy's so damn honest, maybe he'd like to know the law's being broken like a dry twig in a forest, just to save the precious ass of Thomas Jefferson Trice. You think the great and honorable Pete Werner would like to know that?"

Jennifer had her hand on the car door by the time David had finished his answer. "I'll tell you what," she said. "Why don't we just forget the whole thing?"

"What are you talking about?"

"You know exactly what I'm talking about. The whole thing. The spilled drink, the ER records, the Lamplighter House, the damn J.E.B. Stuart suite. You just go back to your loving wife and your big deal job, and I'll go back in that door and run my bar."

He reached for her left arm, trying to hold her in the car. But she was too strong and jerked it free.

"Jennifer, please. Please get back in the car."

"I can hear you fine right where I'm standing. Just make it fast—I've got customers." She kept her right hand on top of the opened door, then leaned her head down under the sill, peering in at David, her eyes suddenly narrowed, her mouth no longer full because her lips were now curled in against her teeth.

"I'm not going to push you any more," David said. "I promise and I'm sorry. All I want is for you to think about what I said. I mean about Pete because I'm really not kidding. The man ought to know what's going on. People go to jail for this kind of stuff—particularly union leaders. All it takes is some little eager beaver in the US Attorney's office, starts sniffing around because hospital records got altered. I've seen it, Jenny. Picking on Teamsters is a national sport with those people."

"You really want to talk to Pete Werner about this?"

"You think of a better place to start?"

He saw some of the tension drain from her face. He was hoping she might get back in the car, so he could at least lean over and touch her hand. But she remained standing and out of reach.

"How about that doctor? You still want to talk to him?"

"Yes, very much."

"Then why don't you just start there? I'll call my sister and set it up for this afternoon, assuming the guy's on duty."

"And Werner?"

"Don't look at me, David. You're a big boy with a telephone."

Harry Greene pointed his silver revolver at a fresh Macanudo and pulled the trigger. He drew the smoke deeply into his lungs, then puffed it out toward the ceiling of his office, like an old humpback whale who had just surfaced for a blow. He was forcing himself to be outraged at the best news he'd heard in weeks.

"I don't want to discuss it, Joe. I really don't. I just want to know how the two of you are going to fix it, that's all."

"What do you mean, the two of *us*? It's the one of *him*, I'm telling you. Dumb kid couldn't find his ass with both hands. I don't know why the hell you let McKeon bail out on this one, Harry."

"I didn't let him bail out, dammit. He did it himself. Said he's in the middle of the Rapid Freight negotiations down in Marietta, so he didn't have time, but Castelli would be great, he said."

"Well, guess what? Castelli's a boob. Rothstein was all over him. Not that it mattered. We'd be in the shitter if the union had Donald Duck for a lawyer. About the only thing useful Castelli did all morning was get the damn thing stopped till Monday."

"What do you mean stopped?" Harry bit hard on the tip of his cigar.

"Right after our star witness couldn't remember what side of the bed he gets up on, Castelli about throws a fit and runs out in the hall. Next thing I know, van Auten comes back in and says we're off till next Monday. Not that it's going to matter any. Case's completely lost."

"Well, it can't be lost, Joseph. You understand that? We're not having that bastard back in here."

"Then you'd better get a real lawyer in there, Harry. And you'd better get him in there fast."

"I'll call Jack."

"You do that. Now, if you don't need me, I've got a warehouse to run."

"Fine."

Harry wrapped his large right hand around the telephone receiver and picked it up even before the door was completely closed. "Shelia, get me Jack McKeon. Tell him it's an emergency."

When she buzzed him on the intercom to say that Mr. McKeon was out of the office on a personal errand at the moment, Harry instructed Shelia to dial his beeper. What he actually said was, "Personal errand, my ass. Beep the sonofabitch, I know where he's at."

Jack McKeon returned the beeper call about a half hour later, Harry asking him if he was still in the saddle because the lawyer sounded out of breath.

"This had better be important, Harry."

"Breitenfeld just left my office. Does that surprise you?"

"I don't know, should it?"

"Should it! You better stop chasing teenage poon tang and start paying attention to business. Today is the Trice hearing, and it isn't even noon yet. So you tell me. Should I be surprised when my warehouse foreman, who's supposed to be downstairs in the most important labor arbitration of his life, plops himself down in front of me at 11:45?"

"Get to the point."

"The point is that your whiz kid, Castelli, managed to get the case continued until Monday. Now what the hell is going on?"

"I don't know what's going on, I wasn't there. Did Breitenfeld say anything else?"

"Oh yeah, the rest was terrific. Carpool could hardly remember his own name. And get this. Breitenfeld said that Castelli subpoenaed Trice's emergency room records, only Trice must have got 'em changed somehow 'cause the chart said he hurt his leg at work on one of my forklifts. Can you believe that?"

"So the company is going to lose, Harry. Just like I said. Now what's the problem?"

"I don't like the extra time, Jack. Who knows what that kid's gonna do?"

"Harry, he's not a magician. So he got five days; there's not a damn thing he's gonna be able to do, I don't care if he's got fifty-five days. It's a minor problem, Harry. A very minor problem."

"You sure?"

"Harry, use your head. Castelli lost his eyewitness this morning. Hell, he lost his only witness. van Auten's not going to care if the kid shows up Monday with the safe from the Titanic. It's a done deal."

———◦◦◦◦———

Shortly after 3:00 PM Castelli entered the emergency room of Garden Spot General Hospital and asked to see Dr. Marcus X. Gerhard.

The nurse on duty took him into a small conference room and told him to wait. The room was totally bare except for a brochure lying on the table. It was for some new drug to shrink prostates, so it had this picture of a big red water balloon with the end squeezed in a clothespin and some drops oozing out. The copy read: "This is how your patient with BPH feels." David suddenly had to go to the bathroom, except he couldn't, because just then the door opened and Dr. Gerhard came in, looking like someone was about to make him sniff garlic.

"Please make this fast, Mr. Castelli. I've got patients."

Dr. Gerhard didn't even sit down. He paced up and back on the other side of the conference table, open lab coat trailing behind him, lapels spotted with blood, stethoscope riding high in the side pocket. David took the ER report from his briefcase and laid it on the table.

"Doctor, I subpoenaed this document for a labor arbitration this morning. I was wondering if you could take a look at it."

Gerhard picked up the report and read it without comment. When he was finished, Castelli suddenly had the doctor's undivided attention. "Where did you get this?" Gerhard said.

"It was produced this morning by your supervisor of medical records."

"That's impossible, Mr. Castelli. This is not my report."

"You remember the patient?"

"Yes, I remember the patient. Said he fell off his motorcycle. Nothing about forklifts. Very unpleasant man."

"Doctor, I take it these ER reports are computerized?"

"They're entered by medical records. We don't save the originals any more. But there's no way anything like this could have been transcribed from my notes, I assure you."

"You have access to the computer?"

"Of course, every doctor on staff has access."

"Then I wonder if you would mind checking out this record."

"You're absolutely right I'm going to check it, Mr. Castelli. This is a very serious matter."

David followed Dr. Gerhard to the nursing station just outside the conference room. He tried to watch over the counter to see exactly how the computerized records were retrieved, but Gerhard's fingers were too quick on the keyboard.

Castelli said, "You have a PIN, I take it."

The doctor nodded his head in the affirmative. "Most of us just use our hospital ID number." Then he stood up. "I can't believe this. Somebody changed this report."

"That's exactly what I assumed, Doctor."

"You assumed? On what basis could you have possibly assumed that this report was inaccurate before you spoke to me just now?"

David recovered quickly. "I have other evidence that Mr. Trice was hurt on a motorcycle. Anyhow, that's not the point. What *is* the point, Doctor, is that I need you to testify next Monday about your meeting with Thomas Trice, and about what you actually did write on that ER report."

"Can't do it. We've got privacy issues here."

"Is that so? Well, we've also got record tampering issues here, so I'm just going to have to subpoena you."

"Do as you wish, sir. But I'm not going to violate anyone's privacy, I'm telling you that now."

"That's too bad, Doctor, because it sure looks like somebody violated yours."

Marcus X. Gerhard had no response.

Two minutes later, trying to balance his file on the tiny ledge below the pay phone in the ER, David was talking to Carol Highsmith at the American Arbitration Association offices in Philadelphia.

"Another subpoena?" she said. "This must be an important case."

"Carol, you don't even know how important."

"That big, huh?"

"Yeah, that big."

"Funny, then, you guys would pick van Auten."

"Don't start me on that subject, Carol. All the cases our office sends you people, you could at least look at those lists before you send them out."

"What are you talking about, that was a good list, David. I made it up myself."

"Greene-Pitowsky and Trice? A good list? Who are you kidding? After Rothstein got finished striking the guys he thinks McKeon owns, and Jack knocked off Rothstein's three musketeers, van Auten was the best thing left. You couldn't have planned it better if the professor was your brother-in-law."

"What about Merten Jorgenson? Nobody owns him. He's the best arbitrator in the city."

"Okay. What about him?"

"Well, Rothstein didn't strike Merten, did he?"

"How could he? Merten wasn't on the list."

"David, yes he was."

"I saw the list, for god's sake. Jack McKeon showed it to me in his office. Merten Jorgenson was not on it."

"You're crazy. I'm looking at the list right now."

In one fluid motion, David let go of the receiver, the headset now hanging down by its cord from the phone, swinging back and forth, and simultaneously spilled the entire contents of the Trice file on the ER floor. He dropped to his knees, rifling through the papers until he had the AAA list. Then he tilted up his head and spoke into the dangling receiver, while the voice on the other end was saying, "David, are you there?"

"Yes, yes I'm here. Who else is on that list?"

"You know who's on it, David."

"Don't argue with me, Carol. Just read the names."

"Okay, but you've got it right there. Felix Gomberger, Oliver Winthrop, Merten Jorgenson, Stuart Blevinsky, Arlene Cohen, G. Arnold van Auten and Triana Smythe."

"What about Scott Mund and Victoria Pershing?"

"For goodness sake, David, you think I'd put all *three* of Rothstein's favorites on the same list. That wouldn't be fair—even to a lawyer as good as you. Is something going on there?"

"No, nothing. Look, Carol, just get the subpoena ready for Dr. Gerhard. I'll send someone over first thing in the morning."

Then David cradled the phone and thought about throwing up.

EIGHTEEN
Thursday, October 6

DAVID HAD GOTTEN TO work at 7:30 AM. There were two reasons he came in early. The most important reason was so he could get out of the house with his overnight bag packed before Leslie got up and started asking a lot of questions. The other reason was to avoid even the slightest chance that Jack McKeon might see him before David could get into Castelli's Lanes, shut the door, and hang the "Do Not Disturb—Genius At Work" sign on the knob.

He had tried to formulate some sort of a plan, but he was simply too distracted to concentrate on anything except the bizarre events of the past twenty-four hours. The packed overnight bag and one night reserved at the Sleep-Tite Motor Lodge (he was on his own money now) were as close to strategy as David Castelli could get.

His first thought after talking to Carol Highsmith at AAA on Wednesday was that McKeon was trying to screw him out of partnership. The only problem was that there was no reason for this, not even within the byzantine sociology of McKeon, Tingham & Marsh. But then, all the other motives seemed even more preposterous. So this morning he had started his own investigation.

The screen on his computer went briefly black, then blue, then filled itself with data. Six columns: Client Number, Client Name, Matter Name, File Number, File Location, Fees Received to Date. David had to tap the "page down" key five times before the file reached its end.

It was Jack McKeon's 1994 client manager list. Not a document ordinarily accessible by an associate—unless that associate happened to know the partner's secret password. Castelli did.

David spoke out loud to himself, in a stage whisper even though no one else was there. "Look at the year this guy's having. Two months to go and he's already got 2.8 million in the book." He pressed the print key on his computer, then got up from the maroon leather chair, opened the office door and walked quickly down the hall to his shared printer. He arrived just as the "ready" light started to blink and 2.8 million dollars worth of billings began sliding out on five single-spaced pages.

Back in his office, David immediately started running his index finger down the list of clients. He reached the next to last page before he saw an entry that stopped him:

NUMBER	CLIENT	MATTER	FILE LOC.	FEES
02836	ORTHO. ASSOC. OF LANCASTER	BREWSTER V	L-781 KK	$64,228.96

A sex discrimination case. Claudia W. Brewster, MD, had been the rising star of Orthopedic Associates of Lancaster, and a gifted young surgeon. The only trouble was that her boss kept confusing Dr. Brewster's bedside manner with her bedroom manner. When her staff privileges at Garden Spot General Hospital were suddenly stripped following an allegedly botched hip replacement operation, she sued Orthopedic Associates for sexual harassment and the hospital for assorted anti-trust violations.

Castelli had paid little attention to the case when it came in. He didn't do very much EEOC work, didn't particularly like it. Besides, he figured McKeon would give the matter to Kenneth Kaye, which is exactly what happened. From what David could remember being said at Labor Department meetings, the case was presently bogged down in some sort of discovery battle. Castelli figured Kenneth Kaye hadn't touched the file in months. Not that such inactivity caused the fees to stop rolling in.

When David had gone to retrieve his printout a few minutes earlier, not a single light was on, except in the hall. So he took the chance and slipped quietly into Kaye's office. *Brewster v. Orthopedic Associates of Lancaster et al.* was tucked against the wall on the floor to the left of the desk chair.

Unlike David's files, which were usually filled with random pieces of paper in no apparent order, Kaye's were the work of a true obsessive compulsive. Each file contained carefully prepared folders, divided by topics: Correspondence, Pleadings, Briefs and Memoranda, Research, KK's Notes, Client's Papers. It was in the last of these that Castelli found the complete personnel file of Claudia W. Brewster, MD. Stapled to the inside of the dark red file jacket was the plastic ID card that Dr. Brewster had been forced to surrender on her last day at Garden Spot General.

She was a pretty woman even in a mug shot. Blond hair tightly curled into ringlets, a broad smile showing white teeth. And under the picture, the vital statistics: "Brewster, C.W., Orthopedic Surg., M.I. #6611."

Castelli stared down at the plastic card, his mouth suddenly dry. He remembered where Jack McKeon's "Out of Office" memo had said the senior partner was on Tuesday, October 4, 1994: Rapid Freight labor negotiations, Marietta, Pennsylvania.

Back in his office, David forced himself to lean in his chair, trying to relax. He felt the morning sun, warm through the window glass behind him now, as it slowly climbed over the Northeast quadrant of the skyline. It was the only part of downtown Philadelphia still stunted by the old rule that nothing could be constructed higher than the statue of William Penn atop City Hall. To the west, the rule had toppled years ago before an avalanche of new towers; but the east—a collage of class B buildings filled with plaintiffs' lawyers, and cluttered stores selling Walkman knockoffs and pizza by the slice and Doc Johnson's Love Products—remained capped at five hundred feet. So the sun could still bake the north windows of the Lincoln Building even before 10:00 AM.

It took several minutes, but his forced break eventually started to work; David actually thought, for a moment, about forgetting the whole affair and just getting back to work. He remembered a John Grisham novel he had read the previous summer, about an associate who discovered his whole law firm was a Mafia money-laundering operation. He had laughed to himself about how preposterous the plot was—this lawyer running up and down the Florida coast at the end, hiding in sleazy motels so the Mafia wouldn't kill him, or worse yet, so the partners in his own firm wouldn't kill him. Yet now, here was David Castelli, convincing himself that a labor arbitration was actually part of some diabolical scheme to wreck his career. What did he think was coming next? A dead body in the office coat closet? It was madness. All of it. He would kick himself for sure, especially when it all turned out to be just a bunch of trivial coincidences, and plain, old-fashioned bad luck.

He kept that thought for at least ten seconds. Then the door to his office opened—without a knock despite the sign on the knob—and Jack McKeon walked in.

"You jerking off in here?" McKeon stood before the desk, absentmindedly playing with Castelli's stapler, then with the pencils in the leather cup next to his blotter, lifting them up and letting them drop on their points, one by one, back into their container.

"You're in awful early, Jack. Can't read signs, either."

"Just thought I'd check on my favorite associate. You busy?"

"Yeah, but it'll wait. What's up?"

Jack McKeon sat down, crossing his legs and cupping his left knee in two perfectly manicured hands, poking out from starched french cuffs held together with gold links. McKeon's Irish blues looked over the tops of his reading glasses. "So how'd it go yesterday?"

"Went fine. You know, usual crap from Rothstein. Gotta go back next week to finish, but I'll be okay." Castelli had made the decision to lie without even thinking.

"Good. That makes me feel a lot better, because when I talked to Harry yesterday afternoon, he said you had quite a rough time down that basement with our friend."

"Harry wasn't there."

"I know. Breitenfeld told him."

"And what, may I ask, *did* Breitenfeld tell him?"

"I wouldn't worry about it. Probably bullshit anyhow. Guy doesn't have enough brains to come out of the rain."

"Well I *do* worry about it, Jack. These days I worry about everything. What did Harry tell you Breitenfeld said?"

"That double hearsay or triple hearsay?"

"It's triple, Jack. But this isn't a courtroom. It's only my very narrow office. Now what did the guy say to Harry Greene?"

"That Carpool changed his whole story on the stand and you threw some kind of fit."

"Anything else?"

"No. Isn't that enough?"

"He's absolutely right, Jack. And you would have been proud of me. Best damn fit I ever threw. Just like you taught me. Witness starts getting shaky, call time out. Right?"

"Okay. So what's the punch line?"

"The punch line is Carpool got flustered, that's all. Guy got his brain scrambled by a metal table. So he was nervous. I bought him some time. He'll be fine by next Monday."

"You know, that's exactly what I told Harry Greene. I said, 'Harry, if David Castelli threw a fit, he had a reason to throw a fit. So just stop worrying.'"

"That's what you told him? Really?"

"I was right, wasn't I?"

"Absolutely."

McKeon had reached the door of Castelli's Lanes when he turned and said, "Good luck, Monday. You want this open or shut."

"Leave it open."

David took the plastic penis out of his center desk drawer, wound it up and let it start hopping around the desk. He was saying "motherfucker" over and over, just beneath his breath, alternately emphasizing the "mother," then the "fucker."

Accepting the fact that Jack McKeon—his mentor, his teacher, his one lifeboat in the unpredictable hurricane of McKeon, Tingham and Marsh politics—had betrayed him, was even more difficult than trying to figure out why. But now there could be no doubt. If Breitenfeld really had talked to Harry Greene, he certainly wouldn't have stopped with Carpool's sudden loss of memory. He would have also told his boss about the hospital records. So, either way, Jack McKeon had been sitting there lying. And, either way, the novel plot was suddenly real again.

While all this stuff was racing through his brain, David's plastic penis had hopped off the desk and fallen to the floor on the other side. Castelli suddenly remembered that it was lying there, in full view of anyone who might happen to stroll by the now open door. With his luck, it would be

Jocelyn Marsh. He quickly got up and retrieved the little pink toy, slid open the center drawer and pushed it in as far as it would go—which caused his arm to stretch out, which brought his head down toward the desk, which allowed his eyes to focus on a single yellow post-it note stuck to the wood. The note, in his own handwriting, said: "Hundred grand *and* job. Think he wants me to murder Johnson. You have to help me here."

She answered on the seventh ring.

"Jennifer, it's David. Did I wake you?"

"I don't know, I'm not up yet."

"I realize it's early, but I have to talk to you. This is important."

"It's 8:15 in the morning, David. I run a bar for a living, or did you forget that?"

"I'm sorry. Really. Should I call you back?"

"The hell with it, I'm up now."

"Look, I'm gonna get right to the point. You remember me asking you yesterday what you were holding back. You do remember that, don't you?"

"Yes David, I remember that."

"Well I'm going to ask you again now. Only this time I'm going to give you a secret word to help jog your memory. You ready? The secret word is Johnson. J-o-h-n-s-o-n. Now what the hell are you holding back from me?"

Jenny had been lying under the covers with the phone receiver resting on the pillow next to her ear. Now she sat up straight, the blanket falling, leaving her naked from the waist up. She reached for the receiver, suddenly conscious of the morning cold on her upper body, in a bedroom still dark from the black shades that she drew each night so she could sleep till noon.

David spoke again. "You there, Jenny?"

"Let me get a robe on and open the blinds."

When she returned to the phone fifteen seconds later she was ready. "David, I don't know what you're talking about. Johnson. That supposed to be some kind of code word?"

"No, it's supposed to be somebody mixed up in the Trice case. You want to hear about it? Maybe it'll refresh your recollection."

"Do I have a choice?"

"No actually, you don't. So pay attention. The senior partner in my firm, his name's Jack McKeon, I'm sure you've heard of him. He's the one trying to make me lose the Trice case. I haven't the slightest idea why, but I know he's involved."

"You're serious, aren't you?"

"Jenny, I couldn't make this up if I tried. Now listen. He fixed the list of arbitrators so the company would have to choose van Auten. Don't worry about how, just trust me, he did it. And I'm also about ninety-nine percent sure McKeon's the one who changed the hospital records; I just can't figure out how the sonofabitch knew I'd subpoenaed them."

"The head of your law firm got into Garden Spot General's computer system? How could he do that?"

"Simple. He's representing an outfit called Orthopedic Associates of Lancaster in a sex harassment case where the plaintiff is a former surgeon at the hospital. Claudia Brewster. He's got her whole damn personnel file, right down to her ID card with her ID number. Right after I left you Wednesday, I went to see that self-righteous resident who took care of Trice. Anyhow I watched him log into the computer system; he said most of the docs use their hospital ID number as an access code. Now here's the best part. Guess where my dear mentor, Mr. McKeon, happened to be on the day before the arbitration?"

"Don't tell me, Lancaster?"

"Close. How about Marietta. What's that, twenty miles away? Plenty of time to buzz over to the hospital, where they know him from the Brewster case because they've been sued in it too. And I'll tell you what really cinched it. Whoever changed Trice's ER record knew enough about Greene-Pitowsky forklifts to know that they used to slip into gear—only not enough to know that Harry just replaced them all with lifts that have dead man switches so they can't slip into gear anymore."

"And McKeon had that knowledge?"

"The knowledge *and* the lack of knowledge. He knew about the damn things slipping into gear from an OSHA case he won for the company about two years ago; but he obviously didn't know Greene replaced them all *after* he won the case. Which brings me to Mr. Johnson."

"What made me think we'd eventually get back to that?"

"I was in the office on Labor Day, what's that four, five weeks ago, right after Trice got fired. No one was there but me, and the phone starts ringing next door in McKeon's office. I figure I'll go answer it, you know, maybe it's some client with an emergency and I'll get brownie points. So I get in there just as the damn phone mail clicks on. I pick it up to see if I can help and there's this guy screaming like a lunatic, saying all kinds of crazy shit about money and a job; then all of a sudden he starts talking about murdering somebody named Johnson."

"Jesus."

"That's good, sweetheart. 'Jesus' is a good start. Anyhow, it was really weird, me listening to this stuff, you know, so after the guy hangs up I go back to my office and write down some notes on a post-it and I stick it to the bottom of my desk drawer. Only I forget all about it. Then this morning, while I'm sitting here trying to make some sense out of why Jack McKeon is trying to ruin me, I happen to pull my desk drawer open and I see the post-it again. But now it means something—or at least I think it means something, because the whole phone message could have been about the Trice case, you get it? And if there's somebody named Johnson involved, then I'm sure it was about the Trice case, and your Mr. Johnson, whoever he is, could be in some real trouble."

David stopped talking. He was almost out of breath from the length and speed of his monologue. Now he waited to see how—or if—Jennifer Alston Delone would respond.

Her voice was soft but still unhesitant despite its low volume. "His name is Steven Johnson; everyone calls him Stuff. He was in the bar with Trice the night of the accident."

"I knew it!" Castelli pounded the desk top with his left fist. "I gotta see the guy today. You gotta set it up."

"You kidding? The guy's in the bargaining unit, David. He's a brother. What am I supposed to do? Go up to him—assuming I can find him in the first place—and say, 'Yo Stuff. How 'bout me setting you up with the company lawyer so you can rat out T. J. Trice?' That gets out, I'll be lucky to have a single customer left."

"But the guy's in trouble. Don't you understand that?"

"Let me tell you something," Jenny answered. "This is a factory town.

Give me a nickel for every death threat I've heard in the last ten years, I retire to Tahiti. Besides, you don't know it's the same Johnson. You don't even know who the guy was who called your boss."

"Does it matter? Whoever called McKeon thought a guy named Johnson was supposed to be murdered. Don't you think that's enough so your Stuff Johnson oughta at least know about it?"

"Then you talk to him, David. Just don't get me involved. Ask your friend Breitenfeld to set it up."

"And how would you like me to start after my friend Breitenfeld sets it up? 'Yo Stuff. I'm the company lawyer and I'm here so you can rat out T. J. Trice?' You think you'd lose customers? I'd lose worse than that."

"But not if I set it up. Is that it?"

"At least you know the guy."

"David, I know a couple hundred guys work down the street. So what? I run a bar for god's sake; I'm not the pope of Local 664."

"No, you're not. But Pete Werner may be."

"Now what am I hearing? You want me to get Werner involved in this too. I think you really are crazy."

"Okay, Jennifer, I'm going to try one more time. So please listen, all right?"

"I'm listening."

"Look, I'm not saying I'm the most experienced lawyer in the world, but I've tried a ton of labor arbitrations. These things aren't exactly candidates for Court TV, you get it? They're Dodge City justice down some basement or in some crummy motel room. Most of 'em take about three hours, somebody wins and somebody loses. No big deal. So all of a sudden I go into this ordinary discharge case, and what happens? The senior partner of my law firm doctors up the Triple A list so I get a turkey like van Auten instead of the best arbitrator in town; then he breaks into the computer system of a major hospital and alters records; and my star witness can't remember his own name. This is crazy stuff, Jennifer. This is *not* business as usual—even in Dodge City."

"All right, it's not like Dodge City. But what's all this have to do with Pete Werner?"

"It doesn't have to do with Pete Werner. It has to do with me. It has to do with me not wanting to lose this case three months before I'm up for partnership, I don't care what Jack McKeon's up to. And Werner can help me. You say he's your best friend. All I've heard from you is how honest this guy is. So maybe he'd like to know his union's winning because somebody's breaking the law."

Jennifer was finished dressing. She wasn't listening before. Castelli was right. She was listening now.

"I almost told him myself," she said. "That make you feel better?"

"It's a start. Keep talking."

"Pete knows there's another witness. He just doesn't know who it is. There's this guy works in the furnace room. Name's Henry Pelletier. Anyhow, Pete told me Henry got up at the union meeting, just before the fight broke out, and said someone else was with Trice when he ran down Charlie, only he wouldn't say who it was. You know, Teamster loyalty. Don't ask me how he knew, but Pete says he's absolutely sure Pelletier was telling the truth. Fact, Pete went down to see the guy at the plant, alone. Tried to get him to talk, but it didn't work."

David said, "And you think the witness is this guy Stuff Johnson?"

"Makes sense. For one thing, Johnson actually hangs out with Trice. That puts him in pretty select company just by itself. Then we get Pelletier saying there really is another witness, and I see Stuff leave my place with T. J. right before Charlie gets hit. You tell me."

"Then, why didn't you tell Werner? What kind of a friend are you?"

"Too good a friend, David."

"What do you think, you're his mother?"

"A little. I just kept asking myself. What possible good would it be for me to tell him about Stuff Johnson? It would twist him into a pretzel. This way, he doesn't know anything, Trice wins the case, union looks good to the members. So I keep quiet."

"Except now there's me in the soup too, isn't there?"

"Yes, dammit, now there's you."

"So what are you going to do?"

She stood up from the bed, twisting the phone cord round and round her right index finger until she could feel it beginning to cut off her circulation. "You know exactly what I'm going to do, don't you?"

"I'll be at the Rat by noon." Then he added, "I love you, Jennifer De-Lone."

"We had a great dinner and great sex. Don't rush it."

⸺∘⦾∘⸺

As David Castelli was hanging up with Jenny, Jack McKeon, in the office next door, was putting his caller on hold, just long enough to tell his secretary that he was not to be disturbed.

"Charlie Carpool did good, Jack. Real good. 'Cept your boy thinks he's some kinda fucking Perry Mason."

"You mean the continuance? Don't worry about it."

"Oh, I assure you *I'm* not worrying about it. What I want to know is whether *you're* worrying about it. He finds out about Johnson this weekend, you and your war buddy could be in some very deep shit—you do realize that, don't you?"

"There's no way Castelli finds out about Johnson. Besides, even if he does, so what? You think that guy's gonna talk to a company lawyer?"

"Hey pal, it don't matter what I think. It ain't my problem."

"Then why do you care if I'm worrying about it?"

"Jack, you hurt me Jack. You don't think I care about you? Of course I care about you. I'm calling you at 8:30 in the morning, way before my usual rising time, just because I *do* care about you. Besides, I wanted to congratulate you on the bit with the hospital records. Very clever."

"What makes you think Greene didn't do it?"

"Because he's too dumb. Just tell me one thing, though. How did you know your boy subpoenaed those records in the first place?"

"Castelli left a phone slip from the Garden Spot General ER on his desk. His stupid secretary wrote down Eeyore instead of ER. You know, the donkey from Winnie the Pooh. I swear, she's about the dumbest woman on the planet. Fabulous ass, though."

"I was interested, Jack. But I'm not that interested."

NINETEEN
Thursday, October 6

PETE WERNER REACHED ACROSS the top of his desk and grabbed a cigarette lighter that was in the shape of a golf ball.

"Rothstein gave this to me. I use it to help members get ready for grievance hearings. Wanna see how it works?"

"What's this got to do with Stuff Johnson?" Jenny DeLone was beginning to regret the whole episode.

"Member comes in all upset. I gotta take him to a grievance hearing down the dungeon where Irene Henderson can mess with his brain. So I say to the guy, 'See this. Now that's a golf ball, isn't it?' What do you say?"

Jennifer took the object from Werner. She had no idea what in the world he was getting at. She placed the lighter in her lap, then folded her hands across it, then said nothing.

"Well, come on. Pretend you're the member. Irene Henderson hands you this thing and says 'Now that's a golf ball, isn't it?' What's your answer?"

"For Chrissake, Pete. I'm talking about a serious problem and you're playing with toys."

"Just answer the question, Ms. DeLone. That's a golf ball, isn't it?"

Jennifer shrugged her shoulders and said, "No, it's a lighter. You happy now?"

"I'm thrilled. You flunked the test. See, you didn't just give me the answer; you went ahead and gave me more than the answer—just like the member's gonna do when Irene starts on him down the dungeon. All I said was, 'That's a golf ball, isn't it?' But you went and said 'No, it's a lighter.' 'Cept I didn't ask you what it *was*, did I? You volunteered that. Right answer's just plain 'no.' Then you shut up. Now, you want to know why I just gave you that test?"

"I can't wait."

Pete Werner stood up, pounded his fist down on the desk as hard as he could, then shouted at his landlady, full volume. "So that the next time I ask you what David Castelli was doing downstairs yesterday not one hour after that joke of an arbitration, you give me a goddamn straight answer!"

"You don't have to raise your voice, Pete. I had an old boyfriend used to do that whenever he got mad. Thought it would scare me. Made me laugh actually."

Werner sat back, deep into his oversized fake leather chair, his shoulders hunched down, along with his chin, which made him look like a puppy who just got caught doing his business on the rug. Jenny let him stew in the silence long enough to make sure the childishness of his outburst had sunk in. Then she released the tension.

"This is hard for me, Pete. I'm not kidding. So just sit there and listen and don't say anything, okay?"

"Deal."

"Castelli was downstairs having a fit because Trice's ER records got switched. He got to see the real ones before he actually subpoenaed them."

Werner let a stream of air whistle quietly through his teeth. "Who does *he* know?"

"No one. My sister got them."

"Your what?"

"My sister. Bettina. She's a head nurse at Garden Spot. I asked her to fax T. J.'s chart to Castelli. He was having his fit because he thought I set him up."

Werner stared straight ahead. He had made a deal; he wouldn't raise his voice. He knew that if he said a word, he would welsh on that deal. So he just sat there and stared over the right shoulder of Jennifer Alston DeLone, focusing on the blue and gold Teamster Horse & Wheel banner mounted on the far wall of his office, between the twin oil paintings of John F. Kennedy and International President O'Dwyer.

When he finally rose from the desk, he walked past the motionless figure in the chair to the closed door of his office. He held it open. Jenny turned in her seat. She could see the knuckles of Pete Werner's large left hand, straining white around the knob. She started to cry.

"Don't do that," he said. "Just get out."

If he had not spoken, if he had stood there at the open door for even a few seconds longer, Jennifer would have left. But he did speak. And that is what gave her the strength.

Now she was the one with her voice raised. "No, I will not get out!" She was out of the chair and around it, almost up against him now, shoving his office door shut with a loud crack that echoed down the narrow second floor corridor of 4641 Hixon Avenue and down the back stairs to the bar, making Axel Kinnard snap his neck around from the table where he sat, playing solitaire.

She pulled his hand off the doorknob, jerking on his arm as she spoke. "You think this is some kind of game here. Well it's not. We're done playing good guys and bad guys. Don't you understand? This has nothing to do with David Castelli or the holy Brotherhood of Teamsters. This is about somebody's life for god's sake."

"You're hysterical."

"No, I'm not hysterical. I'm just angry. You know what it took for me to come up here? Tell you what's going on in this crazy arbitration you got? Tell you there's a guy out there someone's talking about murdering? That happens, there'll be cops all over this place. You won't get re-elected dog catcher."

"All right. All right. Just tell me about you and David Castelli."

"There's nothing to tell. He came in the bar last week, we started talking, he asked me out to dinner, I went."

"And the next thing you know, you're helping him win the Trice case? What do you think I am, stupid?"

"No, and you're not my father, either. I'm forty-five years old. What I do on my time is my goddamn business."

"Not when you're fucking with my goddamn business."

"Okay. I helped the guy because he was down. Maybe I felt sorry for Charlie Carpool. But I wasn't trying to hurt you. You gotta know that.

Anyhow, none of it matters now."

"Why, because you've gone and convinced yourself that someone is going to murder Stuff Johnson?"

"That's not enough?"

"Jenny, you got nothing. Think, for chrissake."

"I am thinking, Peter. I'm thinking that T. J. Trice is one tick away from a psychopath. I'm thinking the biggest labor lawyer in Philadelphia is throwing a case for his biggest client. I'm thinking a guy named Johnson is about the only person left who can keep that case from being thrown, and I'm thinking somebody's leaving phone messages for Jack McKeon about murdering a guy named Johnson. Don't you think that's enough?"

Werner slowly picked up the phone and dialed the number of Greene-Pitowsky Smelting & Battery Company. "Lemme speak to Larry Douglas. He's over the warehouse."

Jenny also returned to her chair. She listened to Pete's end of the conversation with his chief steward.

"Larry, Pete Werner ... Not bad. You know, Rapid Freight negotiations. Jerks'll start moving five minutes before midnight on the last day. Listen, Stuff Johnson there? ... Damn. When's that, two? ... Okay. I'm gonna try him at home, but just in case I miss him, I want you to wait for him before you leave. Tell him to call the hall. It's important ... Yeah, you too."

Then he turned to Jenny. "He's working second shift. Won't be in till two."

"I gather. Problem is David's going to be here by noon."

"What are you talking about, he's coming here?"

"I didn't have a lot of choice. He wants to talk to Stuff."

"And I'm supposed to broker this deal, is that it?"

"Pete, please. Indulge me, okay? Just do it."

———◦◦◦◦———

The woman who opened the front door of Stuff Johnson's tiny Cape Cod house had once been pretty. David could see the traces of high cheekbones buried under years of accumulating fat. And the eyes were still ice blue, though bloodshot and surrounded by puffy skin. She had on purple stretch leggings, the kind designed to accentuate the saddle bags hanging from each thigh, her waistline hidden under a black t-shirt. On the shirt, a woman riding a Harley and the legend "Zero to Bitch in Five Seconds."

David spoke first. "Mrs. Johnson?"

"Don't tell me." She scanned the people on her porch as she counted out loud. "One, two, three, four. Four people. Middle of the day." Her voice rising now, almost to a shriek. "I won something, didn't I? You're that–that–whatchamacallit. Publisher's Clearing House. Ed McMahon's out there in the car, isn't he? I can't believe it. Oh my god."

She turned before Castelli could say a word. "Stuff, come out here, quick. We won a million dollars! Oh my god."

"Mrs. Johnson, please. We're not from Ed McMahon."

The t-shirt was wrong. She reached bitch in two seconds.

"Then who the hell are you?"

Pete Werner stepped around the lawyer and held out a large right hand to his union member's wife. "Mrs. Johnson, I'm Pete Werner from the Teamsters. Is Stuff at home?"

"Oh my god, he's been laid off."

"No, Mrs. Johnson. We just want to talk to him."

"What about, he's not in trouble down there, is he?"

"He's fine, really. We just want to talk to him about Thomas Trice."

"I knew it. I just knew it." She began shaking her head back and forth, her long dirty-blonde hair swinging like a pendulum as she spoke. "I told him to stay away from that bastard. He's no good. I knew it, I knew it, I knew it."

Pete carefully put his hand on the woman's shoulder. "Mrs. Johnson, please. Your husband is not in any trouble, I promise."

"Then what are you all doing at my house?"

"We just have to talk to Stuff. Is he home?"

"He's out back working on his motorcycle. Watch the mud."

He was down on his haunches, facing the Sportster, his back to them as they rounded the rear of the Cape Cod just as he yelled, "Motherfucker!" He was cursing at the aftermarket S&S Super E carburetor that had just slipped out of his greasy hand.

"Hey Stuff."

Johnson turned at the sound of his steward's voice. "Larry, what the hell ..." Then he saw the entourage. "Jenny? Pete Werner?" He stood up, wiping his hands down the front of his jeans so he could greet the Secretary-Treasurer.

"Sorry to bother you at home, Stuff, but we have to talk to you. Your wife said you were out back."

"Shit. I've been laid off."

Werner laughed. "Jesus. First your old lady, now you? No, you haven't been laid off. Everything's fine."

Stuff sat down in one of the green metal chairs that ringed a green metal lawn table that was listing to starboard from one of its tube legs sinking into the soft earth. "We don't get union brass here every day, you know. I guess she figured same as me. Getting near contract time. Greene's gotta look poor, so he lays a bunch of guys off."

"Well he might do that. Just not yet. Stuff, this here is David Castelli. He's a lawyer for Harry Greene."

"Wait a minute. You brought a company whore into my house? What are you, nuts?" Stuff looked at David. "'Scuse me counselor, nothin personal."

"Don't worry about it." David reached down to shake Johnson's hand as Pete started to explain.

"Listen, Stuff. I know this is a little unusual. Kinda surprised me, myself. But I think you should hear what the man has to say. Might be for your own good."

"Yeah, right."

Pete motioned for David to sit down at the table, then he turned to the lawyer. "All right, Mr. Castelli, here he is. Just don't waste the man's precious time, okay?"

David said to Stuff, "I take it you know who I am?"

"Yeah, I know who you are. You're the one trying to dump T. J. 'Cept I heard now it's the other way round."

"You're right, Mr. Johnson. But do you know why?"

"Yeah, 'cause Ike the Kike's tearing you a new asshole."

"It isn't that simple. Now I want you to listen to me, because this is very serious stuff. You may be in danger."

"Pete, what's going on here?"

"Look, Stuff," said Werner. "I know it sounds crazy, but I'm here, aren't I? I brought Castelli with me, didn't I? And Jenny and Larry, didn't I? So just give the man a chance."

David started using his time before Johnson could answer.

"Trice's case is being fixed by the head lawyer in my firm. Probably someone from the company too, but I haven't figured out who yet."

"Now I know you're crazy."

"Look, Mr. Johnson, I don't know what it's going to take to get you to believe me, but why don't we start with the fact that I'm here."

Jenny spoke now for the first time. "The man isn't kidding, Stuff. Just listen to him."

"What, you too?" Stuff picked up the carburetor and started playing idly with it. Castelli went back to work.

"About a week after Trice got fired, I accidentally picked up a phone message that someone left for my boss, Jack McKeon. He's a senior partner in my firm. Whoever was on the line knows you were a witness to what went down with Charlie and he's going to make sure you don't testify. Are you following me?"

"I don't know what you're talking about, counselor. I didn't witness nothing."

"Well I think you did, Stuff. But that doesn't matter. What matters is that someone was talking to Jack McKeon about having you killed. Now do I have your attention?"

Johnson put down the carburetor. Suddenly, the arrogance was gone from his body language, the edge gone from his speech. "Killed? Over a crummy forklift job?"

"I think it's more than a crummy forklift job. Follow me here. van Auten wasn't supposed to be the arbitrator. My boss doctored the Triple A list. Then he got Trice's emergency room records changed, and I know somebody did a number on Charlie Carpool between the time I prepped him to testify and the day of the hearing. Trouble is, I don't have the slightest idea what *is* going on. I figured maybe you did, so I'm here to find out."

Jenny spoke again. "Nobody wants to see you get hurt, Stuff, but you were with Trice the night Charlie got run over. The two of you left my bar together. It's gonna come out."

Then Pete added, "And you told Henry Pelletier too."

Stuff Johnson was silent for the first time since the group circled the back of his house. When he spoke, it was almost in a whisper.

"I don't know a goddamn thing, I swear to God. So there's nothing for me to testify about, right? And if I don't testify then T. J. gets his job back, right? That's what you're saying, isn't it? I don't testify and the whole thing goes away?"

"That's right, Stuff," said David. "The whole thing goes away—until it comes out some day that you were there and whoever fixed this case figures it's too dangerous to take a chance, and then guess what happens?"

"But I wasn't there, I swear it."

"Doesn't matter. Long as somebody thinks you were." David made a slicing gesture across his throat with his right index finger. "Get it?"

"So what the hell am I supposed to do then, mister big shot lawyer? You're so damn smart. Tell me."

"You really weren't there?"

"When T. J. ran over the old man? Not a chance."

"But you know something, don't you?"

"Lemme tell you what I know. I know T. J. Trice is crazy. He finds out I'm even talking to you, I won't have to worry about no lawyer killing me."

"I thought you and Trice were friends."

"We ride bikes together, that's all. I like his sled. Custom Springer. Don't mean I like him, though."

"All right." David took a small yellow pad out of his briefcase. "Forget about testifying. Just tell me what you know about that Friday night. Maybe something will click."

Stuff thought for a moment, then shook his head. "No way, man. 'Sides, ain't nothing to tell."

David turned to Pete Werner. "Can't you do something, here? I'm trying to help this guy."

"No, you're not, Castelli," Werner said. "You don't give a rat's ass about him. Look, I took you here, all right. That was the deal. Now the man says he don't want to talk, he don't want to talk. What more do you want from me?" Then Werner turned to Jenny. "I don't know why I ever let you talk me into this in the first place. Let's get outta here."

Castelli could feel the moment slipping away. He looked at Jenny. She wasn't going to help him any more. Werner was standing up from the table. Stuff was picking up the carburetor. David put the pad back in his briefcase and tried once more. "All right, Stuff, look. No notes, no testifying—just Trice. Tell me anything, anything you want."

Stuff Johnson tightened his lips. "Anything I want? All right, I'll tell you anything I want. There's only one thing."

"Yeah, what's that?"

"I don't want to see you again after today, that clear?"

"You're the man."

"If I were you, Castelli, I'd just go back to Philadelphia and forget about T. J. Trice. This is one crazy motherfucker. They say he's got some kind of PhD or something, only he drives a forklift. How's that? A fucking forklift with a fucking PhD. Twenty-five years been doing it. Shit, he's the one got the union in back in '68. Coulda been whatever he wanted. 'Stead he drives a forklift. Least he did when he worked."

"What do you mean 'when he worked'?"

"Come on, counselor. Most days he just punched in and disappeared. Anybody else, Greene woulda been up his ass like a hot poker. Blew all our minds when Joe B. fired him over Carpool. Hell, we all used to laugh. You know, joking about Breitenfeld being under some kind of orders to look the other way. 'Cept we were wrong about that."

"But what if you were right?"

"About what?"

"About Breitenfeld being under orders to look the other way. Didn't you guys ever think Trice had something on somebody?"

"Yeah, we thought about it. But hell, he had that kinda shit going down, why the fuck was he driving a forklift all them years? He shoulda owned the company."

"How do you know he doesn't?"

"So what's that make Harry Greene, the piss boy?"

"Look, I'm not telling you Trice is really the owner. I'm just asking you to think for a minute. Where'd the rumor ever get started that T. J. Trice is a genius?"

"Ain't no rumor, counselor. It's the truth. I know."

"How's that?"

"'Cause I've been in the man's house, and it ain't no goddamn forklift driver's house."

Castelli almost pulled out the yellow pad but stopped when he saw Johnson stiffen. Then he saw their host relax his shoulders and begin picking at a screw on the carburetor. And then it all started coming out.

"Couple months ago, we were sitting in the Rat on Friday, like usual. All of a sudden somebody puts this song on the juke. Some weird piano shit. You know, lot of notes all at once."

"Oscar Peterson," said Jenny. "It's the only jazz record we got on the thing."

"Yeah, that's who it was. Oscar somebody. So T. J. looks up and says to me, 'Listen to that fat slob. Thinks he can play.' I don't think nothing, you know, just T. J. Only he keeps going on about the piano player having some kind of special piano with extra keys that he hauls around everywhere he plays. Says it's worth about two hundred grand. And then the song's over and T. J. is telling me how he's got the same piano in his house, only he can play it better. So I start laughing.

"Next thing I know, the motherfucker reaches in his pocket and pulls out a gun. Right in the bar. He starts in cursing and asking what the fuck I think is so funny. So I duck under the table and then he puts his head down under there and says if I don't come with him he's gonna shoot my balls off."

"So the both of us leave. All the way back to his house, he's weaving his Harley all over the road. And I'm following him, 'cause I'm too damn scared not to. Some little town called Fivepointville, about twenty miles from here."

Jenny said she heard he built the house himself, out of logs.

"Yeah, it's logs all right, 'cept not inside it ain't. Never seen nothing like it. Place was beautiful. Wood paneling, them Turkish rugs or whatever, like you see in the old movies, and right in the middle is the biggest goddamn piano I ever saw. Trice says it's the same as whatshisname plays."

"Oscar Peterson," said Jenny.

"Yeah, only Trice just keeps calling him a big fat slob. Then he asks me what I want him to play. Like I know or something. He's got music lying all over the place. And he's just ranting and raving and he can hardly stand up.

"Next thing, he starts playing the piano. Never heard nothing like it in my life. I'm just sitting there, you know, 'cause I ain't about to say shit, only I can tell the man is amazing and I don't even know what the hell he's playing."

David said, "I'll bet you couldn't wait to get of there."

"Listen, mister, I'm outta there when Trice says I'm outta there. Sure I wanted to leave. Shit, I didn't want to be there in the first place. But then he starts in with the teeth."

"The what?"

"The teeth. He wants me to tell him how many teeth there are in a dead man's jaw. He's screaming, 'Tell me, tell me dammit, how many teeth in a dead man's jaw?' So I'm just trying to keep him off me, ya know, so I says 'Thirty-two, T. J., same as a live man's jaw.' 'Not true,' he's yelling. 'Eleven are gone, eleven are gone, so there's twenty-one teeth in a dead man's jaw. Wanna see, wanna see. I'm the tooth fair-ee.'

"Then he starts running around the room and all, can't hardly speak he's so fucking drunk. Finally he just sits down square in the middle of one them Turkish rugs and passes out cold right on the floor. I got out. Ask me, Trice don't even remember I was there."

David spoke first. "Well, don't worry, I won't tell."

"Goddamn right you won't." Stuff stood up with the carburetor, turning his back on the group without a word and walking toward the Sportster. Werner and Castelli both knew it was time to leave.

David broke about ten minutes of painful silence in Werner's Town Car, David riding shotgun, Jenny and the steward in the rear. "I realize that was uncomfortable, Pete, but I had to talk to the guy."

"You know he's lying."

"About him not being there when T. J. did the old man?"

"Nah, I think that was straight. I don't think Stuff Johnson'd have the agates to ride through Greene's battery house on a cycle. But he damn well knew T. J. was gonna do it."

"Because?"

"Because Trice doesn't do anything without an audience. 'Cept none of it matters. You got a loser, Castelli. So why don't you just chalk it up and go home?"

"Chalk it up to what? McKeon sticking it up my ass?"

Werner thought about laughing, but he held back. Then, all of a sudden, he just pulled off the road. Pulled into the parking lot of Stoltzfus' Homemade Shoo-Fly Pie. He turned off the ignition. He did this so that he could look straight at David Castelli when he spoke.

"You really believe all this, don't you?"

"Believe what?"

"You know, all of it. Someone getting to your witness. Tampering with the evidence. The phony arbitrator or whatever. Your boss fixing the case. All of it."

"Goddamn right I believe it. I just don't understand it."

Werner stretched his right arm across the seat back. His hand was close to touching Castelli's shoulder, but he made sure that didn't happen. "You know I got opposition next spring?"

"Dickie Romanowski."

"Yeah, Dickie Romanowski. And what do you think Dickie Romanowski'd do if he ever found out I was talking to a company lawyer about screwing a member, right in the middle of the member's discharge arbitration? What do you think he'd do?"

"Would that be before or after he came in his pants?"

"You got that right, counselor. So I gotta be nuts." Then Werner turned to Jenny in the back seat who hadn't said a word since they left Johnson's house. "Isn't that right, Ms. DeLone?"

"It doesn't matter what I think."

"Oh is that so? Well I think it matters a lot. We wouldn't even be here if it wasn't for what you think."

"You're not putting guilt on me, Pete. Just forget it."

"Me put guilt on you? Someone's gonna get killed if you don't help my new boyfriend—never mind you're cutting your own throat. Who said that, Jenny? My grandmother?"

"That's not what I said and you know it."

"But it's close enough, isn't it?"

Jenny DeLone knew it was close enough. And that was why she decided to answer Werner's question and tell him exactly what she thought about his talking to a company lawyer.

"Do I think you're nuts getting involved in all this? That what you want to know? No, Pete, you're not nuts. You're just honest, that's all. Which in your line of work may be the same as nuts, except at this point it doesn't matter anymore because you're in it. We're all in it. Myself included. But, at least you still got a job back at the factory if Romanowski wins. Word gets out Jenny DeLone is helping Harry Greene, I don't sell enough beer to buy chalk for the pool cues, do I?"

Werner picked the perfect way to tell Jenny she was right.

"All right, David Castelli. I want you to listen to this. We had a member once named Epstein. Only Jew this local ever had, far as I know. Worked in the lab. Four, five years ago, whatever, bunch of ties did a locker check and found two lousy glass beakers rolled up in Epstein's stuff. Greene fired him cold. Damn things couldn't have been worth more than five bucks. Didn't matter. Harry said theft was theft and Epstein was out. His own landsman, out on the street.

"Anyhow, we got the guy's job back, and you want to know how? Rothstein got one of the ties to admit on the witness stand that he also found something in Trice's locker that day. A digital scale. Had to be worth a grand. Except T. J. didn't get fired. Didn't even get a warning. That's when I knew Thomas Jefferson Trice ran Greene-Pitowsky Smelting & Battery Company."

"Then how the hell do you explain Trice getting canned over Charlie Carpool?" Castelli said.

"Best I can figure, Breitenfeld just got so carried away he pink slipped the sonofabitch before Harry could stop him."

"So you think Greene is part of this too?"

"Listen, Castelli, Harry Greene is part of everything happens in that plant. He's god down there. You tell me your boss is trying to throw this case? Then I'm telling you Greene's in it too, right down to his Jewish star pinky ring. And I'll tell you something else, seeing as how my career is all but ruined now, anyhow. Someone gets into T. J. Trice's house, I think they start finding some answers. It's just a feeling about that log joint of his. But I've had it for years."

"I think it's right too," Castelli said.

Werner smiled at the lawyer sitting next to him, then turned on the ignition of the Town Car. "Then I guess you want directions?"

"What are you talking about?"

"Directions to Fivepointville. You agree T. J.'s got something important in that log cabin of his, why don't you just break in and find out?"

"Because I'm a lawyer, not a second-story man."

"House only has one floor, you don't need to be a second-story man."

"Come on, Pete, you know what I'm talking about. I can't afford to take a chance like that. Break into Trice's house? Somebody finds out, I could get disbarred. Besides, a man could get killed messing around with that guy."

"You're already messing with him, Castelli. You think for one minute Stuff isn't on the phone right now with your boy. Comes to Trice, Johnson's got a tongue as long as your arm. Romanowski's probably got the story too, by now." Then Werner turned around in the driver's seat and looked at Jenny in the back. "You want an extra bartender down there, sweetheart. I might be available sooner than you think."

No one spoke again until the Town Car pulled to a stop in front of Jenny Rat's and Castelli and Jenny got out. Werner had been thinking about his father, the way he always did when he was about to take it up the ass for trying to help someone out of a jam.

He had been too young to remember when Bill Werner lost his railroad job in Altoona in 1953; too young to remember the family eating beans for dinner; too young to remember moving to Lancaster where his father finally landed a minimum wage job selling cheese at a roadside stand on Route 30. But he was not too young to remember the way Bill carried on when he was drunk, which was almost every night. And he could still picture vividly in his mind the horrible dreams he had as a child, nightmares in which a man named Mr. Clugh—who his father would rave about constantly—came through his bedroom window with a knife and slaughtered everyone in the family.

Werner was snapped back into the present by the knock on his driver's side window. Castelli had a question.

"You don't know anyone who could help me here, do you?"

"You mean break into T. J.'s? No, I don't know anyone. And even if I did, I'm outta this, you get the picture?"

Jenny was standing next to the lawyer. "You're not out of it, Peter. None of us are. Not after that meeting. You said so yourself, not ten minutes ago."

"Well, I was wrong. You two lovebirds want to play James Bond, have a ball. But I'm going home for dinner."

TWENTY
Thursday, October 6

AROUND HIS NECK, HALF-BURIED in tufts of gray chest hair, Harry Greene wore a thin silver medallion. Inscribed on the medallion was a date: June 2, 1983. At one-fifteen on that date, slightly more than eleven years ago, Greene had officially outlived his father.

Harry was thirty-one the day Isadore Greenberg dropped dead at the age of fifty-eight years, seven months. It was May 29, 1956. Harry was home for a Memorial Day cookout at the Greenberg family row house in the Overbrook section of Philadelphia. Shortly after one in the afternoon he heard faint, gurgling sounds coming from the upstairs bathroom. By the time he got there, Isadore had managed to get up from the toilet, his pants like shackles around his ankles. Harry stood helpless as his father staggered toward the bedroom, gasping for air, barely reaching his bed before collapsing on his back across it, ending his life with the simple cry, "I'm going," uttered twice in rapid succession as he fell.

Greene was conscious of the silver medallion slapping against his chest as he pounded the country club stairmaster. Earlier in the morning, Trice had called to say that he would be out in the club parking lot, precisely at three. If Harry pushed it, he could finish his daily workout just in time.

Greene had to yell over the exhaust pipes.

"You said there wouldn't be money this year. You said that."

"Big fucking deal, I changed my mind."

T.J. flipped the chrome kill switch on the Springer, its big twin engine coughing to rest, rhythmically ticking itself cool. Then he carefully thumbed the packet of crisp one hundred dollar bills peeking out of the plain white envelope now in his hand.

"It's all there," Harry said. "Just get the hell out." Greene turned to walk away.

"Whoa, my friend. I'm not finished with you, yet."

"Yes you are."

"I *doubt* it." Trice spit out the second word, along with a lungful of cigarette smoke. "We still got a serious problem."

"In the car then, not out here."

Trice sat in the rear. Greene spoke from the driver's seat, hands on the wheel, not turning his head. "All right, what is it this time?"

"Hey, this lighter don't work. You're not missing maintenance appointments on the Jew canoe now, are you?" Trice put a fresh match to a fresh Camel, then resumed.

"The hearing's off till Monday. I don't like it."

"I don't like it either," Harry said.

"Lawyer's too smart for his own good, Harry. You should've had McKeon do it."

"Look, I already talked to McKeon. He says there's nothing to worry about."

"Oh is that so?" Trice leaned forward, his chin now resting on the back of the front seat, so close Greene could feel the bristly hairs of T. J.'s beard "Now you listen to me, Mr. Greenberg. I decide what's to worry about here. Not you. Not Jack fucking McKeon. And I say you got something big time to worry about here."

"You mean Johnson? He's not going to talk and you know it."

"That's right, Harry. He's *not* going to talk. Now, why don't you guess how I *know* he's not going to talk?"

Greene did not answer—until it hit him. Then he said, "Oh no. Absolutely not!"

"What's the matter, Harry? You don't like 'em still breathing? Is that the problem? I guess it must be, because you sure don't seem to have any difficulty once they're dead, now, do you? How many miles did you take him, Mr. Greene? How many miles with his brains spilling all over the trunk of your car?"

Harry suddenly realized that someone could hear Trice even through the car windows, Harry looking about the parking lot, making sure no one was near, then taking his hands off the steering wheel and shoving T. J.'s foul head backwards toward the rear seat. "That's enough!"

"Shh," Trice laughed. Then he opened the car door, got out, and motioned for Harry to roll down the driver's side window.

"I just found out they went to Johnson's house about two hours ago. Castelli, Werner, sweet Jenny Rat. All of 'em. Now, I don't want to see Stuff in there on Monday, you got that?"

Harry squeezed his eyes shut, as hard as he could, so that Thomas Jefferson Trice could not see that he was crying.

———◦◦◦◦———

"I've got to go to the hall for a few hours. Be back around ten." Pete was saying this as he mopped up the last bit of meatloaf gravy from his plate with a fistful of rolled-up rye bread.

"You said we were going to the mall."

Werner walked to the other side of the dinner table and stood behind his wife. He leaned forward, nuzzling the fine blond hairs on the back of her neck with his cheek, his hands sliding down the front of her sweater until they cradled Dorothy Werner's small breasts. She pushed herself back from the table and stood to face him.

"Come on, Peter, the kids are right in the living room. Why do you have to go in now? It's after seven already."

"I told you why, sweetie. I got stuck with a member all afternoon on some useless grievance, so this is the only time I've got to prepare for Rapid Freight tomorrow. Contract's up in three weeks and we got nothing so far. We'll go to the mall tomorrow, I promise."

Dorothy Werner swiveled around and wrapped both of her arms around her husband. He could feel her hips pressing tight against him as they kissed.

"Whoa," he said. "I thought the kids were right in the living room." Then he laughed and started toward the front door. "But hold that thought. I'll be back as soon as I can."

Two hours later, ready as he'd ever be for Jack McKeon and the Rapid Freight management team tomorrow, Werner was on his way home, hoping that Dorothy really had held the thought. He had EZ-104 filling the Town Car's cabin with Glen Campbell, so he didn't hear the motorcycles until one of them was right next to him, just outside the driver's window. He slowed to let the cluster of bikes pass.

Except they didn't.

The cycle to his left accelerated, pulling back into his lane just inches from the Town Car's front bumper, slowing down now, Pete forced to do the same, instinctively leaning on the horn. And then the other two were upon him.

The second bike cruised up on his left. Werner watched, helpless, as its rider pulled something out from under his leather vest and began smashing it against the car window. Then the third bike ran up the shoulder of the road on Werner's right. Pete turned when he heard it, catching the rider's smiling mouth just as it appeared to break into a laugh. The rider was holding a black pistol against the window with his left hand, gunning the throttle of his mount with the right.

They were on Route 741, halfway between Strasburg and Gap. There was nothing on either side of the empty road except fields and distant farmhouses. There were no streetlights. Only the headlamps of three Harleys and one Lincoln to light up a pitch-dark, cloud-covered night. When Werner stopped the car and reached for the automatic door lock button, a shower of broken glass burst over his upper body. He could feel some of the shards sting at his cheek.

"Get out of the fucking car, asshole." The mouth of Mr. Boneyard, president of the Devil's Disciples M.C., was less than five inches from Werner's ear. The voice preceded a thick arm, chockablock with wraps of leather and silver, reaching though the broken window, yanking at the Secretary-Treasurer's hair, banging his head against the inside doorframe. "Get out of the fucking car, now!"

The other two bikers were already flanking the car door by the time Werner opened it. They were huge men, bigger by at least three inches and probably forty pounds than the man whose arms they now held, one each, pulled back by the elbows until the pain in Werner's shoulders was excruciating.

Mr. Boneyard coughed up a large ball of phlegm and hocked it square into Werner's face. Pete felt it, warm and foul, running down his nose and over his upper lip, with no hands free to wipe himself clean.

"You been paying some visits lately, haven't you, mister big shot union boss."

Werner said nothing. Mr. Boneyard thought this was rude, so he drove his knee into Pete's groin. Werner sucked in breath, then groaned for their pleasure even as he was willing himself to be silent. When he spoke, he could feel Mr. Boneyard's spittle running into his own mouth. "I don't know what you're talking about."

"Well here's a hint, then, fuckhead." Mr. Boneyard balled his fist, then buried it in Werner's stomach. "Man's job's a very important thing, pal. You being a union boss, wouldn't think we'd have to tell you that, but I guess we do, seeing as how you keep fucking with our friend's job. You getting where we're coming from, asswipe?"

"Trice has a problem with me, he can come down the hall like anyone else."

"He did come down the hall. But he said you were too busy to talk to him."

"He's a goddamn liar, then. We're taking his case, just like he wanted."

"Yeah, you're taking it. Taking it down the fucking toilet. What do you think we are, fucking stupid?"

Then Mr. Boneyard's vice president for operations spoke from behind Werner's right arm. "Aw, shit. This is bullshit. I say we waste the mother-fucker right here. He ain't paying no attention."

"That right, Werner?" Boneyard said, again driving a fist into his captive's solar plexus. "Are you ignoring us?"

"No, I'm not ignoring you."

"Well, I'm most happy to hear that. But my brother back there thinks you might need just a little more, uh. Uh. Now, what's the word I'm looking for?"

"Reinforcement?" said the vice president for operations.

"Yeah," said Mr. Boneyard. "That's what you need. Some more reinforcement."

Then the three bikers took turns reinforcing their message. Some sort of a bag went over Werner's head. It felt like burlap and smelled like manure. Blinded, Werner had no way to know when the next punch was going to crash into his face. He had no way to brace himself. And that is what made the force of the blows seem so much harder, and the terror he suddenly felt seem so much greater.

Only after Pete Werner sunk to the ground, unconscious, did the trio decide his reinforcement lesson was over.

The last thing Werner saw in his head before the set faded to black was a series of flashing lights. Which was why the lights he now saw in the distance, bobbing gently up and down as they appeared to draw closer, gave him little clue that he had regained consciousness. That realization came only when he was able to make out the shape of the wagon on which the lanterns were attached.

He could smell the horse, and he could smell the driver, a mixture of body sweat and fertilizer coming from the arm that held the handkerchief that was mopping Werner's brow.

"You all right, mister?"

Pete looked up from the ground into the Amish beard just above him. He tried to stand, but the pain in his ribs and stomach yanked him back down to the road. The Amish man spoke again.

"It was those bikers now, wasn't it. Practically ran me off the road back a ways." The Amish man gestured with his head over his shoulder. "Oughta be in jail, the lot of 'em."

Werner managed to draw himself up to a sitting position. Pain smashed against the insides of his temples, dizzying him, almost making him fall back down. He could feel the gurgle of saliva deep in his throat as he spoke. "God, it hurts."

"Where?"

"Everywhere. Just give me a minute."

The Amish man called out toward the buggy. "Mary, come over here."

Werner was barely conscious. He felt more than he saw. He felt the Amish man's hands, huge and hard, their ends more like hooks than fingers. The woman's hands too. Smaller but seeming just as strong. Pete offered no resistance as the pair lifted him from the road and half-walked, half-carried him to the open back of the wagon, where he fell into a bed of straw and passed out once again.

An hour later they returned him to his car, still parked on the side of the road with its driver's window in fragments. He was fully conscious now, and the smells about him were no longer those of sweat and fertilizer. They were spicy, soothing smells from the poultices and creams applied to his head and neck by the Amish couple. He had drifted in and out of consciousness as they had worked on him in the bedroom of what he thought had been their farmhouse. He remembered arguing as he tried to convince them he was all right to return to his car.

"I don't like this, you know." the Amish man said. "Don't think it's right at all."

"Really," Werner replied. "I'll be fine. You've been too kind already."

"Nothing to do with kind, mister. Just what's right, that's all. You should be staying in a bed, not driving a car."

"I'll be in a bed before you folks are even home. I promise. Just live over in New Holland."

"Well, a man's gotta run his own life. So if that's what you want, you go on ahead. But I still say it's not right."

And then Pete Werner had a thought. His first lucid thought since Mr. Boneyard and his colleagues pulled him over for a chat. "Yes it is right," he said to the Amish man. "What I'm going to do just as soon as you folks are on your way is absolutely right. Please believe me."

"Suit yourself, mister. We'll pray for you."

And then the wagon was gone. Pete Werner knew only that the man's wife was named Mary.

Even with power steering, it hurt every muscle in his upper torso when Pete turned the wheel of the Town Car and headed back up the highway toward Strasburg. But the ride was only two miles, and he sat still in the car for ten minutes after he killed the engine on the shoulder of the road.

Just across Route 741 from the Strasburg Railroad sits the sprawling twin buildings of the Pennsylvania Railroad Museum. Lovingly restored steam locomotives have places of honor inside these buildings, where thousands of people each year pay money to touch their massive black bulks and read the hand-painted signs on each one, recalling their years of service on the railroad. But there are other locomotives at the museum too, unrestored, rusted ones. Train carcasses that may, one day, be polished back to glory, but for now just sit and rust at the western end of the property, in an open grass field spoked from its center with railroad tracks.

It was here, at the edge of that field, that Pete Werner parked the Town Car. A pair of floodlights, shining down from the roof of the building to his left threw just enough light onto the grass field for Pete to make out the ghostly shapes of the locomotives parked outside. He dragged himself from the car, walked over to the chain link fence and peered into the semi-darkness, looking for the familiar hulk of Number 3425, the last K4 Pacific ever built by the Juniata Shops in Altoona, the one whose boiler had been lovingly welded by Gustave Werner in 1928.

About a month before he died in 1958, Gustave had taken eight-year-old Pete to see Number 3425, towed to the grass field from its final run around Altoona's famous horseshoe curve just two months before. Even then, the old steamer had started to surrender to metal death, but enough of the parts were still intact for the boy to imagine that he was the engineer, highballing the 300,000 pound giant down the Main Line from Altoona to Lancaster.

The two had scrabbled up the handholds into the engineer's cab that day, Pete resting his arm on the wooden sill, looking through the peephole down the length of the boiler, trying to imagine the sliver of silver rail that was all the real engineer could see as he piloted the locomotive at 70 miles per hour over the right of way, a consist of twelve tuscan red passenger cars filled with travelers trailing behind. He was too short to reach the throttle lever, but he had managed to wrap his small left hand around the whistle cord, pretending to sound it—too longs and too shorts—at every grade crossing, waving to imaginary children looking up at him as the K4 thundered by.

His grandfather told him that day how he and his fellow welders had crafted the huge boiler, piece by piece as it was raised with a gigantic crane, lengthwise, from the vertical construction pit sunk deep into the floor of the Juniata boiler shop. Over and over, Pete made Gustave Werner describe how the finished boiler, itself over 100,000 pounds, had been hoisted from the pit on two slings of twisted wire thick as a man's leg, then guided, with klaxon horns sounding to warn the workers, to the erecting shop next door to be mated with its chassis.

Many times before that day, Pete had asked his father about how the locomotives were built, getting no real answers. His mother explained that dad just didn't want to talk about it. But Gustave talked of it constantly, even as his dying lungs slowly closed off the old man's speech until it was no more than a whisper, the way it had been on that day in 1958 when the pair finally visited number 3425.

By now, Werner's eyes had adjusted enough to the darkness to begin looking for the hole in the chain link fence that he knew was there, because he had crawled through it before.

He had first crawled through it in 1968, shortly after his high school graduation. He was sitting in the cab when he decided to defy his father and go to work for Harry Greene instead of accepting his scholarship to Penn State. He crawled through it in 1985, a week after he was released from Garden Spot General Hospital, his left leg in a cast from the beating given to him by goons from the Rubberworkers union—payback for Werner's failed attempt to raid the warehouse workers at Armstrong Floors. And, of course, he crawled through it in 1992, the night he decided to challenge Dickie Romanowski for the office he now held in Local 664—the same office that now seemed certain to return to the big Rapid Freight steward in less than six months.

For several minutes after Werner managed to haul his bruised body up into the dark cab, he just sat and stared at the mass of dials and levers arrayed before him—each one rusted shut from four decades of neglect. He leaned forward and grabbed the frozen throttle, the one he could not reach when he sat in this same spot thirty-six years ago, with the bulk of his grandfather wedged beside him. And then, even while he knew it was maudlin, Pete Werner started to talk out loud to a 150-ton metal corpse, and to the ghost of the man who built its boiler over sixty years before.

"Please don't mind if I curse, grandpop. It's just something I do these days. You know the motherfuckers beat me up back there so I'd lay off Trice, and that's exactly what I should do. Just let Rothstein drive the last nail on Monday and put the bastard back on his forklift. And I shouldn't care about the damn election, either. Whole fucking story's gonna come out no matter what I do. Dot wants me to quit anyhow. But, see, I'm not like you. Never was, even when I thought different. You built something wonderful with your hands. I didn't do shit with mine. Just helped a greedy millionaire make more money selling junk batteries. That's why I got out, don't you see?

"But what's left? Sell cheese like the old man? Get drunk every night? I guess that's it, isn't it? I guess that's fucking it. So if you got any ideas, I'm here. Just don't tell me I gotta go back and work for Harry Greene. Okay?"

And then he sat back in silence, his hand squeezing the K4's throttle. He felt like an idiot, a 44-year-old man sitting in the dark in a rusted-out locomotive, waiting for inspiration from foolish Gustave Werner, who died with broken lungs but still loved the company that gave them to him.

Except for one thing. And he would swear later that it was not his imagination. He would swear it came from the throttle in his hand. Through his fingers, up his arm, into his brain. Twenty minutes after Werner climbed into the cab of Number 3425, he knew exactly what he was going to do.

TWENTY-ONE
Friday, October 7

WAITING FOR THE PHONE to ring at 9:15 PM. That is what Werner was doing at this particular moment, sitting in the basement of his house.

In honor of winning Local 664's corner office in 1992, he had decided to reward himself with an office at home. He was an executive now, had to see members at odd hours, discuss important union business. Couldn't do that sort of stuff at the kitchen table. So he walled off a piece of the basement with fake knotty pine, bought some furniture at IKEA and set up shop next to the furnace—which he could still hear during the winter each time it fired up just a few feet from his ear.

He still hurt bad from the night before, and he hated the fact that globs of Dorothy's makeup now covered both of his cheeks and part of his chin; but that had been the only way he could have gone to work twelve hours earlier, once Mr. Boneyard's reinforcement lessons had turned purple-violet ugly across his face. He had stayed in bed until the kids left for school. It saved a lot of questions, and gave him more time to prepare for the breakfast showdown he knew could not be avoided.

"I want the truth, Peter," Dorothy had finally said to break the silence. "You didn't fall off a stool at Jenny's. You know it. I know it. So don't go insulting my intelligence."

"I got beat up, all right? I'm in a tough business, all right? What's the difference, anyhow?"

"The difference?" Dorothy was fighting the tears, because she knew how much it upset him. But she was too angry, and she was too frightened. So they just came out, streaming down her small blond face, suddenly streaked with the red of emotion. "The difference is I want you out of there." She balled up her fists as she spoke, tightening them against her chest until her forearms shook with tension. "Don't you understand me. Out of there! Just give it up. Give it up before it kills us both."

"And do what, sell fucking cheese."

"That's what it's all about, isn't it Peter? That's the whole damn thing. Some crazy idea you're going to avenge your father, take down the railroad even though there isn't any railroad anymore. But you can't do it, don't you understand. Nobody can do it. Nobody gives a damn. You say so every night you come home. The members don't care, the members are worse than the bosses. Don't you even hear yourself?"

"Yeah, I hear myself. And I'll tell you something else, I hear. You're gonna get your wish in about five months. Soon as the Polack kicks my butt. Then I can go back to kissing Greene's butt and we can all live happily ever after. How's that sound?"

Pete stood up from the breakfast table. He already hated himself for the snotty answer, so he reached for his wife and tried to console her. She felt stiff as a board against him, her arms still drawn in tight, her breathing still choked off from the crying. "Look," he said. "I didn't mean that, okay. Really, I didn't."

Dorothy forced herself to loosen into the body language of forgiveness. "I wish you did mean it, you want to know the truth. Anything's gotta be better than this."

Werner looked up at the neon Budweiser clock on the wall behind his basement desk: 9:20. The house was empty when he had gotten home from work two hours earlier. The note on the kitchen table was curt, to the point. "Took kids to mall. Dinner's in the fridge." If only she had signed it "love D" or put a smiley face on it, perhaps the knot in his stomach wouldn't be so tight. He tried to distract himself now, reading again Jenny's handwritten directions to Fivepointville. He remembered what she had said about the drive.

"Once you get on 897, just follow it. It'll wind through a town called Terre Hill, and from there right into Fivepointville. After that I want you to look for the buffalo."

"The what?"

"Buffalo, just what I said. There's a farmer up there keeps them in a field about a hundred yards before a gravel road that leads to T. J.'s house You can't miss 'em."

"Except it's gonna be dark."

"You ever stand next to a buffalo, Pete? They're like elephants. Believe me, you'll see them."

Actually, Jenny's directions were the simplest part of the plan. Three hours earlier, Werner had pulled out the set of lock-picking tools that had been in a drawer of his desk at the union hall ever since Joe Greist left office. He had always wondered what Greist ever thought he was going to do with them. But now, by the time the phone finally rang at 9:25, Pete had managed to open the flimsy wooden door of his basement office three times, though his hands had been shaking on each try, which embarrassed him even though he was alone.

"Jesus," Jenny said, "I didn't even hear it ring."

"That's because I'm sitting right next to it. Is he there?"

"Been in his booth since 8:30. Looks like about six longnecks' worth from here. You got the cell phone on, right?"

"It's in my jacket pocket," he said.

"All right then, you start immediately, it should take about thirty-five minutes. If he leaves, I'll call you and you turn around."

"Don't worry, I'm no hero."

Werner drove in silence, afraid even to turn on the car radio for fear he might get distracted and miss a turn. The map was spread out on the passenger seat of the Town Car. At every stop, he pulled out the cell phone, looking down to make sure the tiny light under the power button was still glowing green, checking it over and over like an obsessive compulsive running up and down the stairs all night to examine the stove. He prayed that the phone would not ring. He prayed that it would.

The two narrow lanes of Route 897 twisted and turned through the darkness north of Terre Hill. Pete strained his eyes, looking to his left for a herd of buffalo. What he saw, instead, was a parade of white signs, rising up on wooden posts into the beams of his headlights, one after the other along the side of the road. "Baptism Is Not Enough—You Must Repent And Be Born Again." "Don't Expect Peace With God Without Obeying His Word." "Hymn Sing, Saturday 7 PM—Cocalico Community Chapel." None of the messages comforted him.

He had just passed the intersection of Route 897 and Dry Tavern Road when the first buffalo appeared. Its huge brown head hung over the wooden fence rails almost into the road. Pete hit the brakes. Then he pulled over to the side, opened his window and killed the engine.

It was so quiet. He could hear them, first one, then two more, dragging their hooves though the grass toward the wooden railing. They chuffed like locomotives, each one trailing a body behind its massive head—a body half-naked, half-covered with ragged fur. Once at the rail, the trio of bovines stood perfectly still, watching Pete watching them. He wondered whether it was good for their health to live in Fivepointville. When he started the car, the buffalo turned slowly from the rail, lumbering back into the darkness from which they came.

Werner was about forty yards away from the end of the wooden fence when he first saw the mailbox. At twenty yards, he could see its red metal flag; at ten, he could read the name on its side: T. J. Trice. He rolled up the window and started to turn in.

But then he stopped, turned the car around and parked it about a block away from Trice's driveway, onto the other side of the road.

There was nothing about the appearance of the road that made him stop and move the car; yet there was an overwhelming sense in his head that he should do so. From here on, Werner decided to proceed on foot.

The driveway was dark and straight. Pete could hear gravel crackling beneath his feet. After about fifty yards, he began to make out objects strewn along the sides of the road: pieces of what looked like broken and rusted farm equipment, the carcass of an old motorcycle without an engine, three tin cans and the bottom half of a glass milk bottle, perched in a row upon a single length of wooden fence. And then the final object: a long, low house made of logs.

He stood next to Trice's pickup. For how long he stood, Werner did not know. What he did know was that he could almost hear the sound of his own heartbeat through his jacket. He checked the phone once more.

Werner walked carefully to the rear of the house. If there was an alarm system, Trice had obviously done a good job concealing it. Nothing in the windows suggested any mechanical security, and the back door looked almost flimsy, anchored by nothing more than a single knob with a keyhole in its center. Pete reached for the small packet of lock-picking tools in his back pocket and extracted the thin metal dowel that had already done the trick three times back in his basement.

Except this time it didn't. What it did do was get itself wedged in tight, deep inside the knob of Trice's back door. Werner pulled on it, then panicked and pulled on it harder, then twisted it, causing the exposed rear point to jam into the flesh below his right thumb. The dowel snapped off in the lock at the same moment.

Pete stood there, in the semi-darkness, under a small yellow bulb glowing just above the doorsill, watching a thin trickle of blood start to ooze from the puncture wound in his hand. The packet of lock-picking tools was lying on the ground at his feet, but Pete forgot all about them now. He moved along the side of the house, pushing up on each waist-high window that he passed—all of them locked. Then he ran back, past the rear door and around the other side, again failing to budge a single window.

Finally he reached the front of the house. The door was large and obviously thick. It had four small casement windows, eye high in a square. It had a round door knocker hanging from the mouth of a brass lion. It had an ornate brass handle, topped with a brass tongue to push down. Pete did that now, and the door, which wasn't locked, swung open.

The tiny red pinpoint of light, which was the only light in the darkened living room of T. J. Trice's house, belonged to a Creek OBH-8 pre-amp that its owner never turned off. Werner moved toward the pinpoint, twice bumping into low-lying shapes that were upon him before his eyes could adjust. By the time he reached the far wall of the living room, Werner was conscious of the throbbing pain in his right thumb.

But he forgot the pain when he switched on a small halogen lamp now in front of him. It was on a thin goose neck, which Werner used now like a flashlight, playing it across the large room. He played it, first, across the gigantic Bösendorfer grand piano. Then he swung the lamp down, panning a single oriental carpet that stretched at least thirty feet, from one end of the living room to the other. Pieces of expensive furniture dotted the carpet, one of them a low coffee table on which sat a large Hasselblad camera, itself a piece of sculpture.

When he finally returned the lamp to its original position, it shown squarely upon a floor to ceiling bookcase filled with compact discs. The case stretched out along the back wall of the living room until it reached the massive granite hearth of Trice's fireplace, the mantelpiece almost as tall as Pete. The bookcase held more recorded music than Werner had ever encountered in a private home.

Werner pulled out the portable phone once more to comfort himself in the green light. Then he began his search. He did not know what he sought, did not even know if he would realize what he found if he found it. But he trusted his instincts, and he could not blot from his mind the vivid picture painted yesterday afternoon by Stuff Johnson. "What," he thought, "had Trice been talking about on the night he passed out drunk on the floor of his own living room?"

It was a one-story house, large of footprint but sparse of walls. Behind the expanse of living room, Pete found only a small, cluttered kitchen, a master bedroom, a bathroom and two walk-in closets, which he checked first. One was practically empty, the other filled mostly with motorcycle parts and what looked like some very old photographic developing equipment. He remembered the Hasselblad on the coffee table.

The bedroom yielded nothing. Just an unmade bed, awash in pornographic biker magazines and an open copy of *Ulysses*. On the floor around the bed, several empty food cans and dirty utensils. In the clothes closet, very little that wouldn't have looked more at home in the laundry hamper.

The kitchen reminded Pete of his own bachelor days: a sauce-crusted stove and a refrigerator full of science projects. But on the kitchen table he saw something unconnected with anything else in the room: a red plastic tray; and in the tray a pair of long wooden tweezers; and under the tweezers an overexposed sheet of eight-by-ten developing paper. Now he was certain there was a darkroom in the house.

He found it within seconds when he pulled open a door to the right of the refrigerator. It opened into a workshop, the kind a weekend handyman might have in his basement. Only this one seemed to be missing many of its essential parts. There was a pegboard, but few carpentry tools hung from it. What was there looked more to Pete like dental instruments. He remembered something Johnson had said, something about "how many teeth in a dead man's jaw." On the back wall of the workshop, a narrow door stood half ajar. He pushed it open and went in.

The room reeked of stale marijuana smoke. Pete fumbled around on the wall for a switch, finding it, throwing it, bathing the area in soft red light. He left the door open behind him, Werner alone now in T. J. Trice's darkroom, barely wide enough for a man to turn completely around without touching the high counter loaded with equipment. When Pete made this turn, his jacket rubbed up against the wooden beading of the countertop, just hard enough to compress the fabric over his right pocket, just hard enough to turn off the power of his cell phone.

Most of the wooden drawers contained only the flotsam and jetsam of an amateur photographer: empty film cans, spent test strips, brown glass bottles of this and that. Near the middle of the cabinet, Werner pulled open a drawer that contained a wooden Cohiba cigar box, the most expensive Cubans made. But all he found inside it were ashes and butts, twenty-five cigars saved in the womb that bore them. For the first time Werner felt fear. For the first time he felt the presence of the sickness that was Thomas Jefferson Trice.

Only the bottom drawer was locked. Werner patted his pockets, then realized he had left the lock-picking tools outside. He was back with them in seconds, willing his hands not to shake as he clumsily wiggled another of the metal dowels back and forth in the tiny opening, letting forth a "yesss" like a hiss under his breath, when the slim drawer slid open and he looked down and he saw its contents.

<hr />

The phone did not answer until the fifth ring. It was twenty after ten. Jennifer said, "Peter, thank god."

"The Lancaster Bell cellular customer you have called is not available. Message twenty." Then it went dead. She pulled the crumbled piece of paper from the pocket of her jeans: 717-334-7676, then tried again, this time dialing more slowly, making certain that she heard the tone after each press on the keypad. "The Lancaster Bell cellular ..."

Frozen, she cradled the receiver and watched from behind the bar as Trice, with Gloria Partridge draped against his shoulder, shuffled toward the front door, then out into the parking lot. She did not move until she heard the big twin cough to life, heard his three quick blips on the throttle with their attendant angry roar, heard the Springer thunder off into the night, down Hixon Avenue.

Then she dialed the phone a third time.

"Good evening, Sleep-Tite Motor Inn."

"David Castelli, please. Room 107."

———————

A thick brown file folder, the words "The Tooth Fairy" carefully printed in magic marker across its cover, was held shut by a red rubber band. Werner lifted it slowly to the countertop, as his right temple pounded through wheat-colored hair newly damp with perspiration.

The rubber band snapped as he yanked it free. Its broken end stung into the back of his hand like a tiny whip. But he did not feel it because the image that confronted him now erased all sensation except a wave of nausea spreading suddenly from within his stomach.

The body in the photograph was definitely dead.

The right arm stretched out on the ground, upwards from the shoulder at ninety degrees, then back across and over the top of the head, draped over the head like a hat with the hand twisted palm side up. The eyes of the head wide open, the ears all but obscured by shelves of dried blood covering each one.

About the ground, and over the torso, Werner could make out glinting pieces of what looked like shards of black plastic, catching light from the camera's flash so that they appeared themselves to be illuminated. And up from between the legs of the corpse, three ropes. Three ropes criss-crossing the thighs, then snaking over the man's stomach until they ended in the wooden shapes of duck decoys, one resting on the body, the other two hanging over its side.

In the next picture, the camera had moved closer, a single decoy filling the entire eight-by-ten image, so that a person looking at it could clearly read the words carved in the body of the duck: "Willis Tucker, R.D. #1, Stroudsburg, PA."

Werner forced himself to continue turning over the pictures. Trice had photographed the body from every conceivable angle, then moved to the background areas: the ground covered with more of the black plastic shards, a wider angle, showing foothills of what appeared to be a large mountain of the shards, and finally the widest shot of all—an asphalt-covered expanse complete with bulldozers, front end loaders. At the top of the picture, the inside facing of a wire mesh fence on which hung green and gold letters that spelled out "YKSWOTIP-ENEERG," and at the bottom, the rubber-booted legs of the victim himself.

After the outdoor shots came the still lifes. Werner counted eleven, each with a dental chart of some kind, a human jawbone, and a typed note, identical in every picture except for the September date: "Season's Greetings to Harry from the Tooth Fairy." It took Pete almost a full minute of picture flipping to notice that each earlier still life had one more tooth on the bone and one less on the chart. The most recent picture was dated this year. The oldest, the one with the date September 9, 1984, had no chart at all, only the jaw.

Images and questions began exploding in his head. A dead body on Harry Greene's property ten years ago. Why was it there? What did Greene have to do with it? Or Trice? Was it still there? He reached into his pants pocket for the small spiral notebook he always carried, now writing in it: "Willis Tucker, RD #1, Stroudsburg, eleven pictures, September 9, 1984."

Werner returned to the brown folder. There was more, under the last picture, a manila envelope. It would take him less than three seconds to open it.

———————————

Castelli was fiddling with the TV remote, trying to distract himself, when the phone rang.

He had logged a lot of time negotiating labor contracts in dens like this one. Motels where you pulled your car up to the room, and opened a metal door, and hung your clothes on an exposed railing, and drank from a plastic cup covered with shrinkwrap. He had joked with his clients in these rooms; raunchy jokes at one o'clock in the morning about women ramming the tops of their heads against the wall, in beds being rented by the hour. But there were no clients this time. Only a solitary management lawyer, still trying to comprehend why the secretary-treasurer of Lancaster County's biggest labor union was, at this very moment, committing burglary on his behalf.

Jenny didn't even bother to say hello. "David, the cell phone didn't answer. I called it twice. Jesus, what are we going to do?"

"What do you mean, it didn't answer?"

"Trice left the bar fifteen minutes ago."

"Do you know where he went?"

"No, I don't know where he went. He left, that's all I know. Him and that woman from Armstrong Floors he's always slobbering after. He left and Pete's phone isn't on."

Castelli felt a sharp twinge of nerves race up his back. But he made himself sound assured as he spoke into the receiver. "All right. Now calm down and let's go through this one step at a time. When did you last talk to Pete?"

"I called him at home. Around nine-thirty. He was leaving for Trice's."

"Okay, let's assume he got there a little before ten. Now, when did Trice leave your place?"

"Jesus, I don't know. Quarter after, something like that."

"So that means if he was going directly home," Castelli looked at his watch, "he'd be getting there in about five, ten minutes. Of course we don't know if T. J. was going home. Fact, we don't even know if Pete ever got up to Fivepointville."

"So you forget it? Is that what you do? Get him to go break into a guy's house, then just do nothing and let him get killed."

"Goddammit, Jenny. I didn't tell him to break into anyone's house. He did that all by his sweet self."

"Except you told him he'd find things in that house, didn't you? I was right there when you said it."

"He said that, not me."

"But you agreed with him."

"Look, I'm not going to tell you I wasn't blown away when he said he was going to do this. Because I was. Damndest thing I ever heard. But this is still his gig. It's not mine."

"So you're not going after him, is that what I'm hearing?"

"That's exactly what you're hearing, and neither are you."

"Don't you think that's my call, David?"

"Jenny, for god's sake. Don't be an idiot. He'll be fine. He's a big boy. Just get over here and we'll wait for him together. Like we planned. He's got this number. Something goes wrong, he'll call."

———✦———

The paper in Werner's hand was onion skin, a carbon copy. It had a date "October 4, 1968." It had a legend, "Third GPS&B wring-out. One week till union election."

The list of names that followed also showed job and shift. Next to the names, five columns numbered 1 to 5, and beside each name an x under one of the columns. Pete scanned the list until he found himself: "Werner, P.W., kettle room, 1st shift, 1."

"They sure got that right," he thought.

Werner knew exactly what he was holding in his hand. He just couldn't imagine how T. J. Trice ever got it. The format was the same one he had been taught to use so many years before. A chart to assess how employees were leaning during a union election campaign. He always knew that management kept the same sort of records; he just never knew they used the exact same form.

A "1" was solid union. Wouldn't vote for management with a gun to his head. Fives were the opposite. These were the employees who would rat to the boss about what went on at the union rally. The twos, threes and fours were the keys, especially the fours, people thought to be leaning toward management, but who still needed some persuasion. In the final week before an NLRB election, knowing which voters management thought were fours could be gold to any union trying to organize a company. And somehow, Trice had managed to get himself a copy of GPS&B's most valuable piece of intelligence, on the very eve of the 1968 election that would give Harry Greene a lifetime of Teamster grief.

The pictures of the dead body had explained some of it. He didn't even have to know who Willis Tucker was, much less how he ended up buried in a pile of Harry Greene's spent battery casings. Just to know that T. J. Trice had these pictures, and apparently sent one every September to Harry Greene, was enough to give the puzzle its first meaningful shape.

But the wring-out mystified him. Especially the handwritten note clipped to the final page. "Call me at home about this," the handwriting began. "We're doing another wring-out forty-eight hours before the vote." And the rest of the manila envelope—or more precisely how Trice ever got the rest of the manila envelope—was most bewildering of all.

Werner laid the papers on the darkroom counter and began turning them over, one by one: 1962 to 1967 audited financial reports of Greene-Pitowsky Smelting & Battery Company; a copy of Harry Greene's 1967 tax return; cancelled GPS&B checks made out to various marinas and resorts in the Caribbean, and caterers, and furriers—the detailed road map of a business owner's excesses. Confidential information guaranteed to pro-duce a landslide vote for Manufacturing and Transport Workers Local 664 on October 11, 1968.

Werner shoved the papers and the wring-out back into the envelope. Then he put the envelope into the Tooth Fairy file, and stuffed the whole affair into the front of his jacket.

The deal had been that Werner would go to the Sleep-Tite and meet with David and Jenny if he found anything. If not, he'd just call over there and sign off. He was sorry now he'd made that deal, even though he sensed at once the power of what was now riding under his jacket against his waist. He thought briefly about just reporting a false alarm, then going home. But, he'd made a promise to his landlady. And, almost in spite of himself, he felt an almost overwhelming need to share the grisly pictures with another human being—as if doing so would make him feel cleaner about having seen them in the first place.

All of this was flying though his mind when he heard the unmistakable rumble of a Harley-Davidson.

In the time it took Werner to pull the dead phone out of his pocket and recover from the burning wave of electricity that seemed to trace his entire backbone, from neck to tail, the motorcycle had traversed the gravel driveway, backfired twice on deceleration, and gone to silence. It took about ten more seconds for Pete to hear the creak of Trice's front door, the sound of heavy boots, and the nasal laugh of a woman obviously inebriated. It was only the last of these sounds that gave him hope.

He could hear them now, even from inside the darkroom, inside the workshop.

"I'm freezing, Tommy. You got anything to drink in here?"

"On the piano."

"I don't mean that shit. I need something hot."

"Right here, sweetie. I got something hot."

"Cut it out, I'm serious. How about some coffee."

"You know where it is, lover. I'm busy."

Pete heard her footsteps approach the kitchen. He moved silently from the darkroom to the workshop door, cracking it barely enough to peer out. He was desperately trying to remember the distance from the refrigerator on his right to the back entrance.

He watched, frozen and barely allowing himself to breathe, as Gloria Partridge fumbled at the kitchen counter. She was a big girl, probably taller than T. J., with a wide derriere looking as if it wanted to burst from the rear of her short tan skirt. From mid-thigh to the tops of her cowboy boots, she showed legs that looked almost too delicate to support the spread that lay atop them. She called out over her shoulder.

"Tommy, I can't get this thing to work. Can't you come in here a minute?"

Werner hoped Trice would ignore her, but he didn't. Then Pete watched as the master of the house entered the kitchen, spun Gloria about and kissed her hard, forcing her back against the counter. Her arms wrapped around his neck as he practically ripped open the buttons of her western shirt and buried his head in her bare chest. She wasn't fighting him.

The act had no mercy, no love. Just efficiency. The skirt pushed up over spreading hips, the black panties pulled down, but not even down to her ankles, caught instead on the tops of her cowboy boots. He turned her around now, forcing her upper torso down on the countertop, as he entered her, almost on his tiptoes to get the proper angle of attack.

He left her to rearrange her own clothes. And also to figure out the coffee maker by herself.

"Ya wanna hear something?" It was T. J. yelling into the kitchen from the living room.

"Billy Ray. You got any Billy Ray Cyrus?" Gloria was hiking up her panties as she spoke.

"I don't mean the fucking stereo, I mean me."

She had given up on the coffee, Gloria now holding two fresh Bud longnecks as she headed toward the front of the house. "Come on, Tommy, it's late. I don't want to hear that shit now."

"Then fuck you, 'cause you're gonna hear it anyhow."

Suddenly, a torrent of notes rang from the Bösendorfer, filling the log house with music of such power and passion that even Pete Werner, wedded for years to a diet of EZ-104, knew that he was hearing something extraordinary. He knew it was his chance to get out, to run through the flimsy back door of the kitchen, into the darkness and down the long gravel road to safety. But for some reason he could not move.

Nothing Stuff Johnson had said could have prepared Werner for what he was hearing. He did not have to know that every strike of the keys was perfect. He did not have to appreciate that T. J.'s performance would have brought down the house at any jazz club in the world. All he had to do was let himself feel, and he would stay in the darkroom transfixed, listening as Trice ripped through the chord changes of Dizzy Gillespie's "A Night in Tunisia"—played it for an audience of two: one union leader in the middle of a burglary and one drunken bimbo who would have preferred "My Achy Breaky Heart."

Gloria handed the plastic jewel box to T. J. while his foot was still on the sustain pedal.

"What the hell's this?"

"It was your birthday present, remember?"

"I thought I threw this piece of shit in the trash."

"You did. I pulled it out last time I was here."

Trice took the compact disc from her hand as if it had Flit sprayed on it.

He rose slowly from his piano bench. "If I put it on, will you blow me?"

"Why not?"

Werner opened the workshop entrance just wide enough to slip through into the kitchen and head for the back door. The last thing he heard as the nighttime chill enveloped him again were the disco sounds of somebody singing "So Many Men, So Little Time." Despite his fear, he couldn't help chuckling to himself, "How perfectly appropriate." Then he dashed into the woods and headed in the direction of what he hoped was Route 897.

It took him about two minutes to reach the road, stumbling through underbrush and whacking his shins on broken branches. Despite the cold, he was sweating through his shirt, wheezing, feeling the Tooth Fairy file pressing into his chest as he gulped for air. He had made for the streetlight as soon as it became visible through the darkness, leaning now against the lighted telephone pole. He had to rest, just for a minute.

He used the time to look again in the file. And when he did, he found the one item that had escaped his eyes in Trice's darkroom. By holding it out so the light shined down upon it, he was able to make out the subject of an eight-by-ten black-and-white photograph. The date on it was November 14, 1968. At first Pete had no idea why Trice kept it locked away with such valuable material. But as he looked more closely at it—at all the detail it showed—he suddenly knew why. He felt the corners of his mouth draw up into the first smile they had formed in days.

Then he walked back down the darkened road to the waiting Town Car, got in, and headed toward the Sleep-Tite. He turned off EZ-104, preferring now to drive in silence.

TWENTY-TWO
Friday, October 7

ANOTHER CAR WAS ALSO headed for the Sleep-Tite. But the driver of this one could not stay on the route. She was too worried about Pete and too angry at Castelli.

Jenny looked at her watch: 10:45. Trice had to be home by now. Was Pete finished with his search? Was he safe? Was he dead? The questions kept going off in her brain like old-fashioned flashbulbs. There was no way she could just drive to the Sleep-Tite and wait there with a man who didn't even care enough about Pete's safety to leave his little motel room. So Jenny found herself heading east toward Fivepointville, foot on the accelerator, hands squeezing the wheel, eyes locked on the road, looking at every car coming toward her.

It was on Route 897, just north of Terre Hill, when she saw what looked like a big Lincoln Town Car coming the other way. She couldn't be sure when it passed, so she swung quickly into the first driveway, turned around, and began chasing the car south. By the time Jenny could finally make out his Teamster bumper sticker, she was sure Pete could see her in his own rear view mirror. He was safe. That's all she wanted to know. She certainly didn't want to be seen chasing him like some little kid's mother. So she pulled off the road and parked on the gravel, waiting as the beating of her heart slowed back to normal.

Jenny's watch now read 11:10. She could race back to Lititz and probably get there in a half hour. But, suddenly, she was in no hurry. She knew

Pete was okay, and she didn't want to see David Castelli. So she decided to stay on the side roads from here to the Sleep-Tite—side roads that were narrow and high bermed, flanked on either side by straight-edged farms now too dark to see. If she were traveling these roads by day, she would have to pull out across the yellow line, over and over, to avoid the Amish buggies. She would have to take special care to leave a wide berth for children in black, pushing along on their scooters, propelled by the rhythmic thrusts of boots against the asphalt.

In the summer of 1963, when she was fourteen, and thinking about boys most hours of the day, she had bicycled down these roads after dinner listening to static and music coming from the tiny speaker of her transistor radio hanging from the handlebars. On clear evenings, the radio could pick up WIBG all the way from Philadelphia, where the Rockin' Bird, Joe Niagra, would play the wonderful songs she danced to after school, alone in her room with the doorknob for a partner.

On one particularly hot evening that summer, as she peddled in her tight dungaree shorts and white dress shirt, tied off to show just the slightest hint of bare skin after she was out of her parents' sight, she had come upon a Mennonite boy catching lightning bugs at the edge of a field.

The insects were so easy to grab from the air, blinking on and off to show themselves in the new dusk, hovering waist high like tiny helicopters. The boy chased one down, right where the field met the road, and because his eyes were fixed only upon his prey, he didn't see the girl on the bicycle until the two collided. Jenny tumbled off the saddle into roadside gravel that instantly imbedded just enough of itself in her knee to send hot pain down her leg. The boy landed square atop the riderless bike, his glass jar splattering on the road. Jenny looked up as a puff of bugs—the boy's entire evening's catch—returned to freedom.

She was not hurt, except for the spot of road rash. Neither was the boy. But the front tire of her bike had separated from its rim, and the case of her new transistor radio had split in two like a melon.

"Are you all right?" the boy said. "I didn't see you. I'm so sorry."

"Look at my bike. What am I going to do?" Jenny rubbed at her knee, brushing gravel out from the striations. The boy took a handkerchief out of his pocket and handed it to her.

He looked to be about her own age but he was tall and already muscled beyond the chronology of his face. "It's just a flat tire," he said. "I can fix that, no problem. Radio too. Needs to be glued, that's all."

She was taken by his speech. Most of the boys she knew at school wouldn't have been able to string three words together in front of a girl, much less actually apologize for breaking something and offer to fix it. But, then, she knew little about Mennonites—only that they were slightly deeper into the twentieth century than the Amish. They drove cars.

He picked up her bike and began walking back into the field. "I've got a wagon just over the hill," he said. "We'll load this on it and take it to the house."

In the open hay wagon, while it was being pulled by a huge horse toward a farm house just visible at the far end of the field, Aaron Mueller introduced himself.

He worked on the bike just outside the open entrance to the family barn, deftly flicking the tube from inside the tire, then patching it. After that, he disappeared into the farmhouse next to the barn with her broken radio, returning almost immediately with the plastic case intact and the tiny speaker playing "Surf City."

"I'm not allowed to listen to rock and roll," he said. "You're lucky." He snapped off the radio and asked if her knee felt better.

"It's fine," she said. "You've been very nice."

"Well I did run into you, you know."

Jennifer declined Aaron's offer to drive her and the bike back to the road. Said she would be fine riding. Then she added, "Maybe I'll bump into you again sometime," delighting in her pun and hoping it would be true. It was.

Two weeks later, on the same road, at the same time, and definitely on purpose, Jenny rode past Aaron Mueller. He was working in the field this particular evening, not catching lightning bugs. He looked much older and more like a man. They talked at the side of the road for about ten minutes, only this time when she left, the two had agreed to meet again the next evening.

By the end of July, Jenny knew much more about the differences between Mennonites and Amish than their preferred mode of transportation. And she knew much more about Aaron Mueller—that he had three older sisters; that he would be fifteen on the day after Thanksgiving; that he went to public school just like she did; that his father let him drive the family car so long as he kept off public roads; and that he never kissed a girl with her mouth open until the day the two of them did it, inside the open door of the Mueller's barn, just as it was getting dark.

The next time they did it—two days later—she had to push his hand off her blouse. He said he was sorry. She said it was okay; they could still be friends. And they were friends, all the way until the last week in August.

They had ridden their bikes long and hard one evening after dinner, chasing each other through the back roads behind Route 30, until they came to the Choo Choo Motel. All the units in the motel were actual train cabooses, tracked in to permanent rest off Route 791, just beyond the Strasburg Railroad. The owner had converted each caboose into a sleeping room, but Aaron knew that one of the cars, the one furthest from the road, had never been made over. It was still just a caboose, completely intact and untouched from its last day of active service on the Reading.

It was almost dark by the time they scrambled into the caboose's tiny cupola below the roof, surrounded on all sides by filthy, narrow windows that the crew once looked through to check on the train. An old cot, with a bare mattress thrown across the springs, took up most of the usable space.

For a few minutes, they just sat on the edge of the cot, catching their breath. It was stifling and Jennifer could feel sweat running down the front of her neck. She was unprepared when he kissed her, but she let him go on.

And then he was on top of her, rubbing himself against her shorts, his hardness digging into her crotch, while she half struggled to get away and half pushed back against him. She let him unbutton her shirt, then push her bra up and over her small breasts. No boy had ever done this to her before. She could feel his other hand reaching down between them, fumbling with the buttons on his fly until she knew his penis was exposed.

The rest happened so fast that when she was back in her room later that night she was not even sure it had been real. Her own hand also pushed between them, Aaron rolling onto his side, Jennifer rubbing her left palm over the length of him, pink and swollen, as he came on both of their clothes almost instantly. She squeezed back the tears as soon as it was over, wanting nothing except to get home and clean herself.

The last thing she saw before running through the rusted metal exit of the caboose was Aaron, sitting up on the cot buttoning his fly. He was telling her he was sorry and begging her to ride past his farm again the next night. But she didn't. And she never saw Aaron Mueller again.

※

Pete Werner arrived at the motel shortly before eleven-thirty. Castelli, who had been peering through the cheap brown drapes of Room 107, scanning the parking lot for the two cars he awaited, had the metal door open before Pete could even knock.

"What happened to the phone?" Castelli said. "Jenny called me almost an hour ago."

Werner looked over Castelli's shoulder, scanning the empty room behind the lawyer.

"Where *is* Jenny?" he said. "She shoulda been here by now. Look at the time."

"Probably stuck at the bar. I told her to come over. She'll be here. Just tell me what happened to the damn phone?"

"Got turned off in my pocket best I can figure. Trice and his girlfriend showed up, but I got out as you can clearly see."

"And you found something in there, didn't you?"

Werner reached into his jacket. "Of course, why worry about some sorry-ass union goon risking his life. Just get to the point, right?"

"Sorry, Pete. I'm just preoccupied."

Werner skimmed the Tooth Fairy file across the bed, some of the eight-by-ten glossies fanning out across the spread like a bizarre hand of cards. "Then preoccupy yourself with that, pal. Damndest pile of stuff I ever saw."

For the next minute, Castelli paged through the pictures of Willis Tucker, the shape of the lawyer's mouth flicking back and forth between wonderment and revulsion. The only words the mouth formed were "holy shit" and "my god." Then he sunk down on the bed.

Pete took up the conversation. "I guess that explains Epstein and the digital scale now, doesn't it?"

"Jesus, look at this stuff. He cut off the guy's head for chrissake. I think I'm going to throw up."

"Well, swallow first, Castelli. Because there's a manila envelope in there too, and I want to know what you make of that."

David forced himself to slow his breathing. He turned the pictures of Willis Tucker face down on the bed, then pulled out the contents of the manila envelope and began turning the pages. He figured out the obvious just as quickly as Werner had in Trice's darkroom. But there was something else Castelli also figured out—something that Werner could not have deduced, because Werner did not recognize the handwriting on the note clipped to the wring-out. Castelli did.

"Win an election, lose a client. I can't fucking believe it."

"What?"

"He says it all the time. We all say it. Except it's supposed to be a joke."

"What's supposed to be a joke?"

"Win an election, lose a client. You know, an NLRB election. Lawyer keeps the union out, that's the end of the client. Union gets in, like you bastards did in '68, company's got labor problems for the rest of time and the lawyer has himself a cash cow, so long as management doesn't blame the lawyer for losing the election in the first place. Don't you get it? This is Jack McKeon's fucking handwriting!"

"You can't be serious."

"I can't? You don't think I've seen that handwriting enough times the last seven years? It's McKeon's all right. Must have sent this stuff to Trice years ago to help you guys win, then convinced poor old Harry there was nothing he could have done. What a sonofabitch." David looked up and let air whistle between his tongue and the roof of his mouth. He shook his head back and forth, trying to make himself believe the evidence now before him.

Castelli spoke in the general direction of Pete. But mostly he spoke to the ceiling. "The man promised me a partnership in three months. And all this time, Trice had him by the balls, same as Harry. No wonder my fucking case— goddammit! That goddamn sonofabitch. Some fucking partnership."

"And what about Tucker?" Werner asked. "You're so smart, tell me what a dead body without a head's been doing in Harry Greene's backyard for the past ten years?"

"I'm lost same as you on that one. But I can just bet how much it must be costing Greene to keep T. J. quiet. My guess is driving Harry's crummy forklift and getting this arbitration fixed must be chump change."

"I just came from the bastard's house, and I can assure you it's chump change."

"So then, what's next?"

Werner walked over to the fake Shaker chair sitting at the fake Shaker writing desk, pulled it out, spun it around, and sat down on it backwards, his arms folded across the back. Then he lowered his head down over his crossed wrists, like a cat settling in to sleep, and spoke to Castelli.

"You know, I always respected your boss. Not sure I can do that anymore. Man sells out his best friend, I don't know. But that's not my problem now, is it?"

"No, I guess it's not."

"Then we got T. J. That arbitrator is going to put him back to work sure as hell. I don't like it, but it is good for business. So what do I get by stirring up that pot? I was thinking first, driving over. I see these pictures, I think shit, there's a murder here or something. Gotta tell the police. But then I say to myself why get involved? I'm a Teamster. First thing you know, cops'll be on my case."

Werner went on. "Who's left then? Harry? I guess that's it. Harry Greene. Poor dumb bastard's got himself in some kind of serious trouble, but what am I supposed to do about that? So where I come out is just leave it all be. I found out what I wanted to know. What else do I need? Just wish I knew where Jenny was."

The whole time Werner was talking, Castelli was looking again at the pictures of Willis Tucker, forcing himself to search the horrible images for some sort of an answer. He picked up the one with the duck decoy.

"Stroudsburg. That's up in the Poconos, isn't it?"

"So."

"So maybe if we went there and checked old newspapers or something, there'd be stuff about Willis Tucker. We got a date here, you know.

September 9, 1984. Might be a good place to start."

"I think you're nuts, Castelli. You got your answer, just leave it."

"Leave it! Don't you understand what this is? Greene's involved with a murder here. And McKeon? Shit. He gets himself disbarred this crap ever comes out—and that's if he's lucky. For all we know, he's connected with Tucker same as Harry."

Castelli put down the decoy picture and walked over to the window, peering into the parking lot, looking for Jenny's car. But he spoke even as he looked out. "You know, you've got an election in a few months, Pete."

"Don't remind me."

"Well I am going to remind you. You think my law firm wants Romanowski running Local 664? The man is a lunatic."

Werner laughed. "Shit, I would think that'd be good for business."

"Well you're wrong. Tough bastards like you are good for business. Lunatics aren't good for nothing—too unpredictable. Course Dickie wouldn't have a chance to win that election if you got Greene to reopen the labor contract early and give away the store. You'd be a hero. Who knows, you might even get him to agree to that crazy clause you keep shoving across the table every three years—you know, the one says a man can't get fired till his case has been through arbitration. Now that, my friend, that would really be good for business."

Werner could feel the heat rising up the back of his neck as Castelli talked. He wanted just to get up and leave. But he was worried about Jenny, and he couldn't bring himself to let Castelli's invitation go unanswered. He even flashed, for a second, on the possibility that the lawyer might be wearing a wire. So he wanted a good transcript, just in case.

"I guess you never heard of Section 302."

Castelli looked puzzled. "Taft-Hartley Act? What of it?"

"What of it? Union guys go to jail, that's what of it."

"For extortion, Werner. For taking money under the table. You'd just be negotiating a good contract for your men. Feds oughta pin a medal on your chest."

"And what about you? What do you get from all this?" Werner couldn't resist pulling on the string, no matter how nauseating the entire conversation was starting to become.

"Well, McKeon's history, that's openers. Pompous Irish bastard's gonna shit himself. But Harry's another matter. I don't see any reason to hassle him, poor sonofabitch. Only problem is, me being an officer of the court and all, I obtain knowledge of criminal conduct I've got this obligation to come forward—unless, of course, the criminal happens to be my own client. Then I've got just the opposite obligation. Besides, Harry's going to need a good lawyer, what with Jack retired and all."

Werner had heard enough. He stood up from the fake Shaker chair, then reached over to the Tooth Fairy file and took out the eight-by-ten black-and-white photo that he'd discovered while standing under the streetlight an hour earlier. "I'm keeping this one for a souvenir, Castelli. The rest of it's yours. Have a party."

Werner walked out to the parking lot, got into the Town Car, and waited in the dark to make sure Jenny DeLone arrived safely. He decided to give her fifteen minutes before starting to comb the roads. With three minutes left, he saw headlight beams swing around the corner and stop in front of Room 107. As soon as she got out and entered the metal door, Pete turned on his cell phone.

He had been thinking about doing it from the moment he saw the pictures of Willis Tucker. But, then, it was only a thought. David Castelli changed that thought into a mission. Pete Werner dialed the home number of Harry Greene.

———⊷∘◦∘⊶———

By the time Jenny DeLone pulled up to the metal door of Room 107 of the Sleep-Tite Motor Lodge it was past midnight. At least five times during the drive, she had almost turned her car around. But each time she remembered Aaron Mueller. Now, thirty-one years later, Jenny was determined to do it right.

She spoke immediately. "Where's Pete? He should be here."

"He was here for half an hour. Just had to leave on account of his wife. But look at what he found in Trice's house. You gotta see this stuff. It's unbelievable."

Castelli was holding her as he spoke, now leading her by the hand to sit next to him on the cheap tan spread. She picked up one of the pictures without even thinking, then quickly turned it face down, willing the nausea back into her throat.

"Oh my god," she said. "What *is* that?

"The answer," he said.

"What are you talking about?"

"Willis Tucker. Ever hear of him?"

"No. Why should I have heard of Willis Tucker?"

"Because part of him lives down the street from Jenny's Rathskeller Bar & Grille. How's that?"

Jenny stood up from the bed. "Look, I only came here because you asked me to be with you. Now I'm glad Pete's all right, but don't you think it's a little late for being cute?"

"Okay," he said. "No more smart ass. Pete found all these pictures in a drawer in Trice's house. There's part of a body buried in battery casings on Greene's back lot. Trice knows it, and apparently so does Harry. When it was alive, I'm pretty sure the body had the name Willis Tucker and he was from Stroudsburg, up in the Poconos. I'm going to check it out first thing in the morning."

"What do you mean check it out," Jennifer asked. She was already beginning to feel uneasy about David's chatty recitation. "You *are* going to tell the police, aren't you?"

"Yes and no."

"Yes and no! David, someone was murdered!"

He came over to where she was standing, closer to the metal door now, still wearing her leather bomber jacket. "Look, Jennifer, there's more. A lot more. Trice has been blackmailing Harry for ten years over this thing. I'm almost certain of it."

"Isn't that something for the police to find out?"

"Not if I'm getting sucked into it."

"You?"

"What are you, naive? Or did you just forget that I'm in the middle of a trial looking like a smacked ass?"

"A trial? It's a crummy labor arbitration, David. We're talking about a murder."

"You don't know that and neither do I. So I'm just going to make a few calls tomorrow, first. Is that all right with you?"

"What kind of calls?"

"Stroudsburg police. Maybe the local newspaper up there. See if they got anything in their files on Willis Tucker."

"And then you promise me you'll turn all this in?"

Castelli circled his arms around her waist under the bomber jacket, pulling her close. She pushed her hips hard against him as they kissed, suddenly unable to resist the delicious tingle in her loins. "Yes, I promise."

On and off for the next three hours, he told her what Pete had said about Trice's piano playing and Gloria Partridge; about the jawbone in the pictures with one less tooth each year; about Jack McKeon slipping information to Trice so Local 664 could win the NLRB election in 1968. And the more he talked, the less she wanted him.

When she would awake five hours later, angry for giving in to her own lust, David would still be asleep in the bed next to her. She would quietly gather her clothes from the floor, slide open the top drawer of the flimsy night table, and take out a single piece of stationery. Then she would carry the clothes and the paper into the bathroom, and finally put closure to Aaron Mueller.

TWENTY-THREE
Saturday, October 8

HARRY'S VOICE HAD BEEN thick with sleep when he answered the phone next to his bed. But it took only seconds for him to comprehend that the call was something very important.

"Do you know what time it is?"

"Yes, sir, I do, and I'm really sorry to be bothering you at this hour, but I need to see you right away."

"What are you talking about, see me? It's the middle of the night."

"Mr. Greene—oh, the hell with it. Harry, get out of bed, get dressed, go to your office, and call the guard at the gate. Tell him to let me in. I'll meet you in a half hour."

"You wanna tell me ..."

"No, I don't, Harry. Just be there."

Harry, his eyes still red with sleep, was behind his desk now, waiting at 1:30 in the morning for a visit from Pete Werner. He rubbed at the stubble on his face, forcing himself to think, knowing instinctively that it must have something to do with T. J. Trice.

As Harry was reaching for the Very Old Fitzgerald bourbon that he kept in a drawer of his credenza, Werner's hulking frame walked through the open office door. Greene turned, bottle and glass in hand, just as the light from his desk lamp played across the swollen features of the Secretary-Treasurer's face.

"Jesus, what the hell happened to you?"

"Some of Trice's playmates decided to play ping pong with my head last night. Would you like to know why?"

"At this hour, Werner, all I really want to know is why I'm here."

"Yeah, well. What's the difference. Union guys just get the shit beat out of them once in a while. Part of the job description, right, Harry?"

Harry was suddenly embarrassed at his own coldness. Werner's face was a mess. And it had to be part of the whole thing, anyhow. So he asked. "All right then, tell me why your face looks like a piece of calf's liver."

Werner sat down hard in the chair opposite Harry's desk. For a moment, he didn't say a word—just shifted his body back and forth, uneasy. "You know, I don't think I've ever been in this office before."

"Well you picked a helluva time to visit."

"I didn't think it could wait—what I have to tell you." Werner saw the bourbon. "Give me some of that. It'll make it easier."

Harry reached into the credenza for another glass. He was wide awake now, suddenly scared. Werner took the offering and drained half in a single swallow. He rubbed his mouth with the back of his hand.

"Trice's biker buddies beat me up because I was trying to find out why his arbitration is being fixed."

"What are you talking about?"

"Oh, Harry, don't jerk me off on this. It's been too long a day. You think I'm stupid? Castelli subpoenas Trice's hospital records, then a fake shows up. Poor dumb Charlie changes his story. You think I don't know a tank job when I see one. I'm in the business, remember?"

Greene forced himself to play the straight man. "So what if it's fixed? Probably one of your clever little shop stewards. Anyhow, if you're right, the union wins. Isn't that what you people want?"

"Harry, it's late. You said so yourself. So let's cut the b.s. We're not talking about a shop steward. A shop steward doesn't break into Garden Spot Hospital's computer. A shop steward doesn't pick a whore like van Auten for the most important discharge case your company ever had. And I'll tell you something else, Mr. Greene, since we're being perfectly frank here, a shop steward doesn't go around blackmailing company presidents with pictures of dead bodies."

In 1961, when he was thirty-seven, a doctor had told Harry that a mole on his back might be malignant melanoma. That day in the doctor's office, Greene had felt a chill course through his body that was almost electric in its intensity. He had heard exactly what the doctor said, understood every word. Still, he had made the man repeat it. It turned out the doctor was wrong, but Harry never forgot the feeling he experienced when he heard the words "malignant melanoma." It would take thirty-three years for him to feel the same chill again.

He said nothing at first. Just stared at Pete—no, past Pete—stared out through the open office door behind the chair where the Secretary-Treasurer was sitting, also saying nothing. Each man fiddled—Pete with his empty glass, Harry with his cigar lighter gun. When Harry finally spoke, it was just like in the doctor's office.

"What did you say?"

"I know about the Tooth Fairy, Harry. And Stroudsburg, Harry. And Willis Tucker, Harry. Where do you want me to start?"

Harry Greene reached again for the bottle of Very Old Fitzgerald. He started to fill his glass. But he stopped. Stopped and just closed his eyes. Then he said, in a very soft voice, the most important thing in his head. "I didn't kill anybody, Werner, I swear to god."

"I believe you Harry. I don't think you're the type. So, what, did Trice do it? Is that the deal?"

"No, Trice didn't kill him, either. He just collects. Same as you, now, right?"

"No, Harry, not right. I don't want your money. I just want the goddamn truth. What does that bastard have on you? Why do you pay him? Just tell me that, so at least I'll know why I've got him as a member."

"It's a long story."

"We've got a long night, Harry. Just start talking."

<hr>

When Harry Greene backed out of his garage shortly after midnight on September 8, 1984, he left behind, in bed, a wife who didn't really believe a word of his explanation.

"I never heard of any Jacob Glick, Harry. You never talked about him, and now you're telling me he can only meet you at six o'clock in the morning on a Saturday?"

"I'm trying to keep a goddamn business going, in case you didn't notice. A guy named Jacob Glick says he's got three acres of junks in an illegal landfill north of Wellsboro, I go. He tells me he don't do business by phone, I go. He tells me it's six AM on Saturday, I go."

He would tell Minna later that they couldn't agree on a price. He'd rant and rave about the bastard making him ruin his weekend, then he'd take her to the club for a big steak and the whole thing would blow over. Until the next time Fontini decided to do it in the middle of the night.

The plane had been due to land at 5:15 AM. It was late. Harry stood huddled in his suede jacket, just behind the tree line at the edge of the field, his feet numb from standing. He felt the wind cut into the back of his neck.

Twenty yards to his right, Harry could see the barrel that was Tony Angelo—no topcoat, no hat, standing motionless against a Canadian front that was already bending tree branches all around him. Behind Tony, shielded from the wind by his bodyguard, Mario Fontini was unsuccessfully trying to light a cigarette.

The three men all heard the Cessna's engine at the same moment. On, then off, coughing its death rattle above the trees as it suddenly fell out of the low cloud bank just a few hundred feet above them.

Tony Angelo yelled, "Stupid fuck, he's gonna crash," then stubbed out his own cigarette just as the Cessna and its pilot and its cargo nosed into a sea of mud and grass less than fifty yards away.

For six hours after Fontini and Tony Angelo had driven off, Harry Greene just sat. Sat on a wooden bench in the cold, empty mess hall that no longer even had a roof, but which had once been the nerve center of Camp Pocono Sunrise.

He wanted to sit in his car, but the thought of what was in the trunk made him physically sick. At the end of the second hour, he had forced himself to get in just long enough to call Minna on the car phone, and roll out a rambling load of bullshit about why he wouldn't be home until after dark. Then he returned to the mess hall, convinced that he could already smell Willis Tucker seeping through the cushions of the back seat.

He figured he wouldn't leave for Lancaster until at least six in the evening, just to make sure that by the time he arrived, Hixon Avenue would be shut down tight for the weekend. The only mistake he made was deciding to kill four hours of the wait in Kitty's Tavern.

Harry found it hard to drive with a dead body in his trunk. He was certain that the latch would pop open and at least one of Willis Tucker's arms would somehow manage to slip out from under the rear deck lid and begin signalling passing cars to come have a look.

He drove with all four of the windows down. By the time he reached the outskirts of Lancaster, he realized he was still drunk from six Cutty Sarks he had downed at Kitty's. He began navigating with the deliberate attention to speed limits that renders an intoxicated driver instantly recognizable.

The flashing lights in his review mirror snapped his head to attention. Harry could feel bile rushing up toward his throat. It only got worse when the red face of Pennsylvania State Trooper Seamus McGrath poked itself through the driver's window.

"Why if it isn't Hixon Avenue's favorite air polluter. License and registration, *Mister* Greene."

Harry looked up at the cop who lived next door to Greene-Pitowsky Smelting & Battery Company and almost passed out. He managed to say hello, but that was about it. When he tried to extract the driver's license from his wallet and dropped it to the floor, McGrath was on him.

"Step out of the car please."

"Excuse me?"

"You deaf too? Or just drunk? I said step out of the car."

It was only McGrath's arrogance that saved Harry from certain arrest. That, and the overwhelming fear in his body, driving out the alcohol, willing him into a state of sobriety.

"Just who do you think you're talking to?" Greene said.

"A drunken Jew. How do you like that." McGrath opened the car door and yanked Greene out and to his feet. He spun the frightened man around and shoved him up against the side of the Buick. "I oughta cuff you right now."

"Look, I'm sorry, all right. It's been a long day."

"Oh is that so? Long day doing what, killing kids with battery acid?"

Greene was determined to get out of this. He concentrated every functioning synapse in his brain on being polite. He had a dead body in the trunk of his car.

"Please, let me get my wallet. I'm not going to give you any trouble."

"That's much better, Mr. Greene. Why don't you just do that."

Harry bent down, then handed his entire wallet to McGrath. The officer opened it up and whistled. "My, my, my," he said. "So how much do you think is in here?"

"Two, three hundred, I don't know."

"Man can go to jail in this commonwealth for drunk driving. You *do* know that, don't you Mr. Greene?"

He desperately wanted to say, "You're the one should know, you Irish bastard." But there was a dead body in the trunk of his car, so instead he said. "Take it all. Just take it."

"Do I hear somebody offering me a bribe?" Then Seamus McGrath started to laugh, a raspy, ugly laugh, mixed with phlegm. Harry could not even look at him. He stared at the ground, away from the officer's tiny pug nose and thin mouth and huge red forehead, bulging out from beneath the tilted back patent leather brim of his cap.

Still carrying Harry's wallet, McGrath abruptly turned and did the one thing Greene feared most. He walked toward the rear of the car. Harry followed. He allowed himself to exhale only when McGrath laughed again, took out his weapon, and smashed Harry's right rear tail light with the butt. "Broken," the policeman said. "Have to give you a ticket for that."

Five minutes later, Harry Greene was waiting for his pulse to return to normal, a fifty dollar ticket and an empty wallet in his hand, his eyes closed in blessed relief. He did not notice the pickup that had also pulled to the side of the road, drawn by the sight of the familiar black Buick, with a vanity plate that said "SMELTER," and its owner being yanked out onto the highway by the police.

The pickup driver decided it might be fun to watch this happy little drama play out. When it was over, he also decided to follow the Buick. There was no particular reason for this, except he was alone on a Saturday night with a beer buzz on, and he just had nothing better to do.

Greene ripped the sleeve of his suede jacket trying to pull open the chain link fence at the rear of his property. He was beginning to sweat now, despite the chilly air. The perfectly clear day had been followed by an equally clear night, with a moon so big Harry was sure he was being watched by half the population of Hixon Avenue. In fact, he was only being watched by a single figure, behind the wheel of a pickup, about a hundred yards to his rear. When the figure saw Harry drive his car right up to the side of the furnace building, then get out and pop the trunk, Thomas Jefferson Trice decided to proceed on foot.

Harry had been trying to prepare himself for this moment since seven o'clock in the morning. He failed. Willis Tucker still looked only like a man asleep, except now the entire side of his face was covered with dried blood. The smell was already rank and sour, making Harry first gag, then rush to the wall of the building and throw up into the weeds. He stayed there, head in the crook of his arm against the wall, spittle dangling from his lips as he coughed himself back to readiness. Finally, he turned and walked toward the front end loader parked about ten feet from his car.

He could still operate the loader—the hand-foot coordination learned so many years ago from his uncle Nate now quickly coming back. He would have to touch the body only once. Had to get it out of the trunk and into the shovel at the front of the loader. The rest would be mechanical—driving the loader into the empty furnace building, positioning it directly over the bucket conveyor leading to the top of Bessemer One, throwing the black-handled lever that would tip the shovel's contents into one of the gigantic buckets, and finally starting the conveyor on its climb to the open furnace top. It would not be Harry doing these things. It would just be the machines.

He threw up for a second time the moment he felt the stiffened body of Willis Tucker, dry heaves now, the contents of his stomach already spent against the side of the building. Tucker's dead weight was enormous, but somehow Harry managed to drag most of his old caretaker up and over the edge of the trunk, letting gravity then deposit the corpse and its tangle of duck decoys into the loader.

The only sounds in the furnace building were deep rumbles from the bellies of the Bessemers, each one with its glowing window of fire throwing a red streak of light across the concrete floor. It would be over eighteen hours before the first shift tenders would come on duty. By then there would be no more Willis Tucker.

He gunned the engine of the front end loader, watching over the hood as its shovel slowly rose until it had cleared the floor far enough for Harry to swing his grisly payload over the lowest conveyor bucket. Then he pulled back on the joystick between his legs, causing the shovel to tilt forward and deposit the dead caretaker into his mobile coffin. Harry could feel his whole body starting to shake. He forced himself to walk to the conveyor control hanging down on its metal electrical cable. He held his thumb over the large green start button, closed his eyes, and pushed. With a loud clack, the chain drive activated, rumbling deep and loud through the empty building. As the bucket containing the remains of Willis Tucker and his beloved decoys began to rise, Harry Greene began to recite the Mourner's Kaddish: "yitgadal, v'yitkadash shmey raba." And that is exactly how far he got before the conveyor jammed.

It was rope from the duck decoys, hanging over the bucket, tangled up in the conveyor mechanism. Willis came to a stop about eight feet up the ramp, which Harry now clambored onto—into then out of the lower buckets—his suede jacket covered with grease and ash, his breath coming in labored heaves mixed with coughing spasms. He was finally in the state of panic that he had managed to avoid for over ten hours. But the panic gave him strength, enough strength to wrestle Willis Tucker from the bucket and push him over the side, then off the belt and into the air. The body thudded to the concrete, dragging its covey of decoys behind like so many kite streamers.

Greene tripped over the last bucket on the way down. He fell hard to the floor, pain exploding in his wrists and knees as he broke his fall on all fours. He managed to stand up, with his chest heaving and sweat matting his hair. He mounted the loader, lowered the shovel, then threw the machine into gear. It scrabbled along the floor now, until it reached the tangled dead body, which it then pushed across the floor, all the way to the base of the Bessemer, forcing Willis back into the metal shovel.

Harry backed up, turned, then drove out the door into the night. He had no idea where he was going. He was lost on the grounds of his own factory, disoriented, totally without a clue—until he remembered the obvious.

Harry was off his chair by now, standing behind his desk, looking at Pete Werner who hadn't said a word since Greene's story began.

"The piles, Werner. The casing piles. And I stuck him in deep. Eight, ten feet. Acid off those cases would have eaten him up in three days. 'Cept the sonofabitch dragged him out. And he cut off the poor bastard's head. Do you hear me, he cut off his fucking head! He actually told me this. Told me just like it was nothing. Went through his pockets, too, till he found something with a name on it. Then he put the rest of Willis back in the pile. And after that he started with those pictures. Every year, just so I'd know he still had a piece of the guy. And I paid him, Werner. Every cent he asked for. A hundred grand a year. What the hell was I supposed to do?"

Then there was silence in the office of Harry Greene.

Pete Werner looked at the owner who was a multi-millionaire. What he saw was an old man with tears running down his face, with two large hands gripping the edge of his desk, with his whole body leaning forward as if in supplication to the big union leader who had finally given him peace.

Neither man said a word for the next two minutes.

Finally, Pete spoke. "Didn't you ever think about having him killed?"

"Every goddamned day for the last ten years."

"But?"

"But it wouldn't do any good. He's got a failsafe."

"A what?"

"A backup. Trice says there's someone else out there who also gets the pictures, and who's going to rat me to the cops the first year he doesn't get his copy."

"And you believe him?"

"Does it matter? I got a business. I got a family. I'm not a murderer."

"I know you're not a murderer, Harry. Anyhow, I know who the failsafe is."

"That's impossible."

"Look, Harry. What I'm going to tell you now is the real reason I came here. Yeah, I wanted to know why Trice sent you those pictures. Who wouldn't? But there's something else I found out tonight. Something not even you know—and you gotta know."

"It's about the failsafe, isn't it?"

"Yes, Harry, it is. Let me ask you something. You ever wonder how the Teamsters got into your place so easy back in '68?"

"All the time, Werner, you want to know the truth. But what's that got to do with anything?"

"Look, Harry. Follow me here. Three hours ago, I broke into Trice's house. Don't even ask me why, because the whole thing was crazy. That's how I found the pictures of Willis and T. J.'s love notes. But that's not all I found. I found out how Local 664 was able to kick your butt so easy. We had all your information."

"What do you mean all our information?"

"I mean everything—your financial records, tax returns, cancelled checks. Shit, we even had your own wring-outs, you know those employee lists McKeon made you keep, showing how the ties thought our men were gonna vote."

"No way. Nobody ever saw those wring-outs during the campaign. Nobody but me and Jack McKeon."

"That's almost right, Harry. Nobody saw them but you and Jack. Until Jack decided to slip the whole ball of wax to T. J. Trice."

"You're nuts."

"Harry, I saw all of it. It was in a drawer in Trice's house. Shit, the wring-out even had a note clipped on—in Jack McKeon's own handwriting."

"How'd you know that?"

"Because David Castelli recognized it, that's how."

"Castelli?"

"Yes, and I'm sorry. Castelli's got the whole file. I gave it to him before I knew what he was going to do with it. I'm pretty damn sure he'll be coming to see you tomorrow—with his hand out."

For the second time since Pete Werner walked into his office Greene felt the chill. Thirty-three years, and now twice in five minutes. Except this time it was worse. "This is all—no. It's wrong. Jack McKeon is my best friend. He saved my goddamn life in a fucking trench in Italy. You know that? I wouldn't even be here wasn't for Jack McKeon."

"You're right, Harry. You wouldn't be here. Of course, neither would the Teamsters. Let me ask you, how much money you think you've paid Jack McKeon since 1968? How many labor arbitrations? How many negotiations? How many OSHA violations and trips to the god almighty NLRB? You think any of that would've happened you don't have a union in here? Don't you get it? McKeon sold you out for the legal business."

Harry got it easily. In matters of the wallet, the man had few peers. But getting it and dealing with it were entirely separate.

"I just don't believe it." Harry was coming back to reality. He stood up and paced around the office. Then he walked back to his desk chair, flopping down into it like a tired old walrus, his head now buried in his hands.

"I'm really sorry, Harry. It must be awful to wake up and find your best friend has been fucking you up the ass for a quarter century."

"Jack wanted me to kill Trice. Kept telling me there wasn't any failsafe."

"Of course, he did, Harry. It all makes sense. Trice has had McKeon by the balls all these years, same as you. Must've made Jack agree to be the failsafe so he wouldn't have to cut someone else in. You get rid of Trice, McKeon's home free."

As Pete continued to talk, Harry Greene the businessman was finally starting to wrench control away from Harry Greene the fool. This was a Teamster sitting across from him, ripping his life open like a rotten tomato. There had to be a catch. A motive. Something. He asked the obvious question.

"Werner, why are you telling me all this?"

"You mean, what's in it for me?"

"Yeah, that's exactly what I mean. You don't like this company, never did. Fact, you couldn't stand it when you worked here; called me a Jew bastard once—right to my face. You probably don't even remember that."

"I remember it, Harry. Week after I got pneumonia because you wouldn't cover the walkway to the kettle room. I was young."

"But you still think it, don't you?"

"No, as a matter of fact, I don't still think it. But the problem is, you do. You believe that's all anyone *does* think about you."

"You can't understand."

"Oh, please, Harry. Let it go, already," Werner said. "You don't think we all come from somewhere? You wanna hear what they called my father in the US Army in '43 because his name was Wilhelm? No, I don't think you're a Jew bastard. Just a bastard." Pete laughed as he said this. Not a snide laugh, just a laugh to break the tension.

And Harry couldn't help the smile that all of a sudden played across his own face. "I'm sorry, Werner. You want to know the truth, I don't think you're such a bad guy, either. You just happen to have a rotten job. But the question is still on the floor. Why did you come here tonight and tell me all this if you're not planning to jump on the tit?"

"You want the truth, I don't even really know myself. Part of it's just a feeling it's better this way. That, and Castelli makes me want to puke. At least Jack McKeon was creative."

"You really think Castelli's coming here tomorrow?"

"Don't bet against it. He knows about Willis Tucker now, same as Trice. And he's a hungry little shit."

"So what do I do?"

"I don't really know what you can do, Harry. But it just seemed to me you'd have a better chance knowing the deal a few hours ahead of time. That's how it seemed, anyhow. Besides, my grandfather probably would have done the same thing."

"Your grandfather?"

"Forget it, Harry. Look, I'm tired, my face hurts, and something tells me you've got a long day tomorrow. I'm going to bed."

Pete Werner stood up to leave. As he did so, Harry also rose from his chair, then leaned across the desk and held out his hand. "Thank you," he said. "I know this wasn't easy."

"It was a lot easier for me than for you. I'd kill the whole damn lot of 'em."

And Werner was gone.

The summer of '43. Harry, alone in his office now, remembering that day in July.

The other Jew in his platoon was a little guy named Sol Sachs from Bayonne, New Jersey. Used to make up stories about himself that nobody believed. Sol the trumpet player who said he jammed with Coleman

Hawkins; Sol the stud who said he fucked one of the Radio City Rockettes; Sol the hood who said he belonged to a motorcycle gang. Sol the soldier who never did anything brave in his life until the day when he suddenly lost it, jumped out of the foxhole, and went running off toward a German machine gun nest screaming "Nazi cocksuckers" at the top of his lungs until a ribbon of bullets tore out most of his chest.

Fifty-one years later, Harry could still see him writhing on the ground. He could still hear him screaming in pain. It was Jack McKeon who had grabbed hold of Harry's right leg that day, hanging onto it with all of his weight, until Greene stopped fighting him and fell back into the hole. "He's dead you asshole! Leave him be." Jack had said this just as the German machine gunner fired a final burst into Sol's already mutilated body, the bullets lifting him off the ground, making him dance like an epileptic rag doll.

Had McKeon already figured out a way to use Harry? He held that thought now, ridiculous as it was, because he needed a new explanation for why the young Irishman had saved his life. Friendship was no longer a possibility. Not anymore.

TWENTY-FOUR
Saturday, October 8

EVEN WHILE HE WAS staring at the Gideon Bible in the open night table drawer, his eyes focusing on the new day, David Castelli didn't realize she was gone.

That discovery would not be made until he stumbled into the bathroom, thinking he would surprise her there with a morning tumble against the sink, and saw her letter taped to the mirror.

He read it without even pulling it down.

SLEEP-TITE MOTOR LODGE
Gateway to the Amish Country

David,

Forgive me, please, but I couldn't do this in person.

It's wrong. Everything about it. I could use the old cliché that you are a married man with a family. But I won't. I knew that the first night I held your hand at the bar and saw the wedding ring.

I am not sad that we slept together last week at the Lamplighter. I am only sorry that I came here. And not because you were waiting, either. I am sorry because yesterday, by helping you, I hurt the best friend I'll probably ever have.

I know you will not be going to the Lancaster police despite
what you said. But don't worry, I won't either. I ask only that
you remember Pete in whatever you do. And remember yourself,
too. It always comes back.

Jennifer

David took a step backwards and stared at himself in the mirror, a naked
body with a piece of stationery for the head. It was a handsome body, fair
and well muscled. The body had no blemishes; it had no scars; it was well
endowed. It had looked so perfect laced together with the taut beauty of
Jennifer Alston Delone.

He pressed his two thumbs tightly against the base of his skull, trying
to stop a throbbing ache that suddenly started deep inside his head. Then
he screamed out loud. "Son of a bitch!" The scream was followed immediately by the right hand tearing the note off the mirror, shredding it, throwing it in the toilet. It was only after he had sent Jenny's farewell to eternal
rest in the sewers of Lancaster County that David Castelli allowed himself
the luxury of regret. Everything she had written was absolutely right.

The phone booth he chose was on the edge of an Exxon station, about
three hundred yards down the road from Lilly's Diner. It was 8:30 AM on
a Saturday morning. Twenty minutes earlier he had scooped up the last
piece of Lilly's Country Breakfast—a dollop of home fries covered with
ketchup—and stuffed it into his mouth. On the way out, he had thrown
seven quarters into a machine by the door and purchased his first pack of
Pall Mall cigarettes in ten years. The initial drag almost made him throw
up.

"Stroudsburg police, Sergeant Hardy."

"I'd like to talk to someone about Willis Tucker."

"Your name, please."

"I don't think so." The phone immediately went quiet. When it came
back, about a minute later, David heard the first beep.

"This is Detective Williams. May I help you?"

"Turn off the damn recorder. Then maybe you can help me." David was invigorated by the anonymity of a phone booth in Neffsville and the second Pall Mall, which wasn't making him sick.

"Okay, pal. It's off." David had no way of telling if it was really off or if just the beeps were off. Detective Williams wasn't waiting for his caller to figure it out. "You got information on Willis Tucker, I wanna hear it."

"I didn't say anything about information. Just wanted to talk to someone about Willis Tucker. That would be you."

"Yes, sir." Williams forced himself to be professional. He already regretted the lapse into cynicism. But ten-year-old open fatals tended to do that. "What can I do for you?"

"It's for my criminology course." David was making it up as he went along, Williams not believing a word of it, David knowing Williams wasn't believing a word of it and was probably trying to trace the call anyhow, but Castelli really didn't care. "See, each student got assigned an unsolved murder somewhere in Pennsylvania, and we're supposed to interview the police, get all the public stuff, you know, then write a report. So anyhow, I was wondering what you can tell me about this one."

Everett Williams had been a homicide detective for seventeen years, long enough to know that you didn't walk away from a thread. Even one that sounded like complete bullshit. Besides, the longer he talked, the better his chance for a good trace.

"Well, sir, there really isn't very much. Practically a complete dead ender. Willis Tucker went hunting on the morning of September 8, 1984, and never came back. Fact is, we don't even know to this day he was murdered, do you?"

David ignored the question. "Then why do you have a file?"

"Regulations. His wife said he liked to duck hunt at this abandoned summer camp where he used to work. Place called Pocono Sunrise. Been closed for years. So we searched the place day after Tucker disappeared. No body. But we did find a duck decoy in the grass near this old coffin blind by the lake. The wife said it was one of his, but we could never find the rest of them. Probably would have stopped there, missing person, that's that. Except the decoy had some interesting prints on it."

"Mr. Tucker's I suspect?"

"His too. But you'd kinda expect that now, wouldn't you? No, the prints I'm talking about belonged to a hood named Tony Angelo. Foot soldier for Mario Fontini. Ever hear of him?"

Everybody in Philadelphia knew the name Mario Fontini. But David had no idea how far north the man's fame had spread, so he picked the safe course. "No, can't say I have."

Williams figured this for another lie. "That so? Well the man just about runs the Philly mob."

"And his boy's fingerprints were on Willis Tucker's decoy?"

"That's right. But that's as far as we ever got. Pulled Angelo in. Wouldn't say a word. Wouldn't even confirm his name. But, now you understand why we never closed the file."

"I guess I do. What about the camp?"

"Searched every inch of it. Only thing unusual we ever found were a few pieces of wreckage in the woods off one of the ball fields. Experts said it came from an old Cessna 140. Except the FAA didn't report anything going down in the Poconos even close to the day Willis disappeared. Besides, it was only a few pieces, not the whole plane or anything."

"You said the camp was abandoned?"

"Over ten years. Traced that down too. Even talked to the owner. Fellow named Harry Greene. Runs a big smelting operation down in Lancaster. Only thing we got there was how sorry he was to learn his old caretaker disappeared. Never even knew the guy was using his land to hunt. That's about all of it."

Castelli didn't bother to say goodbye before he hung up the phone, got into the Accord, and headed for his next stop. On the other end, Everett Williams' people told him only that the call had come from somewhere near Lancaster.

It was enough. The detective pulled out the old cassette of his 1984 telephone interview with the owner of Camp Pocono Sunrise. Maybe something would click this time. Even though he doubted it. His own voice came first.

Good afternoon, Mr. Greene, this is Detective Everett C. Williams, of the Stroudsburg Police. How are you today?

Fine, sir. Is anything wrong?

We're not really sure; but don't worry, whatever it is doesn't involve you?

Then why are you calling?

We want to ask you a few questions about a gentleman named Willis Tucker. Do you know him?

Why do you want to know about Willis Tucker?

Because he's been missing for the past two weeks.

Gee I'm sorry to hear that.

Anyhow, we're just tracking down leads. His wife says he used to work for you.

Christ, that was years ago. Do you know how many years ago that was?

Yes sir. About fourteen.

Then why the hell do you want to talk to *me* about him?

Well, sir, the last place we know he went was your old camp down on Route 191. He was duck hunting.

When was that, detective?

Little over two weeks ago, September eighth. He never came back. We just want to know if you have any information about him, that's all. We really don't want to bother you.

I was in Lancaster two weeks ago. At my office.

Mr. Greene, believe me, your whereabouts that day are the furthest thing from our minds. We're just trying to get information on Mr. Tucker.

Well I'd like to help you, but like I say, I haven't heard from Willis since I closed the camp back in '71. Had no idea he was using the old place to hunt. Not that I care, mind you. Land sure ain't doing me no good.

But you do have it posted for trespassers, Mr. Greene.

Lawyers. They tell me I *gotta* post it so I don't get sued if some schmuck stumbles in there and hurts himself.

Yeah, I understand. Listen. One more thing and I'll let you go. And please don't take this personal because we're asking everyone. You ever have any dealings with a fellow named Tony Angelo? Works for the Mario Fontini mob down in Philadelphia. Ever see him, talk to him, you know?

What are you, Elliot Ness or something? What the hell's Mario Fontini got to do with Willis Tucker. That *is* why you called, isn't it? Willis Tucker?

Yes, sir. Willis Tucker. It's just there may be some connection between Mr. Tucker and this fellow Tony Angelo, so we're asking around, that's all.

Believe me, Mr. Williams, the last thing I need around here is to be messing with those kind of people. This business is tough enough as it is.

Sure. Look, I appreciate you talking to me, Mr. Greene. I really do. Now, anything hits you, I mean anything at all, you call, okay? 717-296-2455. Got that?

Yes, sir. No problem.

Good-bye, now.

Bye.

Everett Williams' eyes scanned the ten-year-old transcript as he listened to the ten-year-old tape. He had probably listened to it close to a fifty times since 1984, and not once had he ever been impressed by Harry Greene's honesty. There was always something about his voice, the edge on it, the timbre. And Williams was always troubled by the part where Greene volunteered that he was in Lancaster on September 8. Said it for absolutely no reason at all. Except one, of course.

Now, completely out of the blue, someone was calling about Willis Tucker. And his people were telling him the call came from near Lancaster.

Everett Williams decided it was time to look up his old telephone buddy.

Number 17 Great Stag Drive. Castelli had picked Harry Greene's address out of the white pages hanging from a hook in the phone booth.

The map on his seat led him to a private road with two stone columns at its entrance and a sign that said "Westbrooke Park." Castelli tried not to think that Harry's house had "Jew" written on it in big neon letters. He felt ashamed of himself for thinking this, but he couldn't help it—even though every one of his parents' Italian friends who could afford bridge toll had long ago abandoned South Philadelphia for similar homesteads in Cherry Hill, New Jersey.

The Greene-a-rosa must have taken up at least half a block. It was a corner property, fake English Tudor, with a boy on a John Deere already carving neat strips back and forth across the massive lawn. Castelli pulled into the circular driveway.

The woman in the hot pink sweatsuit and bracelets stared at the handsome blond figure standing on her doorstep at 9:45 AM on a Saturday morning holding a briefcase.

"We don't buy door to door."

"Mrs. Greene, my name is David Castelli. I'm one of your husband's lawyers."

"Oh my goodness, I'm sorry. Please come in."

He stepped into a white marble foyer. Over the woman's shoulder he could see a large circular staircase, disappearing up to a landing backed by a trio of floor to ceiling panels of leaded glass. The morning sun, angling in through the center pane, almost blinded him.

"You're that young labor lawyer, aren't you?" She didn't expect an answer. "Harry talks about you all the time. I'm really sorry. That was so rude of me."

"Don't worry about it, Mrs. Greene."

"Please. It's Minna." She held out a braceleted hand. "Can I get you something to drink? Coffee? Juice?"

"I'm fine, actually. Listen, I really hate to bother you at home, but I was wondering if I could speak to Harry."

"You just missed him, David. He's at the plant."

"This early on a Saturday. I'm impressed."

"Don't be, he's usually not even up yet. Except last night he made this appointment for some reason."

"Problem?"

"Don't ask me. He never talks about business at home. All he said was he had to meet with some hourly man. Strange. Harry almost never talks to those people. At least not directly."

"He didn't happen to say who the man was, did he?"

"He did, actually. Somebody named Johnson. Tell you the truth, I didn't even realize he knew any of them by name."

It was all David could do to make himself say good-bye before running out to his car.

⸺⸺⚬⚬⚬⚬⸺⸺

Harry Greene had made the appointment with Stuff Johnson late Friday afternoon, hours before his early morning encounter with Pete Werner. And, while he had no reason to doubt what Werner had told him about David Castelli, the only ante actually showing on the table still belonged to Thomas Jefferson Trice. Ever the cautious businessman, Harry had to make certain there would be no Stuff Johnson showing up Monday at the arbitration.

He fiddled with his cigar lighter gun. Picking it up. Putting it down. Not smoking a cigar.

"Stuff. That's your nickname, isn't it? Stuff?"

"Yes, sir."

"I don't suppose you have any idea why you're here, do you?"

He had a lot of ideas. All bad. "Do I need a steward?"

Harry made himself laugh, a big belly laugh, doing his best to make the frightened man feel at ease. "No, of course not. You don't need a steward. Why would you think that?"

"Look, Mr. Greene. How long I been working here?"

Harry looked down at the papers on his desk. "Three years and two months."

"Yeah, that sounds right, three years and two months. Anyhow, this is the first time I ever been in your office. Shit—excuse me—this the first time I ever been in this *building*. So I figure I got to be in some kind of trouble."

Harry stood up and walked around to the side of his desk where Johnson was sitting. He sat down in the other side chair and put his hand on his employee's forearm. "I want to assure you, son, you are not in any trouble. Fact is, Mr. Breitenfeld says you're one of his best workers. You know that?"

"Well, sir, actually, see Mr. Breitenfeld. Well, he ..."

"Wouldn't compliment the damn Pope, right?"

Johnson didn't like to hear a Jew misuse the name of the Holy Father, but he also wanted to keep his job. So he made himself agree. "Well, sir, since you said it, the men don't get too close to Mr. B. You're right about that."

"Goddamn right I'm right. Which brings me to why I asked you to come in this morning. Now, what I'm going to tell you can't leave this room, you understand?"

"Sure, anything you say, Mr. Greene."

"You know about the Trice case I take it."

"Everyone knows about that, sir."

"Yeah, but there may be some things you don't know. So pay attention. I think we're gonna lose that case. Lose it bad. And you wanna know why?"

Johnson already knew why, but this was not the place to demonstrate his intelligence. "Well, the way I hear it your lawyer ain't doing too good against our lawyer."

"That's right, Stuff. That's absolutely right. But it isn't Mr. Castelli's fault. It's Joe Breitenfeld's fault."

"It is?"

"Oh yeah. See, Mr. Breitenfeld jumped the gun here. Very bad for a supervisor. Went off and fired Trice before he actually talked to Charlie Carpool. Did you know that?"

"Not really."

"And this isn't the first time. Look, I'm going to level with you. I've been very unhappy with Mr. Breitenfeld's performance lately. Matter of fact, I've been thinking about letting him go. There's only one problem."

Still the straight man, Stuff said, "And what's that?"

"His age. Joe Breitenfeld is almost fifty years old. I fire him, he sues the company for age discrimination. You know what that is?"

"Something about you can't fire a man if he's old?"

"Close enough. But here's the deal. If we lose this case, like I think we're gonna, then Joe is the one fucked it up. Fucked it up big time. Reinstatement, full back pay. Fuck up like that, I'll *have* to let him go, you understand?"

"But then he'll sue the company. You just said."

"He might want to, but he'll have to find a lawyer first to take the case. Gonna be a lot harder with a black mark like that on his record."

"So why are you telling me all this, Mr. Greene?"

"Because I think you are the only chance left for Castelli to win. And, quite frankly, I don't want to see that happen. Don't get me wrong, now. I think what T. J. did to Charlie Carpool was terrible. But we have to look out for what's best for our company now, don't we?"

"Yes, sir. But I don't see how this has anything to do with me."

Harry purposely took the smile off his face. "Yes you do, Stuff. You think we're stupid? You were with T. J. the night it happened. You left Jenny Rats with him, not ten minutes before the old man got run down. For all I know, you were in that battery house right along with him."

"That's not true, Mr. Greene. He wanted me to go, but I wouldn't do it. It was crazy. I wouldn't ..."

Harry interrupted him. "Now, you see, Stuff. That's exactly what could happen to you on a witness stand. You say that, Trice is cooked. And Breitenfeld saves his job."

"But nobody's asking me to testify."

"And that's just the way I want to keep it. But, I can't control Castelli now, can I? Just think how *that* would look. So what I want from you is a simple promise. If Castelli, or anyone else, contacts you before Monday, you be sure and keep your wits about you, you understand. T. J. left Jenny's. You left Jenny's. He went his way. You went yours. Short and sweet."

For the first time since he entered the office, Stuff Johnson let out a deep breath and smiled. "That's exactly how it went down, Mr. Greene. He went his way. I went mine."

Harry stood up and walked toward the door. "You do this right, we may be talking about your own future with the company. Gonna need a new warehouse supervisor after Joe B. hits the road, you know."

"Mr. Greene, you don't have a thing to worry about."

It wasn't until Johnson had left his office that Harry allowed himself to think about the main event on this morning's card. Was Pete Werner right? Would he soon have another visitor in his office?

———◦◦◦———

What David Castelli least expected to see as he turned his car into the front entrance of Greene-Pitowsky Smelting & Battery Company was a familiar-looking Harley-Davidson Sportster coming the other way. But that's what he saw, its rider throwing a big happy wave toward the guard shack as he roared out onto Hixon Avenue, up past the Rat, then out of sight.

"Who was that guy?" He was asking the guard just to make sure.

"Stuff Johnson, why? You know him?"

He mumbled something that sounded like yes, David distracted now, looking over the parking lot, trying to spot Harry Greene's Buick. When he did, it was the first time David noticed that the car's license plate said "SMELTER." He was sure Harry didn't have any trouble getting that particular vanity plate. Who would want to advertise such a gross business? David also wondered what in the world must have been going through his own mind as he drove to the plant from 17 Great Stag Drive. What did he think he was going to find here, Stuff's head rolling out of Battery Boulevard? Harry chasing Johnson with a machete? He felt like an idiot. Until, of course, he remembered what was in his briefcase.

He found the man in his office, feet up on the desk, barking into his handheld dictaphone. Macanudo smoke rose up in front of his face. Even though he'd seen it before, David couldn't get over the fact that this was the office of a multi-millionaire, with its battered wood furniture and dirty windows and boxes of papers sitting haphazardly on an old linoleum floor of maroon and black swirls. The cheap paneled walls were chockablock with assorted plaques, most of them not even hanging straight: Lancaster B'nai Brith Man of the Year–1987; Who's Who in America–1976; Garden Spot Rotary Club Distinguished Service Award. And behind the desk, in the official place of honor, a large lacquered sign that read "Big Irv Feinstein Buick-Oldsmobile."

"Mr. Greene?"

Harry had been waiting for this moment since two in the morning. But, even so, the sight of David Castelli at the door of his office made him nauseous. Still, he made himself follow the script he had mentally written two hours after Pete Werner had left.

"Christ, you're not on the clock at this hour I hope."

"No sir. May I come in?"

Harry put down his dictaphone, then stood, offering a puffy right hand with thick fingers and leathery skin to his visitor. "This *is* a bit of a surprise now, isn't it?"

"Your wife said you were here. I hope you don't mind my just dropping in, but I really have to talk to you."

"My wife? You were at my house?"

"Well, actually, that's where I thought you'd be. You know, Saturday morning and all."

"Businesses don't run by themselves. I'm in here every Saturday morning by eight. That surprise you?"

Castelli ignored the lie and sat down across from Greene, feeling the springs of the dilapidated armchair as they dug into his buttocks. Harry also sat down. He dragged deeply on the Macanudo, then leaned forward on his elbows, resting his chin in his palm. "Breitenfeld tells me you're having quite a time with my friend Rothstein. I suppose that's why you came here."

"Sort of?"

"What do you mean, 'sort of'?"

"What do I mean, 'sort of'? I mean 'sort of' as in you got a big problem in this case."

"Jack said you could handle it, David. He wasn't wrong, was he? You're not in over your head, are you?"

"I don't think you're listening, Mr. Greene. I didn't say *I* had a big problem. I said *you* had a big problem."

Harry put down the Macanudo for the first time since Castelli entered the office. "Now what kind of a problem could I possibly have, with the most impressive young lawyer in Philly handling my case. You tell me that, okay?"

"Well, maybe the most impressive young lawyer in Philly doesn't like getting a slow hand job from his client."

"What the hell are you talking about?"

"Why don't you tell me?"

"Don't get wise, young man. I can have you thrown out of here in a hot minute."

"Oh, is that right?"

"You're goddamn right, it's right. Fact maybe I'll do it now, you think you're so smart." He reached for the phone.

Castelli was tingling from the sudden change in Harry Greene's demeanor. He liked it. It would make his job easier.

"Put it down, Harry."

"What the ..."

"I know about the Tooth Fairy. That a big enough problem for you?"

Harry Greene then did his very best job of feigning shock and horror. And, as he watched the tiny smile begin to emerge on David Castelli's face, he knew the young lawyer had completely swallowed the hook.

Slightly less than one hour later David Castelli, soon to be the client manager of McKeon, Tingham & Marsh's biggest labor account, got up and left the office of Harry Greene. Harry had followed his script perfectly, but still he was angry. In his head, he played back the final exchange between smelter and lawyer.

"So you get the Greene-Pitowsky legal fee fortune and Jack McKeon just rolls over and dies," Harry had said. "That the deal?"

"That's the deal."

"Then you obviously don't know your precious boss as well as you think. He'll swat you like a fly."

"You let me worry about McKeon, Harry."

"And Trice? Who worries about him?"

"You do. Just like you been worrying about him for the last ten years. Just business as usual." It was then that Castelli had stood up and began walking toward the door. As he was reaching for the knob, he had turned back and added, "Only next time you get an urge to piss on one of my cases, call first so I can assign it to an associate. See how well I learned from the master?"

And Harry had said, "I was right. You are a slimy little prick." But David hadn't heard it because he was already out in the hall.

Still fuming over the young lawyer's arrogance, Greene walked out of his office, drove back to 17 Great Stag Drive, and picked a fight with Minna over how lousy the lawn looked. As was his custom at the end of these skirmishes, he finished by saying, "I'm going to the club."

Then Minna gave her usual snappy close. "Good, and don't come back."

And Harry, his p.s. "You say that one more time I just might not."

But then his wife went off the script. "By the way, who is Everett Williams?"

It didn't register at first. "Who?"

"While you were out. Some guy named Everett Williams called from Stroudsburg. Said it was important. You want his number?"

Harry managed to take the slip of paper from Minna's hand and get to his car before the third electric chill in the last twelve hours struck home. Only this one did not leave him frightened. For some totally inexplicable reason, this chill only left him angry—more angry than he could ever remember in his life. The anger pleased him; it invigorated him. Most of all, it freed him.

Harry Greene actually burned rubber leaving the circular driveway.

TWENTY-FIVE
Saturday, October 8

T. J. DIDN'T KNOW WHERE else to start. Two hours earlier, he had
opened the bottom drawer of his darkroom cabinet.

"Get into the truck and shut the fuck up." Thomas Jefferson Trice was
saying this to Jenny DeLone as he was squeezing her upper arm so tight
she had no chance to defend herself. They were by the rear door of the
Rat, where it was pitch dark because T. J. had just finished disabling the
light over the entrance that he knew Jenny used to sneak into the bar on
Saturday nights, when she was too tired and strung out from the week to
feel like schmoozing with the customers.

"What the hell's going on here?" she said. She pressed herself hard
against the passenger door of the pickup, trying to knead her arm without
him seeing it. The cab smelled of stale beer and non-filtered Camels, mixed
with a chaser of marijuana. She forced herself to watch the useless pine
tree air freshener, dangling from Trice's rear view mirror, swinging like a
pendulum in time to the back roads from Lancaster to Fivepointville.

"It's open." He was standing behind her, gesturing toward the front door.
She could feel him trying to rub against her.

On a scale of one to ten, Stuff Johnson's description had been about
a four. Despite her fear, and the overwhelming desire to be home in her
shower, washing the crude filth of T. J. Trice from her body, she could not
help staring at his living room.

"Surprised, aren't you bitch?"

She did not respond. T. J. spun her around to face him, her lips only inches from the grotesque, squared-off beard. When she turned her head away, he yanked it back.

"I'm talking to you!"

"Please, you're hurting me." She hated what was coming out of her mouth. It sounded so helpless, so weak.

"I wanna hurt you, I'll hurt you good. Now I just want to talk."

"We could've talked back there."

"Yeah, we could've talked back there. But I wanted you to see where I was robbed. Because I think you know something about it."

"I don't know what you're talking about."

"Fucking liar!" He shoved her hard, his hands purposely pushing into her breasts, forcing her to lose her balance and fall into the leather and metal chair just behind where she had been standing.

Trice sat on the edge of the long glass coffee table next to the chair, still close enough to Jenny for her to smell his breath.

"We're going to have a little discussion, now, Ms. DeLone. And we're going to find out exactly what you know."

"About what."

"About the robbery. Something important has been stolen from this beautiful home. Would you like to guess what it is."

"I just want to go home. Please."

"All right, since you're so fucking innocent, I'm gonna give you a hint. I know all about you and Werner and that cocksucker lawyer busting in on Stuff Thursday. That surprise you?"

It should have, but it didn't. She had spent too many Fridays watching the master and his disciple doing their dance in the corner booth. "Nothing about you surprises me, T. J."

"Good, then you won't be surprised at this either."

But she was.

The tiny silver derringer appeared so swiftly in Trice's hand that, for a split second, she didn't even realize what he was holding. But by the time she felt the end of the blunt barrel pressing against the side of her head and heard the smart click of the hammer being drawn back, she knew enough to almost pass out. The room narrowed to a black tunnel in front of her eyes. She squeezed them shut and started to cry.

"Save it, bitch. I'm not going to kill you." He laughed as he stepped away and let the hammer snap back on the gun's empty single chamber. "At least not yet." Then he reached into the front pocket of his jeans, took out a bullet, and loaded it into the derringer. "I just wanted to make sure I had your attention. I do have it, don't I?"

She hated herself even more now, because she could not control the tears. "What do you want from me for god's sake? Just tell me."

"I told you. I want to know who stole my property."

"What property?"

"You're getting smart again, young lady. Only now there's a bullet in here, so I don't think you picked a very good time to get smart, do *you*?"

"We saw Stuff. All right? We told him your case is being fixed by Castelli's boss so that you'll win. And we also told him that somebody left a message on McKeon's phone mail about having your so-called friend murdered."

"Not good enough, Jennifer. I already know all that. And I also know Stuff said he threw the whole bunch of you out on your ass, but see, I don't believe that part, 'cause he's a chicken-shit little boot-licker. No way he's gonna take on three men. No, I figure he told you something. And whatever it was he told you, it ended up getting me robbed. So now you're gonna tell me exactly what it was."

There was no reason why Jenny shouldn't start talking. She didn't owe Castelli. The pictures Pete found in Trice's darkroom couldn't hurt the Secretary-Treasurer—not any more than Pete was already going to be hurt for arranging the meeting with Stuff. But she said nothing. Just sat in the chair and looked at Trice, feeling the tears on her cheeks turning hot as they dried, her fear and nausea yielding, at last, to simple hate.

Trice fiddled with the derringer, a smile on his face until he realized that Jenny wasn't preparing to speak. Then he stood up and cocked the trigger a second time.

"You got nice tits, you know that."

Jenny's mouth opened just enough for the corners to pull back and the lower lip to turn down in disgust. T. J. wasn't phased. "Always wondered what they looked like, too. So why don't you just take off that blouse and let's have a peek."

"You're a sick bastard, you know that."

"Yeah, I'm a sick bastard all right. But you're the one looking at a loaded gun. So if I were you I'd get that fucking top off. And I'd get it off, now!" He screamed the last words, screamed them loud and without warning, in a voice suddenly near the edge. Jenny complied with the order.

"The bra too, bitch. Gotta check them nips."

As she let the garment slide down her shoulders, she crossed her arms over her chest. Trice started to caress one forearm with the cold point of the derringer until she got the idea. He let out his breath as her nakedness revealed itself.

"Very nice. Hard little pencil erasers too. Just the way T. J. likes them."

"Don't flatter yourself. It's only the cold."

"Well then, maybe we oughta warm them babies up, shouldn't we?" He reached down for the pack of Camels lying on the table, still holding the silver gun to her head. Jenny realized what was coming next. And there was nothing she could do to stop it.

He held the burning cigarette just close enough to her right breast that she could feel its heat. His hand was starting to shake, which only increased Jenny's terror. She didn't think he would kill her. But she had no doubt about this.

"Where do you want it, cupcake? On the nipple, or next to it?"

The game was over.

"Castelli's got your sick pictures. You happy now!"

"I'm just thrilled, Ms. DeLone. So thrilled I'm even going to take the little bullet out of my little gun."

And it was good that he did this, because otherwise T. J. might have shot the man who suddenly threw open the front door and screamed at the top of his lungs. "Leave her alone you goddamn sonofabitch."

Harry Greene's voice was so loud that Trice actually dropped the empty derringer, which Jenny then kicked smartly across the floor, sending it skidding under a large sofa and out of sight.

The President and CEO of Greene-Pitowsky Smelting & Battery Company looked like Moby Dick—a hulking figure dressed in a white velour warm up suit. Sweat glistened on his face, already beet red from the confrontation he had been thinking about for the last six hours at the club, the first two spent in the gym, the next four in the member's lounge, throwing down one Cutty Sark after another until he was ready. The last thing he did before leaving for Fivepointville was to steal the large gun that Vince the bartender kept on a shelf next to the sink just in case—doing this while the club host was spinning out a frozen daiquiri in the blender at the other end of the bar.

"You see this?" Harry was waving the piece back and forth. "I don't know a goddamn thing about how to use it. Maybe I oughta learn." Then he pulled the trigger and demolished the right front leg of the Bösendorfer. The gigantic piano crashed down on one of its corners, hammers striking strings in a bizarre chord of accident, as the gun's retort slashed through six ears, leaving them ringing.

Trice was hysterical. "You crazy bastard motherfucker!" He ducked behind the chair in which Jenny DeLone was still sitting, half naked, too stunned to react.

"That's good, Trice," Harry said. "Hide behind a woman."

T. J. spoke from his crouch. "Put it away. We'll talk."

"Talk? That what you want to do? Sure, we'll talk. Here's the rules. You call me Greenberg, I blow your fucking head off. You say one word about Jews, I blow your fucking head off. You touch that girl, I blow your fucking head off. You getting it?"

Trice stood up now, hands down and palms up in the universal gesture of surrender. He spoke first to Jenny. "You can get dressed now." Then to Harry. "Whatever you want, man. You're the man."

Harry Greene made Trice get on his knees and clasp his arms behind his back. "Get the fuck over here. And don't stand up." T. J. waddled like an amputated duck until he was directly in front of Harry. "How do you like it, asshole?"

Trice said nothing.

"How many years you think I've been waiting for this?"

"You know what happens if you fuck with me."

"Yeah, I know. Your secret partner turns me in." Greene reached down under Trice's beard with the tip of the gun, then pulled up until the kneeling man's face was eye to eye with his captor. "There's only one problem with that. Something tells me your secret partner is about to get some very bad news of his own from his favorite associate. And I think you know exactly what it is."

"I don't know shit. And neither do you."

"Please. Spare me the crap, will you. Just once."

"How do you know it's him. Could be anybody."

"No it couldn't, mister fucking genius. Jack McKeon is too perfect. My guess is you didn't even have to cut him in, did you? Just blackmailed him about the Teamster election, same as you blackmailed me about old Willis."

Then Harry turned to Jenny. "You know what's going on here?"

She was standing behind them now, by the door, thinking of nothing except how to get out alive. Playing dumb seemed like the best idea. "I don't know anything, I swear."

"Well then, maybe you'd like to hear, seeing as how Mr. Trice so kindly invited you over for cigarettes. What do you think, Thomas, should I tell Jenny?"

"Fuck you."

"He said 'yes.' Did you hear him? Mr. Trice would like very much for me to tell you the whole deal. But I don't think I'm gonna do that. No, I think you'd better wait in my car."

She didn't have to be asked twice.

Then Harry said to Trice, "By the way, Thomas, what kind of a gun is this, anyhow?" He shoved the bulky piece closer to the kneeling man's face.

"It's a Sig, what of it?"

"A Sid? I've got a gun named for my Uncle Sid?"

"I said 'Sig.' Sig Sauer nine millimeter." Trice was trying very hard to sound calm, but the sweat running down his forehead was blowing the facade.

Harry pulled back slightly so that he could sit on the edge of the glass coffee table, which promptly sprung a foot-long crack under his weight. "Did I break that? I'm really sorry, specially seeing as how you're not going to be buying any new ones. See, that nice annual bonus you've been getting for the last ten years. That's going to stop."

"No it's not," T. J. said. "Not unless you kill me, which I don't think you're gonna do."

"You don't know that. Besides, Uncle Sid here might go off by accident.

No, I think the bonuses are going to stop. They're going to stop because you get paid with cigarettes in jail, not cash." He was on a roll.

"Ten years ago, you saw me bury a dead body in one of my casing piles. Of course, you didn't know shit about what happened, but what did you care? Just dug the poor bastard out, cut off his head, then started sending me pictures of his teeth. And I paid you to shut up. All these years, I paid you because I was a schmuck. You said if I ever tried to do anything, there'd be someone else starting in with the pictures. And you'd go to the cops. Make yourself a deal to testify against me and give them more pictures of poor old Willis Tucker lying on my property."

"And I still got copies too," Trice said.

"So you made copies. You think I give a shit? Well, I don't because now I got Castelli up my ass, too. And your precious little failsafe isn't gonna do shit. But there *is* someone out there who will. Ever hear of Mario Fontini?"

"Philly goodfella. What of it?"

"I'll tell you what of it. He's the one that killed Willis. I've got this property up in the Poconos. Used to run a summer camp, but I closed it in 1971. Fifteen years ago, I needed some money. My good friend, Jack McKeon, said he'd help me find a buyer. Only thing was, the buyer turned out to be Mario Fontini, and he wasn't a buyer. Just a renter. Made me let him use Camp Pocono Sunrise to land little planes full of cocaine. Made me go with him to meet the planes and paid me by the trip. Then, one day in 1984, there was a crash. Willis was duck hunting on my lake. Wrong place at the wrong time."

Trice said nothing.

"Anyhow, Fontini's button man, Tony Angelo, decides to put a bullet in Tucker's brain, and Mario decides I can stop being his landlord for one little favor. Get the picture? Only problem is, the Stroudsburg cops know Angelo was on my grounds. Damn if I know how they figured it out, but there's this detective up there named Everett Williams who called me when Willis turned up missing. All of a sudden, ten years later, he wants to talk to me again. Called me at home this morning.

"Except now, maybe *I'm* the one gonna make the deal. Maybe I'll turn the whole bunch of you in. I actually kind of like it. Harry Greene, star witness. Tell 'em all about Tony Angelo, the murderer; Thomas Jefferson Trice, the blackmailer; Jack McKeon the blackmailer's best bud; David Castelli, the new *consigliore*. That ought to be enough for them to give up on one old man who buried a body that was already dead, don't you think?"

"You don't have the balls, Harry."

"Is that so?"

Harry stood up from the broken coffee table. "I want you to ask yourself something. Why did I come here?"

"The fuck should I know?"

"Oh, you should know. You of all people. I came here because I'm actually a little like you. It's the drama, Thomas. Of course, I can't play the piano. But, that doesn't matter. I still like the drama. I go to the cops nice and quiet, you just get arrested one day. No fun in that. But, this way, you can stew in it. Choke on it. Wait for it to happen. Same as you been doing to me for the last ten years. Matter of fact, I'm even planning to write it all down on a piece of paper." Harry reached into his sweatsuit with the hand not holding Uncle Sid and took out an envelope.

"Read the address, Trice. Because that's the person whose going to be *my* failsafe. Don't you just love it? I might not even go to the cops. Then again, I might. Only thing is, you fuck with me, this letter is going to tell my man to send a carload of really good stuff to Everett Williams."

Trice stared at the envelope in Harry's hand. What he wanted most to do was hock up a big lunger and deposit it squarely on the middle of the address. Uncle Sid reminded him that this wasn't such a good idea. So he went the other way. "Harry, I gotta hand it to you, I really do."

"No you don't, you Nazi piece of shit. You hate my guts. All you're really thinking right now is 'Jew.' But that's okay, because what I'm thinking now is so disgusting it would even make you throw up."

Harry started backing toward the door, still waiving the Sig Sauer at his host. "By the way, just in case that faggot arbitrator puts you back to work next week, let me save Joe Breitenfeld the trouble." Harry had his hand on the doorknob now. "You're fired."

Trice stood up and looked at his beloved Bösendorfer, its listing body surrounded by sheet music that had fallen to the floor. He watched a river of Remy Martin still trickling from the lip of the toppled crystal decanter.

He made himself think. He knew nothing of Everett Williams, but the man couldn't have much. Not after ten years. And T.J. still had Jack McKeon on a short leash. The senior partner of McKeon, Tingham & Marsh would never risk disbarment proceedings, not with his ego. The only wild card was David Castelli. He had the Tooth Fairy file; he knew about the NLRB election. Maybe Trice could make a deal with Greene for them both to lean on the lawyer. Castelli had a ticket to practice law, same as McKeon. Being in possession of stolen property, knowing about a crime but not talking—maybe it was enough to cost him that ticket.

The pieces were just starting to fit together, when Trice picked up the odd one, the one that had no edges to match up. If Castelli knew what was in the Tooth Fairy file, did Jenny DeLone know what was in it too? He suddenly remembered the night he and Romanowski found Castelli in the bar talking to Jenny. Then he thought about the name on Harry's envelope.

For the first time in his life, Thomas Jefferson Trice started into motion without a finished plan.

Greene heard the unmistakable noise behind him even before he noticed that the vehicle closing fast in his rear view mirror had only one headlight.

"The bastard's chasing us!" He increased the pressure of his right foot, making the big sedan jump forward and begin swaying back and forth on the curves of Route 897.

"Take it easy, this road is dangerous." Jenny had already turned her body around in the seat so she could monitor the progress of their pursuer. When she did this, her knee knocked a black plastic object to the floor.

"What the hell is that?" Harry said.

"Trice's distributor cap. I took it off his truck. Forgot about the damn motorcycle."

"Well you better start remembering, because there's no way I outrun him."

"Then just pull over. This is crazy."

Harry ignored his passenger. He was oblivious to everything except the pitch black road, twisting by sections into the beams of his lights, then disappearing under tires that were now squealing to hold their purchase. When they crested a small hill that sloped down toward a rare straightaway, Trice used the section to pull even with driver's side door. Harry could see him now, the cyclist's left hand reaching over, gesturing toward the Park Avenue.

Trice tried to yell over the roar of his illegal drag pipes. "Open the fucking window. We have to talk."

Then Harry was sure he saw something silver in T. J.'s hand. He turned the Buick's wheel slightly left, making its black body slowly ride Trice across the yellow line of the road

Jenny screamed. "Stop it! Stop it now!"

"He's got a gun."

"No he doesn't," she said. "You're crazy."

But Harry wouldn't listen. Trice realized what was happening. He slowed the cycle down, but Harry did the same with the Buick. Then T. J. downshifted, the Harley snapping forward now as the end of the straightaway rushed toward them. Greene mashed his foot on the gas pedal as hard as he could. The Buick was no match for the Springer, but Harry still managed to hold his left front fender even with Trice just long enough that the cycle had no chance to recross the yellow line before entering the sharp right hand curve.

All the instincts T. J. had acquired in thirty years of riding rushed from his brain into his hands. He thrust the left handlebar forward, countersteering the big Harley into a frantic left lean. The right turn was impossible now. His only chance was to get the bike to the left shoulder of the road before it intersected with a suddenly appearing set of oncoming headlights.

Harry saw the oncoming car fly by his window, its brakes squealing. It started to slide sideways on locked wheels. Harry saw this, too, from his rear view mirror. He didn't see Trice's Harley, but he was sure he heard metal hit metal. The car disappeared from sight around the curve.

Harry's first instinct was to keep driving. He was safe, now. But, was he? He had to know. He couldn't bear the thought of Trice roaring back behind him. So he pulled the Buick quickly to the side of the road and killed its engine.

There were no sounds.

As Harry started to reach for the driver's door, Jenny grabbed his arm.

"Now what," she said. "Haven't you had enough?"

"I don't trust the bastard. I think that car hit him, but I've got to be sure."

"Sure of what? Sure that he's dead? You're out of your mind, you know that?"

"He had a gun. He was going to kill us."

"What, from a moving motorcycle? He didn't have gun. He wanted to talk. Didn't you see him with his hand. He wanted you to roll down the window."

"Yeah, so he could shoot us. Just stay here and shut up."

Harry got out of the car and walked across the empty, silent road. There were no signs of a motorcycle or a rider. Had it been light, Harry would have seen the skid marks, angling off the asphalt at 45 degrees to the road's edge, marking the course of T. J.'s Harley from highway to sunken ditch. It would have been good for Harry to have seen these skid marks, for it would have at least prepared him for the sight he was about to encounter.

At first, he didn't even notice the ditch. Just thought the road butted directly up against the cornfield that stretched out now before him, all the way to the horizon. But he realized the error when he heard a voice coming from the dark, somewhere beneath his feet.

"Please, somebody. Help me." The voice was strained and thin. It was a pitiful, crying voice.

The ditch was only a couple feet deep, running parallel to the highway, and about five feet wide. It was just deep enough and just wide enough to hold the prostrate body of T. J. Trice, pinned underneath a steel blanket of twisted Harley-Davidson.

The teal blue tank, chrome accents glinting even under cloud-spotted moonlight, lay on its side across the man's lower abdomen. The arms stuck out flat on the ground, still as death. One of the legs, obviously broken horribly, splayed from the underside of the bike. The other was still wrapped around the chassis.

Trice looked up at the man who was now standing over the ditch. "I can't feel my legs, Harry. I can't move."

"You were trying to kill me."

"No I wasn't. You ran me off the road, fucking sonofabitch. You gotta help me."

"What for, Trice? Why should I help you?"

"Oh Jesus, Harry, I'm paralyzed. Help me for god's sake."

"For god's sake? What god is that? Yours?"

"Just help me. I'll say it was an accident. You weren't anywhere near here."

"That's not what you'll do. You'll fuck me again."

"You can't leave me here like this, Harry. I'm begging you. I'm fucking paralyzed."

"Begging me? T. J. Trice is begging Harry Greene?"

The broken man's voice was turning to gravel now, blood beginning to trickle from the corners of his mouth. "Just get it off me, goddammit. Get it off me and call someone."

Greene leaned further over the lip of the ditch, trying not to lose his balance in the darkness. "Where's the gun, Trice. I wanna see it first, you want me down there."

"There isn't any gun. I swear to Christ. I just wanted to talk to you."

"So start talking."

"Get me out of here, Harry, and it's over. All of it."

"It's already over. I told you that back at the house."

"You want the fucking money back, is that it?"

"What, a million dollars? You don't have jack shit left of that."

"Whatever I have, it's yours. Just get down here and help me. Please, Harry, you gotta."

Greene knew, even there in the darkness, squinting down at his broken tormentor, that there wouldn't be any money. He wanted to walk away, just leave the man to his own painful end. But he could not. Even T. J. Trice was a human being. So he started down the side of the ditch.

Except he couldn't see. It was too dark. He remembered the Zippo in his pocket, pulling it out now, flicking it to flame, holding it out over the hole to help him find some solid ground for his left foot. Two steps down toward the wreckage of a man and his bike, the old metal lighter suddenly grew hot in his hand—terribly hot. The sudden upward motion of his arm, reacting to the pain, was instinct, not plan. He heard his own voice yell "look out," as the little silver box , its windproof flame still aglow, clattered down into the exposed guts of the Springer.

Harry barely had time to clamor back up to the road before the Zippo and the gasoline dripping from Trice's custom painted tank united for the big Harley's final roar. Then he bumped squarely into the onrushing body of Jenny DeLone.

She fell backward onto the asphalt. "I was too late, Jenny. There was nothing I could do." He said this while helping her up.

"What did you throw down there. I saw it. I saw it."

"I didn't throw anything. I was trying to help him."

"That's a lie, Harry. I saw you. You threw something burning in there."

"It was my lighter for god's sake. But I didn't throw it. I swear. I was trying to see the bastard. It just got too hot in my hand."

"Oh, Harry. Don't even try. I don't believe that, and neither will the police."

"What do you mean, police. I saved your life back there. What the hell's the matter with you?"

Harry reached out to grab her arm, to talk to her, reason with her. But she was too strong, breaking away from him, running back toward the flaming wreck in the ditch, screaming at the top of her lungs. "Oh, my god. He's on fire!"

Greene knew there was nothing he could do. Nothing except get into his car and drive away.

TWENTY-SIX
Sunday, October 9

EIGHT FEET HIGH AND twenty feet long.

David Castelli could never help thinking about those dimensions whenever he stepped between the rows of files in the basement of McKeon, Tingham and Marsh. There was a safety switch imbedded in the floor. It always worked, of course, but the machine still made him nervous.

He listened as the gears began to turn, separating the huge cabinets so that David could walk between them, down the aisle that now appeared from nowhere. He retrieved the Greene-Pitowsky Smelting & Battery Company 1968 NLRB Election file as quickly as he could, then scurried upstairs to his office.

Castelli always liked to linger over the old files. He particularly enjoyed the letterheads—stepladders of names that so accurately chronicled the fortunes and failures of those who came before him. The firm had only twelve lawyers in 1968, yet Jack McKeon's name was much farther up the letterhead that year than his age would have suggested. He sat below only Marsh himself and Pennfield Smith, now the firm's oldest living lawyer, whose one remaining daily challenge was not to dribble on the men's room floor.

It took only a few minutes for Castelli to find the original wring-outs. He took the next to last one from its binder and held it up against the window, where the bright morning sun made it almost transparent. Then he opened the Tooth Fairy file and held Trice's copy of the wring-out over the original. The two pieces of paper matched perfectly.

When he turned back toward his desk, he saw the red light blinking on his telephone. David had retrieved his messages less than seven hours earlier. So this one had to have come between midnight Saturday and seven AM Sunday, which is what it was now. The voice on the phone sounded almost frantic.

"David, it's Jenny. I've got to talk to you. I couldn't find your home number so I'm leaving this at the office. Call me as soon as you get it. I'm at home."

She answered on the first ring. He didn't wake her up.

"Trice is dead. Harry killed him."

"This is a joke, right?"

"No, David, it's not a joke."

"Come on, Jenny. What do you mean, he's dead?"

Her voice got louder. It sounded strained, and with an edge he hadn't heard before. "What do I mean? I mean dead, as in not living anymore, as in burned up in a ditch on his motorcycle. Jesus Christ, David, I was there. I saw it."

"Who knows about this?"

"That's what you want to know? 'Who *knows* about this?' A man is murdered and all you want to know is who *knows* about this."

"That's not all I want to know. It was just the first thing came out. You're all right, aren't you?"

"No I'm not all right. He kidnapped me, David. Are you listening?"

"Who kidnapped you?"

"Trice, dammit. Last night. He took me to that crazy house of his and threatened to burn me with a cigarette if I didn't tell him who stole his pictures. Harry stopped him."

"So Greene killed him in self-defense?"

"I don't know. I don't know. It was horrible, that's all."

"All right, just calm down a minute, get your breath, and tell me exactly what happened."

Then Jenny gave him most of the details in one long rambling sentence without any pause. Even though it was difficult to understand exactly who did what to whom, when she was finished, David knew one thing clearly.

Derringer or not, Harry Greene was in some very serious trouble.

"I'm coming out," he said. "Right now."

"No, I don't want you to come out. Just stay put."

"Listen, Jenny, I didn't call you—you called me. You didn't want to see me, why didn't you just sneak into Philadelphia and tape a note to my car window?"

"I'm sorry about the note. It was the best I could do."

"Well it stunk."

"All right, I said I'm sorry. Anyhow, that's a whole different issue."

"No, it's not a whole different issue, goddammit. You don't do something like that to a person who loves you."

"You don't love me, David. Grow up. It was a roll in the hay and you know it. You've got a family. What were you going to do, give up your career and come run a bar?"

"Then why did you call me?"

"Because I'm scared and I didn't know who else to call."

"What about your precious friend, Mr. Werner?"

"This has nothing to do with him, David. He's not planning to blackmail anyone."

"That's really low, you know that?"

"It is? Then why don't you tell me why you're refusing to go to the police about Trice?"

"I'm not refusing to go to the police."

"Then when are you going?"

David said nothing. When the silence had lasted long enough to be an answer, Jenny said, "Well I'm going. And I'm going this morning. It's already been on the radio."

"About Harry?" David was suddenly very uncomfortable.

"No, not Harry. Just Trice. How could they know anything about Harry? All they said was the police found T. J.'s body in a ditch. They had to identify him from the license plate on his bike. As far as I know, the police assume it was just a motorcycle accident."

"But you want to go and make it a murder."

"It *was* a murder, David. He set the man on fire."

"That's not what you said a minute ago. You said Harry thought Trice had a gun so Greene ran him off the road, then he went over to the side and when you got out of the car the bike was on fire."

"And I said I saw Harry throw his lighter into the ditch right before the thing blew up. I told you that. What are you, his defense lawyer all of a sudden?"

"I don't know what I am, Jenny. Right now, I really don't."

"Then maybe you ought to just sit there until you do. I'm sorry I called."

"Wait a ..."

She hung up.

When she didn't answer after ten rings, Castelli slammed the phone down and yelled "bitch" as loud as he could. Then he buried his head in his hands and tried to think. But the only thoughts he could muster were of how many laws he had broken in the last twenty-four hours: accessory to breaking and entering, obstruction of justice, blackmail, and so many violations of the Code of Professional Responsibility that he quickly lost count.

He pictured Jenny spilling her guts to the Lancaster police, and Isaac Rothstein filing a gigantic complaint with the Pennsylvania Supreme Court Disciplinary Board. He began pacing up and down the length of Castelli's Lanes, muttering "oh, shit" over and over to himself—until he finally made himself stop, which he did by actually saying the words—out loud, on the empty twenty-fourth floor of the Lincoln Building.

"Stop it! This is fucking nuts. You're hysterical."

Then he returned to his desk and made himself think. He remembered something he had said to Jenny the day he had first convinced her to help him with the Trice case. Something she could have denied but didn't. Jenny DeLone needed Harry Greene. Because without Harry, there would be no company, and without Greene-Pitowsky Smelting & Battery there would be no Jenny Rats. Jennifer DeLone was not going to pin a murder rap on her meal ticket.

———✦———

Early Sunday evening, David made the call from the phone in his bedroom at his mother's house. He had managed to slip upstairs just before the spumoni, feigning a touch of indigestion.

"I cook all afternoon and it makes you sick?"

"It was delicious, mother. Honest. It's just the case."

The last thing he heard, going up the steps two at a time, was Mrs. Castelli lecturing Leslie on the proper care and feeding of the Italian son.

"Are you sure nothing's wrong?" McKeon said. "You don't sound right."

"I'm fine, really. I just have to talk to you."

"It can't wait till tomorrow?"

"No, Jack, it can't. You gonna be home?"

"I guess. What time you going to be here?"

He looked at his watch. Figured to leave about five. Half hour to run Leslie and Ashley home, then make up some bullshit about needing to go back to the office. "Six, six-thirty. That all right?"

"I'm going out at seven. This going to take long?"

Castelli forced himself to smile at the innocence of it all. "Not long at all. I promise."

His mentor reeked of aftershave.

Castelli eyed the tiny man up and down. Cole Haan tasseled loafers, butter-rum colored slacks, some kind of Italian sweater that looked like it had nothing but skin underneath. He wondered whether tonight's main event was over thirty.

McKeon flashed the Irish blues. "Come in. Get you something?" The senior partner looked down at his own half-empty martini glass.

"No thanks, just finished dinner."

"Of course, the Sunday ritual."

McKeon turned and led David into his large study that overlooked the Delaware River. The older man stood by the picture window behind his desk, looking out across the shiny black water to the lighted shores of Camden, New Jersey.

"Even that sorry excuse for a city looks good at night, don't you think? Can't see the moolies *or* the spics."

"How about the micks, Jack. Can you see them, or are they all just lying drunk in the gutter?"

"Oh my, somebody sounds like they need a nap. What's the matter, you nervous about tomorrow?"

"Case is off tomorrow. That's what I came over to talk to you about."

"I don't get it."

"I think you oughta sit down, Jack. I want your undivided attention."

McKeon felt the muscles in his neck tighten just the slightest bit, the animal in him not quite sensing danger, but not fully relaxed either. "Okay, I'm sitting. So let's have it."

"The union is going to withdraw Trice's grievance tomorrow. Would you like to know why?"

"I can't wait."

"T. J. Trice is dead."

McKeon put down his martini glass and gripped the edge of his desk with both hands. "Dead? That's impossible."

"You think so. Well, I suggest you think again, because it's true. T. J. was the main ingredient in a serving of Harley flambé last night. Burned to a fucking cinder."

"I still don't believe it. Something like that happened Harry would have called me. I was home all day."

"I don't think Harry's gonna be calling you anymore."

Now the animal knew something was terribly wrong. "David, I'm not in the mood for games here." He looked at his watch. "I've got to meet someone in ten minutes."

"Then slam it in your desk drawer, Jack. She's gonna have to wait."

"I don't find this the least bit amusing. Now, if there's something wrong with Harry Greene, I want to know about it."

"Oh, you're going to know about it, my friend." David sat down in a leather armchair across the desk from the man whose Irish blues had suddenly gone out as if they were connected to a light switch. "But first, you're going to answer some questions for me." Then David added, "You no good fucking sonofabitch."

"Who do you think ..."

"Question number one." David pulled the first piece of paper out of his briefcase, then flicked it across the naked desk top. "How did you get that Triple A letterhead, blow in Carol Highsmith's ear?"

McKeon picked up the paper as if it were a bomb about to explode. David went on. "That's right, I got her to read me the real list last week—the one with Jorgenson on it, and Stuart Blevinsky and Triana Smythe. The list of arbitrators we *should* have been picking from. I'm surprised Rothstein didn't offer you a blow job."

"I can explain this."

"No, you can't. You can't explain shit. So let's move on to question number two." The next piece of paper flew across the desk. McKeon looked down at the emergency room record of Thomas Jefferson Trice, his eyes immediately focusing on the phony description of T. J.'s forklift accident.

"The question, Mr. McKeon, is how could you be so careless? Harry Greene replaced all his old forklifts just last year with brand new models. Models with dead man switches so they can't jump into gear and pin guys' legs against piles of pallets."

McKeon began talking on autopilot, the lawyer filling up space until he could think of something to rehabilitate the witness—which in this case was him. "Look, just be quiet a minute and give me a chance. This stuff is nothing. You're going to be a partner in three months. We'll laugh about it."

It wasn't working.

"Oh, Jack. These are just the appetizers. This is just the stuff that's gonna get you disbarred. You wanna blow smoke up my ass, you can at least wait till you see the stuff that's gonna land you in jail."

"What are you talking about, jail?"

"Well, let's see. Wanna start with Mario Fontini's cocaine highway up in the Poconos—or was that just a coincidence, like you been telling poor dumb Harry Greene for the past fifteen years? Of course, if you don't like Mario, we can discuss having Stuff Johnson murdered. You oughta tell your old war buddy not to go leaving Labor Day messages on your phone mail."

McKeon was trying his best to make a quick recovery. "What I told Harry about that camp deal was the truth, goddammit. I didn't know it was the mob."

"Oh is that so? And I guess you also told Harry the truth all these years about Trice not having a failsafe." Castelli tossed the manila envelope clear over the top of McKeon's desk and into his lap. "Those are just photocopies, but I'm sure you've already seen Willis Tucker's originals."

McKeon didn't have to open the envelope.

"It's over, Jack. I know everything. So what do you think the ticket is for obstruction of justice? Two, three years? Maybe probation if you cop?"

"Then you know why the case had to be fixed." McKeon suddenly saw a tiny crack of light showing through the darkness, and he was running for it now at full speed. "He came to me, David. Trice was going to drop a dime on him if he didn't get his job back. I only did it for Harry."

Castelli slowly rose from the leather chair. He walked around the desk, turning his back now on John Joseph McKeon, who slumped in his seat as Castelli talked to the plate glass window.

"What was that you said a minute ago about Camden? 'Can't see the moolies or the spics.' That's right, Jack. You can't see them. But they're out there just the same. Everything's out there—it's just sometimes hard to see because the light's not right. Or maybe the light is right, but you really don't want to see. That was me, Jack. I didn't want to see. I wanted to believe in you. Jesus Christ, I wanted to believe you were my mentor, maybe even my friend. But you let me down, didn't you? Just like you let Harry down."

David heard the desk chair creak behind him. "Don't get up. Just sit there and listen and don't say a word. You didn't fix this arbitration for Greene. You fixed it for Jack McKeon. You fixed it because Trice had your balls in the same vice he had Harry's. What was that famous line of yours? 'Win an election, lose a client?' Open the envelope, Jack."

Then David turned to watch McKeon look at the wring-out with his handwritten note clipped to the top.

"He told me you saved his life in Italy, you know that? He loved you, you know that? For a while there, I loved you too. What an asshole I was."

"I did him a favor." McKeon spoke softly, his voice barely audible even in a silent room. "He was going to get a union in there sooner or later. At least you can deal with the Teamsters. They're not like the Steelworkers or the Rubberworkers."

"That wasn't your decision to make, Jack. It was Harry's. And he didn't think you did him a favor."

"You told him?"

"Goddamn right I told him. Don't you think the man's been through enough? I think he's been through enough. That's why he killed Trice last night."

"No!"

"Yeah, he killed him. Ran him off the road, then set the bastard on fire when he found him pinned under that fucking Harley. Jenny DeLone told me."

"Jesus H Christ. Who else knows about this?"

Castelli winced as he heard his own words coming from the mouth of Jack McKeon. Then he remembered what he had told himself about Jenny DeLone. He walked behind the old lawyer's chair, looked down at the man who now appeared so small, and whispered, "Besides her? No one knows about it, Jack. Just Harry, me, and you. And you can make sure that's all who's ever going to know."

It took David less than thirty seconds to rattle off his terms. Jack McKeon would announce to the firm tomorrow that he had decided to take early retirement at the end of the year. David Castelli would become the client manager for all of the senior partner's business, and would be guaranteed a partnership, effective January 1, 1995.

David refused to shake hands before he left. More than anything else about the evening, that is what ate at McKeon's gut long into the night.

———⚬∞∞⚬———

Castelli had one more stop to make before returning to his palace in the shadow of the Echelon Mall. He had meant to dictate the memo when he had been at the office earlier, but he was just too distracted. He could have chosen now to wait until Monday, but this time he was just too elated.

He sat behind his desk at the end of Castelli's Lanes, turned in his swivel chair to face the blinking lights of North Philadelphia, his feet up on the standard issue associate's metal file credenza. His first thought had been to demand partnership immediately, not even wait for the turn of the year. But the second idea was much better. It had symmetry. It had style.

He picked up his dictaphone and began:

Maribeth, prepare this memo for Mr. McKeon's signature:

To Eleanor Rice, Office Manager, from Mr. McKeon, re David Castelli's office. I was in Mr. Castelli's office the other day and noticed that its dimensions appear to be rather narrow. Upon checking the plans, I discovered that the build-out crew had obviously misplaced the dividing wall between his room and mine when we did the twenty-fourth floor renovations. Please contact them and have this corrected ASAP. If there's no money left in the punch list budget, you may charge this minor renovation to my personal account.

He tossed the microcasette into his out box, then took out the little plastic penis, wound it up, and let it hop around his desk. This time, when it hopped off onto the floor, he didn't bother to pick it up.

TWENTY-SEVEN
Monday, October 10

PETE WERNER COULDN'T SLEEP.

There was probably not a single member of Manufacturing and Transport Local 664 whom he personally hated more than Thomas Jefferson Trice, but that didn't matter. News of a brother's death always troubled him, all the more when that death was as sudden and gruesome as T. J.'s.

He had been outside working in the yard when Dorothy had called through the kitchen window that he should come quick and listen to the radio. The story was over by the time he arrived, but Mrs. Werner gave her husband the details. When she was finished, he made the sign of the cross over his chest.

He jumped up at the sound. It was the thud of a car door, directly below their bedroom window in his driveway. A car door, followed moments later by the rumble of a large engine revving up to speed, then moving off into the night.

"What the hell was that?" Werner sat up and spoke into the darkness.

Dorothy mumbled something that sounded like, "Nothing, go back to sleep," and the episode ended. But Pete Werner was now most definitely awake. He lay in the pitch-black room, listening to the ticks of the night outside: a tree branch tapping against the window, the wind of early fall beginning to blow the first dead leaves to the ground, the bark of a distant dog. It was his car door. He knew it. It troubled him.

The clock radio said 3:47 when he finally succumbed to the urge.

Barefoot, and dressed only in the t-shirt and shorts he used instead of pajamas, Pete Werner walked silently down his stairs, through the kitchen, and out the back door to the driveway. He saw nothing out of the ordinary. Just the Town Car at rest. He was about to dismiss the whole thing as stupid paranoia, when something made him open the driver's door. The dome light snapped on, throwing its single beam squarely on a large white envelope now resting on the front seat. In magic marker the words: "TO BE OPENED ONLY BY PETE WERNER." And in the upper left hand corner of the envelope, the lightning bolt logo of Greene-Pitowsky Smelting & Battery Company.

Werner emptied the contents of the envelope on his kitchen table: a handheld dictaphone with a microcasette inside, a second loose cassette, a single sheet of tablet paper filled with neat printing, and a photograph. He felt a chill run through his body at the sight of the picture. It was a crude snapshot with the date September 15, 1984, scrawled across it in blue ink. The picture looked down into a hole in the ground. In the hole, a large open metal container. In the container, the same headless body draped with duck decoys that Werner had first seen in the Tooth Fairy file.

There was a post-it note stuck to the dictaphone. "Play this first" was written across its yellow surface.

He recognized the voice on the tape immediately. Harry Greene spoke clearly, in a monotone Pete had never heard before from his long-time adversary.

"Pete, I've never been a very good writer," the voice began. "I do better by talking, so pay attention.

"The picture you're looking at was not taken by Trice. It was taken by me, a week after Willis got shot. All these years, Trice thought the rest of the body got eaten by acid, but I came back the next week and took it out of the pile. It's still buried just inside the hole in the fence on Sharpe Street. I thought someday it might help someone. Maybe now it will. Maybe the police can find something on it to help nail Fontini and that bastard Tony Angelo.

"You were right about Castelli. He came to see me Saturday and threatened to turn me in if I didn't use him as my lawyer for the rest of my life. But he didn't know that I got it all on tape. I was pretending to dictate a letter when Castelli came to my office. So I just left the machine running when I put it down on my desk. Play it and you will hear everything the bastard said. Just promise me you'll turn this over to the people who can take his goddamn law license away—him and McKeon both.

"By now you probably know that Trice is dead. What you don't know is that I killed him. But it wasn't on purpose. I swear to God.

"When I got home yesterday morning, my wife said the Stroudsburg police were back looking for me. She didn't know it was the police, of course, and don't ever tell her. But it got me so mad I decided to go after Trice. When I got to his house last night, he was torturing Jenny, trying to make her tell him who took his pictures. I probably saved her life. But then I killed him. He was chasing us on his motorcycle and he ran off the road. He was in a ditch, calling for help. I tried to get him and my lighter fell. Jenny thinks I threw it in. But I dropped it—I swear.

"So now it's all over. The Stroudsburg police are going to get me on account of Willis, and even if they don't, Jenny is going to tell the Lancaster police what happened with Trice. I was going to blackmail Trice with all this. That was my idea. Get him back. But he's dead and Jenny says the cops will never believe I dropped the lighter by mistake. I just can't take any more of it.

"That's why the last piece of paper is for you. Give it to a lawyer and hopefully it will be good. My signature is on the bottom. I have a wife and two wonderful kids. But they could never run a business. So I'm giving fifty-one percent of the company to Local 664. I named you the president. You always told me that the men could do a better job running the place than I could. Now you can find out if that's true. The only thing I ask is that you make sure my family is taken care of.

"Please don't feel sorry for me. I've already outlived my father by eleven years, so I'm probably on borrowed time anyhow. And I made a lot of money, but it was all by luck. I know that. I've always known that. Trice was bad enough. Now there's Castelli. And Jack McKeon. He was my best friend and look what he did. But the worst thing is, another man got killed last night on account of all this. Are you listening? A human being! Even Trice was still a human being. Except I'm not a murderer. You got to make sure they know that.

"Promise me, Pete Werner. You're the most honest man I ever knew."

It was only at the end of the message that Harry Greene's voice cracked.

Werner practically ripped the phone off his kitchen wall. He knew what the answer would be, but it didn't matter. Minna Greene answered in a voice heavy with sleep.

"Mrs. Greene. This is Pete Werner. I've got to speak to your husband immediately."

There was silence on the line at first. Then he heard the phone receiver strike the ground. In the background was her voice—soft, then frantic as she realized her husband wasn't lying in the bed next to her.

"Oh my god," she said into the phone. "He's not here. What's the matter!"

"Don't move from the house, Mrs. Greene. Stay put."

"What's this about? What's going on."

"I'll be there in twenty minutes. Just do what I say."

He didn't give her a chance to reply, before he hung up the phone and bolted up the stairs to throw on some clothes.

Dorothy Werner was wide awake. "Jesus, Pete, what the hell's going on?"

"I think Harry Greene's trying to kill himself. Call 911. Tell them 17 Great Stag Drive and no goddamn sirens."

The police arrived before Pete did. Three patrol cars, their light bars turning Great Stag Drive into the Fourth of July, had already pulled into the circular driveway.

Werner could see two officers silhouetted by the hallway light, just inside the open front door. One of them appeared to have a slightly built woman draped against his chest. Pete could see her body heaving against the man. Five feet from the door, another officer halted Werner's progress.

"Are you Pete Werner?"

"Yes, sir."

"Your wife call 911 about a half hour ago?"

There was something in the tone of the officer's voice that made Werner realize the question was irrelevant. So he said, instead, "You guys were too late, weren't you?"

"We found him in the garage. The motor was still running."

The police were willing to let Pete Werner see for himself. What harm could it do? They even let him look inside the envelope that was resting on the seat next to the body.

There was a silver medallion in the envelope, with a note that said only "For Eric." On one side of the medallion was the date June 2, 1983, beautifully engraved in the metal. On the other side a second date appeared, this one crudely scratched on, as if by hand.

March 10, 2025.

TWENTY-EIGHT
Tuesday, October 11

WERNER SKIPPED WORK ON Monday. He spent most of the day just listening to the news radio station for something about Harry. But they never even mentioned him. The late edition of the *Lancaster Times* at least gave him an article obit., even though he didn't rate a picture. The text was mainly about his air pollution battles with the EPA.

Several times Tuesday morning, alone in his office with Harry's tablet paper deed to Greene-Pitowsky Smelting & Battery Company, Pete had picked up the phone to call Rothstein about it. But each time he stopped before he could finish dialing the number. He promised himself he'd do it Wednesday.

In truth, he didn't even want to come to work. And he would have taken the extra day to nurse his wounds, except for the one task he actually looked forward to doing, despite the pain that still throbbed in his face. The task arrived at the hall slightly after ten.

"Axel called me at home this morning. Said you had some shit to see me about was important. Better be 'cause I gave up a good mileage run to Pittsburgh."

"Sit down, Romanowski. Sit down and shut up."

Werner eyed the Rapid Freight steward with a particularly strong stare of contempt. Dickie's fat bulk oozed into the chair across Pete's desk. Romanowski reached into his pocket for a cigarette.

"Not in here, pal. You know the rules."

"Rules till March, buster. Then we're gonna have ashtrays all over this hole."

"Dickie, I want to know what you think about scabs."

"What the fuck is this all about?"

"It's about the election, what the hell did you think it was about. See, I want to know if you think our membership would vote to put a fucking scab behind this desk?"

"What the hell are you talking about, Werner. I missed a good run today."

"Just answer the question, Dickie."

"No, they wouldn't elect a scab. Wouldn't piss in his mouth if his throat was on fire."

"Then I suggest you go buy yourself a water cooler, buddy, 'cause your throat's gonna be mighty dry. Where were you working in '69?"

"1969? How the hell should I remember?"

"Well, let's try you should remember because a loyal Teamster should remember running picket lines for Harry Greene. Don't you think a loyal Teamster should remember that."

Pete Werner picked up the eight-by-ten picture that he first saw under the streetlight on Route 837. "Mr. Trice really was a good photographer, Dickie. Too bad he's dead." He held out the photo for Romanowski. "Oh, and don't even think about tearing it up. This one's just a copy. The original's down at the printer for next month's newsletter."

Even with the long sideburns and Beatle haircut, the driver in the window of the truck was unmistakable. The man on the ground beside the driver's door, brandishing the picket sign that read "Death to Scabs" had unwittingly done Werner the supreme favor of standing just far enough from the truck window so that the driver's entire profile was visible. The other item visible in the photo was the logo on the door: "Greene-Pitowsky Smelting & Battery Company, Lancaster, Pa."

Romanowski's lower lip began to tremble visibly.

"It's you, Dickie, isn't it?" Pete said. "Twenty-five years old, but it's still you. Just as fat then as you are now. No, I don't think the members are going to have any trouble at all recognizing that ugly face. You agree?"

"This is fucking bullshit." Romanowski was on his feet, waving the eight-by-ten back and forth like a fan. "Who the fuck do you think you are?"

"I know exactly who I am, brother. I just never really knew before who *you* were. Trice took that during the '69 strike down the street. 'Cept I figure, you scabbed for Harry, you must have done it for lots of people. So I checked."

"What do you mean, checked?"

"Social security records, Dickie. I lied. Said I was you on the phone, needed to get some employment dates from the sixties and seventies. Wanna guess what they told me? No, don't. I'll save you the trouble." Werner tossed another piece of paper across his desk. "We'll be printing this too. Right under your fat face."

Romanowski grabbed the list and just stared at it. Pete couldn't resist. "Manheim Resistor. How long was that strike, Dickie? Eight weeks? How many men's jobs did you steal then? And how about the Food Wizard Stores? I think that one lasted ten weeks. Or was it eleven? What do your records show?"

"You motherfucker. I oughta kill you right here."

"Forget it, sport. Too many witnesses downstairs. No, I suggest you just get your ass out of this office and don't ever come back. If you're a good boy, I won't get you fired down at Rapid. How's that?"

Romanowski took the list and the eight-by-ten picture, crumbled them both into a ball, then threw them back across the desk at Pete. Then he stomped out of Werner's office and thudded down the stairs. Werner couldn't help thinking how much Romanowski resembled Baby Huey from behind. He picked up the phone and punched intercom.

"Yes, boss."

"Axel, what time is it?"

"Ten-thirty, why?"

"You don't think that's too early for a beer, do you."

"Never too early, boss."

"Good, and get one for yourself too, Chopper. Put it on my tab."

Two days later, Minna Greene finally figured out March 10, 2025. On that date, Eric Greene would have lived for 25,545 days—the exact number in the life of his father.

She decided not to give the medallion to her son.

Printed in the United States
215995BV00001B/165/P

9 780979 520426